DEATH TRIP

DEATH TRIP

Mark Littleton

MOODY PRESS
CHICAGO

To Mom and Dad,
who taught me to love words and use them well,
who encouraged me to revel in the magic of the story
and to retell it with spirit and soul,
and who helped me learn to listen
for the truth between the lines,
for there one finds the wisdom that heals.

ACKNOWLEDGMENTS

Much thanks to the many people who have offered help, suggestions, and guidance as I wrote this novel: Duncan Jaenicke and Jim Bell of Moody Press, who first encouraged me about the idea; Paul Wieland, Carolyn Males, Bonnie Crawford, and Don and Lynn McCorkel for reading it in various stages and offering very helpful lay-editorial opinions; Al Brown of Hill Management for his grand tour of the top floor; Paul Lochstampfer for his information on funeral homes and cremation; Petty Officer Jerry Gamble of the Towson Navy Recruitment Center for his information about the Navy SEALs; Nicole and Alisha, my daughters, for playing quietly while Daddy pounded away on the word processor; Curtis Lundgren, my agent, who set me and kept me on the right path repeatedly; and to Anne Scherich, Joe O'Day, and Ella Lindvall of Moody Press who brought it all to a worthy conclusion.

A man's experience should be to him the laboratory in which he tests the medicines he prescribes for others.

—Charles Spurgeon

We live by faith, not by sight.

—Paul to the Corinthians

You must insist that their experiences are rotten, that their joys are delusive, although they may have been rapt up into the third heaven in their own conceit by them, unless the main tenor of their lives be spiritual, watchful, and holy.

—David Brainerd

One should be careful to get out of an experience only the wisdom that is in it—and stop there; lest we be like the cat that sits down on a hot stove lid. She will never sit down on a hot stove lid again—and that's well; but also she will never sit down on a cold one any more.

—Mark Twain

PROLOGUE

The Late Sixties, New Jersey

Eight-year-old Ray Mazaris eyed the shark-mouthed Chevy as it jumped and jolted in position. "Johnny's playing drag race again," Ray muttered as he turned to the muscular black lab sniffing the grass in the front yard.

"Barney, hurry up. I want to get back inside."

The dog snuffled for what seemed the millionth time the oak sapling recently planted by Ray's father. For an early evening in June in south Jersey, the air was remarkably cool. With rising irritation, Ray jerked the leash. "Barney, you've had long enough!"

The blue and gold '57 Chevy roared again. John Godwin, the seventeen year old in the driver's seat, was the local juvenile delinquent. In any comparison Ray's father made of good and evil, Godwin always figured heavily on the side of evil. Ray often watched the car nut work on the Chevy in the family's backyard garage. Ray had tried to like John Godwin. But something about the boy's fake Elvis sneer and the mumbly monotone he always used when talking gave Ray an uneasy feeling. He knew messing with cars did not a life make. Not the kind he wanted, the kind he hoped to find in the navy as a commando, frogman, or captain of a battlewagon, like his father was.

9

Barney pulled on the chain and scrabbled forward on the thick green grass, straining on the leash. Ray allowed himself to be pulled along.

Behind them, the tires screeched and pebbles flew out behind the spinning wheels. Ray and Barney turned again, gazing with some amazement at the slit, half-snarling front of the Chevy. Godwin was pulling his usual hot rod tactic. Floor it for about ten feet, then crunch to a stop before actually breaking a law.

Ray turned back to Barney. "What are you doing, saving it up?" He instinctively rubbed his belly under his green T-shirt. The grass felt cool and nubbly under his bare feet, but he wanted to get back to playing with his soldiers. He had a major battle going and was picking them off with a rubber band gun.

The chunky dog twisted his head and yapped gleefully. Godwin stopped the car, and it bounced up and down in the road as he pressed and released the accelerator. More than once Johnny told Ray how he wanted to be number one, to be the best so that his picture got on the cover of *Sports Illustrated*. Ray's parents said he'd sooner end up in prison.

Suddenly the dog's back stiffened. He stopped and fixed his eyes on something across the road. Ray looked up. It was a gopher, standing erect, ears twitching, nose wrinkling. Its fat, brown, knobby-skulled head dipped and jerked, then it turned and waddled back a few feet toward the woods. Ray sighed. "Barney, it's a woodchuck. You've seen two million of them. I want to go back in the house. Now hurry up."

He gave the chain another jerk.

Up the road, the car roared. Then John Godwin's Chevy hurtled down the gravelly asphalt for another few feet. But this time it kept going. Illegally. Ray stared, then felt a sharp tug on the leash as Barney launched himself at the woodchuck. He dragged Ray off the curb.

Ray didn't have the right balance, and he swung to his left, putting his back to the supercharged machine accelerating down toward both of them.

"Barney!"

The leather thong slipped off his wrist as the dog bolted.

Ray fell forward.

Somewhere a horn blared.

John Godwin, for all his callous attitudes about people, dogs, and everything else except being number one, hit the brakes.

The chrome fender struck Ray broadside. He felt nothing else. As his slight body hurtled through the air, something else ripped away inside him. Then suddenly he was watching his small, sweat-shirted form roll through the air and crack down in the middle of the street like a rag doll. To his left, he heard his mother scream. With astonishing lucidity, he spotted his little brother Terry standing behind her in the doorway, still wearing his pajamas from a nap.

The car skidded to a stop on the front lawn of the house down one from the Mazaris's. Ray watched in fascination, now standing about twenty feet away from the curb.

"How can I see myself—" he began to ask.

John Godwin threw open the left front door and jumped out, shaking his head with dispassionate aggravation. Ray noticed the grease on John's hands and a smudge on his nose. Ray's eyes seemed to have improved 1,000 percent.

Then he looked again at the body that once was Ray Mazaris as it lay still in the road, splayed out. The boy's eyes were closed. His brown hair hung in a drape out from the left side of his head.

With a sudden, searing jolt, Ray realized he was dead.

"Mom!" he shrieked. But his mother bolted past him to the little body in the street.

"Mom! Something's—"

A moment later, someone stood to his right. Ray turned to look. The man was tall, Indian-looking, with a broad back and a small waist. Long, black hair covered his shoulders. Two huge green jewels burned on each arm. Ray began to say, "Who are you? Did you see what happened? Am I dead?"

The being touched him kindly, then moved soundlessly past Ray, saying nothing. He bent over the body in the street. Ray ran to catch up with him.

"Am I really dead? How come I'm here? How come I can see myself?"

The stranger turned and smiled at him. "You are dead for the moment," he said. Then he reached inside Ray's chest with one hand and with the other, he touched something inside Ray's skull. Pressing his thick bronzed lips to Ray's scratched and bloody mouth, he breathed out and spoke several words Ray didn't understand.

Ray's mother knelt by the body, and Ray looked from her to John Godwin to another man, Mr. Martin, from across the street. His mother wept, caressing the body's forehead. Ray shouted, "Move back. He's trying to help me."

No one seemed to hear him or see him.

His mother cried, "Please, somebody, do something. He's dying."

Another neighbor appeared, a Mrs. Collins. She said, "I called the police. They're sending an ambulance."

The Indian continued working on Ray's body, still invisible to everyone else. Mr. Martin felt the boy's still flesh for a pulse. Ray's mother bent over him and cradled his head in her lap. "Please, honey, don't die. Please don't die. You'll be all right. I know you will. I know it." Ray watched as her tears dropped onto the body's face and shirt. Instinctively, he wiped at his own face and noticed a strange, hot sensation. He looked at his hands and realized he could see through them.

"Am I alive?" he cried to the Indian.

The being ignored him and bent one more time to press his mouth to Ray's lips. Out of the corner of his eye he looked at Ray and nodded. "You will live," he said.

Ray watched as the body suddenly twitched once, twice. Ray's mother held him tighter and prayed again. John Godwin stayed behind them, staring impassively and saying nothing. Mr. Martin fumbled with a first-aid kit.

Then the Indian stood and smiled. "Farewell," he said to Ray. "Several ribs are broken, and the arm. Your mind will be all right. There's no other damage."

Ray watched in amazement as his body jerked again. "Who are you?" he yelled as the Indian began to walk away.

The tall, bronzed man turned and waved. "I am Trell."

"What are you?" Ray cried again.

Trell turned. "A servant," he said and disappeared into a fog. Ray strained to see where Trell had gone, but suddenly something tore at his back. An instant later, he exploded back inside his body, pain searing through his chest like a burn. He opened his eyes.

"Ray, Ray honey? Are you all right?" His mother dabbed gauze on his face.

Ray winced. "It hurts. I can hardly"—he fought for air—"breathe."

Mr. Martin produced a vial of Mercurochrome from the first-aid kit. Ray heard a siren somewhere in the distance. John Godwin looked down on him, his greasy black hair hanging out from his face, his sharp blue eyes cool and dark.

Mrs. Mazaris glared at John and pulled Ray's head to her chest. "If I have anything to say about it, Johnny Godwin, you'll go to prison for this. Or reform school."

He looked at her with little interest, then his lips twitched with a mean smile. Finally, he turned and began walking back to his car. He murmured, "What's the deal? The little punk's all right."

The ambulance arrived, red and white lights flashing. The siren turned off with an eerie burp. Wrenching corkscrews of pain stabbed through Ray's chest and side. But something else crowded his thoughts: what had happened to the raven-haired being? He looked around wildly and cried, "Where is the Indian?"

His mother's face hovered over his, caressing his face. "It's all right, honey. Just be quiet."

Ray said, "Mom, I saw someone. He helped me. He was invisible. I was apart from my body."

Mrs. Mazaris rocked Ray in her arms. "It's all right, honey. I'm sure you saw lots of things."

The ambulance attendants asked her to let the boy down so they could get him onto a stretcher. They checked his blood pressure and heartbeat, felt for broken bones. Orders shot back and forth around him. Ray sensed a dizziness, and things began to blur. He heard a grizzled man with a crew cut and purplish nose say, "He could have a concussion, ma'am. We're taking him to the general hospital."

13

"I'm going with him," Mrs. Mazaris said. She turned to Mr. Martin. "Would you watch Terry and call my husband from the house? And take Barney in." The dog stood in the road, his tail drooping, his eyes appearing worried and sad.

Mr. Martin wrote down the number.

As Ray was wheeled toward the back of the ambulance, he looked up at his mother as she held his hand. "Mom, I saw an angel. There was an angel. Right there."

Mrs. Mazaris brushed the hair back from his scratched forehead. "Your guardian, I guess." She squeezed his hand.

The attendants locked the stretcher in place and showed Mrs. Mazaris where to sit. Ray waited quietly on the stretcher, absorbed in thought, ignoring the sharp pains in his side.

"Who are you?" Ray asked in his mind, expecting a voice to resound from heaven.

No one answered. His mother caressed his cheeks. Ray nestled down under the warm covers. "Thank you," he said, and closed his eyes. "I'm going to meet you again," he whispered. "I promise."

PART 1

The Experience

I know a man in Christ who fourteen years ago was caught up to the third heaven. Whether it was in the body or out of the body I do not know—God knows. . . . He heard inexpressible things, things that man is not permitted to tell.

—Paul the apostle to the Corinthians

CHAPTER ONE

Twenty-five Years Later
Brinton, Maryland

1

A scrub-clad attendant scrutinized the telemetry unit and said, "Three minutes to alpha, Doctor."

Dr. Hiro Nakayami, head of research at TWI, Inc., nodded briefly and rubbed his thin, dark eyebrows. He let out a breathy sigh of weariness. This was the fourth and last test. The completion of this exercise would put a cap on the work he'd started over thirty years before. Now on a cool day in September he would knock open the door. That made it a little easier to ignore the numbing ache in the back of his head. He tapped his clipboard and nervously sucked his lip.

One of the interns rushed up and pressed a computer printout into his hand, then rushed off.

Nakayami perused the printout. He smiled with relief when he reached the bottom figures. All thananauts in an earlier episode had returned within ten seconds of the prescribed four-minute limit. No chance of brain damage or anything else.

The doctor gazed over the five reclining chairs that held the five adventurers they called "thananauts"—travelers in the realm of death. Nakayami snapped his finger, and an aide rushed to his side.

"Yes, Doctor?"

"I want printouts on all five when they're back, but just give me Listra's immediately after the test. The tape recorders are on?"

"Yes."

"Defibrillator's up and the oth—?"

"We won't need them, Doctor."

"I know. But I don't share your absolute optimism."

"All the equipment is ready and waiting."

A voice called out over the loudspeaker. "Two minutes to alpha."

Nakayami looked back at his notes. "All right. Let's make it work."

The aide disappeared into the throng of doctors, psychiatrists, nurses, and aides that swirled around each thananaut. At the far end of the room, Nakayami looked at the austere portrait of Gordon Watt, presumably presiding over the proceedings. Gordon Watt founded The Watt Institute— TWI, Inc.—ten years before after building a powerful evangelistic machine and organization. He had inaugurated the two schools connected with it—Atlantic Bible College and Seminary—in the early sixties.

Nakayami scanned his notes one more time, then studied the face of the redheaded woman in the sending apparatus. Even without makeup, her cheeks glowed with that youthful peach color he'd always admired in well-scrubbed American children. Of course, this woman was well into her forties, but plainly she retained not only spiritual appeal, as did all those working at TWI, but sex appeal, something Gordon Watt always preferred in his staff. Watt himself had said, "Christians should not only be beautiful on the inside, but on the outside as well. We must present a pleasing portrait to the world." Nakayami's boss and the heir of the kingdom, Martin Croase, kept that principle in force for every TWI applicant.

This woman, though, was Martin Croase's wife, Listra. She was only one of the five they were sending out this time into the world of clinical but not irreversible death. In this case, though, she had "traveled" over ten times herself and was acting as the "guide" in the operation. Watt called the process "thanatravel," from the Greek term for death, *thanatos*, but everyone referred to it as "traveling." Nakayami hoped Listra would be able to keep all five together and not be separated at alpha point, as had happened so many times before.

She was a key to the present success of TWI and the venture it was now involved in. Gordon Watt had personally recruited both Listra and her husband, Martin Croase, who was CEO of The Watt Institute, its evangelistic organization, and the two schools, as well as WCN—Watt Christian Network—a television and radio empire that provided cable programming to more than 2 million homes.

Watt was possessed of a serious fascination for dramatic Christian experience as the final proof of true religion. During the turmoil of the sixties, he pushed back the lines on the mystical/experiential side of evangelicalism, cashed in on the Jesus Freaks and charismatics, broke into radio and television, fashioned an incredible money machine during that time, and finally achieved complete legitimation as a "fringe" evangelical stalwart because of his prominence, conservative theology, and sheer money-making punch.

"One minute to alpha, doctor," the attendant intoned.

Nakayami didn't move. In his rumpled whites, he did not look like a man with three earned doctorates. He stood about five-two, distinctly Japanese, with a sharp, straight nose and thick lips. Though not a handsome man, he carried himself with high dignity.

The doctor blinked at the hot lights over Listra's head. Listra smiled and gave him a thumb's up. She wiggled her poised and sensual shape on the leather-covered reclining chair and affectionately made another face at him. When he didn't respond, she stuck out her tongue and laughed. To Nakayami, she was a remarkably girlish woman, almost childlike at times, yet he had long ago recognized her solid inner conviction of eternal destiny.

"Listra, don't make fun."

"This is fun," she said, rolling her eyes. "This is the greatest. You're a genius, Hiro."

Nakayami winced and looked down at his notes. He did not like Listra's using his nickname around the other attendants.

"Now don't give me that look, dear Hiro," Listra said. "You know I love this and I love you. I love everybody." She blew the people in the room several kisses. The doctors and nurses who noticed smiled.

"I feel so full of energy every time I go out," she said again. "Like I'm bursting to the seams with joy. I just want to kiss people. Want a kiss, Hiro?"

The doctor gave her a stern look and made a pretense of going over his notes one more time. But he did like Listra. For all her ambition, she had color and life. Not like many of the others he worked with each day.

"And just think, dear Hiro," Listra said. "I'm going to be dead soon. In . . ." She looked up at the digital time clock on the wall. "In thirty seconds. And I'm not even upset about it!"

It was in the early eighties that Watt hit on the idea of the NDE—near death experience—as the ultimate Christian "proof." He was one of the first to capitalize on using testimonials in his crusades by people who died and "went to heaven." As a result, he financed research directed on finding a way to scientifically produce repetitive NDEs, first in rats and rabbits, then dogs, monkeys, and in the end, it was hoped, in human beings.

Watt never saw his goal achieved. He died in the middle 1980s—though not before he had carefully entrusted the organization to the able hands of Martin Croase, a marketing and management genius who interned under several of the potentates at General Motors and Boeing and finally made a big splash at a biochemical lab called Lambda Research.

It was during that time that Watt also hired Nakayami, one of the preeminent researchers in thanatology. Nakayami had three Ph.D.s, one each in biochemistry, biogenetics, and computer science, the first two from Stanford and the third from M.I.T.

"What's the matter," Listra called. "Cat got your tongue?

Or something else?" She rolled her eyes suggestively.

Nakayami pursed his lips tightly and blew frustrated air through the thin cleft.

Shortly before coming to TWI, Nakayami had tired of the money-grabbing atmosphere of business and the government sycophancy required of university scientists. Quite accidentally Nakayami heard Gordon Watt preach several times in the evangelist's twilight years. The old man possessed a raw mystical charisma Nakayami had never witnessed before. He eventually became enamored of Watt's philosophy, and when Watt offered him $5 million in research funding a year, no questions asked, Nakayami took it.

In the past year, the Japan-born scientist had managed to develop a drug—TUT—that induced an NDE and internally resuscitated the subject after four minutes of clinical death. In other words, he had found a way to explore the regions of death at will and then come back to tell about it.

It was the stuff of which Nobel Prizes are born.

"Ten seconds, doctor."

The room became dead quiet. Each doctor shoved the pneumatic gun for injection against the upper arm of one of the five travelers.

The thananauts closed their eyes as they lay still and quiet on the reclining chairs. Around them, the equipment Nakayami used for monitoring thanatravel beeped and blipped. Electroencephalograph wires and electrodes hung out of the top headrest and pricked each scalp. An EKG machine sat to Listra's left, all the leads carefully adhered to her chest and back. The numerous other machines for recording blood type, taking temperature, and measuring heart rate were all hooked up to the master computer that synthesized the information in a readout.

"Five, four, three, two, one, injection."

The five doctors pressed the buttons on the pneumatic injection guns, and the cool blue liquid hit each arm simultaneously. There was a pause as everyone waited for the TUT to erupt inside the hearts of the thananauts. Then suddenly the faces of the five travelers went rigid. A moment later, their eyes rolled back.

"Alpha," said one of the doctors next to Listra.

"Alpha," echoed each of the other doctors at the other chairs, stethoscopes poised over each heart.

"Begin the four-minute countup," Nakayami said gruffly.

In the background, the same cool voice enunciated the seconds: "One, two, three . . . "

Nakayami sucked air noisily through his lips. His headache battered him behind his eyes. He knew he needed sleep soon or he would suffer a convulsion or something worse. When this test was over, he told himself to get to his apartment and conk out.

He brushed back his thinning gray hair. His thick upper lip dripped with sweat. He watched Listra's still face and glanced at the man standing against the wall behind her, David Hughes, one of the security people. He often walked in when they were doing testing to watch.

Nakayami smiled reflectively. He studied Listra's reposed face. Even in clinical death she was beautiful. He wondered what stories she would tell this time. It was always some incredible secret or revelation she brought back. Of all Nakayami's thananauts, Listra was preeminent, and not just because she was the boss's wife. She had been the first to travel, the first to guide. What next?

Nakayami already knew. The wall. Listra wanted to go beyond the wall.

He smiled. Maybe soon she would, he thought. He also wanted her to get beyond it. Then all mankind would know, once and for all. And not just from the lips of others. Anyone, anywhere could use the TUT to experience life beyond the grave. That was his hope, his mission, TWI's purpose, Martin Croase's inspired and determined message, and Gordon Watt's dream.

It was coming true before Nakayami's very eyes. "If only Gordon had lived to see it," he muttered as he turned to head for the door.

As the upcount continued over the speakers above his head, Nakayami knew already that the TUT was proved. Martin Croase would be all for announcing it to the rest of the world in a short time.

Listra Croase rose majestically and confidently above her still body on the chair. She immediately motioned to the other four she saw ascending. "We must all enter the tunnel simultaneously," she said, not verbally but mentally.

The other four twisted and, gaining their ease in flight, moved toward Listra.

"Forward, into the dark first," Listra said as the four spectral spirits joined her. "Everyone OK?"

"Fine here," Mark Jacobs said, one of the interns. The other three answered similarly.

"The tunnel will appear in a moment," Listra told them.

They waited, moving through the floors of TWI until they rose into the air above the building. Then Listra saw it. She pointed. "Follow me."

A moment later, they were inside it, whooshing together through the undulating curls of the gray-white smoky substance Listra called the tunnel. Once inside, they accelerated without any sense of fear or pain. Having shed their fleshly bodies, nothing restrained them from attaining speeds that Listra believed were beyond the speed of light. "You move at the speed of thought," she often said.

All five people were easily recognizable. Even without human, earthly bodies, their spirits retained a "look" that was a mixture of form and personality. The faces were almost the same, but younger looking. Listra figured her thanabody looked around thirty-two, the optimum age in an earthly sense. But the feeling of power was tremendous, as if once you became accustomed to the environment you could go anywhere in the universe you wanted merely at the mental suggestion.

There was no sensation of flying. No need to stretch out like Superman blazing across the sky. The tunnel curled and danced around you, but you moved through, whether prone, standing up, sitting, or balled—each of the other four had taken one position to see how it affected the journey—with no hindrance.

The journey seemed to last less than a minute. But the moment she touched down on the grassy meadow that ap-

23

peared at the end of the tunnel, Listra knew they had traveled beyond the known universe. She turned to look back down the tunnel as the other four alighted. An inner tremor like rushing water shot through her. This was the glory of death: the peace, the joy. As though nothing could ever be wrong again.

"When will he get here?" Mark Jacobs asked Listra as the five stood together in the meadow.

"Sometimes not immediately," Listra answered. Mark's face was young, radiant, like an Olympic god. They were all dressed in embroidered tunics that appeared to be fashioned of a different kind of light from their bodies. Listra had tried to explain this effect to others. In this place, everything was composed of light. There was no material, no earth, no flesh. She supposed this made it possible for the incredible speeds of travel and the mental communication.

Yet, on previous trips Listra's garments were nothing like these. Each time it changed. On one occasion she wore blue jeans and a Texas-style shirt with pearl buttons that glowed and danced as she moved. Another time, it was a long flowing dress. She had not yet figured out why this happened.

"Something's coming," Mark Jacobs said, turning to the horizon.

Listra looked up. Far up across the high meadow, someone touched down and seemed to be sprinting toward them.

"Is it him?" Jacobs asked.

"Rafa," Listra said.

"Will there be more?"

"I never know." Listra stepped forward toward the tall, august creature descending the meadow toward them. His cloak shivered with spangles of light, and his face was dark with blue eyes and long, glowing blond hair. A moment later, he stood towering over them.

"You have come once again."

"Yes, Rafa. I have brought friends." Listra motioned to her four fellow travelers.

"Mark Jacobs, yes. We have expected you. And Kerry, Linda, Harold. You are all welcomed with courtly honors."

24

The being's lips did not move as he talked. He placed his arm over Listra's shoulders.

"Things are well. Soon there will be many more who have traveled among us."

"Yes, Rafa. Many more. We hope to bring hundreds, thousands, even more. The TUT is a marvelous gift."

"It is something that has been saved for the last days." Rafa led them through the meadow. They walked without touching ground. But they did not have to move their feet at all.

"So we really are in the last days?" Listra said, glancing at the other four.

"It will not be long."

"And then?"

"The end, and the beginning."

Listra stopped and faced Rafa. "What about the threshold? What must we do to get past it?"

Rafa nodded, his long nose and sharp chin seeming to make the air sizzle around him. "The threshold is not yet. You must wait. There will be time."

"Soon," Listra said.

"Soon," Rafa answered.

Then there was a sharp pull on Listra's back, and she turned in time to see the other man and the two other women jerked backwards. She started to say, "We must leave now," but she didn't finish her sentence. With a blink, she imploded the universe, Milky Way, solar system, earth, TWI, and her body. She knew all had been passed. But she opened her eyes into the rays of the dazzling fluorescent lights above the recliner.

Dr. Nakayami watched as Listra's eyes opened. Her dark green irises sparkled with happiness. "We did it," she said softly. Nakayami knew she was probably still fighting the dizziness that accompanied the first few minutes back.

"You stayed together?" one of the doctors asked.

She shook her head slowly up and down. "More. We will soon be able to get past the wall, the threshold. I saw it again—at a distance. But soon. Soon, he said."

"Who? Rafa again?" Nakayami asked.

"Of course Rafa. I'm in rapture." Listra threw her hands over her head and stretched. How she could treat it all so blithely was always a sharp shock to Nakayami's sense of decorum, but it made him feel good. That was Listra's gift: making a person feel glad he was alive, and in her presence.

But behind them one of the doctors called out, "Jacobs isn't coming around."

"Code Red!" shouted one of the nurses.

Several monitors began stuttering with the defibrillation signal of permanent death.

"Get the adrenaline injection," another doctor shouted.

One hovered over Jacobs's still body. The other four thananauts stepped off their recliners and gathered around as everyone held his breath. So far there had been no deaths, though a few times this kind of thing had happened. A shot of adrenaline usually did it.

A nurse ran over with the syringe, but one of the doctors began administering CPR. "Just give me a second."

After pumps on Jacobs's sternum and a breath of air, Jacobs suddenly coughed, jerked, threw out an arm, and revived. The whole room broke into cheers. Jacobs sputtered for a minute, then getting acclimated to the situation, shouted, "I stood at the wall."

For a moment, Listra's face registered shock, then instantly she was at his side. "What did you see?"

"It was like rocks. Stone on stone. Rafa said I could not go in, though. That was when I finally got pulled back."

"Almost didn't return at all," the doctor who had administered the CPR said.

"Aw, you guys know what to do," Jacobs said.

Listra patted his arm. "Who knows, you could have gone all the way in if we'd given you another minute."

"Another minute and his brain would be dead," the doctor said. But everyone was full of cheer now that nothing catastrophic had happened.

Dr. Nakayami wondered, though, what Martin Croase would say. The TUT still was not ready. He braced himself for a tirade. But as he watched Listra practicing the genteel encouragement she gave people when she spoke in person, in chapel, or on television, he felt better.

"Dr. Hank, I saw you wink," Listra said to Dr. Hank Perry, one of the researchers, as she began walking out of the sending room. "I'll remember it. You have such a marvelous wink."

Perry turned a light shade of pink.

Voices in the room rose as the four other travelers excitedly recounted the experience into the tape recorders. They were required to record precisely what was going on in their minds upon awaking, so that tended to take the edge off of their initial euphoria. But Nakayami knew Listra was not about to be deterred from her other goal in life, which was to help everyone realize they were the crown of creation and nothing should ever stop them from reaching their dreams, even if Jacobs had almost died.

Listra hugged a nurse, Julie Callas, in the doorway. "I have something important I want to tell you, Julie."

Nakayami watched as they walked away, Listra's arm over her shoulder and Julie beaming as though she'd just been featured on the cover of *Time* magazine. The Japanese doctor wrote down Listra's initial responses on his clipboard. He knew they might change with time and perspective. Coming out of thanatravel was in some ways like awaking from a dream. The intense ideations that struck just upon breaking out of deep REM sleep disappeared in a few minutes, never to be regained. Fortunately, the tape recorder had taken it all down for each of the travelers.

After punching in a final period on his notes, Dr. Nakayami turned to leave the room. Everyone was all right at least. The TUT was still a bit dangerous. But the TUT-B would be another matter.

Nakayami knew that getting beyond the wall—which Listra was determined to do—would require a far heavier and deeper dose of TUT than the present version. And that might cost lives.

The thanadrug, TUT, was so called because the chemical name—TetraUlamicine-Thyocrinoprafin—used those three letters. It was euphemistically referred to by TWI personnel as

"The Ultimate Trip," and was deemed safe enough by Martin Croase that much of the equipment on the reclining chairs was no longer necessary. Only the pneumatic arm for injecting the TUT was now required. And soon that would also become obsolete. But Nakayami was much more cautious, and he knew restraining Croase would be difficult.

The Japanese researcher pushed open the door.

"Dr. Nakayami," someone called, "should we go through the usual questions?"

The doctor waved his right arm without turning. "Of course." He hurried to the elevator to the twelfth floor. Martin Croase would be waiting there—if he wasn't in the barn, practicing his shooting.

2

Raymond Mazaris pumped his legs furiously for the last quarter mile. Just over a minute later, he stopped, panting and wheezing at the end of the track in front of the piled up hurdles. He glanced at the stopwatch, shook his head, and murmured, "Even my time is getting worse."

After running a few wind sprints and then doing forty-six push-ups and eight pull-ups, he headed for the Atlantic Bible College and Seminary men's locker room. He was a second year student at Atlantic Seminary. He took a long hot shower, then stood in the bathroom rubbing the fog from the mirror with his right hand. The cool gray eyes, tousled brown hair, and jutting jaw that once marked him with resolution looked faded, ragged. "The SEALs would laugh," he muttered. "I've got to get out of this funk."

For a long moment he gazed into the mirror, blinking and trying to force out the pictures that began clotting his mind. And then he was there.

Briny air pummeled the faces of the twenty-eight SEALs as they silently paddled to the beach near Paitilla Airport, Panama. The radio crackled for the hundredth time. "Final recon: Noriega still at large. Panamanian forces waging attack on U.S. troops in Canal Zone. Secure the Lear Jet."

Captain Ray Mazaris stared forward to the desolate, hard dark mud at the end of Paitilla's runway. The low grass wasn't much cover. The thirteen men in his platoon crawled forward. They could all see the Panamanian Defense Forces moving far ahead under the control tower. His two best friends, Torpedoman's Mate Second Class Bill Clager and Boatswain's Mate First Class Jess Ross, were nearby in Golf Platoon, and Ray felt secure that they were there: two of the toughest and sweetest guys he'd ever known.

"Stagger and cover," Ray whispered along to the men. "Bravo Platoon first. Stop, cover. Then Golf Platoon. Move."

Mazaris's Bravo Platoon hustled forward, crouched and ready with the formidable weaponry they carried—.50 caliber machine guns, M60 light machine guns, M16A1 rifles, grenade launchers, rocket launchers. They could not fire until fired upon. And they had to be wary of accidentally killing civilians. A support gunship helicopter, lights out, whined overhead.

Two minutes of movement and they were in position to go for the hangar. Mazaris looked through his night-scope, searching for signs of ambush. He wanted to send just a couple of men scouting ahead. But there wasn't time. He had to make the decision. Crack Jossen, Mazaris's lieutenant, whispered, "We've got to go, sir."

"I know," Ray answered. "All right, Golf, do the hangar. Bravo covers."

The first squad of eight men rushed forward, spread out.

The Panamanian ambush was perfect. A hail of gunfire strafed the eight men as Mazaris watched, his throat constricting. Seven men went down.

Someone yelled, "Heavy wounded!" and Ray knew they had to gain fire superiority to get in the medics. Mazaris hand-signaled to his men to move up and cover.

A bullet punched Ray's webbing, and he fell over. But the bulletproof vest underneath had held. He quickly got on his belly. "Around," he motioned.

Three of his men crawled to the right. Then Ray clearly saw the machine gun nest the Panamanians had set up. He had a grenade launcher. It was now or never. He stood.

Fired. The machine gun nest blew.

More men moved in. The gunship above began leveling the Panamanians farther in. Ray sprinted forward, firing a light machine gun he had picked up along the way. Then one of the rockets crashed and exploded Noriega's Lear Jet. It was over.

As his men mopped up, Ray returned to the scene of the seven downed SEALs. Four lay dead, stretched out. It took him only a second to recognize two of the faces: Clager and Ross.

Ray's eyes burned as he stared into the mirror. "If we'd only had one more minute to do recon. Was it a bad order?"

He didn't know. He'd never know. He'd only have to live with it. Which was what he was trying to do.

The eight-year-old Ray Mazaris who had died and then been resuscitated by a supernatural being named Trell had matured into a lanky, broad-shouldered man with a ready smile, a steady hand, and a dark sense of foreboding about an evil, mixed-up world.

Ray stifled a curse in his throat and continued toweling off. He rubbed the mirror again and bared his teeth. A moment later, he snorted with disapproval. "Get a life, man."

It wasn't just Panama that had thrown a nuclear bomb into Ray's otherwise cool, calm spiritual machinery. His mother had died when he was ten—bone cancer tearing to pieces her thin, broken body; and nine years later his father had been mugged on a side street in Philadephia. After nearly a month in a coma, he lived another ten years as a near vegetable in the VA Medical Center in Washington, D.C.

As Ray sat quietly in the locker room wishing something would knock him out of his own spiritual coma, he thought for the thousandth time about the hot, inky anxiety that sometimes yapped out of its basket like a cobra and sank fiery fangs into his soul. Why had God saved him from death at eight if that same God was going to take away everything else that mattered?

As always, no answer echoed in Ray's mind. Deep down, he wondered if there were not some curse on his life, some dread decree of God that said nothing would ever turn out for Ray Mazaris.

"I should have been a Catholic monk," he mumbled into the damp bathroom air.

A moment later, the metal locker room door banged open, and two other men entered talking. The taller one, someone Ray knew as David Hughes, a rather cocky ex-cop involved in TWI security, said to the other, whom Ray had seen around but didn't know, "You think we ought to try it? Listra says it's incredible."

"When Croase is ready for guys like us to do it, we'll do it. Don't push it, Dave."

Ray instantly zeroed in. He'd heard some of the news on campus about TWI working on a project concerning death, but he knew little about it. He had few friends and fewer who confided gossipy campus details to him. He was considered at times a little too holy, a little too unapproachable.

"Croase'll be announcing it soon anyway," Hughes said. "I'm psyched."

Suddenly, Hughes saw Ray. "You're Mazaris, the military guy, right?"

Ray looked up, trying to act nonchalant. "I don't think I'm alone in that category." He had on his blue jeans and a light blue navy shirt. He was about to pick up his gym bag and leave.

"Yeah, you're the ex-SEAL."

Ray grabbed the purple gym bag. "I was in the SEALs."

"You pick up on what we're talking about?"

"Not really."

Hughes was down to his underwear and seemed to be challenging Ray for some reason. Ray had no idea why. Hughes was well built, muscular, definitely the type that worked out a lot. Every now and then Ray had a run-in like this.

"Death trips, man. Croase is sending people to the stars."

"Not something I'd be real interested in at the moment." Ray started for the door.

"Better get interested, ex-SEAL-man. Martin Croase likes to have lots of backers when he gets into a project."

31

At the end of the aisle was the small, enclosed foyer to the outside. Ray stopped, combed his hair as he looked in a mirror, and got ready to go.

"Hear that, SEAL-man?"

Ray turned around slowly. "It's still a free country, unless I missed something this afternoon."

The bigger man stood naked now, obviously showing off for his friend. The other man stood with his hands on his hips, watching the whole scene.

"Yeah, well, what're you in such a big hurry about?"

"I've got a blind date." Ray opened the door.

"Who with?"

Ray stopped, feeling more and more irritated. "One of the secretaries."

"Which one?"

He snorted and eyed Hughes with exasperation. "You want to go out with her?"

"Just tell me the name. I'll give you the line on her."

"Don't need any line."

"The name, SEAL-man?"

"Forget it." Ray started to go.

"What—you too big a man to let us know?"

"Guess so." The dank air of the locker room and Hughes's pushy style made Ray want to exit quickly. He rammed open the door.

Hughes called after him. "Give me the name, and I'll give you the line on her."

Ray let go of the door. As it closed, he heard Hughes say, "Some tough guy. He's a flake, like most of the rest of the people around here."

The just cooling September air felt good, and Ray drew a deep breath. For a moment, he thought about what Hughes had said, then he shrugged it off. "No use in fighting that kind of baloney," he said to himself.

He ambled up the sidewalk, knowing that he still hadn't popped the sour mood. "This could be your last chance," he murmured. But then he laughed sardonically. "Yeah, I've probably already had my last chance. I just don't know it yet."

3

Andi Darcasian stood at the sink of the fashionable, filled-with-every-latest-gadget kitchen. She was finishing the last of the dinner dishes as her ten-year-old son, Tommy, described the events of the day at school, where he was in the fourth grade. It wasn't her house; she was sitting it while the owner, a Bible college prof, was on sabbatical. She was more used to cheap, three-room apartments, so being here was a real boon to her sense of motherhood and femininity. Cleaning the fine maple and walnut Victorian furniture, polishing the Revere silverware, and making the beds in the spacious upper rooms was a small price to pay for some comfort and relief from the rigors of single motherdom.

She was five-six, with long black hair that curled meticulously at the ends framing a tanned and friendly face. Her given name was Andrea, but everyone called her Andi.

"I didn't do so great in math this week, Mom," Tommy said with some hesitation.

"What did you get?"

"You won't get mad at me, will you?" Tommy's eyes behind his thick glasses looked small and worried. If there was anything Andi longed for it was that Tommy would discover that all people weren't out to hurt him. Since Andi had come to work at the campus and taken classes, Tommy had experienced quite a bit of rejection and name-calling from several of the faculty children who considered themselves much more spiritual than he. She'd thought about leaving, but that was impossible.

Andi turned from the sink and looked at Tommy. "I will never get mad at you if you try, honey."

There was a long pause. "What if I didn't really try?"

Andi rubbed her hands with the towel. "Then I'll just have to help you learn to try."

Another long pause. "I got an F."

He pulled out the paper. His rosy cheeks almost flamed. For all his awkwardness, he was a friendly kid, eager to please. She'd discovered that early on, even when he was a baby. He rarely cried, and when she put him to bed he always obediently closed his eyes when she said, "Night, night."

Andi took a few minutes to sit down and discuss the paper. When she was finished, she took Tommy's hands in her own. "Tommy, look at me."

He raised his eyes slowly.

"You've got to believe I want the best for you. And I'll do all I can to make it happen. Do you believe that?"

His hands trembled in hers.

"Do you?"

"I—I guess so."

She gave him a quick hug, then said, "Well, we'd better get ready for tonight. We get to meet the famous Ray Mazaris, you know."

"Who's he?"

"Some ex-military guy they say. He was in the Navy. Some special group or something. Commandos, I think. Green Berets or something. I don't know. Real macho person. You'll like—"

"What's macho?"

Andi laughed. "Nothing worth thinking about, believe me." A friend named Holly Quinette, one of the married secretaries, had set her up with Ray. She was a good friend and frequently kept Tommy when Andi wanted to go out. Andi snagged a ruffled red dress from where it was lying over one of the chairs in the kitchen and held it up to her chin. "Like this?"

Tommy moved his head briskly up and down, jostling the thick glasses on his nose. His curly blond hair, uncombed as usual, moved slightly.

"Hurry up, then. We only have about thirty minutes. We shouldn't be late."

While Andi dressed upstairs, Tommy clumped into the leather easy chair in front of the TV in the family room. He hit the remote switch, and the television flickered on. An afternoon sitcom argument had started on one of the programs.

Andi walked back into the room wearing a blue velour robe. "Tommy, please get dressed."

Tommy scrunched up in the chair staring wearily out the

34

window. She knew instantly he was in a mood and it would not be easy to knock him out of it. She decided to let him sit for a few minutes.

When she came back, he was still crumpled up in the chair, looking tired and worried. She had on a sheer blue skirt and powder blue blouse buttoned to the chin with ruffles and long sleeves, having changed her mind about the red dress. It was one of her more stylish outfits. On an impulse she sat down on the arm of the easy chair and touched Tommy's blond hair.

"What's troubling you, hon?"

"I don't know."

"Yes, you do."

He kept his eyes on his hands and fidgeted.

"Tell me."

"Do you think you'll ever get married?"

She laughed. "That one is too hot for me to handle."

He bowed his head. She realized he was deeply worried.

"Tommy, believe me, I'm not getting married."

"What if the person doesn't like me?"

She riffled his hair, trying to effervesce him out of the mood. "Believe me, if I decide to get married, you'll be in on it long before it ever gets to that point."

"I would?" He stared up at her, true amazement in his eyes. She knew it was a dangerous thing to say. But she had decided long ago he would be a part of everything. If he didn't like someone, if was as good as over.

Andi held out her fist. "Go ahead."

He put up his fist slowly.

"Punch it."

He punched hers lightly, a little ritual she'd started several years before for making an unbreakable agreement. She smiled. "OK, that settles it. Now please get dressed. I can't keep Mr. Macho waiting, and you've got to go to Holly's house."

4

Martin Croase stared at the gray wood of the huge barn, then bashed it with his foot and jumped in, swinging an Israeli Uzi into readiness. The first dummy appeared to his left. He fired, splitting it to smithereens with half a clip. The sound of footsteps resounded behind him, and he knelt, whipping the automatic around and strafing a wall until the 9 mm bullets emptied and pinged into the sign face that grinned at him from the projecting arm.

He reloaded with a 32-bullet clip, cracked it into place, and stuck the nose of the submachine gun into the darkness of the next door. He was about to fire at a woman who stepped in front of him, but he realized she was "friendly," and he pulled back. He moved past the dummy.

The sound of a semiautomatic pistol hammer clicking into place.

Croase spun, fell, lay prone.

Imaginary bullets ricocheted over his head. He pulled the trigger. Fifteen shells destroyed his quarry, this time a terrorist in a gas mask. He started to get up when he heard voices.

"Dr. Croase!"

Croase swore under his breath, stood, and brushed himself off. "Why does business always interfere with fun?" he murmured as he walked to the doorway. "I'm in here. Come in. I'm on safety."

He saw Dr. Nakayami enter with Ken Strock, his head of security, and two others. Strock was thickset and paunchy with watery green eyes, short-clipped, blondish hair, and a nose that looked like it had been the only thing on his face never broken. Croase pulled the Uzi strap onto his shoulder and let it dangle. He eyed the doctor, then said nonchalantly, "So you feel we're ready?"

Nakayami shook his head. He was still in his scrub greens. "There are problems."

"What problems now?"

"We had one misfire this evening."

"Oh, garbage, Hiro. That's not a problem. You give them a shot, and they're all right in a second. Forget it."

Nakayami didn't move. "Martin, this is a serious problem."

Croase turned to Ken Strock. It was Strock who planned out Croase's "barn games." The ex-cop and Vietnam vet had an interest in antiterrorist warfare and had been hired specifically to head up security and provide Martin Croase with a little fun. A barn in the woods on TWI property, but over a half-mile from the campus, was selected. Croase spent at least one evening a week there, after Strock set it up. He said to the burr-cut security man, "I want to start finalizing the plans for mass production and introduce it to the board, our primary donors, and those we can trust."

Nakayami started to protest, but Croase waved him off.

Strock said, "I think we can go ahead with it now, no problem. We've got two groups lined up, several faculty, several students. All checked out."

Nakayami stared at the two men, incredulous, then said, "It is not ready."

"It is, Hiro," Croase said. "There's no problem. We have plenty of doctors, nurses, everyone on hand. We do it in the sending room, or the place out at Fisherman, and we're all right. Ken, do you see any other problems at the moment?"

"Only thing I'm worried about is the FDA. But you said that was all handled."

"Yes, it is." Croase pushed the Uzi up, cried, "Hit the dirt," and all four men around him fell to the ground as he let out a burst of shots over their heads at a mechanical hand that had just appeared on the far wall. When it was over, the men dusted themselves off, still squatting. "Sorry, guys, but you meet me here, you take it as it comes." He held out his hand to Dr. Nakayami.

He said to Strock, "Legally, we think we're all right. It's not a medicine. It's not used in medical practice. It's not an over-the-counter drug. And we're defining it as part of religious worship. Plus, we have our loyal Senator Garvey always ready to go to bat for us. So I think we're in the clear. At least at this point. As long as we keep the information flow within the confines of the campus."

"That's my job," Strock said.

"Right. By the way, how many students and faculty are there in residence here now?"

"Twenty-two hundred, give or take thirty."

"So we have a captive audience. It's perfect. Anything else before we get moving on this?"

Strock got to his feet and scratched his burr haircut. "Boss, one thing. Where are we going with this? I mean, I understand you trying it out on campus first. But I'm not real sure what it's supposed to do in the long run."

Croase smiled. "Leave that to me. I've got it handled. You just keep security tight. I really think that if we can get people to try it, just try it, I think we're home free."

He leaned on the wall again and let out the empty clip, replaced it with a third from his belt. "What do you think, Hiro?" he said, not looking up.

The quiet Japanese researcher sighed with a classic Japanese hissing noise. "I don't think we should go ahead with anything mass."

Croase snorted. "I don't pay you to think about that. I mean, about the idea. We work in ideas, right? What do you think of the idea of the research project as a means to transform lives? That was Gordon Watt's vision. A drawing in of all faiths into the one true faith. And this will make it possible."

"Still," Nakayami went on, "I do not think we're ready."

"Why not—besides the one problem you keep harping on?"

"Everyone we have used has been required to be free of drugs for one month, including vitamins, aspirin, cold medication, everything. We do not know—"

Croase snorted with exasperation. "Hiro, you're being overly cautious. The TUT is proved."

"For people with no drugs in—"

"So we tell everyone that they have to be off all medications. So what?"

"There's always a chance someone will not listen."

Croase looked at Strock and the others and rolled his eyes, then jerked his thumb in Nakayami's direction, joking. "Japanese guy need to eat his Wheaties, I think."

Strock and the others laughed, but Nakayami didn't respond.

"All right, people, get this thing in motion. Plan out some weekends at Fisherman. Get the right people selected, high-visibility-type people, whatever. That's my order."

There was a brief pause. A clock ticked in the background. Instantly, Croase dove forward, rolled, and came up on both feet, firing at a figure that appeared in the loft. Straw flew out of the dummy's belly as Croase unloaded the whole clip at its chest.

"Nobody messes with me," Croase growled, smiling to the others. Then he laughed. "Don't mind me, guys, I'm just having fun. Ta-ta." He bolted back through the doorway with a whoop, and soon automatic weapon fire began rattling throughout the back of the barn.

5

After a movie in Gaithersburg, Ray drove to the large mall down the main drag and he and Andi walked around the mall talking. She was definitely the fox that Kalimer had said she was, and Ray couldn't help wondering what the "line" was on her. He had chosen to take her to a movie because he thought that would mean less need to talk. But as he warmed up to her, he found himself wanting to talk more.

They window-shopped and conversed about clothing, music, mutual friends, and the movie for a few minutes, then Andi said, "I hardly know anything about you, Ray. What's your life all about anyway?"

"Not much to tell." They were both staring at the best-seller pile of books in the B. Dalton window.

"Oh, don't give me that. I heard your testimony."

Ray winced. "I had hoped you hadn't."

She looked surprised. "I thought it was dynamite, really. All those military operations, and you becoming a committed Christian just before the invasion of Panama."

Ray nodded and led her away from the window. The mixed aromas of pizza, fresh donuts, hamburgers, and Greek tyros battered his nostrils as they sauntered around. They aroused his hunger. He thought they might stop for some ice cream, but he said, "Actually, I'm beginning to think it's a lot of hype. Every time I tell it, it seems to get bigger and better. Sometimes I wonder what really happened."

She laughed. "Yeah, that's what happens. You start off telling the bare truth, then you get a laugh sometime about a genuine exaggeration, but because it got a laugh you keep it in. I know all about that."

He looked at her, then smiled. "So you've given a testimony or two yourself?"

"Yeah, but you're ducking my question, Ray Mazaris." She gave him a cocked eyebrow, reproving look, and he smiled sheepishly. "There must be a lot to you to get through all that—even if it has gotten a little exaggerated. From what you say, just the entrance exam sounds grueling."

"You have to be in shape," he answered, nodding his head with the memory. "Swim five-hundred yards in ten minutes, then a two minute rest, forty push-ups, two minute rest, fifty-six sit-ups, two minute rest, then a one-and-a-half mile run with full pack in ten minutes, and finally eight chin-ups."

"You did all that, huh?"

"That's what they say." He licked his lips and looked around for a place to get ice cream.

She looked him up and down, as if to measure his physique. "You look like you could take it." She suddenly touched his upper arm and gave it a squeeze. "Yeah, you could do it."

He laughed. "You don't hold anything back, do you?"

"Just having fun at your expense, that's all. Come on, aren't you going to invite me for a burrito or something?"

"How about some ice cream?"

"Great. Show me the way."

Crowds of people hurried past as they took the elevator to the main floor and walked along, looking for a Friendly's or a take-out counter.

"What was it like in the SEALs, Ray—really?" She gazed at him seriously. Her deep brown eyes and long lashes, the angular face with the high cheekbones, and her lovely dark hair pulled back in barrettes made him squirm for a moment with the desire to grab her.

"Believe me, the hard part isn't the initial physical test. But it does weed out a few. Lots of guys think it's a lark. But the SEALs are serious people. Real serious. And dangerous. Twenty-five weeks of intensive training after you get in. And the trainers do everything they can to make you quit. They don't want anyone in who doesn't want to be a SEAL more than anything else in life. They make life a royal hell, and every day it gets worse. You make a mistake, you have to run off the pier at Coronado—the base in California where you're trained—into fifty degree water and swim a mile—in your clothing. Two guys make the same mistake, the whole platoon has to dunk.

"Then there's 'hell week' at the end. You get about four hours of sleep a night. Running in full pack for miles each morning. Then swimming—in cold water for hours. Demolition. Blowing up imaginary enemies. Constant physical and mental exertion, then weapons training. I think I could shoot just about anything with a trigger now." He laughed. "You end up almost becoming a fish. I distinctly remember drowning four or five times during hell week."

She gazed at him, incredulous. "You're joking."

"Yeah. But that was only the beginning. Then there's the constant training, always on call. It's a tough life. I wouldn't want it now."

She stopped at a toy window, peering at a Nintendo game display. "Tommy wants this for Christmas."

"Don't they all?"

A loudmouth walked by, using vulgarity, and Andi turned, looking at him. "You'd think people would learn to keep that kind of talk private, but no more."

"The world's gone crazy," Ray said, touching her arm and steering her in the direction of the eatery.

"So how did you become a Christian, Ray?" Andi asked quietly, swinging her arms as they walked. She had a fluid, easy-going grace that he liked.

He shoved his hands in his pockets and spotted a Häagen-Daz ice cream stand. "My parents became Christians under the preaching of Gordon Watt when I was a kid. I had this experience when I was eight—an actual near death experience like you hear about on TV—"

"I didn't know that."

"I haven't told many people." He looked into her eyes, and she returned his gaze with cool intensity. He liked her style. She might even make a good SEAL.

41

"So what TWI is doing really must intrigue you?"

"In a way. I don't know much about it."

"Yeah, neither do I. Lots of talk, though. Very mysterious. But what happened to you?" They stood with a group in front of the counter and waited to make an order.

"I hope you're not a chocolate freak," Ray said.

"I am. It's luscious. Why?"

"Because when I get done here, there won't be much left."

"Let's destroy the place," she said, grinning.

Ray stepped up to the counter and ordered a double dip Belgian Chocolate Chocolate cone, and on his recommendation, Andi tried the same—single dip.

They walked away toward a small fountain. She sat down on a ledge, and he joined her. Pulling out a coin, he threw it into the fountain. He handed her one. "My weekly tithe," he said.

"You make enough to throw in that much, huh?"

"Less." As they sat on the ledge, Ray told her about Trell and the resuscitation. When he was finished, she looked at him wide-eyed and earnest.

"I've probably thought about it once a day ever since."

"I bet."

He gazed off at the opening to a department store. People were moving back and forth, smiling, joking, laughing, looking serious and preoccupied. Every expression imaginable lit on a face somewhere. Ray cleared his throat. "I became a Christian during that time—at least, I prayed the prayer and accepted the Lord. Later I was baptized, but it wasn't until I joined the navy and the SEALs that any of it began to click. My testimony about Panama is, well, it leaves out some things."

"Like what?" She licked her cone and looked at him sideways. She had a determined, suck-out-all-the-flavor look as she ate.

He suddenly wanted to put his arm over her shoulders, to drink in her warmth, to listen to her heart beating. For a brief second, he realized how desperately lonely he was. But he forced the thoughts away. He told her about the assault on Paitilla.

When he finished, he swallowed and looked off over the open spaces of the mall, his eyes suddenly, burning. "Two of the ones who died were my best friends." Ray's voice became husky, and Andi touched his shoulder sympathetically. "So after it happened, when it was time to recommission, I quit."

She had stopped licking her cone and gazed kindly at him.

He looked down at his hands. "Sorry, I didn't know we would get into this."

"It wasn't your fault, Ray," she said, suddenly letting her knee touch his. "I'm sure of that. Things like that happen."

"Not to Navy SEALs." He shrugged and looked past her to the fountain. "It's another thing I think about every day." He coughed into his hand. "Anyway, I don't want to depress you. Ever since, I've kind of felt like a cop-out. I shouldn't have quit, at least not like that, but I was, well . . ."

"I'm glad you told me."

He nodded, then said quietly, "That's why I hate that testimony. I don't tell about my mistakes in it. They just want to hear the good stuff."

"I think you should tell it the way you want to tell it."

"Oh, you know when you get on one of those TV programs or in front of a crowd, the Croases always want everything down to the letter." He looked away from her and crunched into the cone.

There was a long silence as they finished the ice cream. "What about your family? Any of them live around—?"

Ray sensed that his face had clouded because she stopped.

"I'm not opening up another disaster area, I hope?" She looked at him, anxiously. "I'm always getting too personal. I'm sorry. Please forgive—"

"No, it's OK." He shrugged. "Most people don't ask me about these things. I'm glad, so don't worry about it."

She waited for him to continue.

"My mom died when I was ten. Cancer. We kept praying that God would do something miraculous, either take her quickly and gently or heal her. He didn't do either. It seemed she just went on and on in pain."

For a second, Ray visualized the scene shortly after her death.

"Daddy, why did God take Mommy away from us?" Ray asked his father.

Ray's dad, a brusque, blue-eyed navy commander, replied with his usual terse finality. "God didn't take her away from us, son."

"But if God really cared—"

"God cares, Ray. But we live in an evil world."

"But why did God let it be evil, Daddy? Why didn't He make it good? And why didn't He let Mommy stay with us?"

His dad pressed Ray's shoulder and grimaced. "It was His will, son. That's all. He decided to do it that way."

"But it's not fair. We need her, Daddy. She did every-thing . . . " Ray started to cry, and when he looked up he no-ticed his father's chin quiver. But the man shook it off and resumed his usual unflinching calm.

Ray stared forward. Even at ten, he had a penchant for asking hard questions. His brother, Timmy, sat by his side in the back of the big Chevy, swinging his legs back and forth. As he looked out the window, Ray murmured, "Why do I have to love You, God, if You took away my mom?"

Ray licked his lips and concluded the story, glancing at Andi and licking the cone, though for a moment it began to taste like sand. "My dad was a navy captain—in Korea and then Vietnam—he suffered a major stroke when I was nine-teen and away at college. First he went into a coma. When he came out, he had serious brain damage. My brother, Timmy, and I had to make some hard decisions, so we had him put in a VA Medical Center in Washington, D.C. He died there about four years ago."

"Man, Ray, you've really been through it."

He cleared his throat and looked over the fountain at a woman pulling a reluctant toddler to her feet. "No worse than anyone else."

He stood and helped her to her feet. She pulled on her sweater. They walked along in silence, and he wondered what she was thinking. She was definitely refreshing, a happy change of pace. They began window-shopping again, talking about school and sports and the latest movies. The mood changed, and he felt buoyed up on her scent and warmth.

As they walked along, chuckling about the anecdotes they shared about high school, she said, "Not to change the subject, but do you know what the girls call you at school?"

He turned and gave her an OK-I-can-take-a-joke look.

"Mr. Macho."

He rolled his eyes. "Yeah, I guess I've heard that."

She slipped her arm through his. "Well, now I for one know the truth about it, and I promise I'll set them straight in the future."

"Oh yeah? And what's the truth?"

"That you're macho-decent. It's a new male hybrid never before known. Super-tough for the bad stuff, and super-understanding for the women-stuff. Maybe I'll do a study of it for the psych department."

He laughed and enjoyed the closeness of her arm in his. They went through the mall, then out to his car. On the way home, she asked another of her high-powered questions. "So why are you here at seminary, Ray? You really don't seem like the minister type."

He turned onto the main drag where he could catch the road out to Brinton and her house. "I guess it comes down to that ever since I was eight, since that near-death experience happened to me, I've felt God's hand on my life. I've believed that He saved me for something special. But when all these things happened to me—Mom, Dad, Panama—I've always wanted to know: Am I wrong? Is all this God and Jesus stuff just a fantasy? Was I really preserved for a purpose? Your basic philosophical questions, I guess. But they're real enough to me. I don't want to be a minister that much. It's just that I had enough money saved up, I already have a B.A. and a B.S. if I want to do something with them, and I figured it's now or never. If anyone influenced me to come specifically to Atlantic it was Dr. Kingston. He's sort of my mentor."

"Good man, I hear," Andi said.

"You're right about that. Anyway, there you have it—a true nut in his shell."

"Ah, a pun. Don't tell me you're one of those?"

"A punster? No, serious all the way."

"Not serious. Mysterious."

"Oh, so you're the real punster?"

"Some say I'm a real punny girl."

He groaned. She chuckled. "I promise, no more tonight. Anyway, when are you going to start asking about me?"

He glanced at her as he drove and smiled. "I thought you must be doing research for my biography."

"No, I'll leave that to Kitty Kelley."

"Can't wait." He noticed her perfume again and thought about asking what it was—it stirred him—but he said, "All right, why are you here at the school?"

"Do you really want to hear it?"

"Sure."

"Well, don't be too horrified. I got pregnant with Tommy in college and refused to marry the fraternity crumb that got me where I was. I was stupid and young and a real fool. But these things happen. I considered an abortion, then felt it would be wrong. Tommy was born, I never ended up finishing college, and I worked several office jobs, eventually coming here as an assistant administrator. My parents supported the ministry of Gordon Watt for many years. They're just your average couple, retired now. My dad and I had a real falling out when I got pregnant, but after I became a Christian a few years ago, things have gotten better. They're helping me pay for part of school. Very proud parents, you know, despite my many sins. If I graduate, I'll be the first woman in my family with a college degree. I think they want that more than I do."

"So you really want to finish?"

She smiled wistfully. "Yeah. But I'd be lying if I said I didn't want to really settle down, give Tommy a solid foundation. Still, I've got a lot of questions. Not in the same way as you. I want to learn about Christ, though, and I'm thinking seriously about nursing. But I want to have a real home, make some money, be independent, and try to serve God in some practical way."

"Judging from what I know of you tonight, I'd guess you have far more than a 'real' home, Andi."

She was looking out the side window to her right. "Yeah, but not like I want. Tommy's the most important person in my life. I want him to find his place in the world and put some roots down somewhere. My parents gave that to me, and I want to give the same to him."

For the next twenty minutes, they talked about school, courses they'd taken, profs they liked or disliked. Finally, Ray pulled into her driveway and hurried to get around to her door before she got out herself.

She waited for him. When he opened her door, she said, "Being the gentleman."

"Trying to."

Holly, the baby-sitter, had brought Tommy home and met them at the door. Tommy came running out from the kitchen, and Andi introduced Ray to both of them, then asked Tommy why he was still up. He said, "I came down for a drink," but Holly whispered when the boy went out to the kitchen that he'd been watching in the window.

When they were alone, Ray felt too nervous for a kiss, so he finally smiled, touched her shoulder, and promised to call. She watched him from the doorway until he was out of the driveway, then waved. As he headed down the street toward the campus, he felt more alive then he'd felt since leaving the navy.

CHAPTER TWO

1

The Fishermen's Bible Conference Center near Hagerstown featured all that was best and little of the worst of Christian campgrounds. A hundred-and-twenty-room hotel stood at its heart, three stories high, and as plush as anything Hilton or Marriott thought of offering. Listra Croase herself oversaw the original layout and interior decorating, which was strictly top of the line furnishings. One wing strung together twelve conference rooms that could be opened up for larger gatherings, or sized down for the typical smaller ones during the fall and winter seasons. It was the perfect place for Martin Croase to introduce his world-changing experience.

Ray Mazaris took a seat in the back of the small blue room facing the lake through sliding glass windows. Already fifteen people had gathered. He knew most of them by sight—students, their spouses, and a couple of faculty members—but none personally.

Quietly, Ray opened his pocket Bible and began to read Philippians, a book he had begun committing to memory. He was working on the first chapter when he sensed someone standing behind him.

"Hi!"

He looked up. Tommy Darcasian stood behind him to his right. It had been three weeks since his blind date with

Andi, and he still hadn't called her. Tommy said, "I didn't know you'd be here."

Ray patted the seat next to him. "I didn't know *you'd* be here. How are you doin'?"

"OK." The boy didn't move into the aisle.

"Is your mom with you?"

"Sure." Tommy looked behind him to the door. "She's talking to someone as usual." He smiled hesitantly. Ray moved over two seats. He suddenly felt his face get hot, but he hoped she wouldn't be upset.

Tommy took the seat, kicking his short legs back and forth. "We don't get many vacations like this," he said.

A moment later, Andi walked in wearing faded blue jeans and a denim jacket. "I see you've already found a friend," she said to Tommy. "I told you you would." She looked at Ray and said, "Hi."

Ray smiled. "Have a seat."

Andi took the chair to Tommy's right with Tommy between her and Ray. "You as nervous about this as I am?"

"Probably."

She draped her arm over Tommy's shoulders. "Well, I didn't expect to hear that from you."

He sighed and looked at her askance. "I'm sorry I didn't call. But I'm glad you're—well . . ." She was gazing at him again with those lovely brown eyes, and he found himself barely able to think. He stammered, "I think it'll be a good weekend, nice spot anyway. I'm sure no one has to try this monumental experience the whole campus is fluttering about."

"What have you heard?" She cuddled Tommy, and the boy squirmed, then she let go. She whispered over his head, "Doesn't like too much mothering nowadays."

Tommy gave her a sudden fierce look, but she shrugged and he turned to Ray with a "Moms are weird" look.

Ray said, glad she didn't seem upset about his not calling, "I haven't heard much. It's obvious somebody's got an iron hand on this. Probably Martin Croase. I've watched him work a little. He knows how to get things rolling but without losing control. He's like one of those demolition people who can collapse a building without lobbing a speck of dust onto the high-rise next to it."

"That's an encouraging analogy." She crossed her legs and bounced her right over her left knee. She dangled her penny loafer from her toes, revealing a slender, shapely foot. "What do you think of our Dr. Croase?"

"He's OK, I guess. Something about him, though."

"Something fake, right? He kind of reminds me of one of those sleazy guys with greasy hair and a broken nose who made good and now's trying to be completely respectable."

Ray raised his eyebrows with surprise, then laughed. "Better not let them hear that. He has done a lot for the school, though."

"That's what I hear." She opened her pocketbook, took out a notepad and pen, and set it back down.

He often wondered about Martin and Listra Croase. They had this aura of cable television's golden couple. Listra had her own show—"Heartlines"—and Martin's messages in chapel were broadcast on Sundays. On camera and before the world they could inspire, make you want to give and help. But on campus, they seemed to control everything. After a year at Atlantic, Ray had almost had enough.

Someone began testing a microphone up front, and Ray spotted Listra and Martin Croase outside one of the sliding glass windows. They were dressed casually, both in colorful slacks and shirts.

Ray could smell Andi's perfume—one of those celebrity name fragrances. His mood had changed radically for the better the few days after their blind date. He decided to try to spend some time with her and Tommy, if they were willing.

Andi said, "Do you think this'll be some arm-twisting thing like the fund-raisers?"

"I figure it'll be no worse than going on one of those free vacation weekends where Happy Vacations or some such thing tries to sell you a time share in their condo."

"Oh, I've been to one of them. I almost did it, and then they found out I was destitute. They skittered away like cockroaches when the light comes on in the bathroom."

"Oh, you have them?" He leaned back on the chair, enjoying the banter.

She sighed dramatically. "No. Alas. I'm all alone, except for Tommy here." She smiled, and for a moment, their eyes met. Instantly, his heart quickened. Her clear-eyed gaze was friendly, but on another level almost seductive. It was an unexpected feeling for Ray. He sensed she wasn't trying to be that way, but he suddenly realized how strongly attracted he was to her. *Those eyes,* he thought. *I could look into them all day.* He hid his feelings though, and coughed into his hand, looking away.

"You OK?" Andi asked, wrinkling her brow.

"Sorry. I was just thinking about something . . ."

"Anything I'd want to hear?" Andi said, raising her eyebrows with mock seriousness.

"No." He paused. "Well, just that you're a very attractive lady."

Again, their eyes met, and Andi returned his gaze sincerely as if searching his eyes for something. "Thank you," she said suddenly. "I didn't expect to hear that today."

He nodded, feeling as if his whole face burst into flames. "I think I've just been cooped up too much in my room."

"That happens." She pulled back her hair again and looked at him out of the corner of her eyes, grinned, and patted Tommy's knee. "Everybody has to get out sometime, right, kiddo?" She looked back at Ray. "You mean if you hadn't been cooped up, I wouldn't be as attractive?" She arched her right eyebrow, obviously meaning it as a joke.

Someone came to the podium and called for attention. Ray gave her a roll of his eyes, then looked forward. The Croases stepped in through the sliding doors, and everyone took a seat. One of the administrators began welcoming the group, now over forty or fifty people.

Martin Croase began to speak, looking dapper and composed, always in charge. After some introductory remarks, he said, "You are aware, of course, that the supernatural is the quintessential of the Christian life. We possess it. We own it. Above all religions, we are plugged into the divine, the supereminent, the omnipotent. That means a humdrum, shabby, nonmiraculous, nonexperiential religion is a travesty. Listen to me now."

Croase paused and briefly roved the crowd with his crystalline blue eyes. Like sapphires, Ray thought. Croase's charisma was something Ray had to admire, if reluctantly.

"We want to push back the barriers, blaze the trails, cut across the horizons of life until all men must stand back and reckon with the reality of God. What happens to us should so magnetize the world around us that they will scream for a similar experience. They'll want what we have." Croase's hand banged on the podium.

Ray sensed Andi tensing.

"They'll want it, they'll cry for it, they'll pray for it and pay for it, if only as a gift of their intense gratitude." Croase looked over the group, now hanging on every word. "TWI has pushed back the barriers and moved into a realm never before explored by men of faith. That realm is the realm of death. You know this probably from things being said on campus. But I want to spell it out for you now in detail."

Croase let the words sink in. "Death is the final enemy, the last battleground. Even with Jesus' miraculous resurrection in 32 A.D., man has always feared it, cowered before it because it's the unknown, the great mystery. But what if men found a way to explore it, to study it, to dive into it and swim in it, and then jump out—just like out of a swimming pool—still wet with the magic of that realm, but able to think and meditate and tell about what has just happened? What if mankind found a way to go into death and come back out without permanent loss of life?"

Croase waved his hand over his head. "Now I know, you say yes, there have been people who have had experiences where they went to heaven. They had a heart attack, or something went wrong on the operating table, or they fell from a building, or a horse kicked them"—there was a titter of laughter—"and they died for a few minutes, then someone revived them and they came back to tell us what happened. Yes, that's true. I've heard the testimonies myself. But those are—excuse my lack of theology—chance experiences. They can't be duplicated, or studied, or planned, or even anticipated. They just happen. But what if we could make them happen at will?"

He put his fingers to his temples and closed his eyes. "What if I could close my eyes and die—for a minute, for two minutes, for four minutes—and go to that place just to see what it was like? A sort of house-hunting expedition. A little museum tour. What if I could do that? What if you could do that? No cost. No possibility of harm. Everything carried out under perfect conditions. Would you want to do it?"

There were a few amens in the group. Ray stirred uneasily. He had not really known what the hubbub on campus was all about, but this was definitely not what he'd expected. This weekend had been announced as a special retreat opportunity and update on TWI.

"Did I hear an amen?"

Several people said it louder.

Ray watched Croase's face. It was almost too animated. He seemed to be glowing. *Radioactive* was the word that flitted into Ray's mind. It made him smile, but as he listened he became more uneasy. Croase was just too confident, too cool. How could he believe that a group of Christians would go along with this?

And yet, clearly they were. There were now more than sixty people gathered to listen. It was nuts, Ray thought. Nuts.

Croase went on, "I want to present you with an awesome truth: TWI has now perfected a way to do it. We have probed the celestial. We have sent men and women, yes, and a few children to heaven. They will be giving their testimonies in a minute. But the beauty of it is that this experience is available to all of us. Right in this room. This very afternoon. You can have it. Just like going to Disneyland. Except this is into the most mysterious realm in human consciousness. I tell you, people, you, today, this afternoon, can go into the regions of heaven, have a look around, and come back. Furthermore—"

Ray's body felt hard, as though he were afraid to move. Was everyone in the room really going to do it? If not, would Croase force them? Ray suddenly sensed that this might not be a little "it's-up-to-you" situation. He glanced at Andi uneasily. She was sitting erect, her eyes fixed on the speaker. Her face looked dark and anxious.

Ray turned back as Croase went on, "It will transform your spiritual life. My lovely wife, Listra, whom you all know personally, has taken this little vacation over ten times now. Her attitudes, her outlook, her life has never been happier, better, more perfectly honed for serving the Lord."

Croase nodded with understanding. "You will have questions, naturally, and we'll answer them. But for now, I want you to hear some testimonies. Listra?"

Dr. Croase's wife walked up to the podium. Her red hair looked like a flame above her head, and her face shown with undeniable joy. "What Martin is saying, ladies and gentlemen, is that we all believe the Lord wants us to use our gifts to the maximum, both to advance His kingdom and to bring the lost home where they belong. As you know, Gordon Watt wanted above all that Christians experience all that God has for them in this world. He believed that Christians should, as a rule, see the supernatural as a normal and vital part of life. He was tired of the desiccated, disappointed, disillusioned, depressed version of Christianity we see so prevalent in our age. He gave us a vision to do all we could to raise the experiential horizon for Christians so that their faith becomes rooted deeper and stronger and can never be dislodged. Isn't that what we all want?"

There were more amens.

"I can understand any fear or worry you might feel in the face of this. It's all so fast. But let me tell you my story—in brief. I've been a Christian since I was five. But it was never real to me. It never gripped me. Oh, sure, on 'Heartlines' I sounded wonderful and could really tell a ripping good story. But I always wondered if it all was true. Then one day I got a chance to visit heaven—just visit, mind you, not stay—and I took it. It's utterly transformed me."

"Heartlines" was Listra's show on WCN, the Watt Cable Network, a television network that offered Christian programming from nine in the morning till eleven at night. There were several specialized shows such as Listra's that featured interviews, contemporary music, and a talk program. Somehow the network managed to go on unscathed despite the televangelist scandals of the late eighties because Gordon Watt and then Martin Croase had managed to build a loyal audience of over a million donors.

"I've felt real excitement since this happened. A personal sense of destiny. Power to overcome sin."

As Ray listened, his fear diminished. No, they certainly wouldn't force anyone. Listra was too classy, too genteel for that kind of tactic. She was indeed a lovely woman, with a trim figure and a resonant, embracing voice. He'd seen her many times in her element, encouraging students, taking aside some bedraggled soul and cheerleading him back into commitment.

Still, as she went on, like her husband, something about her struck Ray as false. He didn't know how to take them. So many people on campus praised the Croases as though they were the last great hope. In many ways, they had all the things Ray didn't—security, friendship, love, loyal followers. Yet, the way they could both be so dramatic, so intensely sincere, bothered him.

He wriggled nervously in his seat, glanced at Andi, then closed his eyes and rubbed his eyebrows. When he opened them, Listra was saying, "I was an insomniac for years. It's gone. I rarely have to wait more than ten minutes to go to sleep. I have a genuine feeling of inner security. Tell them, Martin, what a basket case I was all those years. Worrying about everything. Five miscarriages. Three adopted children. Now I'm as cool, calm, and collected as could be. And I had such a problem with anger. But patience has just zoomed into my life. Someday I'm convinced I will actually meet Jesus in person."

When she finished, an older couple, a prof and his wife, spoke. Over the next hour, Croase paraded six more people, including two children, before the group. One boy, named Jess, twelve years old, was especially enthusiastic. "It's helped me make better grades than I was getting," he said. "My mom and dad are really happy about the changes they've seen in me. I don't spend all my time with the Nintendo and watching

TV like I used to. It's just not that interesting anymore."

Others spoke of increased time and enjoyment in prayer, a greater dedication to the work of God, a fervent intimacy with Christ that pulsed with new life. Ray fought off the feeling of being mesmerized. It sounded perfect. It was truly what had happened to him at age eight. Here he could do it again, under laboratory conditions without fear of mishap. But both Listra and Martin Croase made him feel uncomfortable. How did they really know what they were opening themselves up to?

His arm was rigid, his hand gripping the chair like a salt water fishing rod with a marlin on hook. Tommy fidgeted between him and Andi, and she tried to quiet him. Ray was sweating. Suddenly he knew he didn't want to do this, be a part of it. God's choosing to save him at age eight, for whatever reasons, was God's choice. To go into death like a Disney World space ride was downright foolish. For a moment, he thought about leaving that night.

Martin Croase opened it up for questions. There were the usual queries about God's will, was it biblical, was there any chance of actually dying permanently, and could it be demonic, to the more in-depth arguments about God's sovereignty, Gordon Watt's obsession with mysticism, and other fears. Listra and Martin Croase and others answered them all deftly, confidently. As Ray listened, he could detect not a single note of dissent. More people were saying, "Amen," and many appeared quite excited about the prospect.

At the end, Croase said, "We can only take you up in groups of five, but the marvel is that we will send a guide with you who will lead you into that realm and offer help if any is necessary. We understand, it's like taking your first roller coaster ride. There's fear, worry, gut-wrenching terror. But believe me, this is totally safe. We've tested it over and over and have suffered not a single problem. We only ask that you not take any medications between now and the time you travel. That could cause complications, though nothing serious."

As if downplaying his last statement, he hurried on. His level eyes moved about the room with eager confidence. "You all know what we're about at TWI and the seminary and the Bible college. You've trusted us with your education, your money. Now I want to ask you, will you trust us one more time—enough to let us give you the most life- and spirit-enhancing experience imaginable?"

There were amens all over the room. Croase nodded with a wide smile. "Then we will begin tonight with the first two groups, and tomorrow we will continue. Believe me, none of you will regret this."

Ray stared in silence as Croase finished. Croase was going to press all of them to do it. He sensed it in his gut. He'd just have to tell them he wasn't interested. He'd done that enough times in life. But suddenly he feared for Andi and Tommy. Would they be strong enough to go against the flow?

As people filed out of the room, Tommy turned to his mother. "Mom, I don't have to do this, do I?"

"Of course not, honey."

"Are you?"

She glanced at Ray uneasily. "I don't know, honey."

Tommy looked up at Ray, who was now standing. "Will you, Mr. Ray?"

Ray shook his head. "I want to think and pray about it. I'm not convinced at all."

Andi started pulling on her jacket. "Can I come with you? This has made me feel rather anxious."

"Sure."

The three of them filed out. In the cool night air with the sounds of water lapping the shore in front of them, Ray took a deep breath. All the anxiety he'd felt listening to Croase vanished. Andi's lovely presence sent a surge of excitement through his abdomen.

When they stepped onto the lawn in front of the lake, a boy named Billy stopped Tommy. "My parents are doing it first, and if they think it's OK, I'm going to do it tomorrow. Isn't this gnarly?"

Tommy stepped closer to Andi under her arm. "We're thinking about it."

"I'll go with you," Billy said, then turned and headed toward the group that was filing up the path. The boy named Jess who had given the testimony stood on the porch alone.

He said to Tommy, "I'll go with you too, if you're a little afraid."

Ray noted the hint of sarcasm in his voice. He didn't like it. He touched Andi's back and said, "Let's take a walk."

□ □ □

Tommy picked up the long silver flashlight and flicked the switch twice. "Mom, can I take this into the woods?"

His mother stood with Ray outside the conference center. "Sure, honey. Go ahead. But stay nearby."

He glanced at Ray trying to stifle a smile, then pushed the button on the flashlight. A beam streamed from the lens, and he swung it about making circles across the leafy darkness. "This'll show them," he murmured and headed for the trail. He looked back to make sure they were following. His mother and Ray walked along, talking and smiling. Tommy told himself this time it would work, this time the man would get married to her, and this time he would have a real father. But he had to prove he wasn't afraid. That was the important thing. If he wasn't afraid of the dark or monsters or anything else, then Ray would want to marry her.

It was always his fault they didn't. He'd heard people say that.

As he scurried up the trail, keeping Ray and Andi in sight, he remembered what his uncle had said: "You and your little bastard are not welcome here. He's an illegitimate little coward."

Tommy turned the words over in his mind again. *Bastard. Illegitimate. Coward.* Sometimes kids at in school used that first word. It meant someone no one liked. He thought that must be because he got so afraid so easily. That was the third word, *coward.* His uncle often said Tommy was "such a coward it turns my stomach." That was what made people not like him. He was just afraid the things in the dark would get him.

So now he had to prove it. Once and for all. He'd go out into the dark. He'd stand there and face it. Then Ray would like his mother and he'd have a real father.

Then something screeched in the path ahead of him.

Tommy froze, the hairs on his neck prickling. *Just stand still and it won't hurt you,* he told himself.

The thing screeched again. What was it?

Suddenly two somethings skittered through the leaves. Tommy jumped back, waving the flashlight in their direction. They stopped. Didn't move. What was it?

Then his flashlight caught two yellow eyes. Tommy's heart was booming. *Don't move. Don't be a coward,* he told himself again. Where was his mom? It looked like a raccoon. Yes, it was a raccoon. Tommy breathed with relief.

Then the raccoon hissed at him, baring its fangs.

The flashlight fell from his hand and clattered to the ground, going out. The thing hissed again. Tommy didn't wait. He turned and ran back down the trail. "Mom!"

The boy almost collided with Ray as he and Andi came around a corner.

"A huge raccoon!" Tommy cried, trying to catch his breath. "It was gonna bite me. It was huge."

Andi stooped down and looked into the terrified eyes. "It's all right, honey. A raccoon won't hurt you. Not around here."

"But it might have rabies or something."

"I don't think so."

She glanced at Ray, then patted his head. "Where's your flashlight?"

"I dropped it. I'm sorry. I'm really sorry."

"We'll find it. Don't worry."

Ray tousled his hair. "Don't worry, we'll get that raccoon if it does anything to your flashlight."

Tommy knew now he'd blown it for good. He did everything wrong. That was another thing his uncle said. "I wish the kid wouldn't be so clumsy, Andi. He's broken half your aunt's drinking glasses."

Forcing back his tears, Tommy walked silently beside the other two. A three-quarters moon through a cloudless sky lit their path. Small buoys dipped and swayed in the water.

Bright lights across the lake reflected off the waves. He searched the path for the flashlight. Then he saw it, glinting silvery in the moonlight. He ran to pick it up, then flicked the switch. It came back on.

This time he had to prove it, once and for all. "I'm going up ahead a little again," he said.

His mother answered, "Just be careful, honey."

☐ ☐ ☐

"Do you think it's real?" Andi asked Ray, as they walked along.

"I'm not sure." Ray watched Tommy disappear up the trail. The flashlight jumped back and forth ahead of them. "It's kind of intriguing. But—"

Andi nodded. "That troubles me quite a bit."

"That it's intriguing?"

"That Dr. Croase makes it sound so good. How can something so good, so important supposedly for spiritual growth, not have been even hinted at in Scripture?"

Ray nodded and pointed her to the left down a stony path. "Yeah."

They turned around when they reached a small point of land jutting into the lake. Andi called Tommy, and they headed back. As the boy ventured down the path, Ray remarked, "I'm a little surprised he's being so brave in the dark."

Andi called to Tommy to slow down. "Yeah, it's really gotten into him the last few days. I've heard him practicing in his room. Being brave."

"How come?" Ray turned to look at her in the moonlight. Her hair shone in gentle waves of deep umber.

"He's not good at sports. Not real coordinated yet. I have a relative who has completely rejected him, too. And he is sort of a fearful kid. Actually, I'm kind of amazed he's so animated tonight. But I think there's a reason."

"What's that?"

"He heard about you."

Ray frowned. "Not the whole SEALs thing?"

"He listened to your testimony on tape. He pestered me

so I brought one home from the library—after our date." She gazed at him with a hint of laughter in her eyes. "Well, you are one tough cookie."

Ray groaned.

"So now he wants to be a SEAL," she said, obviously enjoying ribbing him. She called to Tommy again. The boy ran up this time squealing about seeing a deer. He wanted to take them to the spot, but Andi said, "We're talking, honey. We've both seen lots of deer."

"Aw, Mom, it was cool."

"I know. You go tell the deer how cool he is yourself. We just want to walk for a few minutes."

Tommy gave her a wry look, then suddenly darted back toward the woods. Ray smiled to himself. One minute terrified, the next on top of the world. That was a little how he'd been as a kid.

Kneeling down, Andi picked up a stone and pitched it into the water. The splash broke the silence. "So what do you want, Ray Mazaris?"

He crouched beside her, fingering other stones. When he found one, he threw it out sidearm, skipping it across the water. "What do I want?"

"Right. What is it you're looking for?"

He threw out another stone, skipping it five times, then stood. "If you want a serious answer, then I guess what I want most is a family, some peace, and a job where I can feel like I'm doing something for the kingdom of God. Nothing spectacular."

"No more military interventions, huh?"

"No, I've had enough hair-raising adventures in that category." He looked into her eyes. Her brow was furrowed, but in the moonlight, her eyes were dark and mysterious.

"Well, I'm not going to do this death trip thing, that's for sure." She looked behind her and called Tommy again.

"Neither am I."

"I'd leave tomorrow morning, but I came with a friend, and from the looks of it, I don't think she'll want to leave."

He watched her lips move and the way her eyes flashed darkly. "I'll be glad to give you a ride."

"You would?"

"Sure. I think I'm going to leave too. This isn't turning out to be much of a vacation. After lunch tomorrow?"

"That sounds good."

She called Tommy. When the boy appeared at the edge of the woods, Andi suddenly leaned over and kissed Ray on the cheek. "Thanks for walking. I feel better. Something about that whole presentation tonight really unnerved me." Tommy hurried toward them, swinging the flashlight.

When he reached them, she put her arm over his shoulders and said, "You need a bath, young man. And I need to get some beauty sleep." She winked at Ray.

They went back inside. The warm air of the conference center cheered them instantly, there was a fire roaring in the fireplace in the foyer, and several groups of conferees sat around tables drinking coffee and talking. Ray and Andi both had a cup of tea and some cookies. As they sat quietly at a table, they overheard one group talking about how eager they were to try the TUT the next morning. Andi looked tense, and Ray worried she might somehow be corralled into doing it when he knew she didn't want to. He escorted them back to their room and at her door she suddenly asked him, after she got Tommy inside, "You don't think there will be a problem about us leaving tomorrow, do you?"

He didn't want to tell her about the signals he was picking up. "It'll be OK."

She sighed and looked up and down the hall nervously. "I don't know. Dr. Croase can get pretty forceful at times— when he thinks something is essential. And everyone else seems to sure."

He waited till she looked back into his eyes. "Just tell them you're not doing it. I'll back you up."

"I was hoping you'd say that." She suddenly smiled. "Anyway, how well does a super macho, hard dude, ex-commando hug?"

His heart throbbed, but he began to embrace her. As they held one another in the doorway, he could feel her heart beating against his and drew back. "I like you a lot, Andi."

"Already?"

"Already."

She started to smile, but he drew her close and kissed her on the lips. In his arms she felt soft and gentle and beautiful, and his heart beat wildly. Then he let her go, and she drew a deep breath.

"Wow!"

He laughed. "It's been a good time, Andi. I should have called you before this."

"See you tomorrow." She gazed at him evenly, then lowered her eyes and closed the door.

Back at his room, Ray undressed and lay on the bed in his underwear. He hoped there wouldn't be too much pressure about the NDE thing the next day, but he wasn't sure what might happen.

"Just don't do anything stupid," he murmured as he pulled up the sheet and rolled onto his side. He prayed for a moment, then let his mind drift. For a minute he thought of Andi and love and her sense of humor and how he'd felt when he'd been with her and Tommy. "Please don't take her away, Lord," he prayed as his mind moved toward slumber. "Just promise me that. Don't let anything bad happen to either of them."

The next morning Billy Rafer's father, the staff psychologist, led off the meeting. "I feel rejuvenated," the dapper, tweed-jacket clad man said. "Both my wife and I were so invigorated last night afterwards, we spent half the night talking about the fears we've most recently been struggling with. I went back to things I've worried about since childhood. I feel as though last night put an end to them. There's just no more uncertainty about my faith."

His wife followed up with more jubilant words of encouragement. Forty-two people still remained who hadn't tried it. Ray and Andi took another walk by the lake.

Tommy hung onto her sleeve. "You promise you won't make me do it?"

"I promise I won't make you do it," Andi said. She looked into Ray's eyes. "I'm just not into this, Ray. Maybe I'm paranoid, but even with all these glowing testimonies, I'm not convinced."

Ray agreed. "Like I said, I'm not changing my mind from last night."

"Do you think they'll let us just go home?"

Ray slipped his hands into his pockets and jingled some coins. "I don't know why not. We don't even have to tell them. We can simply leave."

"All right, after lunch. It'll take me ten minutes to pack, and I'm out of here."

2

Johnny Goge sat quietly in the battered red pickup surveying the Hilltown Heights custom housing development in Portland, Oregon. He was clad in black leather pants, a gray turtleneck, and a dark blue peacoat with a blue knit pulldown cap. In the early morning darkness, he would be almost invisible. Under a tiny penlight he looked over the message he'd scrawled in black ink. Everything was just as it had been described—the dark streets where rich Oregonians kept away from the troubles in the inner city.

Cold stilettos of air poked at his raw cheeks. The shiny, green-lit digital clock signaled 5:25 A.M. Carl Hasekker would be out of his house in fifteen minutes, if the message was really correct. Goge had seen him do it the day before just to make sure. This would be his second heist, and already the adrenaline gushed through his lean body, over a hundred-eighty pounds of Kenpo-karate-built muscle.

Years before, he learned killing in the special forces as a front line grunt in Vietnam. There, he'd personally eliminated eleven Vietcong, face to face. That didn't even count the dozens he'd killed at long range.

Now, at forty-five, he realized how much he'd missed the squeeze of a trigger and the vacant, half-surprised look of an unsuspecting victim, even though he'd done it a half-decade before in the employ of a Chicago Mafia boss named Carlos Giotto. His new boss, though, was very different, and he wasn't sure how to read it.

But he put any question out of his mind. He was getting 10 percent and this could prove to be a very lucrative operation.

As he sat in the car, he smiled, then slid a custom-made noise suppressor—a "silencer"—onto the barrel of his 10 mm Colt "Delta Elite" semiautomatic pistol. It always made him laugh the way Hollywood and many best-seller writers portrayed killers with "silencers" going about their bloody business in nearly perfect quietude. To anyone in the business it was all lies. There was no such thing as a true "silencer." But one of the thugs working for Giotto was also a master gunsmith and could fit pistols like Goge's with the right kind of equipment to effect real "silencing."

The first element was, of course, the silencer itself. For the 10 mm the gunsmith reamed the pistol with threads in the barrel to screw in the six-inch suppressor. It was a standard variety with an internal perforated tube inside a larger outside pipe barrel. Between the tubes were a series of baffles and wipes sandwiched between coarse steel wool. Goge could get about ten shots before the silencer began making too much noise.

The Colt was also designed so that although it was automatic, the slide was held in place when the gun was fired. That prevented it from sliding back and "clapping" too loud when metal struck metal. It meant that Goge always took only one shot, unless he prepared otherwise. Years of practice gave him the ability never to need another. He rarely tried to take anyone out at more than ten feet, and he preferred the muzzle under the chin and bullet out through the top of the head as the best method for inducing certain death.

Carl Hasekker was scum. That was all Goge needed to know. He ran unlaundered crack and cocaine dollars out of the Projects out into the country to a major drug baron's headquarters south of Portland. Hasekker could be carrying anywhere from a hundred grand to half a million dollars in the smart black attaché case he used. The man, apparently, was smart. Nondescript, operating a home cleaning supplies business, no one suspected him of running money for a mafia drug lord. The money was sent to Hasekker by Federal Express, UPS, mail—all the normal means by which a home business operator would receive his wares. He'd conceived the methodology, sold it to Mickey "Dike" Pallamini, and had been operating for several years without so much as a parking ticket from the police.

But this was the end of the road for Hasekker.

Goge's watch beeped 5:30. He hit the button that turned it off and glanced around, worrying that someone might happen up the sidewalk or come down Morrow Street and see him. After looking around, he murmured, "What are you worried about?" So far the directive from headquarters had been perfect. Not a miss yet.

He left the window down and pressed the unlock button to his left. Both door locks jumped. He opened the door and closed it silently, then hurried across the silent street. From the pitch-black driveway up to the house, Goge watched the front door. His nostrils flared as he took deep breaths through them to calm his hammering heart. He felt certain there would be no trouble.

The sound of metal on metal broke the quiet. Hasekker, a bit pudgy and cherubic looking, stepped out into the early morning darkness. Goge heard him take a deep breath and then a whisper that ended in the word "rat." He ambled bouncily down the path, the attaché case in his right hand.

Goge counted in his mind. *Five—four—three—*

He could hear Hasekker humming to himself now.

Two—one—zero.

Goge stepped out from the dark of a pathway bush and aimed the Colt with both hands at Hasekker's chest. "Carl?"

The hapless money-runner looked up, unafraid, unsuspecting.

Goge pressed the trigger. His target's chest shattered, flinging blood and bone in all directions while Goge was left to contemplate the single *pffft* emitted from his suppressor. Hasekker catapulted backwards, throwing the attaché case

66

into the air. Goge always used hollow head rounds, which at 225 grains in a 10 mm mushroomed perfectly.

Goge hurried into the light, transferred the gun to his left hand. He checked the pulse on Hasekker's neck. Nothing. Usually he would put a bullet through his brain, but there was no reason to do it. The man was still. As always, his aim was true. Right through the heart.

Goge took out a single lock blade Schrade knife and quickly cut the letter *A* into the man's cheek. Why the boss wanted that, he wasn't sure, but Goge didn't question why he was doing it now. For a moment, he surveyed the cherubic, rosy-cheeked face and imagined what would happen when the body was discovered. How they'd try to make some connection with the letter and the man. How the newspapers would tell the story. And the weeping relatives on the news. "He was a good man, a hard worker, a community participant." And the adjectives about the death: hideous, terrifying, irrational. But by then Johnny Goge knew he would be far away.

Shivering with the cold, he picked up the attaché case and hurried over the lawn to his parked car. He knew a talk with the boss would be in order and then possibly a short high before heading off to the UPS office to mail the case east, that is, after he took his 10 percent, or a little more if he felt like it.

But he decided to be honest at this point. It was good business, and there was no sense in ruining it for a few extra dollars. The boss might know the true amount anyway.

3

After he finished packing, Tommy asked if he could get a Coke. Andi told him to meet her at the dining room.

On the way to the snack room, Tommy saw Jess, the twelve year old who had given his testimony the night before. He leaned against the stairway railing to the porch and grinned as Tommy went by. "Hey, Darcasian, you want to see where they do it?"

"Do what?" Tommy turned and looked at the taller boy.

"See where the people die and come alive. They're done this morning. Guess your mom is wimping out, huh?"

"She is not."

"She didn't go with any of the early groups."

"She didn't want to."

"No wonder you're a wimp, Darcasian. You have a wimp mother."

Billy Rafer ran across the pine needle strewn lawn to the two boys. "My mom and dad are real excited abut it. They said they met Jesus."

Jess nodded. "It's definitely the coolest thing I've ever done. You want to see the room?"

The younger boy opened his eyes with wonder. "We could see where they do it?"

"Sure, come on." The two boys started off across the lawn. Then Jess turned, "You coming, wimp?"

Tommy hesitated. He knew he didn't have to go. But he knew that even if he was a wimp, his mother wasn't. He looked back from the west wing to the two boys. Then suddenly he bolted toward them. "I'm no wimp," he murmured.

☐ ☐ ☐

The room was empty. It was on the first floor of the south wing. Jess tested the handle of the door. It turned.

Inside, five blue reclining chairs stood before them. Jess hopped onto one of them. "See," he said, "it isn't anything. Just like going to the dentist." He turned around and set the small cap on his head that held the EEG leads. "This reads your brain. And this"—he picked up the leads and electrodes for the EKG—"tells when your heart actually stops beating. I met an angel when I went out each time."

Billy watched with fascination. "I wish I could do it."

"You want to?" asked Jess, looking from Billy to Tommy.

The younger boy gulped. "You know how?"

"Sure, I was in it two times already, and I watched some others. It's simple." Jess looked at Tommy. "I could do both of you, no sweat."

Tommy backed up. "No, my mom won't let me."

68

"Oh, don't tell me about your mom. She's just wimping out on you. Anyway," he turned back to Billy, "we'll leave this coward to himself. Get up on the chair."

Billy hesitated a moment, then grinned mischievously and jumped on the chair. "My mom was really excited."

The older boy set up the equipment while Tommy watched. Inside Tommy's mind, a fire was building. *Wimp. WIMP. WIMP!* He couldn't seem to get his breath. Something in the back of his head told him to leave, to get out, and find the adults. But he wanted to be like Ray. He wanted to be a SEAL. Ray had been brave, hadn't he?

But even Ray didn't want to do this. He said it was dangerous.

Then if you do it, you'll be braver than Ray.

Tommy gulped. He stepped forward. "I'll go too."

Jess turned around. "Oh, so you're going to be brave after all. All right, get on the next chair. I'll do Billy first."

Taking off his glasses, Tommy climbed onto the chair and lay back. It was much more comfortable than a dentist's chair, the leather plush and soft. He listened as Jess explained.

"Now I shoot the stuff into your arm with this." Jess swiveled the injection gun around and placed it against Billy's arm. He then turned around and took a small vial off the table. It was marked "TUT" and looked a deep blue to Tommy. He noticed that it was the last one on the shelf.

Jess loaded the vial into the gun, then flipped several switches at the base of the chair. The EKG and EEG began recording, a tape recorder switched on, and a computer started warming up. Jess tapped the clock on the side of the chair. "The moment your heart stops, this times you. You'll be gone four minutes. It'll stop automatically. Ready?"

Billy nodded enthusiastically.

The big, black-haired boy swiveled the gun around into position, leaning it against Billy's bare biceps. "I'll count down—that's what they do. Ten, nine, eight . . ."

Tommy's heart banged in his chest as he watched.

"Two, one, zero, blast off." Jess pulled the trigger and Billy's arm flinched. The boy looked violently ahead at something on the wall, then his face twisted and he lay back, his eyes still open but unseeing.

"He's dead," Jess said. "Now wait. This will be rad."

The timer clicked off two, three, then four minutes. Two seconds after four minutes, Billy's face twisted again and his eyes popped open with life. He groaned, blinked, then slowly turned to Jess. "Wow!" he cried. "Wow! That was really something. I met this person made of light and everything."

"I told you it was something." Jess laughed, then turned around to face Tommy. "You ready, wimp?"

The word made Tommy gulp, but he nodded. Jess walked over to the counter. He looked around and then cursed. "That was the last one. You may be outa luck, kid."

Tommy sighed with a measure of relief, but Jess said, "Wait a minute, I know where they keep it." He hurried to a cupboard at the end of the room, opened it, and looked in. Tommy could see the shelves were full of vials. Jess reached up and took one off the top shelf. "We'll give you the top of the line, kid."

The vial was blue like the other, and Tommy lay back, trying to relax. Jess fed it into the slot on the injection gun. "Now just relax, buddy. You won't be a wimp anymore after this."

He flicked the same switches, and the equipment jolted into action. Jess began the countdown. Tommy's heart was deafening. Then the gun was placed against his arm. The tip was cold, almost frozen. Tommy closed his eyes. *Please, God,* he prayed in his mind. *Don't let anything bad happen.*

Then he heard a short pneumatic wheeze and the freezing liquid hit his arm. He turned to look at Jess. Then it happened.

☐ ☐ ☐

Tommy sensed a sudden tearing. A moment later, he hovered over his own body. Jess and Billy were looking up and pointing. Jess said, "He should be up there somewhere." He waved. "Have a trip, wimp."

70

There was a sensation of cool air and something else pulling him up and away. Tommy moved around effortlessly. It felt like a completely mental action—will it and it happened—and he peered into a huge hole in the air, like a tunnel. He was not afraid. He floated toward it until it engulfed him, drawing him inward and upward.

A surge of pleasant sensations like the excitement before Christmas burned through him. He noticed his arms and legs—they looked bigger—was he an adult? He didn't know. The sides of the tunnel coiled about him like giant smoke rings. He floated through it, gaining speed until it was little more than a blur around him, like looking directly at the pavement underneath you in a speeding car.

The tunnel was dark, but now and then sparkles and spangles of light ricocheted off the sides, whizzing around him and jolting him with internal jumps of happiness. *Am I really dead?* he wondered.

Far out ahead, the tunnel flattened until it looked more like a road with a wide panorama of sky above it. Then he realized he was slowing; finally he floated down and began running on the surface. A slash of green lay on the horizon. He sprinted toward it. No weariness numbed his limbs. He could go as fast or as slow as he wanted.

Underneath him, the tunnel turned to a blue-green color, then solid green. Soon he realized he stood on grass. A moment later he stopped in a huge pasture. No cows or other animals appeared. But all was quiet, unearthly, peaceful. Joy surged through him. Would he meet an angel? Would he meet Jesus?

He looked around and began walking. All was silent. No one appeared. Where was he?

He moved his lips. No words came out. Then he spoke inside his mind. *Is anyone here? Where am I? Anyone here?*

No one answered. He stooped down and touched the tips of the grass. They were soft, like slightly stiff wool. Grabbing a blade, he tried to blow it between his fingers, but he couldn't grip it. Frustrated, he stood up, shielding his eyes from the light glowing over the horizon.

"Is anyone here?" he called again.

He jumped forward, imagining himself splashing in puddles of water.

Then suddenly a glowing form of light started toward him from the edge of the horizon. Tommy stared at it and stopped. The form wobbled, and he thought uneasily of something he'd once seen in a movie—was it *The Wizard of Oz?*—he couldn't remember. Things felt blurry. The thing glowed and wobbled, became bigger and brighter. Then he made out arms, shoulders, a face. An angel?

He gulped, and suddenly it stood before him. "Welcome," the being said.

The voice was deep and shivery, as though the being was very old. As Tommy looked into the dark blue eyes, all the fear vanished.

Who are you? Tommy asked mentally.

"I am a friend," the being answered. Tommy could make out a form underneath the waves of light. A person with long silver hair, no beard, a red robe. There was something hanging at his side, glimmering. Was it a sword?

The light being motioned him forward. "Come. I will show you. Would you like to meet your great-grandfather?"

Tommy swallowed with wonder. "Great-grandfather Darcasian?"

"Yes."

"Sure."

In the distance, Tommy saw a man stand and walk toward him, smiling. He looked like a picture Tommy had seen of him that Andi kept on her bureau.

□ □ □

"He should be back any second now," Jess said confidently to Billy as they watched the clock tick off the last few seconds. "Four minutes," Jess said. He opened his arms and waved them over Tommy's body. "Come to life!"

Jess laughed and Billy said, "Gnarly."

Tommy didn't move. His eyes were still open in a death stare.

"Come to life," Jess said, a little less exuberantly.

72

It was ten seconds past four minutes.

The older boy swore.

"What's wrong?" asked Billy, his face turning white.

"I don't know," said Jess, his face darkening and his lips twitching. "I don't know!"

☐ ☐ ☐

Tommy sensed immediately that he'd reached a barrier. His great-grandfather told him, "It's wonderful here. The most beautiful place in existence. Is my granddaughter all right?"

"Who?" Tommy stared at the man, trying to discern the precise shape of his body. It kept changing and moving before him like a slow flame.

"My granddaughter? Your mother, Andrea?"

"Yes, she's doing great."

Suddenly Tommy wanted to go back to her. "When will I come back to life?"

Tommy, the being, and great-grandfather Darcasian stood looking at the fence. It seemed to be composed of stones, but the stones were jewels, glittering in the light like rainbows, like the kaleidoscope he once played with.

"Where am I?" he said to the light being.

"The gate," he said. "Do you want to go through?"

"Can I?"

"You may."

"What is on the other side?"

There was a long pause. "Are you afraid?" The being was smiling compassionately.

"No."

"Then go forward."

Tommy stepped to the cleft in the jeweled wall. He recognized the colors of various jewels—diamonds, rubies, and emeralds, other gems he didn't know the names of. It glowed and danced before him like something liquid and alive. It appeared to be an alleyway, yet it was not dark and foreboding; rather, beautiful and inviting. He turned again to the light being next to his great-grandfather. "Am I really dead?"

The light radiated calm. "Humans call it that."

73

"But where is God?" Tommy said again. He remembered the many times he and his mother conversed about God and Jesus Christ. Tommy had become a Christian that spring.

"Go through the gate," the light being said. There was a strange electricity in the voice that made Tommy pause.

"If I go through, then I will never go back. Is that right?"

"Correct."

"So they killed me."

"Yes."

"Why?" Tommy didn't feel grieved. He even wished he could bring his mother and Ray there.

The light didn't answer.

Tommy said to his great-grandfather, "Will I ever see my mom again?"

"Of course," the old man said.

The light spoke quietly into his mind: *Go through the gate.*

Tommy moved effortlessly to the edge of the jeweled stones. He turned to look back a moment, but the light and his grandfather were gone. Then he went through.

☐ ☐ ☐

Jess rushed back and forth around the chair, making sure all the wires were plugged in and all the machines were on. It was now past five minutes on the timer.

"He really is dead!" Jess yelled. "He's not coming back!"

"What should we do?" Billy cried, ready to bolt for the door.

"My dad'll kill me!"

"We should get someone!"

Jess paused. He seemed to be thinking of something. Then he said, "All right. Go get them. Get anybody."

Billy sped out of the building, yelling for help. When he was gone, Jess went to the door and looked out. No one was in the hall. He slipped out and turned in the opposite direction. "It's my word against his," he said as he darted into an alcove and disappeared out a side door opening onto the lake.

□ □ □

All was silence in Tommy's mind. The country was lush with flowers, trees, mown hedges, fields of corn. He stopped to look at one, and it was perfect. "No bugs here, I guess," he said to himself. He wondered if anyone would come out and greet him. What had happened to his great-grandfather, and that other person?

But no one appeared. The country went on for miles. Then he saw a house. Someone stood out in front of it. Tommy hurried toward him. He wanted to ask the person a question.

□ □ □

Billy ran up to several members of the staff. "Something happened in the death room. One of the kids is hurt!"

A staff member bent down. "What are you talking about?"

Billy started crying. "Jess and me, we went into the death room. Jess sent me up, I mean I was dead, and then I was alive again. And then we sent Tommy Darcasian up. But he didn't come back. Not after five minutes even."

The worker stood and said immediately, "Somebody get Dr. Croase and Dr. Nakayami."

□ □ □

"Are you Jesus?"

The being was tall, handsome, slim. His face was bronzed and his hair long and golden. He placed his hand on Tommy's shoulder. He must have been eight feet tall. "No," he said. "You are one of His?"

"Yes—I guess. I mean, I think so." Tommy instinctively put his hand over his eyes, though he did not need to do that to look at the person.

He smiled broadly with bright white teeth. "Come, then." The being began walking deeper within the green country. Tommy and he passed more houses. In the distance, Tommy saw more people, like the one who was with him, all working, building. Tall, beautiful, powerful-looking creatures in jeweled tunics.

Then he began to worry about his mother. Would she miss him? He was supposed to go back. That was the way it happened. This wasn't supposed to be permanent. He touched the being's arm.

"Please, sir, can you tell me if I'm ever going back?"

The being looked deeply into his eyes. "Some do go back from this country. Rarely. But a few do."

"Will I?"

The being stood and looked off toward the horizon. Someone else moved toward them, brighter and larger. The being said, "Maybe we will soon find out."

"Code Red!" the worker shouted. "Get the defibrillator."

Several nurses were shouting, and doctors poised over the body of Tommy Darcasian. One man physically pumped his heart. Another held an oxygen mask over his face.

"Fire up!" yelled the doctor bent over Tommy's limp form. "Breathe!"

At the door, Dr. Martin Croase stood with a little throng of people. He glanced uneasily around to see if Andi Darcasian was present. Then he saw her and Ray Mazaris hurrying across the lawn. Croase motioned to one of the security men, David Hughes. "Get this crowd out of here," he said when Hughes was in whispering distance.

Hughes immediately began moving people away from the door. "Everything's under control, folks. Just relax and stand back. The boy will be all right." Hughes was tall and lanky, with a long, brown handlebar mustache that he turned up at the corners with fresh waxings each morning, hard, brown, nutlike eyes, and a long scar under his right ear, down his neck. He said he'd got it in a knife fight. People like Croase believed otherwise. Hughes was a big talker.

Ray and Andi ran up, her face red. "What happened?"

"There's been an accident," Croase said, stopping her. "But Tommy will be all right. Let our staff handle it."

Andi pushed past him into the room. A team of doctors and nurses worked on the still, unresponding boy in the transmission room. Ray gave Croase a hard look, but said nothing. He stood next to Andi and waited.

"I knew this would happen," she cried.

Ray took her hand and gripped it.

"He's been gone eight minutes now, doctor," one of the nurses said. Only the doctor's angry eyes answered. Another nurse wheeled up the defibrillation equipment. One doctor peeled away the boy's shirt, while another hurriedly placed the two electrodes over his chest. "Two hundred volts!" he yelled.

A nurse flipped a switch and electricity shot through the small boy's rib cage. His whole body lifted off the table. Andi screamed, then placed her head against Ray's chest. "Dear Jesus, please, please don't let him die."

The nurse called out, "Nine minutes, doctor."

At the door, Croase clenched and unclenched his fists. Hughes had managed to get the crowd back with several other security people helping him. Croase's forehead was wet. He watched with steady, angry eyes.

For a few more moments, Andi watched, holding her fist at her mouth. "It can't happen," she whispered. "Please don't let it happen."

Ray held her and tried to pray, but his mind was on fire.

Doctors hovered over the boy. The nurse called out, "Nine and a half minutes."

The room was dead quiet except for the thrust of the electricity through the defibrillator. The nurse intoned again, "Ten minutes, doctor!"

Finally, the physician working on Tommy stopped. "We've got to call it." He swore, glanced at Andi, then looked away.

Andi wailed, "Nooooo!" Ray held her tightly and as she squirmed in his arms, he yelled, "There must be something else you can do!"

The doctor shook his head. "I'm sorry. There's nothing else." He began to pull a sheet up over the boy's head. Andi screamed again. As she did, Tommy suddenly jerked and his eyes popped open. Everyone froze, then the group gasped as one and the boy coughed. Someone cried, "He's alive!" Tommy twisted on the recliner.

A nurse jumped forward, to help him sit up, but Andi bounded past the doctors and grabbed him. "You came back! You're alive!"

The boy began crying. "I'm sorry, Mom. I'm really sorry. I didn't mean—"

Andi closed her eyes and hugged him fiercely. "I don't want to hear any more about it. You're alive and that's all that matters."

Ray edged up behind her and looked over her shoulder at Tommy. "You OK, Chief?" he said, giving the boy's shoulder a squeeze.

A moment later, Croase hurried over to Andi and put his hand on her shoulder. "We'll have a complete physical done on the boy. This is a major miracle!"

Someone in the crowd cheered, and soon everyone was shouting praises and bravos. Croase gave Andi and Tommy an enveloping hug. "Come on, let's get him back to the examining room and see that everything's OK. The Lord really came through. Let's shout another praise."

He stepped back to rev up the crowd, but Andi suddenly whipped around and glared at Croase. "I'd like to have a few moments alone with my son. Now please leave. This won't be the end of this, Dr. Croase."

Croase returned her gaze, then set his eyes and walked out past Ray and the others. There was a stunned silence, then everyone moved quickly out. Andi grabbed Ray's arm as he turned, "Please don't you go, Ray."

He nodded and put his around both of them. "We're getting out of here," he whispered. "Let's just make sure everything's OK, and then let's go."

"I'm there," Andi said heatedly, then her chin quivered and she burst into tears.

Outside, Croase said to Hughes and Nakayami. "Find

78

out what happened here. Right away. We have to make some big decisions."

4

Croase paced in his office after hearing the report from the two doctors who examined Tommy, and a second from Hughes. Several other key personnel sat around him in the large room, including his wife. They'd all learned about Tommy's taking the Actifed, which they thought explained the near disaster. But now there were other problems.

After some angry discussion, Croase said, "We can't let them go. She could sue. Her father's an important donor."

"But what can we do?" an aide asked. "We can't force them to stay. And we certainly can't keep them from going to the police."

"I have the perfect solution," Listra Croase answered when everyone else had a say.

All the faces turned to her.

"Martin and I will take them to meet Rafa himself."

Nakayami started to protest, but Listra turned on him. "You and your idiotic team have done enough. This time Martin and I handle it."

"But how?" Hughes asked.

"Gag them. Tie them up! Whatever it takes."

"I will not do this," Dr. Nakayami shouted. "It's wrong!"

"Then don't!" Listra said. "Go back to Brinton and make the TUT-B work. We don't need you here."

Nakayami stared at Martin Croase, looking for some support. But Croase was smiling. "I think it might work."

"It will work," Listra said with clipped precision. "Now let's do it."

5

"Ready," said Dr. Lew Reed, who was chosen to take Nakayami's place. "We proceed in five minutes. They will be ready in two."

One of the nurses said, "Hold him tight."

Ray Mazaris lay gagged and handcuffed on the reclining

79

chair. He blinked angrily, and muffled sounds emitted from behind the gag. When a nurse started to remove the tape over his mouth, Reed waved them off.

"We can start," said Reed. There was a crackle over the speaker system, and a voice came on advising the people in the room what was happening. Andi Darcasian lay on the far chair, also gagged and handcuffed. Martin Croase lay in the one of the middle chairs, with Listra next to him.

Croase said to Ray, "I didn't want it to be like this. But in a few minutes you'll understand. What happened to Tommy was an accident, and it won't happen again. You have to understand that. Once you've gone through it yourself, you'll see why it's so important."

Ray wriggled on the chair, but he was strapped firmly into place.

At the other end, Listra spoke softly to Andi. "There's no need to be afraid. We'll all be back in four minutes, and you will be as excited as I am about the TUT. Don't fight it, and all will go well."

Angered sounds broke from an edge of Andi's gag. One of the nurses leaned over and pressed it tighter against her mouth. Andi jerked her head back and forth, obviously trying to yell.

Finally Croase nodded to Reed. "Get on with it."

As Reed checked the monitoring gear and other hook-ups, he nodded in approval.

Telemetry units beeped, and a nurse and doctor stationed themselves at each bed. Not in Ray's eeriest moments had he thought Croase would go to this extreme.

The nurses moved the injection guns into position. The whole room seemed to stop breathing. Ray heard his heart like a deafening hammer banging on a thick leather drum inside him. Then each nurse simultaneously pulled the triggers on the guns. As they did, all four of the subjects throbbed in the familiar moment of breech. Andi's face went almost blue with fright. The four monitors bleeped within moments of each other. Then someone said, "They're traveling."

The freezing liquid nailed Ray Mazaris in place.

"What?" he heard himself shout against the tape over his mouth.

A moment later, he began rising above the recliner. He could see the other three still bodies, their eyes closed, the monitors still. A strange warmth infused him, and he turned to his right, rising higher. He felt as if he was swimming in air. He saw the dust above the lamp over his face.

Then: "My face!"

He stared down over the lamp and recognized his own body looking weak and cold on the white, stiff bed.

What is this? he screamed. But his voice seemed inside his mind. The thoughts rapped outward, telepathic.

One of the nurses looked up, smiling. "Are you there?" he said and winked, then gave Ray a thumbs-up.

"Do they see me?"

He looked off to the right. Andi, Martin Croase, and Listra hovered over their bodies making the same apparent inspection. As though in unison, everyone looked up and at one another together.

"What's happening?" Ray's mind said to no one in particular.

Croase, without a voice, but his mind sharp and plain said, "Come with us."

Listra called to the others mentally, "We must stick together."

Andi surged after them, giving Ray a look of terror and despair. Seconds later, Ray began skidding at high velocity up a dark, spiraling tunnel. The darkness was eerie gray, then lighter. Ray noticed an inner sense of security he'd never felt before. He'd read about out-of-body experiences, but this was not how he remembered the episode when he was eight years old.

Like a scientist taking measurements, he peered at the walls of the tunnel, wondering why he never touched them. What was guiding him along through it so perfectly?

As a youth he'd got involved with marijuana and co-caine, even LSD a couple of times. But this was nothing like that. In a way, it felt like a dream, yet far more than a dream. Still, no one else hovered near him. They were out ahead of him, getting farther apart.

His speed increased. Time no longer existed. The medium he zoomed through was unearthly, another dimension. Somehow he enjoyed it, feeling like a lone passenger on a subway careening through a tunnel at night alone.

When he came out, he remained alone. The whole scene arrayed before him in a pungent, beautiful green and white light. A soothing breeze flowed over and through him, yet without the sensation of air. His mood reflected an intimate, almost jubilant, joy and peace. Something within him wanted to shout, to scream happy, victorious cheers into the air. Waves of subtle, marvelous emotion trembled through him. In his mind was the thought *Perfect love.*

Before he could gather in his surroundings, though, he saw a clot of light like a star wobbling and rolling towards him. He moved forward in anticipation, partly afraid, partly in wonder. He knew the light somehow would not hurt him, though he wasn't sure how or why he knew it. As it drew near, the light spoke mentally, directly into Ray's own mind. "You are welcome, Raymond Mazaris."

"Welcome?"

"You have been expected."

"Expected? Where am I?"

"You don't know?"

"They told me, but—"

"You didn't believe them."

Ray hesitated. Then: "Well, no."

The being did not seem to pass judgment. In fact, Ray sensed that it was smiling at him. "Come. I will show you."

Ray turned. The light seemed to enfold and enwrap him in a strange sensation he could only identify as love. As his sight focused—he could not say he personally had eyes, yet he saw more clearly and at greater distance than he ever had—he thought he saw someone looking vaguely like his mother moving toward him, then his grandmother and grandfather.

"What is this?" he cried.

They were weeping.

The being waved in their directions. "Your family."

A moment later, Ray was surrounded by more than fifty people. He recognized his grandmother and grandfather. They touched him with a feathery softness.

"Grandmom, I—"

"We were told you were coming."

"But how did you know?"

"They know everything here."

"Who?"

"God, of course. And His servants. You will be very happy."

The light being said, "Please come with me."

The crowd parted, and Ray moved forward. "I'm to go back, aren't I?"

The being said, "That is not for me to decide. There is someone you must meet."

In the distance, Ray saw another bulb of light approaching, this one more radiant, like a sun. But he did not have to shield his eyes.

"Who is this?" Ray asked.

The first being said, "The Master. You must bow."

Ray stared at the person approaching. Ray was not sure what was expected of him. He looked back at the first being and could now see the outline of a body. His face was dark and friendly, with a large nose. The hair was red, bright. The arms and legs were long and his whole body slim but powerful looking. Strange bubbles of fear percolated through Ray's mind.

Then the second being stood next to him. "Do not be afraid," he said. Ray felt the strange pulsation of the being's fingers pressed into his shoulder.

The first being bowed. Ray started to kneel, but his mind suddenly seemed to fog inside. He fought to regain some comprehension of what he was doing. Suddenly he blurted, "Are you Jesus?"

The second being flared momentarily, then rose before him, high, powerful.

Ray said again, "Who are you? Are you Jesus Christ?"

A raw silence rose between them. Anger crackled through Ray's mind. Why was he to bow? What was this? Who was this person? "I said, 'Are you Jesus?' I want to know."

The second being immediately closed in on himself as if a furnace door had suddenly bolted. He looked into Ray's eyes. The cool blue orbs burned through Ray's soul. He felt himself quaking at the power that pierced him. The second being said, "I am—"

The last word was muffled as Ray was jerked backward. The tunnel disappeared behind him. His flesh seemed to explode, and he trembled, an earthquake rattling through his bones. A moment later, his eyes wide with fright, he saw the light above him beaming back silently. A nurse and doctor stood over him.

"How was it?" Dr. Reed said with a smile. The tape had been ripped off his face. His cheeks still tingled with a burning sensation.

Ray stared into the doctor's green eyes. He noticed his heartbeat, then that his fingernails were digging into his palm. He said, "What hap—?" He had no strength to utter anything else.

Martin Croase's voice rang out next to him. "We meant to keep together, but that's not always possible. Are you OK?"

Ray stared at him, then past him to Andi. She struggled to sit up and seemed to be fighting to keep her eyes open.

"Great, everyone had a great trip," Martin Croase said. "Let me have something to drink. I'm dry as the Gobi Desert."

CHAPTER THREE

1

A nurse took Ray on a gurney into a small recovery room. The handcuffs were removed. A few minutes later, Andi was brought in.

Ray spoke immediately after the guards left. "Are you OK?"

She was trembling, her face white. "No." Her voice quavered and she blinked, as though she were fighting back tears. She said evenly, "I just want to find Tommy and get out of here."

Ray stepped off the gurney and touched her face with his hand. She flinched.

"Andi, I didn't think they would do this."

"Neither did I." Her lip trembled. "I just pray Tommy's all—"

Instantly, they were in each other's arms. He patted her back, and she burst into tears again. "I just want my son back. That's all I care about."

He ran his fingers up the nubs of the bones in her back and worked at finding the right words to say. But nothing came into his mind. She pulled back from him, wiping her eyes. "It was horrible, Ray. It wasn't like they said at all."

Shrill fear was reflected in the deep brown of her irises.

"What happened to you?"

She shook her head, her hand at her forehead. "You don't want to know."

"It's all right. Whatever happened, you're all right now."

"No, I'm not."

Ray looked anxiously at her, then helped her into a chair. "Just sit tight."

He peered out the small square window in the recovery room door. Two guards stood outside, talking. Both were wearing side arms. He ran his finger along the frame of the door. Croase had to be crazy, he thought. What was he doing to people?

Then he saw Listra and Martin Croase walking down the hall toward the room. Ray stepped back from the window as the guard opened the door and let them in.

Listra spoke the moment she and Martin stopped inside. "Well, I hope your feelings are not too badly hurt."

"I just want to see Tommy," Andi answered. She looked red-eyed but unafraid.

Ray said with controlled fury, "I think the best thing is to let us get home at the moment."

"You didn't like it?" Listra asked incredulously. She was dressed in green slacks and a light green shirt. As always she looked perky, like a movie star just returned from a beauty treatment.

"I didn't say that," Ray answered. "Do you really think you have a right to use us like in some godforsaken experiment?" Ray clenched his fist. A guard moved forward, but Martin Croase put his arm out and stopped him.

"Ray, we just thought you were being unreasonable."

"Me being unreasonable? I don't believe this."

Croase turned to Andi. "We did not mean to scare you or anything like that. We just felt you needed to know what happened to Tommy. We knew it was safe, and we were sure once you saw it all yourself, you'd be quite relieved. We were only concerned for your psychological and spiritual well-being."

"I don't call this concern!" Ray shouted.

Listra took Martin's arm. "Honey, let's let them talk and cool down. Now's not the time to preach."

Croase hesitated, looked at Ray one more time, then agreed. "OK, we'll bring in Tommy, and if you want to leave, we'll let you leave. But I hope you won't drop out of seminary or anything like that. Good grief, son, we just want to give you the best theological education you can get anywhere."

"I'm not dropping out of seminary," Ray said with sudden finality. "Just let us go."

Listra walked over to Andi and took her hand. "Are you all right, darling?"

"Just let me see my son." She was sniffling, her head bowed. To Ray she looked vulnerable and beaten, a look he'd never seen in her.

"Immediately!" Croase answered and motioned to the guard. "I'm very sorry it had to happen this way, but in a few days, you'll see it all differently, I assure you."

Listra hugged Andi and spoke softly into her ear, but Andi kept her arms at her sides. As Croase started to leave, he said, "We're on your side, Ray. Both of your sides. Please believe that."

Ray said nothing and let them go out. When they were gone, he stooped in front of Andi. "Are you really OK? What happened out there?"

She caught her breath. "It was hellish, Ray. I never thought what happened could happen to me." She shook her head, shutting her eyelids tight with the memory. "I must have passed through a half-dozen places, and they were all torture chambers. It was awful. I feel so—." She started crying again. He crushed her in his arms, patting her back and talking softly.

Gradually, she calmed down, and when he started to pull away she whispered, "Please hold me. Just please hold me and don't say anything."

He wrapped his arms around her tighter, and she cried softly on his shoulder. He listened as she murmured, "Dear Jesus, just bring me my son and let us go home. Please just grant us that."

Tears burned into Ray's eyes. Whatever happened now, he wasn't going to let them hurt or Tommy again. Whatever Croase tried to do to him didn't matter. He didn't have anything to lose anyway. But neither Martin Croase nor Listra nor God Himself was going to hurt Andi or Tommy again. He swore to it.

2

Johnny Goge lay still on the bed of his motel room. The air quieted around him. Not even the sound of breathing disturbed the silence.

Then his whole face jerked like a body tic. A moment later he shook his head and blinked. He placed his right index finger on his temple and breathed out twice. He sat up, caressing the Colt lying under his left hand.

"Bold!" he yelled and exhaled heavily again.

He shook his head, sighing hard as though trying to blow out bad air. He had changed his clothing after the hit in Portland and was wearing a pinstriped shirt with chino pants. With the thick curtains shut it could be night. But he knew it was still daylight, only minutes after he'd entered the room earlier at noon.

He stood, flicked on a light, and turned and faced himself in the mirror. He carefully combed his reddish brown hair so that it fell over his ears. "It must be my lucky day," he said, smiling and revealing the silver tooth he'd got as a teenager. It was a side tooth, though, not visible unless he bared his teeth. He did not like anything that could be used by an onlooker to easily identify him.

As he eyed himself in the mirror, he twitched his eyebrows, slit his eyes, and tried to affect a penetrating movie star once-over. He picked up the mirror sunglasses off the dresser and placed them carefully over his eyes. Then he looked at the pile of money on the dresser. "Thirty thousand big ones!"

He laughed as he juggled one wrapped pile in his hands. "This kid is going to fly tonight."

Suddenly, the sound of voices on the walkway outside startled him. He listened, catlike, tensing. The rap of several feet clicked down the concrete walk. They passed, laughing.

Goge lay the Colt in a green gym bag with giant white *M*s on either side, packed up a few toilet articles, washed his face, then headed for the door. "Got to get in touch with the boss." He smiled. "Wonder what letter it'll be this time," he said again. "Maybe I'm gonna go through the whole alphabet."

As he turned the handle, he made his face sink back into a sober, emotionless mask. Behind the mirror sunglasses he felt invisible. A woman in a white skirt and pink tennis top with a sweater and a man in jeans walked down toward him. They passed him without a second look. As he watched them go by, he thought, *You don't know the powers that are watching.*

He chuckled again and walked to his car.

CHAPTER FOUR

1

Lou Miles, on the verge of retiring from the FBI at age fifty-seven, arrived at the Hillside murder site at 8:30 A.M. to inspect the body. Miles was bald, with a circle of short-cropped gray hair around a pink top. The body was covered with a blanket. Police had draped yellow line tape to keep a growing crowd of spectators back from the scene. Already, several people had been questioned. Miles worked out of the Portland FBI office on Southwest First Avenue and had been called in because of the letter carved into Hasekker's face. Normally, the FBI only got involved in such cases if the local police requested it.

Lou stooped by the blanket and lifted up the top right edge. The blood in the "A" cut clearly into his right cheek was dry and dark. The incision was deep, enough to make sure whoever looked at the face knew the killer was conveying a message. Lou winced, but didn't move.

"Nothing else like this in the city in recent weeks?" He looked up at Lt. Lilly, a gaunt, haggard-looking homicide man.

"First one this way."

Miles squinted through the hanging darkness. The early morning shadows were long and cold. Several detectives searched for whatever evidence might be available around the house.

"Looks almost like an underground hit job," Miles said. "Except for this letter in his cheek. He wasn't robbed or anything? No sexual molestation, so it's no gay revenge situation. Why would someone whack this guy? He was a banker, right?"

"Here's his wallet." Lilly handed the brown alligator skin billfold to Miles.

Miles looked through it and said, "His family?"

"We're trying to reach them now. He was a bachelor, apparently."

Miles wiped his forehead. Even with the cool Pacific air, he felt hot. "Somebody going door to door?"

"We have two men on it. So far, nothing."

"They think around five-thirty this morning?"

Lilly nodded. He had his hands jammed into a heavy tweed coat. "The coroner said it couldn't have been more than an hour before it was reported."

"Who first reported it?"

Lilly waved to a young woman from the crowd of people sequestered by the police just outside the taped off area. She had short brown hair, turned up nose, freckles. She wasn't pretty, just average. She had obviously been crying. When she came over, Miles questioned her gently. She had come out to deliver Hasekker's paper. She saw Hasekker, thought he'd fallen, then when she saw his face and bloody chest she called 911. Miles smiled and let her go. "Thanks." She went back to the group.

"We think the killer was hiding in the shadows over here." Lilly pointed to the row of bushes at the end of the walkway. "Must have known what time to be there. It has all the signs of a contract killing. No randomness about it."

Miles proceeded with all the usual questions: drugs, gangs in the area (though from the look of the houses, he knew that was preposterous), threats against the neighborhood, people who knew of possible enemies. No one had a clue. "Why would someone put a contract on a guy like this?"

"Everybody's got a secret or two." But Lilly was obviously as befuddled as Miles.

The FBI man stooped again and looked at the rest of the body, examined the books lying about. "OK, file the report. Send a copy to my office." He gave Lilly a card. "Let me know right away if anything comes up on the community canvas."

Miles walked to his blue Honda Accord. His paisley tie, still unknotted, hung around his neck like a scarf. He hated cases like this. Why someone would pull a classic hit on a pudgy accountant type made little sense on the face of it, though he knew there was probably a very logical explanation. Hasekker, theoretically, could have been into something very dangerous. A nice house in a nice neighborhood could cover for anything.

Ultimately, he knew deep down, to someone this killing made plenty of sense. So much so that as he stepped into the car, he heard himself mutter, "There are going to be others."

2

As Ray took his extra socks and shirts out of the dresser drawer to put in his suitcase, there was a knock at the door. He called, "It's open."

Martin Croase stepped in. "Ray, I hear you're leaving."

"Yes."

Croase had a sheet of paper in his hand. He waved it briefly at Ray, then said, "I know this probably will seem a bit out of order, but I'd like you to sign a release form before you go."

"Oh no you don't." Ray stared at him coldly, the anger building.

Croase clicked his fingers and a tall, blond man appeared with a seal in his hand. Croase grabbed Ray's shoulder and turned him around, then gazed Ray sternly in the eye. "For our protection," he said. "And yours. We wouldn't want anything unseemly to happen to our friends. So put off your natural sense of resistance and unwillingness to cooperate and sign it."

"It would never stand up in court."

"Let us worry about that."

Ray chewed his lip. He knew he couldn't prevent Andi from signing one, and Croase's people were probably wrangling her into doing it, too. He had to get Andi home, that was the important thing.

"And if I sign it, you're going to let us go back home, no questions asked."

"Of course."

"What's your purpose in making me sign this?"

Croase's eyes went up and down over Ray's face, then he smiled. "You have some, er, background with the police, do you not, Ray?"

Ray knew he had to be referring to two arrests a year before during an antiabortion sit-in. Neither the seminary nor Bible college had supported such activity, and he'd done it on his own. He felt he could not compromise principle just because his superiors frowned on it. He answered, "Nothing important."

"Actually, we know all about the arrests, Ray. Of course, we would not bring them up at all, but you have taken a very different and difficult position in this. We don't quite understand your or Andi's reaction. Tommy is fine, you both seem to have survived your experiences, and I for one do not comprehend your sudden antagonism. This is just a formality. Everyone who takes the TUT signs it. That's all. I'm not making a threat. Forget I brought up the arrests."

It was apparent to Ray that Croase wanted Ray to know he knew about the arrests without making it seem it was important. A fury raged inside him, but on the outside he prevented any of it from showing. It was a reaction he'd learned in the navy, something he'd fought hard to gain and now wished he could lose.

He looked at the paper, clenching his fist. "I thought you were a Christian, Dr. Croase."

"I am. Gordon Watt selected—handpicked me—on the basis of both my administrative ability and my faith. At some of the rallies I've spoken at, hundreds of people have come forward to receive Christ."

"Why do you want me to sign this form?"

"We consider it insurance."

"How?"

Croase shifted his weight impatiently. "You figure it out, Ray. As you said, it won't stand up in a court of law, so there's no danger in it. Please sign the form, and we will be getting on with letting—I mean, you and Andi and Tommy can go."

Ray ground his teeth a moment and slowly raised his fist. The svelte man before him looked almost like an apparition suddenly, as if Ray could see beneath the surface of his face. But the feeling disappeared a second later, and Croase grinned before him like an engraved photograph.

"You don't need to use violence, son. This isn't the navy. We're brothers in Christ. Let's act like it."

Ray slowly put down his fist. *Croase knows just what buttons to push.* "Give it to me," he said.

As Croase pressed the paper into his hand, he smiled toothily. "You're making the right decision."

After Ray had signed and Croase checked the signature, the tall blond man notarized it and left. Croase extended his hand and said, "I hope you and I aren't going to become enemies over this?"

"I hope not, too."

"You know, Jesus said, 'Love your enemies.'" Croase chuckled. "So we're required to love each other even if we don't much like each other."

"I guess you have a scripture for everything."

Croase frowned. "Ray, think about this. It's not that bad. Everyone's OK, you personally had a wonderful experience, and the whole group here is pulling and praying for the three of you. That's what it's all about."

"Is it?" Ray stared into Croase's deep blue eyes. Croase didn't flinch, but returned the stare. Then his eyes flickered, and he shifted uneasily on his feet.

"You're a military man, Ray. The SEALs are a tough outfit. I've heard your testimony many times. Military men tend to think certain problems have to be solved in less than conventional ways. I hope you won't be thinking of using those kind of tactics against us. It would not be wise."

"You're incredible!" Ray answered. "This is such hypocrisy it makes me puke."

"Call it what you want. That doesn't make it that way. We're doing important work here. We don't want it compromised." Croase reached out to touch his arm, and Ray stepped back. "Ray, come on. This is not something to shout about."

The two men faced off against one another. Finally, Ray said, "I just want to get Andi and Tommy home and situated. Believe me, I'm not thinking of using SEAL tactics on Atlantic Seminary or anyone else. So just relax. Now I'd like to finish packing."

Croase smiled. "Good. I knew you'd work it through." He clapped Ray on the back, then turned to leave. "If you need anything, let me know personally. I'll do all I can."

Ray said nothing more until Croase shut the front door.

When the bolt clicked, he looked up at the ceiling and said, "God, what are you doing? You can't be in this. You can't." After a long pause, he said with firm conviction, "You'd just better get Andi and Tommy out of this, or You're done. That's all I've got to say."

He threw the last shirt into the suitcase and jammed it shut. The fury grew larger until it suddenly exploded. "You hear me? You hear? They don't get out of this OK, then I'm through with You, with Christianity, everything. You hear me?"

His face quivered, then he composed himself and went to the door.

□ □ □

When Andi had finally put on her seat belt in Ray's Toyota and Tommy was safely ensconced in the back, Ray closed his door. A crowd had gathered to give them a send-off. Everyone told them they were praying and to let them know if there were any problems. Ray promised he would, then pulled the stick back into drive.

Out on the road, he said, "Everyone all right?"

"I'm just tired," Andi said. "Mind if I don't talk a lot?"

"Get some rest. Both of you."

Ray turned around and looked into Tommy's eyes behind the glasses. "You perkin' up, Chief?"

95

Tommy's lips flickered with a slight smile. "A little."

"When we get home," Ray said, turning back to the front, "you and I are going to do a little football together."

"We are?"

"Sure. You'd probably make a great end or tailback, maybe a halfback, fullback, whatever. What do you think?"

"Can I, Mom?" Tommy said, undoing his seat belt and leaning forward.

She nodded wearily. "Let's just get home first. Put your seat belt on."

He hovered over the back of the front seat. "I know of a park near us."

"Great. We'll do it."

Ray winked at Andi. He tried to be upbeat, thinking it would get everyone feeling better. But she was pensive and quiet. After driving for a while, Tommy lay down and began snoring quietly. Andi asked him, "Did they make you sign . . ."

Ray cleared his throat. "I signed it. You?"

"Yes. What else could I do?"

"What about Tommy?"

"They didn't ask him."

Ray kept his eyes on the road ahead. Then he said, "Did Croase make any threats?"

"Several."

"Do you want to talk about it?"

"Not right now."

"Maybe later?"

She bent down to pick up her pocketbook. "Maybe later."

He licked his lips and set his eyes on the road.

☐ ☐ ☐

An hour later, Ray pulled up to Andi's house. A jarring ache throbbed in the back of his head. His eyes felt as if they would shut and never open again. The air outside, though, was cool and woodsy. Pine. Andi had fallen asleep; she awoke when he stopped. He said, "Well, we're really home. This isn't a dream."

She rubbed her eyes.

"Come on, I'll help you get everything in." Ray turned around and patted Tommy's head. "You OK, Chief?"

The boy yawned and said, "Better."

A heaviness glued Ray to the spot. He stepped out into the cool air. As he moved about, the heaviness began to lift. He rolled his head around and kneaded his neck. Andi got out on her side. Across the roof of the car, she said, "You won't drop out or anything?"

He stopped twisting his head back and forth and sighed. "I don't know. No decisions till I've thought this through."

"You'll tell me whatever you do?" She no longer looked anxious, just wrung out. But he appreciated her concern.

"You'll be the first to know."

Tommy looked back and forth from Andi to Ray. He then went around to the trunk and said, "Mom, I'm really hungry."

Andi arched her eyebrows in Ray's direction. "Childhood calls."

Ray opened the trunk, then carried their bags up to the front door.

☐ ☐ ☐

The phone was ringing when they stepped inside. Andi picked it up off an end table in the antique-furnished living room.

The voice said, "It's Listra. Get home all right?"

Andi mouthed "Listra" to Ray. He slumped in a blue easy chair, then leaned forward, looking at his hands.

"We just arrived home," Andi said.

"I want to apologize, Andi. I'm very sorry all this has happened. Martin and I want you and Ray and Tommy to come over for dinner Monday night. Would you please consider it?"

She held the receiver to her chest and told Ray what Listra wanted. He looked surprised, then said, "Let's think about it. Why don't we discuss it and call back tomorrow night or so?"

97

"That sounds good," Andi said and took the mouthpiece off her chest. "We'll give you a call Sunday night."

"That's fair. Again, please forgive me if anything bad happened."

Andi blinked, then said, "Don't worry about it, Listra. I'm OK."

"Good. We'll be waiting to hear from you."

When she hung up, she walked over to Tommy and spoke soothingly to him, then said, "Why don't you take a long shower? It'll make you feel better."

The boy huddled apprehensively. "I'd rather stay out here with you."

She ran her fingers through his hair. "You think you're OK now?"

"Sort of."

Andi looked at Ray over Tommy's head and said, "Take off your coat. Would you like a cup of coffee?"

"Just like a glass of cold water for now."

With a quick pat on the head, she sent Tommy into the kitchen to get the water. "And put ice in it," she said. "Any that drops on the floor you throw away."

Ray suddenly laughed. "Hey," he said, "after that ice hits the floor once or twice it gets a little flavor."

She wrinkled her nose in disgust. "He's always doing that. Wouldn't be so bad if it was just for him, but he does it for everybody. He can be awfully thoughtless at times."

"Oh, it makes sense to him."

She rolled her eyes with exasperation.

When he heard Tommy out in the kitchen, Andi suddenly whispered, "Ray, I feel terror-stricken. Do you think they'll try to do anything else?"

Ray spoke low. "I don't know. We should probably prepare for anything. It might be good just to hole up somewhere for a few days. What did Croase threaten you with?"

"He said that ultimately even the U.S. government can't protect me and Tommy from everyone, so I should just trust him."

Ray gazed at her compassionately. "I'm afraid he's right, Andi—about the government, not about trusting him."

"I know. But—well, I think we could just sit tight for a few days anyway. It might be best just to get back into the flow of things. I think Listra realizes it was a mistake. Maybe they'll just leave us alone."

"Yeah." Ray began to think of what he might do in the SEALs, but this was not what the training was for. If it had involved "fast-roping" fifty feet down a thick rope from a helicopter onto a barge and setting up a .50 caliber machine gun, or swimming a mile underwater and fixing plastic explosives to the underside of an oil platform, he'd be quite prepared. But SEALs weren't private investigators, or the FBI.

Who knew what kind of money and power Croase really wielded? Obviously, he knew how to conduct a rather suspicious operation without its being compromised.

He felt angry and, for the moment, impotent. Still, he liked Andi's style, and he decided she'd be a good ally. She was gritty, a team player. That might matter more than anything for the three of them.

Andi was gazing at him when he looked up again. She patted Tommy's back the moment he walked back in with the glass of ice water. "Come on, hon. Go upstairs and take a shower, or do you want to take a bath?"

He handed Ray the drink, then said to his mother, "Will you come with me?"

She didn't return for nearly half an hour. Ray looked around the room. It was obviously a thoughtfully decorated house, with Victorian furniture, mauve drapes that stretched to the floor, silver ashtrays and fine wooden boxes and knick-knacks everywhere on the tables, mantle, shelves, and sills, and fine blown glass lamps. He wondered what Andi's family was like and if she had brothers or sisters. He suddenly realized how little he knew about her. He thought through several questions to ask her when things were settled.

When she walked back down the stairs to the main floor, she sat down. "I got him into bed. I know it's only afternoon, but he's dead tired. Ray, tell me honestly. How could they do that to us? To anyone?" She gazed at him with hopeful, trusting eyes. It gave him a strong, solemn feeling, a sense of meaning that he hadn't felt in years.

She went on, "I don't know whether to spit, swear, scream, or weep. I'm mad, I'm terrified, and I feel like punching someone."

He nodded with a lengthy sigh. "I think there's a lot more to this underneath the surface. I don't know what TWI or Croase or any of them are up to, but it's far more than providing Christians with a unique 'spiritual' experience. We have to be real careful about this." He stood and went to the fireplace, then turned, his hand on the marble mantle. "What did happen to you out there?"

She looked down and her hair fell forward, then she faced him and swept her hair back. "I think I went to hell—for a few minutes, anyway."

"But what happened?"

As Andi began to talk, the scene unfolded in her mind.

"Ray!" Her voice was eerie, as though it did not come from her lips but from somewhere inside her. She stared at the tunnel and watched as the Croases and then Ray were pulled into it. She started to move toward it, then suddenly it disappeared.

Heat crackled against her face, and she realized she stood on the shore of a vast, bubbling lake. She stared at it. Her first thought was of a volcanic eruption. The path underneath her feet was charred and black, like unlit charcoal briquetts. She bent to look closer.

The horror of it filled her with a shriek. "Bones!"

She began running away from the lake, tripped, fell.

A moment later, she had the sensation of hurtling downward. But there was no weight to her body. Her feet struck something—a ledge—and she turned around. A vast opening yawned before her, a cave. She stepped forward, her thoughts wild with terror. The hot, fetid air hit her face like a brick. Then the voices. Wailing. Screaming.

"My God! Enough. Please enough!"

"Help me. I didn't mean it. Get me out."

"The pain. The pain is so great. Please!"

"I don't understand. Why? Tell me—why?"

Andi gasped and strained to see into the darkness. She could see nothing. The darkness was as deep and impene-

trable as sheer rock. Listening, she realized the voices could not hear one another, or at least no one responded or talked to the other. They were all wailing about their own pains.

Then something cold and terrible grabbed her shoulder. She froze, then slowly turned around. A grotesque creature with warts and scars all over his dark face leered at her from the ledge.

"Come," it said. "You will see. You will tell."

Claws gripped her arm, and the creature led her out onto the ledge. They stepped off and were suddenly both walking straight down into the pit as if defying gravity.

"Who are you?" Andi screamed.

"Shut up!" The creature gave her a fierce, angry look, slapped her, then gripped her arm even harder. She could feel the cold, steel-like claws drilling her spirit.

She let him pull her downward. Soon they were walking across another bubbling, glowing river. They stepped on stones, but when she looked down, she realized the stones were faces staring up at her and murmuring without being heard.

She screamed again, but the creature said, "Shut up and come."

"I shouldn't be here!" she screamed behind him. "I'm a Christian."

The creature snickered.

"But God said—"

"God says many things."

Andi looked up and cried, "Please, dear Jesus, if you love me, get me away from here."

She felt the creature's claws dig deeper into her arm, then suddenly above her a light shone, like shafts of sunlight. She knew she had to reach it. She kicked the creature. It growled and let go. She ran toward the light. Then just as suddenly she was ripped away, pulled through stone, fire, char, and the bodies—she passed through it all and a stench filled her nostrils.

A moment later she opened her eyes into the lights above the reclining chair.

When she was finished, Ray's chin had dropped and he had no idea what to say. He'd read about such experiences, but had never known anyone who'd had one.

101

She gazed at him through teary eyes. "Am I even a Christian, Ray? If I die, will I go to that place?" She put her head in her hands and sobbed. Ray knelt in front of her, his hands on her knees. She wiped at her eyes and trembled. "I've tried to do what's right. I've believed. But why did I go to that place?"

As she gazed at him helplessly, he knew she was expecting some final answer that would explain it all. He took her hands in his. "Andi, look at me. If you've believed in Jesus, you're a Christian. If you're following Him, there's no question about it. He said, 'Whoever comes to me will not be cast out.' You've come to him?"

She shook her head. "Yes. Absolutely."

"Then regardless of what happened, you belong to Him. Nothing can snatch you out of His hand. I can't explain why you went to that place or what it was. But according to the Bible, you couldn't have gone to hell. Maybe it was a kind of death hallucination—maybe all these experiences are hallucinations."

She choked. "You just don't know all of it." She pulled a handkerchief out of her handbag and dabbed at her eyes. "I haven't told you everything about myself, what kind of person I used to be."

His heart suddenly began banging inside him like a pile driver, and he felt as if everything he loved about her was about to crumble. But he stilled his fear and gently asked, "OK, do you want to tell me?"

She sniffled and choked and coughed into the handkerchief. "When I got pregnant, I really hurt my parents. I lied to them. I had been into drugs. I blew everything. They were helping me go to college, spending nearly every cent they had, and I simply spurned it. I took complete advantage."

She shook her head and wiped her eyes. "I just treated them so shabbily. And partly, I've been trying to make up for it now, by going to school, by working toward my degree, by being responsible. But maybe . . ." Her voice cracked and Ray gripped her hand.

"Maybe God just wrote me off, Ray."

"Never! That could never happen. God is not like that."

"But look at King Saul, and Esau, and Judas Iscariot."

"You're not Judas Iscariot or any of those others." Ray stood up. "Look at me."

She blinked, then looked into his face, her eyelashes wet and her cheeks streaked.

"I don't know why that happened to you. But it's not because God has rejected you. Good grief, if He did that to you, He'd have to do it to everyone who's ever lived."

"But I've done such awful things."

Ray laughed. "Andi, what have you done? You made a mistake—you got pregnant out of wedlock. OK, it's done. You've repented of it, you've trusted Him. Maybe without the mistake you never would have trusted Him, so in a way the sin itself led you to Christ."

She nodded her head thoughtfully. "That's true."

He smiled. "So just relax about it. We'll find the explanation if there is one, but don't crucify yourself because of it. Maybe the computer program that transports people from earth to heaven got switched in your case, who knows?"

She laughed. "Computer program. Yeah, right." But she was smiling. Ray felt as though they'd had a breakthrough in their relationship. She trusted him. He could see it in her eyes.

After a few minutes, she sighed. "I'm such a crybaby. I hate this. You must think I'm a complete child."

He pulled her close. "What you and Tommy have been through this weekend—I think you are one outstanding woman."

She leaned against his chest and gradually a great calm came over them. "I knew I had to tell you. You were so honest with me, and I just knew I couldn't keep it all a secret from you. But I don't want to hurt my mom and dad. If we went to the police or anything, they'd be crushed."

Her warmth and her streaked face and her closeness made him feel hotly protective. "Well, I wasn't thinking about going to the police, not yet anyway. So don't worry about that."

There was a long silence, then she nodded. "Thanks."

"All right, let's get to work. We have to figure out what we're gonna do first."

They talked into the evening, and when Tommy got up they had some dinner. Finally, after offering to stay for the night, Ray agreed he should get back to his room. At the door, he hugged her hard, then winked as he tousled Tommy's hair. On the way to the dorm, he thought again about Martin Croase, about Andi's situation, about the NDE. He prayed, half to himself, half to God, "Well, You're doing something, Lord. What, I don't know. But somehow I feel confident we're going to get out of this alive and kicking."

He smiled as he drove. He wondered if he was falling in love with Andi. And suddenly he realized he had probably fallen in love with both her and her son.

3

Dr. Nakayami stood in Martin Croase's office at the conference center looking angry and unapologetic. It was past nine o'clock on Sunday morning, just before the church service they held in the chapel. He laid a file on Croase's desk. "It was security's mistake. The door should have been locked. But we found out what happened."

"Yes."

"It was the TUT-B, not the Actifed, though we'll test that out again. There were several vials of the TUT-B on the top shelf. One of the aides wanted to try it on several of the pigs at our research farm. They shouldn't have been there. But it happened exactly like it was supposed to. The boy was dead for ten minutes, precisely as long as the TUT-B is supposed to work."

TWI had been working on two versions of the TUT. The standard, already in use, induced death for four minutes, give or take a few seconds. That was the crucial juncture for any thanatraveler. For many years, medical people recognized that oxygen deprivation to the brain did not normally cause damage until after four minutes. Thus, that always seemed the right point of return.

But Dr. Nakayami hit on the idea of a second level of TUT that would induce death for longer periods without brain damage. In the normal TUT the drug insulated the cells of the body through a special "chemical shield" from which they derived the acronym.

It was this "shield" that prevented brain cells from physically dying while the subject was clinically "dead." The drug was a combination of the chemical components of a lethal poison—hydrocyanic acid, or cyanide. It included amyl nitrite, sodium nitrite, and sodium thiosulfate that were delivered sequentially in time release coated spheres injected with the serum. These chemicals counteracted the effects of the cyanide, which through an enzyme reaction prevented red blood cells from absorbing oxygen. Somehow—neither Nakayami nor the TWI people knew how—the TUT element of the formula both protected the brain cells and also facilitated immediate radiation of the entire brain in a few seconds so that no brain cells actually died permanently.

It was thought that this state could be enhanced so that the shield lasted even longer. Thus, the TUT-B. But until the day before, nothing, not even a rat, had survived a dose.

"So he's the first one who has lived through it?"

"The only one. The only human it's ever been tried on."

"And it hasn't worked in the lab?"

"Right. Not even once. We were going to try the pigs because their endocrine system is close to that of the human."

"Well, then, maybe it's a clue," Croase said.

Nakayami stared at his boss. Croase looked at the file, then leafed through it quickly. "OK, the boy got TUT-B," he said. "Maybe it's ready to go then. We need to begin trying it on others. Maybe it won't work on animals."

"But it could fail. People would die. We can't use people for this." Nakayami's face was gray, the light brown skin drawn on his cheekbones.

"I'll take care of the people issue. You get ready to test it. If the kid could do it, so can anyone else. We've got to get beyond the wall, Hiro."

"But this is not like the TUT, Martin. It is very dangerous. It—"

"Then maybe this kid himself is the answer we're looking for. We study him, find out what elements combine to make him compatible, then try it on someone else."

"But who?" Nakayami wailed. "It could be immediate death!"

Croase leaned forward. "I said, let me worry about that. All right? Now do your job and don't worry about nonissues." Croase pulled a package of mints out of his right pocket and popped one into his mouth, turning to other papers on his desk.

Nakayami gave him a hard look, then sighed and went out. When the researcher was gone, Croase put his fingers up to his forehead and closed his eyes. "I need to talk," he said out loud. "But first the service."

He pulled on a navy blue sports coat and strode out to the chapel where he would deliver the final address of the weekend.

4

Lou Miles looked over Carl Hasekker's file at the Portland First National Bank office. A Kool lay in the ashtray in front of him, sending a ribbon of smoke upward. Hasekker was nothing spectacular. Joined the air force at eighteen. Four years. Got out and went to college and became a CPA. Started with First National in the middle eighties. No record. Not even a driving ticket. His parents lived in Seattle. He also had two brothers, both younger.

What was the A?

The question kept reverberating in his head. Obviously it was a message, but what? Was this guy some kind of new serial murderer? Going to write a message on people's cheeks? Or was he just pulling a single job and doing his own little dance in the wind? Was it related to drugs? Was it just a diversion, something to misdirect the investigation? Was it a cult?

A cult.

He'd seen that sort of thing before. All the way back to Charles Manson, which he'd done a little legwork for in August 1969 when the Sharon Tate murders took place. Over the years he'd had a specialty in cults for the FBI. There were plenty of them in Oregon where he was based. Rarely, though, had they hired professional killers to do their "work." They home grew their own. This guy was obviously a professional.

106

The phone rang.

"Miles."

"We got the bullet." It was Lt. Lilly. "10 mm."

"Uncommon, huh?"

"Yeah. Maybe he watched "Miami Vice." The lead character on it wielded a 10 mm Bren Ten. Colt makes one. There are others. We haven't ID'd the make."

"Hard to get ammo, too."

"Yeah. We're checking local stores. But if this guy is a pro, he probably has his own sources."

"Probably." Miles drew on his cigarette and expelled noisily into the air. Several years before, the FBI had signed a big contract for 10 mm Smith and Wessons, but it began to crumble when problems with firing and ejection developed. "Anything else?"

"We're interviewing people who knew him. He definitely wasn't a loner. A lot of friends. People at the bank thought he was a real whiz. Smart. No enemies that we've been able to dredge up."

Miles sucked on the Kool. "What do you think the *A* is?"

Lilly didn't respond.

"You got any idea?"

"I don't like it."

"Yeah. It looks like there're gonna be more."

"Right. Maybe we ought to put out something on it on the PD computer." Lilly sounded like he was in a phone booth somewhere. Miles could hear cars going by.

Miles stubbed his cigarette out and reached for another from the pack in his pocket. "I'll send out a bulletin by the KEY network to every FBI office in the country. I'll also put a bulletin on the LLEAS."

FBI KEY was a highly sophisticated computer database that linked every FBI office to the same internal information. Any Special Agent with a computer and modem, his ID number, and the answers to the personalized series of questions the computer gave to anyone seeking access could retrieve in-depth information about nearly any person in the United States as well as internationally. LLEAS was another, more recent information database system available to every police agency in the country.

Miles went on. "Any prints?"

"Nothing. It was definitely a pro job."

"That's what I'm afraid of. A pro job, a message to the public, and the boding of more to come. A pro serial murderer. Just what we need."

Lilly breathed evenly into the phone. Miles swore.

"OK," Miles said. "Thanks."

When he hung up, he took a long drag on the second cigarette, then picked up the file and gazed at Hasekker's picture. A little pudgy. But not a bad looking guy. "Why Hasekker?" he said again.

He was sure Hasekker had been selected. It wasn't a random hit. Chances were he wasn't involved with drugs, or something from the military—spying or illegal information. Crime was a possibility. But what was he doing? And could they find it out soon enough to prevent another murder and possibly apprehend the killer?

5

Ray went over to Andi's house for lunch on Sunday afternoon. Tommy seemed less withdrawn, but behind the thick lenses, he blinked with anxiety. "Hi, Mr. Ray," Tommy said as Ray stood in the doorway, leaning up against the jamb.

Andi called from the kitchen, "Make yourself comfortable, Ray. Tommy's willing to go out, if I go with him. We'll just have a bite before we go."

Ray smiled, happy he didn't have to stay inside and play a board game. Though he enjoyed Monopoly, Boggle, Trivial Pursuit, and others, he far preferred heaving around a basketball or football, or just running. He played on at least one intramural team at the seminary each season.

Andi had worn a blue chiffon dress for church, but after they had a lunch of meat loaf and macaroni and cheese, she went upstairs to change. Ray said to Tommy, "I've got a football in the car. Let's go."

As Ray looked into his serious, expectant face, for a moment he thought about the possibility of marrying Andi and adopting Tommy as his son. *I could do that,* he said in his mind. After the boy pulled on a jacket, he pretended to make a handoff to Tommy and then tackled him on the living room floor. Both were laughing when Andi skipped down the stairs, dressed in blue jeans, a flannel shirt, and sneakers. She had pulled up her shiny brown hair in the back with a leather barrette. She looked to Ray like some yuppie mother. "Let me just visit the ladies' room, and we'll be off," she said, passing Ray quickly and squeezing Tommy on the shoulder.

When she had left the room, Tommy said, "She likes you."

Ray tried to act nonchalant. "She likes everyone."

"No, she likes you special, I can tell."

"Well, I like her, Tommy. And you too."

"Do you think you'll marry her?"

Ray coughed. "I don't think it's at that point yet, Chief."

The boy looked down into his hands. "Guess I shouldn't be talking about this, huh?"

Ray put his hands on Tommy's shoulders and squared him up so he could look into the boy's eyes. "Listen, Chief, you can talk about anything you want to with me but especially your mom, OK? But getting married is something that takes a long time."

Tommy shook his head. "No, I went to one once. It only took about an hour and all they had to say was 'I do.'"

The boy was so sincere and direct, Ray burst out laughing. He decided, though, he'd better change the subject before Andi walked back in and discovered her son and this ex-military grunt were conspiring to marry her off in an hour. Ray said, "So you ever play much football?"

The boy looked down at his feet and pointed the tips together. He murmured, "A little." Then wiped his nose on his sleeve. "I'm not real good at it. I like computers." This time he looked directly into Ray's eyes.

"Oh yeah? What kind of computers?"

"We have Apples at school. And an Amiga. And a Macintosh, too. For the older kids. But I learned some programs on the Mac."

"Like what?"

Ray realized it was not easy for Tommy to talk to him. He wondered why. Tommy answered, "I made up my own database."

Ray raised his eyebrows, impressed. "What's in it?"

"A list of everything we have here."

"You mean all the furniture and kitchen stuff?"

"And clothes, too. Please don't tell Mom."

Ray grinned. "It's a surprise?"

He smiled and shrugged. "Yeah. I even checked out how valuable our stuff is. So now Mom can know how much she's worth—even though it isn't her house."

Ray peered at the boy. He thought of what Andi had told him about her father. Maybe that was part of it. Had Tommy understood what was happening? Ray said, "So did you count you and your Mom in it?"

Tommy's eyes flickered and he looked at Ray directly, then flinched away. "Me and Mom?"

"Well, those are the most valuable things, right? You should put them in too. Make them worth two billion dollars each."

Tommy made a wry face. "Not that much."

"More," Ray said. "Three billion. Four."

"Maybe for Mom."

Ray winced. It suddenly made him mad. For a long time he'd thought the whole self-esteem cult was baloney. But he knew a lot of people who considered themselves little more than garbage. It angered him to see so many people thinking that God made them wrong or that He was some kind of cosmic Mengele who created less than perfect people for kicks. Worse, some thought He didn't care at all, that He just let it all happen however it happened. Even with the doubts he was battling at the moment, he knew God could not be like that.

Ray said, "Tommy, believe me, you're worth far more than all the money in the world. Especially to Jesus."

Tommy gazed at him unbelievingly. "To Jesus?"

"Jesus didn't buy you with money, Tommy. He paid for you with His life. That's what He was doing on the cross. When He died there, He was buying us back from sin, from

110

being sentenced to hell. No amount of money could have paid for that. So you're worth the same to God as Jesus is."

Tommy stared at him. "I am?"

"Definitely." Ray tousled his head. "Come on. Let's get going. Where's your mom?"

"I'll get her." Tommy left the room and bounded up the stairs.

Ray stood at the bottom of the stairs thinking about Andi's situation and the things Tommy's uncle had said. How could people be that way? The more Ray thought about it, the angrier he felt. It wasn't right to put Andi and Tommy through that. He closed his eyes and prayed that God would work things out, perhaps giving Andi what she desired without forcing her to make decisions just to please others.

A moment later, the sound of clicking fingers snapped in his face.

"Hey, space man, you out in the wild blue yonder or something?"

Ray opened his eyes and blinked. "Sorry, guess I'm a lot more tired than I thought. I was just praying, and then I sort of veered off."

She smiled at him and pulled on a sweater. "Must have been pretty heavy. You looked like you'd gone to the great vacuum cleaner bag in the sky."

"When I pray on something important, I really do it."

"So what were you praying about?" She called to Tommy to hurry up.

"Just the situation for all of us."

She nodded. "I've been praying a lot too. Seems like the only thing to do at the moment. Tommy!"

Tommy hurried down the stairs. Ray said to him, "All right, Chief, let's go and wing that football and show your mother what real men do when they have fun."

He winked at her, and she rolled her eyes. "I'll take both of you on any day," she said. She made a fist and grimaced. "Women can be tough, too."

"Yeah, right," Ray said, twitching his eyebrows at Tommy. "But men prefer them soft and sweet."

111

"That too," Andi said with a little pouty shrug. Then she smiled and led them out.

On the way to the park, Andi chattered pleasantly about school and courses she'd like to take. Ray wondered if she'd suddenly forgotten what had happened over the weekend. But he realized she might just be trying to put it out of her mind. He decided not to bring up anything about the experience. After some more talk about the school, she began questioning Ray about profs he liked and didn't like.

"Doc Kingston's the best I know of."

"Oh, I took one of his classes. He's good."

"What one?"

"Apologetics. He's got a clear argument for everything. I learned a lot."

"Yeah, that's his specialty."

They walked on. Ray sank down into his thoughts again. As they stood at a corner, waiting for the light to change, he said, "I think I'm gonna talk to him about all this."

The air was brisk, and a slight wind riffled the grass and leaves. Andi responded, "He'd probably give the right kind of help."

"Yeah, he'd help me think it through."

She laughed.

"What's so funny?"

"'Think it through.' Dr. Kingston was always saying that in the class. You say that a lot too."

Ray grinned sheepishly. "Like teacher, like disciple."

They crossed the street. In the park, Ray called plays while Andi and Tommy went out for passes, ran end-arounds, and rushed. They played alone, but it felt exhilarating to Ray. Tommy did have a hard time. Most of the time he dropped the ball. But he learned quickly. Ray sensed that he was trying to be what he imagined was a kid version of a SEAL. Andi caught a few passes, even pulled one down that was over her head.

They meandered home, joking and laughing. Once inside the house, Tommy excused himself to visit the bathroom. Andi went into the kitchen, and Ray followed.

"Guess I'll have to stock up the Spam around here. That is what they eat in the navy, isn't it?"

"Hah, you should see what we get. The best vittles in the world. Course, nothing like your meat loaf this afternoon, and of course I haven't seen your complete repertoire—"

"Oh, trying to make sure you will?" She backed up against the sink and grinned at him playfully.

Suddenly, he leaned over and grabbed her, kissing her on the lips. When they both caught their breath, she said, "You are one good kisser." She squeezed his cheek, then wriggled out of his grasp. "How about a Coke to cool off?"

Ray smiled. "I think I should go. I'll say 'bye to Tommy on the way out. You don't have to show me to the door. Thanks for the lunch and everything."

"My pleasure." She gave him another quick kiss, then turned back to the sink. "Lock it, would you please?"

"Sure."

After giving Tommy a pat on the back, Ray drove home, thinking about how much this new relationship with Andi had revitalized his feelings. He wanted to be with her—and Tommy. He wanted a family. They were together more than he'd ever hoped for.

But another thought nagged at him: what if God took it all away—again?

He clenched his teeth as he drove. He knew he couldn't threaten God. He only wanted understanding. And hope.

Above all, hope.

His thoughts came back to the near death experience. For a moment, he relived it and then he gasped. "Grandpop! How could he have been there?"

☐ ☐ ☐

An hour and a half later, in Dr. Kingston's home library, Ray paced back and forth before the revered professor and mentor. "Doc, everything's going wrong again. I can see it happening all over."

Kingston raised his bushy eyebrows and leaned against the shelves of books that lined the lush study, spaciously laid out on the top floor room of the two-story town house. It was a fashionably decorated library, with glowing mahoghany

113

paneling and bookcases with elaborate crown moulding around the eight-foot ceilings. The house was filled with antiques, several different book collections—one of the Civil War, another of the Reformation—and several fine original paintings from local rising artists.

Kingston was a widower of over ten years. His wife, Bea, had died of cancer after thirty-six years of marriage to him. At the time it hit Kingston badly. But her mark had been left on his life. She was an impeccable homemaker, with a degree in interior design. Though their home was small now—after their children exited and went their three ways, they bought the stylish town house—she managed to turn it into the castle Kingston talked about on the religious "family life" lecture circuit.

Kingston said, "Ray, God did not take your mother or father or those friends in the navy to punish you, or hurt you, or anything. He doesn't work that way."

"Then why does it all go wrong for me, Doc?"

"Hey, if it did, what about me? Why am I still here? Wouldn't He have taken me away from you too?"

Kingston was still handsome, even at seventy, with a mane of stark white hair. He remained robustly healthy. He was taller than Ray, too, who at six-one was no dwarf. Semi-retired, he taught only one class and spent a lot of time on the road, speaking at seminars and conferences around the country. He was one of those larger-than-life professors who could wow an audience with humor, pathos, spiritual power, and dynamic insight. Many young men eventually came to the seminary because of an encounter with Kingston. Ray was one of them.

Ray sighed and ran his fingers through his long, brown hair. "I honestly feel you're safe."

Kingston leaned back and roared. "So this is how you really feel about me—I'm safe! That's edifying. Here I was thinking it might have something to do with my looks, or my intellect, or my stocks and bonds."

"I'm not joking around, Doc."

"All right, I'll give you the benefit of the doubt." He grinned and fingered a pen lying on the blotter. "Still, I'm certain God is not disciplining you or anything like that by killing off people in your life. I can't conceive of a God that works that way, much less the God of the Bible."

Ray shook his head adamantly. "But Doc, lots of Christians feel that at times. They're afraid God will take away something dear to them because they've put it before Him, or they're afraid He'll make them do something—be a missionary, go to darkest Africa, get killed by being skinned by cannibals—it's not like I'm the only one. God can let some bad things happen to people, and it often appears for no good reason."

"I'll give you that. But God doesn't have to explain Himself. He's running a universe, not a good time Charlie bar."

Ray sat down with frustration. "It's just that I'm afraid to—what? I don't even know. I'm afraid that if I really get involved with Andi and her son that something will happen to them. Something bad. And I'm afraid if I don't help them out, that Croase is going to go even farther."

"What would Martin Croase do?" Kingston gazed at Ray with sudden consternation on his face.

"I haven't told you what happened last weekend." Ray gave him a quick rundown of the events.

Kingston's chin dropped, and his face reddened with anger. "I had no idea Croase was doing this kind of research." He questioned Ray for a few more minutes, but his obvious rage only deepened. "This is incredible! How could they be doing this kind of thing and keep—" He slapped his hand down on the desk. "I'm calling Hawkins and Pirelli immediately. The board should know what's going on."

Ray grabbed his hand as Kingston reached for the phone. "Hey, slow down, Doc. I came here to talk about this with you, not start an uprising."

"That is sure what this calls for."

A phone rang somewhere, and Kingston waved it off. "Next door town house. They keep the blasted phone cranked up to ten decibels. He's always in the cellar."

He slumped in his seat, obviously avoiding looking at Ray. "I'm sorry, Ray. I had no idea. What can I say? They keep me on the road so much now, and things have changed in the last few years. Even if I did go to the board—I hardly know the people on it now. For all I know, Croase has stacked it in his favor. And what with Bea gone and the kids all married and rearing their own families, well . . .”

“I don't blame you, Doc,” Ray quickly answered. “Look, we can think about what to do later. Right now I just want to know your opinion. Do you think this could really be from God? Nothing like this ever happened to me except that experience when I was a kid—the one I told you about when I was hit by a car.”

Kingston nodded emphatically. “I remember. We've discussed it a few times.”

“Right. Well, in a way, I'm almost drawn to doing it—multiple times. I mean, maybe I could get some answers. But in another way, I feel as though it's not what Croase says it is.”

“I think it might be exactly that—something far removed from real Christianity, something very possibly demonic.”

Ray nodded forcefully and stood, pacing back and forth, gesturing, pointing, clapping his fist into his left palm. “The biggest problem I see, Doc, is that my grandfather was there. It just hit me this afternoon. Not that I'm not glad, but he was a Unitarian, probably really an atheist, nothing even close to a believing Christian in any sense of the word. What was he doing there? Sure, maybe he had some kind of deathbed conversion, though I've never heard anything about it, and I doubt he would have—but if what the Bible says is true, then sad to say, my grandfather should never have entered into heavenly bliss. And if this is really a spiritual experience as some people say it is—and Andi's experience was even weirder (she thinks she went to hell!) what gives? What am I supposed to think?”

Kingston nodded and pressed his fingertips together, deep in thought.

“And there's all this stuff in the news, people talking about ‘out of the body’ experiences and meeting ‘ascended masters’ and things, how do I know who or what that person Trell was when I was eight? And how do I know if this is even close to being Christian? I mean, it's powerful—monumental—when you go through it. I didn't tell Andi, but when I came back to and cleared my head, I felt like I was Superman. Don't laugh. I did."

Dr. Kingston's lips twitched. Behind him, sunlight beamed in through the window and outside Ray could see a couple of kids throwing a frisbee on the wide lawn in front of the town houses. Kingston said, "From what you tell me, I think it's almost certainly demonic."

Ray chewed his lip. "Maybe, Doc. But that's awfully glib to just write it off. But let's say it is—then what's God doing with me? I feel totally confused. Like I'm half-afraid God's going to let Andi and Tommy be hurt badly because of me, and then I'm afraid this whole NDE thing is just another piece in the long line of ridiculous Christian demands for a bigger, better, more supernatural experience. I know Listra and Martin Croase seem to think it's 'Christian' and all. But frankly, if anything, it goes way beyond 'Christian.' In fact, it puts the whole Christian faith at risk. It's a total destruction of Christian teaching—and it's real. You're there. You see it unfold before you. Doc, I feel like I'm losing it."

Kingston sat up and stared at Ray. "Your faith?"

"Yeah." Ray nodded furiously. "This has really got me. And if I lose that, I lose everything. I can't live without believing there's a real God up there who's going to make this world into something decent, and make my life decent along with it."

The old man stood and sucked on his lip, peering anxiously at Ray. "Well, let's put that one to rest. You can't lose your faith if you really have it, Ray. That's the end of that matter."

"But what if I never really had it?"

Kingston shook his head. "Ray, you have it. Believe me. You're the kind of guy I look for every year when I teach here. You've got what I call gutsy faith. You're not afraid to push it to the limit. None of this namby-pamby stuff. When I met you, I knew I had to get you here, or I'd go nuts. You're a prof's dream."

Ray sighed. "Thanks for the vote of confidence."

The old man's hand crashed down on the desk. "It's no vote of confidence. Boy, you *have* it. You're like my Timothy. You lose it, and I go with you."

Ray took a deep breath and sat down. "OK, but what is this all about? There has to be some explanation."

The old man sat down again and leaned back, looking up at the ceiling. "I've thought about the problem a lot, I'll confess to that. Ever since we've been marauded by Hollywood with life-after-death movies. I think Satan's making a big move, Ray. That's what it comes down to."

"But what if it's not demonic, Doc? What if that's the way it really is?"

Kingston eyed him quizzically. "You mean, Christianity's completely untrue?"

"Yes." Ray nodded with emphasis. "That could be, you know."

"Not possible, Ray."

"Why not?"

Kingston sighed. "You're trying to tell me everything I've taught and believed all my life is wrong?"

"That's basically what we're telling the rest of the world—that most of what they believe, live, and die for is falsehood."

After scratching his neck a moment, Kingston nodded slowly. "OK, I see what you're saying. But it will always come down to faith, Ray. That's the way God has made it. 'Without faith it's impossible to please Him.' We believe because God has personally opened our eyes. Even if our experience seems to contradict it, even if the so-called facts militate against it, we choose to believe the Scriptures are the truth and wait for God to deal with the so-called facts. Sooner or later, He always sheds some light on the issue."

"Sure, sure. But in a way, Croase is offering the ultimate means to faith, to really trust God. Suddenly, we can literally see Him, feel Him, talk to Him."

Kingston leaned forward, fixing Ray with burning, fearless eyes. "And maybe that's the Achilles heel of the whole idea. We learn to trust God by trusting Him, Ray. It's as simple as that. We live by faith, not by sight. We trust Him for something little in the rigors of life. He works on the basis of our prayers and our faith. Next we trust Him for something bigger. He works that out. Maybe not the way we expected or wanted, but He truly does bring good out of bad. The only way any of us is going to trust Him is by actually sticking our necks out and believing. Some harebrained experience isn't going to do it, I'll assure you of that. Like Proverbs says, 'Trust in the Lord with all your heart and do not lean on your own understanding.' That's the core, Ray. You trust that the truth works even if at the moment it sure doesn't look like it does."

Ray sighed with frustration. "I know all that. In my head at least. But why am I so scared?"

The old man laid his hand palm up on the desk. "Look at that hand. You're not doing anything that hand hasn't already been through. You're scared because you're facing issues that are shaking you to your roots. When you get out of this, you'll be stronger than ever."

"If I get out."

"You will. And I'll do it with you. And your friend Andi and her son, too."

"But what if God just decides to zap all of us?"

The old man's hand was swift and loud. "Ray, God doesn't work that way. Bad things happen because of the kind of world we're in. God works around them, through them, under them, over them. But He doesn't stop them from happening. I know that's hard to accept, but that's the way it is."

"If God would just do something."

"You can't go through life expecting God to part the Red Sea again."

"I know." Ray stood up. "I just don't know what to do."

"Then think and pray on it. God will speak. Just let Him."

After a long sigh, Ray said, "What does God want from me, Doc?"

The steel blue eyes gazed back at Ray evenly. "To glorify Him and enjoy Him forever. That's it."

"I wish it was that simple."

"It is."

Ray returned the Doc's cool stare, then nodded, "Yeah, I know, it's just . . ." He looked at his watch and blew air out of a tight lower lip. "I'd better get going. I want to see how Andi and Tommy are doing."

"So you're dating her?"

"Sort of."

Kingston smiled. "I'm glad to hear it. You were getting too—"

"Like a monk?"

"Exactly."

Both men stood and embraced. As they went downstairs, Kingston said, "Do you want me to talk to the board?"

Ray rubbed his chin thoughtfully. "Not yet. You may find they're in on it. No, we've got to play this one soft and slow."

"Keep me informed. This has really rattled me."

"Me too."

At the door upstairs, the old man paused a minute, looking into Ray's eyes. Then he said, "Ray, I'm with you in this."

"I know, Doc." Ray's eyes burned a moment, then he left, fighting a taut hardness in his throat. "Teach me, God," he prayed. "Teach me to trust You."

5

Ray suggested the Croases meet with him and Andi at the student lounge Monday evening. When he arrived, Andi and Tommy were already there. Tommy was quiet and would not leave Andi's side.

The lounge was in the main floor of Steringer Hall, one of the dormitory buildings for girls. It had several rows of back-to-back plastic leather sofas in several shades of green and blue. Late at night, a few students could be seen there, waiting for the chance to do some hugging and kissing with their dates. It was known on campus as "the passion pit." A row of food machines covered the side wall, and there was a large, stone fireplace opposite.

"So how's it going?" Ray asked Tommy when he arrived. "Ready to throw more bombs in the park?"

"I guess." Tommy glanced uneasily at Andi. She fixed her eyes on Ray and mouthed, "Go easy." Ray moved his head almost imperceptibly in response.

Just to make small talk, he said, "By the way, do you ever type papers for students?"

120

Andi answered, "A dollar twenty-five a page. For you, a dollar thirty."

"Oh?"

"I've seen your handwriting."

She smiled. "Just joking. I'll accept whatever donation you're willing to impart."

"That's fair. Did you go in to work today?"

"Yes. It wasn't too bad. Everyone said they were 'praying for me.'" She rolled her eyes. "Maybe I ought to pray for them." She patted Tommy on the back. "You OK, kiddo?"

Tommy nodded and sat a little more erect. Ray hoped Andi wasn't going to spoil him with too much motherly clucking and attention.

"I feel tired a lot at the moment," she went on. "The miraculous transformation hasn't hit yet."

He studied her face as she talked. Her dark eyes flashed, but her skin looked drawn, tight. Yet, he recognized the fighting spirit in her. The navy had taught him to separate the fighters from the riders. "Commuters," the SEALs called them. Guys who were in the navy to get a free education, or get off the streets, or because they had nothing else to do. They were passive, half-hearted types who, if they ever tried out for the SEALs, would never pass the first test. If anything, being a SEAL had taught Ray about endurance, something he also found true of genuine Christian faith. Even in the church he could spot the riders—those just hanging on the side of the bus—and the fighters, the people in it for true love of God. Fortunately, the navy didn't enlist many riders, though he'd noticed the church had plenty.

Ray suspected that if he wanted to get close to Andi, he'd have to be rigorously honest. She wouldn't take either lip or bull from him or anyone else. Already he'd discovered a strange fascination in simply watching her face as she talked. The way her nose turned up slightly. The high cheekbones. The little natural red in her cheeks. But those eyes. Very dark, mysterious. Almost black. He thought her name must be Greek. Maybe Armenian.

He was part Czech. His paternal grandparents had come

to the U.S. in the early thirties, during the depression. His mother was English, a governess until his father met her.

Ray fidgeted. Andi seemed different from the previous couple of days. She was definitely acting more reserved. But it might have simply been the stress of all that had happened. So far he'd had no more blackouts. He strained for something to say. "By the way, how long have you been at ATS?"

"Three years now."

He cleared his throat, then said, "Are you dating anyone?"

Andi chuckled. "They line up at my desk." Then: "Sorry. Actually, there are always students coming by and asking me out—the older ones. I don't go out with hardly any of them. They're all very serious about finding a minister's wife. I don't think I'm the minister's wife type."

Ray stifled a grin. "And what type are you?"

Andi's lip curled a moment as if she was going to say something caustic, then she shrugged. "Some guys have told me I'm a real backbreaker."

Ray raised his eyebrows with amazement, then laughed. "I can see that."

Andi nodded with wry agreement. "I don't like being pushed around, that's all. Most of these guys around here harp on submission and a 'woman's place' as though God gave Eve a waitress costume after they sinned in the garden instead of a fur coat. I don't buy it."

For a moment, he listened to the buzz of the machines, and Tommy got up to walk around. She went on, "I resent the men around here thinking women don't have a thought in their heads. Keep them barefoot and pregnant, that's their motto. Not all of them, but an awful lot. Some of the girls really hate it. But then there's always some special guy who comes along and whisks them off to never-never land."

"You haven't found him, though."

"Oh, no, I have. He just doesn't know it."

He laughed dryly. "OK, I get it."

The door behind them opened. Listra and Martin Croase stepped in. They both looked fresh, perfectly groomed. He was wearing a suit with a tie. Ray figured they were probably going out afterwards, some high rolling place in D.C. Martin shook his hand, and Listra sat down next to Andi, putting her arm over her shoulders.

"Are you both doing better?"

Andi nodded, but Ray could see she had tensed up. "We're OK. Tommy's still a little frightened."

Martin Croase looked at his watch. He looked as though he'd just had a haircut and a manicure. "I'm afraid we don't have much time. Something came up. But we do have a few minutes."

Listra turned to Ray. "So how do you feel now? I know we made a bad decision about letting you two go through with it. But you need to understand, we thought we were helping you."

Ray's throat tightened with anger, but he told himself to stay calm. *Letting us go through with it?* he thought. But he said, "We're all right."

A male student walked in and went over to the Coke machine, dropped in a couple of quarters and went back out, after giving everyone in the silent group a good eye-over.

When he was gone, Listra beamed her flashy smile. "You know, before I became a Christian, I was involved in drugs—cocaine, marijuana—well, I guess you've heard my testimony . . ." She looked around at everyone. When she seemed satisfied that everyone did indeed know about her heart-rending testimony that she gave once a year at one of the chapels early in September, she went on, "Well, as you may suspect, I know this was nothing like that. Far better, and far more real. So it has never felt like foreign territory to me. Or to Martin." She looked up at her husband. "Right, honey?"

Her husband grunted in agreement.

"But we shouldn't have let you do it. We know that now. It has to be entirely voluntary. So that was a mistake, and we'd like to ask you to forgive us for doing that. We're all agreed it was a bad decision."

She looked up at Andi and Ray. Her look appeared so sincere and so truly repentant that Ray felt a searing of guilt run up his spine.

"Will you?" Listra said. "I speak for both Martin and my-self and everyone else who was involved."

Ray glanced at Martin Croase. The CEO was looking at his hands and turning them over, obviously slightly bored. Ray wondered if this wasn't another complex strategy to get something. But he said, "No problem. So long as Andi and Tommy are OK, I'm not going to rage about it or anything."

Andi gazed at him, and he felt uncomfortable. But Listra did appear genuine. What was he supposed to do?

"And you, Andi?"

She looked up at Listra. Ray could feel the anger behind her eyes. "Yes, I'll forgive you, all of you, but I think it's all downright illegal, if you want to know the truth. I'm not threatening you or anyone, I just think Christians shouldn't be involved in this sort of thing."

There was a long, nervous silence.

Then Andi said, "I don't mean to be nasty about it. I'm sorry. I don't know if I'm right, but—" Ray could tell the guilt had suddenly descended on her, too. What was it about them that people like the Croases—especially Listra—could seem to summon guilt from the heavens and through it make you do anything?

Listra went on, "But I'm sure you can admit that the experience is, well, intriguing. Even inspiring. There is so much that is worthwhile in it. And God does work all things for good, right?"

Ray peered at his hands as if they would reveal some-thing germane to their conversation. He stared across the table at Andi for a moment, but she appeared deep in thought.

Listra's eyes flickered from face to face. When no one answered, she said, "Anyway, that's what we wanted to say. We would have liked to have said it over a nice steak din-ner—filet mignon would have been appropriate—but since you wouldn't come, we felt this was best."

The way Andi turned and glared at Listra gave Ray such an unpleasant feeling that he suddenly realized what rank manipulation this was. The hum of the machines behind them filled the uneasy silence. Listra twisted her long fingers with silver-pink paint on the nails. "Anyway, perhaps you should consider doing it again, just to give it one more chance. Many on campus are saying—"

Ray dropped his jaw. Andi's eyes hadn't moved.

"Are you nuts?" Ray said. "Try it again? That's crazy. Next time we might not come back. Tommy almost didn't."

"Oh, give me a break," Listra snapped. "It's perfectly safe. And anyway we have discovered what happened to Tommy, and what happened was also perfectly safe, just longer. So don't give me that."

Ray stared at Listra, then turned to Martin. "None of us is doing it again. Now I think I'll give Andi and Tommy a ride home. Excuse me for being a little seminary student, but I'm beginning to think you people are totally off the wall."

Both of the Croases gazed with hard eyes at Ray as he spoke. When he was finished, he helped Andi with her coat. In the doorway, Andi said, "Believe me, Tommy isn't doing it ever again as far as I'm concerned, and neither am I. That's final. I don't think you should use your position to try to persuade people like us to do something which, frankly, I consider against my conscience."

Listra raised her eyebrows diffidently and began to rise. Martin Croase said to Andi with a nervous smile on his face, "Obviously, we're quite out of line again and please forgive us. This has put quite a strain on all of us. I'm sorry. We will not ask you to do it again. I promise."

He walked over to his wife and took her hand. "We would still like to have you to dinner," he said, suddenly relaxing and appearing as if the situation had all been perfectly friendly.

As they turned to go, Tommy suddenly said, "Mom, can I have a Coke?"

Andi glanced at Ray, then began walking past the Croases to the machines. Ray stood in the doorway as the couple went by. Martin Croase punched Ray lightly on the arm. "Hang in there, Ray. We'll be praying for you."

Ray said nothing. Then he walked over to the machines where Tommy had just pushed the Coke button. When the can clattered into the tray, Ray said to Andi, "How do you feel—?"

"They're the two most hypocritical people I've ever met," she snapped. "I'm so angry, I could spit in their faces."

"Then why didn't you?" Ray suddenly poked her in the side, hoping to defuse her anger. She crumpled up and away from him.

"I'm not joking about this." She pulled back her hair and blew out a stream of frustrated air.

"Sorry. I just—"

She closed her eyes and sighed. "Yeah, we need to lighten up. This is tearing me—us—up."

As Tommy opened the Coke can, Ray said, "How about going out for a little ice cream or something? On me."

"All right!" Tommy said. "Can we, Mom?"

Andi threw up her hands. "All right, I give up. Obviously everyone's going to try to humor me about this. So lead on, Mr. Macho."

Ray grinned and said to Tommy, "So what do you like, Chief? Peppermint ice cream with fudge on top?" Then he said to Andi, "I'm not trying to humor you, Andi. I just think—"

"We need to keep away from those people."

"Something like that."

She nodded and they stepped out into the cool Maryland night air.

6

Johnny Goge pushed a tape of Tchaikovsky's Violin Concerto in A Minor into the cassette player. "Do it to me," he cooed. He had dumped the truck just outside Portland, stolen a Honda Accord, and changed plates. He made sure this one had a cassette player. It also had cruise control, which he put on. The Honda whooshed through the rain south through Salem toward northern California. It would be a long drive. He'd probably stay overnight at a hotel along the Interstate. He hummed along with the New York Philharmonic as Isaac Stern's bow screeched out the famous tune of the concerto. It was Goge's favorite, though he also liked Beethoven, Brahms, Puccini, Handel.

Johnny Goge until four years ago had worked for Carlos Giotto, a Chicago thug heavily into the cocaine market. Before Vietnam he spent two years in a special reform school, then joined the army and went to Vietnam. When he returned to the U.S., he wandered aimlessly, performing odd jobs. He spent a lot of time strung out on grass, LSD, mescaline, PCP, all the stuff that had been available in Da Nang where he fought with the 82nd Airborne. He'd learned to take out a gook with every weapon imaginable. He came to prefer night raids where you crept up on unsuspecting guards and immobilized them with a twist of the skull, snapping the neck. With a quick knife slash of the jugular, the man was gone.

He missed that close contact. Hitting now involved mostly semiautomatics behind the head. You didn't feel the victim's last breath on your fingers. It was cleaner, but less intimate. Still, Hasekker in Portland had been satisfying. He could well imagine the soul sluffing off from the body and meeting one of those light beings a moment later. Several times he thought about trying a simultaneous entry—taking the TUT a moment after he pulled the trigger. But it was too risky. His new boss demanded complete obedience. If Goge was ever going to get the kind of power he wanted—and the money—he had to obey him.

Goge craved the idea of power over people's minds. To stand in front of an audience and hold them in the palm of his hand. To incite a crowd to action. He'd never been able to speak rousingly. As a child, he stumbled over words. Even now, though he didn't stutter or stammer, he found it hard to articulate. He tended to speak in a monotone. Yet, he'd seen it in Vietnam, in Giotto, in the men he knew and worked for. With words they had human power to command, to lead, to explode a situation toward a goal they had in mind. It was something he'd always craved.

Then about ten years ago, Carlos Giotto had a long talk with him. Giotto talked about The Power, and how it had come to him as a young man. It was something that happened to Giotto when he first became involved in the organization, after a killing he'd pulled off. The mafioso lieutenant hadn't been a hit man then, but he performed a special hit at that time. Afterwards he'd gotten drunk and had the vision. A man came to him in the night and spoke. He didn't know whether it had been a dream, nightmare, or something else. But the man told him he'd been selected. He would have The Power to crush or exalt men.

Goge craved it. Then he'd met Martin Croase. The eloquent man promised Goge that he would soon have The Power—the ability to hold a mind, many minds, to hold sway so that they did your bidding.

Goge hadn't been able to do that with even his wife—ex-wife, actually—or his kids, whom he hadn't seen in seven years, since his wife had left him and gone into hiding.

But Martin Croase promised to give him that power—to win women, to persuade politicians, to run an organization. When Johnny Goge spoke, people would listen. Like that commercial he always played over in his mind. That was what he would be.

Of course, the TUT was helping. Through it, Goge had built his confidence incredibly. He was no longer afraid of death. And now he was in the process of ridding society of the real scumballs—the ones even society didn't know were scumballs.

That was satisfying. Always before it had been hoods killing hoods. But this was ordained. This was advancing the kingdom. This was accomplishing good for all.

Goge smiled as he drove. Slashing rain pounded the windshield, then smoothed off as the wiper squeaked across the glass. He was sensitive to sounds. Always had been. Even as a youngster he heard things no one else detected. Twice, in his neighborhood in New Jersey, he'd heard break-ins happening several apartments down the hall and had alerted the police. At one time he wanted to be a policeman. But they turned him down. He passed all the fitness tests. But they said he failed one of the psychological tests. They didn't tell him him which it was.

Years later, working for Giotto, he had it checked out. He found out the psychologist's name—Dr. Bernard Colwell—then on a trip to New York he had murdered Colwell, along with the errant dealer Giotto had sent him there for in

128

the first place. Before he twisted Colwell's neck the way he learned in Vietnam, he had questioned him at length about the exam. Of course, Colwell had no idea who he was. He'd seen hundreds of such tests. Goge had just said, "Well, now you can say you knew one personally." Colwell's vertebrae snapped easily. He was a slight man. Not an especially satisfying kill. But knowing who he was had been enough.

In Vietnam, Goge figured he'd killed over eighty gooks, more than a dozen in hand-to-hand combat. He kept a collection of earlobes. A sergeant in his battalion tanned them for him. They preserved nicely. He still had them at his apartment in Chicago, except for the two he'd had made into earrings for a Vietnamese prostitute for whom he was a regular. She liked them and showed them off to all her friends. Another set he had on his key chain, but he stopped using it when he realized they were a point of identity. Not good for a hit man.

Goge popped open a Coors Light and drank a long draft. The fizzy first rush scratched at his throat as it skidded down. He liked the first taste especially.

Two times he looked at the map of California, then a close-up of Los Angeles. Somewhere near Disneyland was where Croase wanted him to go this time. He'd never heard of it. A woman named Janice Koppers. A pimp-madam—one who organized a whole legion of pimps and they in turn their hordes of women of the night. Apparently very professional. And sitting on several hundred thou in cash. This time Goge was to use the letter B. It sent chills down Goge's spine. He really was going through the whole alphabet.

He wondered if twenty-six was the magic number for power. He wondered where Giotto had got his power. And people like a U.S. president, or Hitler, Gorbachev, Mussolini, Al Capone. And Croase.

Now there was a mystery. Head of a seminary of all things. But Croase had explained it once. "Sometimes God has to destroy in order to build," he'd said. "God works within the parameters of the world's rules. He's not afraid to heft a gun if that's what's necessary to get the job done."

It made sense to Goge. Croase was the first Christian that ever had made sense to him.

Isaac Stern had reached the monumental conclusion of the Concerto. The notes leaped and prickled inside Goge's skull like the feel of neck after neck snapping. He tensed. The crescendo was coming.

The prickly flush struck as Stern hit the last soaring notes.

7

The phone rang in Martin Croase's office on Tuesday morning. He was in a sour mood. Only minutes before another revelation had rocked his otherwise solid foundation. Nakayami told him one of the best researchers, a young man named Klaus Morgan, had tried an unauthorized dose of TUT-B. He was found dead that morning. The police were looking into it, but it appeared to them to be a heart attack.

"Why would he do such an insane thing?" Croase seethed.

Nakayami answered in his clipped English. "Because it's very addicting. The ones who have tried TUT want to go further."

Croase swore, and when the phone rang he waved Nakayami out.

"Martin Croase here."

"It's me, honey," the voice said. Listra.

"What's up, babe?"

"I want the TUT-B finished soon."

"It can't be done that easily, dear. I just got some real bad news. One of the researchers tried it last night. They found him dead this morning. Permanent dead."

Listra gasped.

"Yeah, so now how soon do you want to do it?"

"Soon! That boy—that foolish little boy has gone past the wall. You know I can't allow that to happen for long."

"Honey, we don't need you dying on us—permanently, that is."

"Dearest, I'm not going to die. I'm never going to die. Now get the TUT-B finished. Push Nakayami. The man doesn't work hard enough, if you ask me."

Croase rolled his eyes. "Love, it's not that simple."

"Get it done, Martin. That's all I have to say about it. I want the wall." The phone clicked off. Croase swore. He didn't need a fight on the home front in addition to everything else.

CHAPTER FIVE

1

Andi stood in the spiritual life section of the ATS library. It was just past 7:30, Wednesday night. She'd spent the early evening reading sections of books by Gordon Watt, books she'd never seen and hadn't even known Watt had published. They were dusty paperbacks, yellow with age.

She started up toward the wide front desk, her high heels clicking on the floor. She felt the eyes of some of the men on her as she passed.

Then she saw Ray, stuck back in one of the gray metal desks along the back wall. He was reading. She hesitated, then headed for his desk. As her heels ticked on the linoleum, he looked up and smiled.

"Hi," she whispered. "How are you doing?"

"OK. I'm catching up on a paper—when I can concentrate."

She stooped, eye level with him. For the first time she noticed his eyes. Silver gray, but more silver. There were glasses lying on the desk—horn-rim, intellectual glasses. "I found something interesting," she whispered. "Did you know Gordon Watt didn't believe in hell?"

"Where did you read that?" He turned and looked at her with consternation.

"In one of his books. In the stacks. I was astonished. He

132

had it all laid out, and it was published in the fifties."

"Could you show it to me?"

"Sure. Follow me." She led him back to the books. She had left the one on hell—it was called *Some Things We Shouldn't Believe*—lying on top. "It was self-published, I guess. At least I don't recognize the press."

Ray looked at the title page. "No, never heard of them. It looks like that kind of book though."

She paged through to the passage she'd found. It was underlined, with a pencil-scrawled comment on the margin that said, "Makes sense." Part of the passage read, "Hell is a pernicious doctrine, born in the fire of the partially inebriated mind of Martin Luther and his henchmen. Jesus would have none of it. Then what did He mean 'gnashing of teeth, wailing,' and so on? Nothing more, nothing less than the recognition that once death enfolded the lost soul, he recognized his foolishness and bit his tongue in repentance, then ascended to the master. Hell is not a doctrine any true Christian should give credence to."

When he was finished, he leaned against the shelf and gazed at the shelves pensively. "Well, one thing's for sure—if Watt is right, then that explains why my grandfather was in heaven."

"Your grandfather?"

Ray explained about seeing him during the episode.

"Then you don't believe in hell either?"

Chewing his lip, Ray shook his head. "No, but now suddenly I'm not sure. It's kind of contradictory—what happened to you and my grandfather up there in heaven, or wherever—that way. It doesn't make theological sense—at least to me. What else does Watt not believe in?"

"I don't know. This just about put me through the floor. I'm astonished. Why don't they tell us about that?"

A student at the end of the aisle muttered in Ray's direction, "Keep it down in there."

Ray motioned to Andi to follow him back to his cubicle. The aisle there was empty. He said to her, "The truth is that rejecting hell disregards conservative Christian teaching completely. Some scholars don't believe in it, I know. But the teaching is all over the Bible. Why would Watt believe such a thing, much less publish it?"

Andi gripped her bare arms and shivered. "It gives me the creeps. Here I thought he was one of the great Bible teachers of the twentieth century."

"Well, how many books of his have you read?"

"Just two or three. You know they're hard to get. Most are out of print, and a lot of them that are available are compilations of his sermons, edited by people on the faculty."

"I wonder if Doc Kingston knows about this." Ray sat down in the chair at his desk and turned it around. Andi swiveled the seat opposite and sat down. She stared at Ray with wide eyes.

"Do you think Gordon Watt could have been a complete charlatan?"

Ray shook his head emphatically. "How could he establish this seminary and Bible college and everything?"

"Well, that is another thing I read in another book. I should have marked it. But something to the effect"—she closed her eyes and concentrated—"'The depths of theological understanding are not to be plumbed by the average seeker. God places the great gifts on the top shelves. But the masses will never, should never, know them. They are secret things for only the educated to understand and enjoy.' That's far from an exact quote, but that was the gist of it."

Ray frowned. "That's definitely wrong. The Bible teaches that the Spirit is a teacher—for all of us. Where was it?"

She pulled out several books and leafed through them. "Here it is." He read it, then she said, "It has to be some mistake. Maybe he changed later or something. That book was also published in the fifties."

"Well, Watt was an evangelist back then. But as I understand it, his movement was very different from Billy Graham and those people. In fact, I've got the impression he was really shunned by them."

"But my mom and dad," Andi said. "And weren't yours converted under his ministry?"

"Yes," Ray said with a sigh. "Man, this is almost too much. How can these things happen?"

"It has to be a mistake, that's all. It has to be. Look at the teachers here. Some of them come from very reputable seminaries."

"That doesn't guarantee anything. And besides, a lot of people have left here in the last few years. That has to be significant." Ray gripped his chair. Andi watched as he closed his eyes and shook his head. She touched his hand.

"It must be a mistake. We should talk to somebody."

"Who—the Croases?"

"What about Dr. Kingston?"

Ray turned around and picked up his Bible, then looked back at Andi. "Frankly, I'm almost afraid to talk to him about it, for fear of what else I might find out."

"But we have to get to the truth, don't we?"

He flipped through his Bible to the passage in Matthew where Jesus spoke of hell and "weeping and gnashing of teeth." "It says 'where the worm does not die, and the fire is not quenched,'" Ray said. "That was gehenna—the place where the people of Jerusalem threw their garbage. It was always on fire and full of foul worms." He flipped back several pages. "And here He says, 'How will you escape being condemned to hell?' And what about the parable of Lazarus and the rich man?"

Andi stopped him from turning pages. "You don't have to prove hell to me, Ray. I've always believed in it since becoming a Christian, and especially after going to that 'place' out there, whatever it was. People like Martin Croase are going there, I'm convinced. And if they don't then God is the real charlatan."

"I just thought all of a sudden that maybe I was missing something."

"Don't rationalize it away. We may not like the teaching, but it's there and we have to deal honestly with it. Watt didn't even seem to do that. He simply denied it even existed."

Ray sighed with frustration. "This really troubles me."

"Well, I've got an even worse problem." She folded her arms, glanced around, and whispered, "Tommy's having nightmares. Bad ones. I'm worried. I think I might have Dr. Harrison talk to him."

"From the pastoral counseling department?"

"Yeah, I hear he's a regular psychiatrist."

"He is."

They glanced furtively around, speaking low, just above a whisper.

"What was in the nightmare?"

"He can't remember. He just woke up screaming the last two nights. He kept saying it was dark, he was in the dark and couldn't get out. I don't know what to do."

Ray chewed his lip. She noticed a scar below it on the right side. A fine white line, just barely visible. He said, "I don't think we should tell anyone what we're thinking and doing. No one. Not even the Doc." He gazed at her, his silvery eyes unblinking, a solid 'I don't lie' look. She didn't feel as though he was looking into her as she did with other students at the seminary. *He's not the type who's always trying to figure out what you think of him,* she thought. *That's refreshing.*

"OK, I can live with that." She sighed. "I guess when Jesus said, 'Be as shrewd as snakes and as innocent as doves,' He knew what He was talking about."

"Yeah, He knew what He was talking about all right. And that passage about wolves coming to you in sheep's clothing. I have a feeling—well—"

"That we're right in their lair."

"Could be."

There was a sudden thump, and both of them looked up. A man was standing at the end of the stacks a few feet away from their desk, apparently looking at a book. But he'd dropped it. It was David Hughes, the security man, the same person Ray had encountered in the locker room. *What is he doing here?* Ray thought nervously. Had Croase been watching them for some reason?

"Let's get a cup of coffee." Ray avoided looking at Hughes. He and Andi walked by the man without saying anything.

When they reached the coffee room downstairs in the library, she said lightly, "All the secretaries will be talking. Andi Darcasian lands Macho Man."

Ray didn't laugh. "I don't think David Hughes is interested in campus romance gossip."

136

"You know him?"

"Not really. But he's in security here on campus. Don't you remember? He was there when Tommy was being revived—organizing things—and I've had some run-ins with him. I think Croase may be having us watched."

She stared at him a moment, then her voice cracked with fear, "I'm going home right now to make sure Tommy is OK." She turned and hurried back to her seat where she'd left her coat and books.

Ray followed her. "I'm going with you."

They went back upstairs to get their things and hurried out into the night.

☐ ☐ ☐

Tommy greeted them both with a rousing Hi. He was watching a cartoon television show. They had some cake, and at 9:30 Andy took Tommy upstairs to bed. Ray sat in the living room and tried to find books by Gordon Watt on the well-stocked bookshelves. But there were none. He finally settled down on the couch with something by a radio preacher out West that he frequently listened to.

When Andi came downstairs, Ray hopped off the couch. She said, "He's all right. Do you want another piece of cake? I think we'll be OK."

"Good. No, I've got to get rolling. Keep the door locked. You don't think we're being paranoid?"

"No. Just be careful." She led him to the front door, and they kissed briefly. When Ray pulled back she said, "Oh, is that all I get for giving you half my evening?"

He grinned at her. "Just remember, I'm a navy guy."

They kissed passionately a moment, then he twisted out of her arms. "All right, I definitely have to go."

"Thanks," she said as he opened the door and hurried down the brick sidewalk.

After locking and dead-bolting the door and checking all the other doors, Andi went upstairs to her bedroom, changed into a nightgown and crawled under the covers. She read for about ten minutes, then punched the pillow and rolled over.

"Lord, please keep Tommy OK," she prayed, "and Ray and me and this campus, and let this all work for good. In Jesus' name."

She closed her eyes and began to doze.

The next thing she knew, something was standing in front of her dresser. Shining. He had something in his hand. She felt him before she saw him.

Her eyes opened, and she turned immediately in his direction. His mouth moved. He raised his gloved hand. Was he pointing? Was it a gun? A knife?

Her heart hammered. She couldn't speak. A mist seemed to hang around him. Then he moved toward her.

Get it over with, her mind said. *Just kill me and be done with it. I'm not afraid.*

Then she cried out, "Who are you?" Her voice came at her from a distance, as if she was deep down inside her body looking out. "What do you want?"

It didn't answer. The body shimmered. It began to swirl. It was going to suck her up. It came toward her. She would be pulled in, she knew it. The grotesque mouth opened. She couldn't move. She only hoped it wouldn't hurt.

"Who are you?" she cried again.

Then her door opened and light beamed in. "Mom?"

Her mind cleared. She saw the reflection of the street lamp in her dresser mirror. No one was there. It was a dream.

No, it wasn't a dream. It couldn't have been. Someone was there. She knew it deep down.

"Mom? Are you all right?"

Tommy stood in his pajamas shivering. He had on his glasses, and a bat was in his hand. The light from the street lamp flickered off the silver surface.

She threw off the covers, still shaking. "Yes, I'm sorry, honey. Did you hear me?"

"I thought there was someone in here. You were shouting."

She told herself to be calm. She'd never been prone to nightmares. Never anything like this. "I'm OK, honey. Let me tuck you back in." She hugged him.

Still holding the bat, he didn't move.

"I guess you're not the only one having nightmares, are you?"

"It's them," he said. "They've come to get us."

"It was just a dream, honey. A nightmare. Don't worry about it."

He shook his head. "They're going to get us."

She led him out of the bedroom and flicked on the light in the hallway. Outside she could hear cars passing on the street. She told herself not to worry as she directed him to his room. After setting the bat back in his closet, he crawled under the covers. She turned off his light and sat on the edge of his bed. "There's nothing to worry about, honey. God will take care of us. He's not going to let anything happen to us."

"Then why did He let them do that to us? Make us all die?"

She brushed back his hair. He was a handsome kid. It was too bad he had to wear those thick glasses. Maybe she could get him to try contacts.

"God does things we don't understand, honey. We just have to trust Him."

"Will He let them do it again?"

She swallowed and looked out his window. The street below now was silent. Several cars sat in neat rows around an island. Sometimes she wished life was like parked cars. Everything in its slot. For a while as a Christian, she thought that was the way it was—God worked out everything so it all moved in harmony. But she soon found out there were at least as many questions, paradoxes, problems, and contradictions in Christianity as in anything else. How did you explain that to a ten year old, when every week in church he heard how God loves us and protects us and watches over us?

She put her hand on his chest and patted it. "We're going to do our best not to let it happen again."

"But what if God decides we have to?"

She hugged him tightly, her eyes suddenly brimming with tears. "Then we'll have to cross that bridge when we come to it," she whispered into his ear. "That's all we can hope for."

139

He pushed back from her and gazed into her eyes. The pole light from the street shone on his face. It lit the tawny down on his cheeks. "I'm afraid to go to sleep. They might come again in it."

"Why don't we pray then?"

He nodded. She prayed, then he did. As she stood, she said, "Think you'll be all right?"

He tried to smile, but she could tell he was still afraid.

"Just remember," she said. "I'm right next door. If you call, I'll be there in a stitch."

He turned on his side. "I love you, Mom."

She patted his head and kissed him. "I love you too, honey."

She went out of the room. For a moment, she stopped at the phone, thought about calling Ray, but it was past 2:00 A.M. "What is happening to us?" she said as she pulled the covers over herself. As she closed her eyes, she noticed she was still trembling.

CHAPTER SIX

1

David Hughes and Ken Strock cruised through Northwest Washington toward Georgetown. They were driving an older model Chevrolet Caprice, brown, four-door. As Strock drove, he spotted a suitable specimen along Connecticut Avenue. "How about him?"

Hughes nodded. "A thou?"

"That's what the boss said."

The homeless man was unshaven, wearing dirty clothes, picking trash. Hughes figured him for fifty or so. He had gray hair sticking out under a stained, navy blue, Greek fisherman's cap. He didn't look strung out.

Strock stopped, and Hughes pressed the passenger seat window button. It slid down and he called, "Hey, buddy?"

The man paid no attention.

Hughes yelled louder. "Hey you, with the hat."

The man turned and gaped at him with liquid, shimmering eyes. He started to turn back to the trash, but Hughes called again, "How would you like to make a thousand bucks, fella? Easy money?"

The man stopped in his twist and paused, then slowly turned back and eyed him, saying nothing.

"A thousand dollars," Hughes said giving Strock a knowing glance. "Just for helping out a big company."

The man blinked, then rasped, "For what?"

"Just taking a little medicine. Experimental. Nothing dangerous. But we want to know your opinion."

The man started to turn away.

"A thousand dollars and a case of wine on top of it," Hughes called.

"I don't drink," the man said and looked back at the trash.

Hughes looked at Strock with exasperation. "This is such a pain. What am I supposed to say now? Why does Croase want us to do this?"

Strock snapped his fingers. "Just think of the half K we get for each one we bring in. Try drugs."

Hughes tried it. The man waved him off and started off down the street. Hughes cursed. "Come on, what's the angle?"

Then he smiled and yelled to the man again, "A thousand big ones and a couple bags of rags and a whole Dumpster. All to yourself. We'll guard."

The man eyed him. "Where?"

"Anywhere you want," Hughes said, grinning.

The man moved toward the car, shuffling with a slight limp. "How much do I get now?"

Hughes recoiled from his breath. The bum smelled like a hot afternoon Dumpster at a ham factory. "A hundred right now." Hughes waved a sheaf of tens in his face. The bum tried to grab it. But Hughes pulled it away and opened the door. "Get in first."

The bum looked him up and down, then inside the car. "I can open the door myself," he said. When he got in, Hughes handed him the hundred as he leaned in the window, then shut the door and got back into the front seat. He twitched his eyebrows at Strock and stroked his mustache. They headed back into the southern flow of traffic.

"We have to take a ride for a while," Strock told the bum, "but it'll go quick. Make yourself comfortable."

The man closed his eyes and huddled in a corner. In a minute he was snoring.

2

Nakayami stood before Croase, anger knitting his eyebrows. "Why are we suddenly using these homeless people?"

Croase banged his fist on the desk with unanticipated fury. "I told you, they can't be traced. That's the way it is here. They're bums. They're junk. They're meaningless. God doesn't give a rip about them. And neither do you. We're doing the world a favor. It's all in the advance of the kingdom, the way I see it. Just get on with the experiment."

Nakayami stared at Croase, astonished.

Croase knew from long experience the look meant that though Nakayami didn't like it, he'd do it. In the name of science and the glory of discovery. But the CEO made a mental note to have the Japanese researcher watched for a few weeks. Just to make sure of his loyalty. Croase suddenly leaned back in the chair, putting on his friendly face. "Hiro, we can't use the normal means of experimentation for this. You know that. Unfortunately, homeless people, bums, derelicts, whatever you want to call them, are the best choice. So long as they're not deranged or something. Most of them are glad of the money. If they die, we'll be relieving them of a lot of misery. They'll be with Christ in any event, and that's all that counts."

"This is twisted," Nakayami said acidly.

Croase cocked his head in a lecture stance. "Hiro, you know things happen. That's the way it is. Even in normal drugs. So don't give me that."

"Too many things are happening in this. Five dead people now."

"What is your objection, Hiro? Is it unethical? Is there any place in your outlook that allows a few deaths for the good of mankind? For the good of the kingdom?"

Nakayami snorted and hissed air through his teeth. Croase knew he had him on that point. Nakayami had no real ethics that Croase knew about. At least he'd never argued the point. Though Nakayami was educated as a youngster by Baptist missionaries, and even though at one point he'd been interested in Gordon Watt's ideas, nothing had ever jelled in

143

the researcher's outlook that was truly Christian. It had always been enough that he was an agnostic with an interest in thanatology.

When the small, thin Japanese didn't answer, Croase said soothingly, "You know we make them as comfortable as possible. We don't give their bodies to those medical mercenaries to be dissected afterwards. You know we do all we can."

Nakayami's face twitched, but he remained silent. Croase stood and walked around the edge of the desk. He clasped his fingers in front of him and beamed at the slight man before him. "He'd die on the streets in a gutter, Hiro. Think of that."

"You insist we continue this?"

As he turned to look out the window, Croase shrugged. "Of course. We have to break the threshold consistently. That is paramount. If we can do that, our research will leap forward light-years."

"Five so far have not come back."

Again, Croase turned around and looked into Nakayami's dark eyes. The slight man wouldn't look at him. "I know." He stretched out his right arm and put it on Nakayami's shoulder. "I grieve that that is the price we must pay. Jesus grieves. But it's the threshold, Hiro. Think of it. Going beyond it—for anyone. Think of the psychological effects. People no longer fearing death, knowing *by their own experience* what it is. Knowing that Christianity once and for all is the truth. It will change the face of the world."

For a moment, Nakayami stood still. He didn't shake off his hand. "We proceed in an hour," he said and marched out stiffly.

Croase smiled as he watched him. "Another tantrum handled expertly," he murmured as he went back to his desk, checking the clock. He sat back in the chair and closed his eyes, holding his finger and thumb hard against his brow. Images fluttered through his mind.

"Four o'clock today. I'll be there," he whispered, then punched the intercom to his secretary.

144

□ □ □

By then they knew his name was Bill. That's all he would give them. He lay on the bed without fear in his eyes. All the monitoring equipment had been hooked up and was in place. His watery eyes didn't flicker as they administered the proper dose. He had confessed to making money in exactly this manner, so he wasn't afraid.

The moment his heart stopped and the telemetry equipment ceased beeping, one of the nurses kept time. Croase watched nervously from the amphitheatre outside the eighth floor sending room. Only a few others were present. Until TUT-B was proved workable they would not introduce anyone outside the upper leadership to what they were doing.

"Three minutes," the nurse called out.

Croase stiffened. He was also sure that Tommy Darcasian could do it again and again, if it came to that. But Croase wasn't ready to bring him in again until he'd figured out how to do it without discovery. Nakayami thought the TUT-B had this effect on Tommy because of skin tissue they'd found in Tommy's bed from a cut he'd got the weekend at the conference center. His tissue showed precisely the shielding effect they wanted. But they didn't know whether it was a genetic abnormality, something in his body chemistry, or plain luck.

Nonetheless, they were making progress. They'd discovered Tommy's blood type was B negative. Bill had the same blood type. But no one was sure that was the only factor.

"Four minutes."

Croase leaned forward, watching Bill's nostrils. Everything was quiet. They all knew this was a critical juncture. Thirty seconds passed. No blood appeared on Bill's face.

Then it happened. Bill jerked, blood burst from his nose. His face twitched twice. Finally, he lay still.

The doctors began pumping Bill's heart.

"Six minutes."

Again Bill jerked, for a moment his eyes registered recognition, then blood exploded again from his nostrils and mouth. Nakayami stood stock-still, his clipboard horizontal in his hand, jammed into his chest. Croase waited at the win-

145

dow, his face almost pressed up against it, watching in amazement and terror. The doctors fought frantically to get a heartbeat. But in another minute the EKG read flat. He was dead.

They worked for another thirty seconds, until Nakayami said, "Call it."

A nurse said, "Nine-thirty-two."

Nakayami spun around, looking at the mirrored wall. Croase knew he was staring in precisely the spot where Nakayami knew he should be. Nakayami mouthed a curse, then wheeled and hurried out of the sending room.

□　□　□

The Japanese scientist was yelling before he even stepped through Croase's door. "Never again! It's impossible. It's not tested properly. No more!"

Croase stood looking out the window over the parking lot. From twelve floors up it was a majestic view. He didn't turn around. "Sit down, Hiro."

"No more! Not until we've tested on more nonhuman subjects."

"Sit down," Croase said calmly.

Nakayami stood in the middle of the room, unmoving, his clipboard still pressed into his ribs. "Don't 'sit down' me. Six people dead! Kapush!"

Croase whipped around. "Then we go to the boy."

"No. No boy. No human."

Croase slapped his open hand on the desk. "He's our best chance."

"We don't know why the B worked on him. It could be an accident. He could die. I say no."

"And I say yes."

The two men squared off across the room. Croase's eyes flickered, and a moment later he switched back to his consoling, coaxing tone. "Hiro, need I say it again? The boy can go beyond the threshold anytime he wishes. Perhaps for five, six minutes or more. Think of the knowledge we could gain. Think, Hiro." Croase pulled a smile onto his face.

146

Shaking his head adamantly, Nakayami said, "We don't know why the boy survived."

"But he did survive. And he will again. I can feel it. Hiro, trust me."

"Trust you! Trust you? For what?"

"Hiro, we are on the brink of it. The boy can do it."

"Just give me several days."

Thinking a moment, finally Croase nodded. "All right. Several days. But you will continue with the others."

Nakayami turned and sped out. Croase sighed again, turned to the mirror and grinned. "I may have to think about some changes if this persists," he murmured and went out of the room in search of a cup of tea.

3

Johnny Goge surveyed the staid house on Donna Street in Los Angeles through slit, tired eyes. Before he slept he simply wanted to see it. He liked to get a job going as soon as possible, once he knew about it and there were no immediate time constraints. He parked the car on Carlsbad and stepped out onto the curb. The bright sunlight made him wince, but he chose not to wear sunglasses. He had on dark dress pants, a blue dress shirt with a striped tie, and tan blazer. He was sure he looked like a patron at the very worst.

He walked up the pavement toward the stucco building with a tan Naugahyde briefcase in his left hand. Door-to-door salesmen probably stopped all the time like this and he would be no different. People meandered by in little groups, not paying him any attention. Goge wasn't an attractive person. His cheeks ravaged from teenage acne, huge, popping eyes, and a limp from a wound in a botched hit made him the kind of person few people liked to look at directly, at least when he could return the stare. Still, he had learned long ago how to walk, bend, and move with his shoulders slightly hunched and his chin tucked just a hair so that no one could gain a sense of his powerful physique. At five feet eleven, he could look imposing—he could easily bench press three hundred pounds—but he managed to cover it up in public.

Goge figured that Croase got the information from the "angel" Croase said guided him. Goge didn't know whether this person was an angel or not. Of course, when he used the TUT, he met various spirit beings. But he liked the high more than the talk. They had not as yet offered him anything remarkable. Croase was the one with the power to move men.

As always, Croase's information was precise. The house looked just like Croase described. As a result, Goge knew where the woman kept the money. All he wanted to do now was see what kind of lock the front door had so that when the time came he could pick it. Croase had already provided him with an inside layout.

A woman answered Goge's ring. He could see she was a fairly high class whore from the model look she affected. Probably the type who serviced the high rollers. That was how Janice Koppers managed to sock away over a quarter mil in an upstairs safe.

"Yes?"

Goge affected a tired voice. "You wouldn't be interested in an insurance quote?"

The girl giggled. "That's one lousy line for a man who wants to make it big in insurance."

"I'm tired. Been a long day." Goge quickly took in the locks on the door, but he knew from long experience he'd have no trouble with them. "I guess you're not really interested."

"Not really. Thanks." She closed the door.

Goge walked down the street, then returned to his car, cruised down the back alley once, and laid out his plan.

He returned that morning at 4:10 A.M. in a tight, dark outfit, wearing thin, black gloves and carrying a large valise. The money was supposedly in large stacks of bills. He easily picked the lock, opened the door, and went inside. No lights were on, though he did hear some giggling in a back room. He quickly mounted the stairs. He was wearing black sneakers with a special cushion sole that was extremely quiet.

Janice Koppers would be on the third floor.

He reached her apartment and turned the handle. It was locked, but the jamb was wide and he easily slipped a card behind it and sprang the latch. He opened it quietly and shut it behind him.

The apartment was plush, red velvet. He could see that in the light from the streetlamp. He saw the bedroom door in the back, crept over, opened it. The woman's long blond tresses lay over her pillow. She looked like an aged Mae West. *What was she doing with a name like Janice Koppers?* he wondered.

He stood at the side of her bed, placed the gun with the silencer under her chin, and said, "You'll like it there. It's very peaceful."

Her eyes opened, and he fired. He easily cut the large B into her rouged cheek, then went to the dresser and took a small penlight out of his back pocket. He pulled out the middle drawer. Inside he found the release with the penlight, just as Croase had advised. He pulled it and something snapped. He went around to the side. A panel in the wall had popped open.

The panel squeaked slightly on its hinges, so he opened it very slowly. Then he turned the light onto a large brown metal safe inside. He looked at some numbers he'd written on his wrist and quickly spun the large dial. A moment later, the safe creaked open.

Piles of money lay inside, wrapped in rubber bands. He opened the valise and lay the money inside, trying to figure how much it must have amounted to. But it was impossible to tell. There were all denominations, even some stacks of thousands. Croase had said it was $625,000, rounding it off, as of the previous Friday.

The money safely cached in the valise, Goge closed the safe and the panel and replaced the dresser drawer. He gave Janice Koppers one last look and whispered, "Hope you enjoy the visit," then headed to the door. The house was still quiet.

There was no disturbance on the way out, and Goge reached his car without incident. He easily found the beltway, pulled off at a rest stop, and changed in the back seat. Then he figured he would find a hotel and get some sleep.

4

Ray settled down in front of the TV at Andi's house. She'd invited him over for dinner. He and Tommy had thrown around a football in the tree-lined front yard where there was a wide, grassy area divided only by the front sidewalk. Tommy was learning to catch.

Ray thought again about Croase's intimidating style. In a material sense, Croase had it better than most people ever dream of. But there was something else besides the TUT that he was interested in. But what? What did he really want?

Andi clumped down on the couch opposite Ray. "It'll be ready in thirty minutes."

Ray opened his eyes and smiled. "What is it?"

"Pork chops. Good for your cholesterol level."

"Yeah, I need some more gunk in my arteries."

She pulled her feet up onto the sofa and hugged them, with her chin resting on her knees. "Actually, they're made out of turkey."

"You're kidding."

She raised her right hand. "They have them at the supermarket now. They're not bad. Let me know how you like them."

NBC News flashed onto the screen. The anchorman began, "Another letter murder has occurred in Los Angeles."

Ray and Andi watched as a reporter briefly recounted the two murders. "Authorities know the murderer is the same person. After analysis, they determined that the bullets used in each case were from the same gun and the letter cut into the cheek of each victim was done with the same blade. No description of the murderer has been reported. The FBI is still looking for a motive. In the Middle East today—"

Ray turned to Andi. "It gets worse every day."

He glanced up as Tommy walked into the room from his bedroom where he'd been playing a record. His shirt was half out and his hair a mess.

"You been sleeping?" Ray said.

"I haven't gotten much at night."

Ray patted the sofa. "Well, have a seat, Chief. We need to talk about some things—especially these nightmares."

Tommy jumped up on the couch and curled in a corner. "What do you want to know?"

□ □ □

Johnny Goge watched the news in his motel room. Afterwards, he called Croase at his home.

When Croase answered, Johnny said, "See the news, big boss?"

Croase's voice was suddenly low and angry. "I told you not to call me here."

"Hey, I expect better treatment than this, with all the dough I'm making you."

"Was it all there?"

"Just like you said. Couldn't have been better laid out."

"OK. Put it in a box—after you take out your ten percent."

"Hey, it's gone up to twelve, boss man. You see the fibbies are in on this? I don't like this letter stuff. It's a bad way of doing business. It could get me a bad name, and a whole team of fibbies after me."

"Don't worry. That's the way Benreu wants it. Something he says is important for the kingdom. Look, take your twelve percent and mail it to me at the P.O. box. Pack it in newspapers this time."

"Got it. Did the man upstairs tell you to do it that way?" Goge laughed.

"Just do it. Call me tomorrow at the office after six, the special number. Anyone else answers, ask for Mr. Reeves and then say you're sorry, it must be a wrong number."

"Got it, boss man. Just doin' the work of the kingdom. See you tomorry."

There was a pause. Then Croase said, "Look, Johnny. I want to help you get what you want. But don't throw religion at me, all right? Christianity is a tool, just like anything else. People use it to get what they want. People want happiness, you give them happiness, and then they give you what you want."

"So what do you want, boss?"

"That's none of your business."

151

"Hah, it's written all over everything you do."

"What's that?"

"Money, man. That's you. You want money."

There was a pause. "What if I do?"

"Then don't go giving me no lectures. I'm getting you your money. But we have a deal. I get more than just a percentage."

"I assure you, Johnny, the resource we have tapped will take you all the way to your goals. I learned a long time ago some hard facts about religion. People believe what they want to believe, what makes them feel life is worth living. And if someone can make a buck off of giving them that, I'm all for it."

Goge laughed. "You're my kind of guy, boss."

"Just do the jobs I give you. That's all I ask."

Goge hung up and roared. "I don't know why I believe this guy. I don't know why." He laughed hard until his eyes teared. Then he got up, pulled a beer off the six-pack he had laid on the dresser, and drank it all down in a single chug.

◻ ◻ ◻

"Do you remember what happened after you got past the wall?" Ray asked Tommy, searching his eyes.

The boy shook his head with frustration. "There was someone—two people. But it's all fuzzy inside my head. I was scared, then I was not scared. I just remember I wanted to come back. And he let me."

"He let you?"

The boy kicked his legs and lay back with his arm over his head. "I think he let me. I just don't remember." Tommy glanced at Andi, then said, "Can I have a carrot or something?"

"Just one, until dinner."

When he went out into the kitchen, Andi said, "What do you think?"

"It's strange," Ray answered. "I wonder if he met Jesus or an angel or something—if that's even possible. But maybe they do something when you return—like what Paul said, he saw things in heaven that men are not permitted to tell about. Maybe God induces some kind of amnesia."

"Then why do we remember what happened to us?"

Ray shook his head. "I don't know. I think I'm gonna have to really study up on this thing."

Tommy came back in, chewing on the carrot. Ray said to him, "If you remember anything, you'll tell us?"

"Sure." Tommy went to the television. "Are we going to eat soon, Mom?"

"Soon."

CHAPTER SEVEN

1

Hughes stood on the loading dock with Strock. Two body bags lay on the concrete ready to go into the truck for the journey out to the funeral home on Georgia Avenue.

"The guy we picked up yesterday—what was his name?" Strock had his hands deep in his pockets.

"Bill something," Hughes said.

Strock kicked the right-hand bag. "And who might this be?"

"The bag lady. Sadie."

Strock laughed. "I kind of liked her. What on earth are they doing up there? This makes—what—eight in the last week?"

"Seven. They still have one up there. In a coma."

Strock snorted. He and Hughes did a lot of drinking together. They hadn't actually tried the TUT, though they had the opportunity. Frequently they discussed who would go first. Neither offered.

"Well, let's get on with it," Hughes said, hefting the lighter load of Sadie onto the truck. It was made up as a regular panel van, white, nondescript, Chevrolet. There was nothing inside except a bare floor. They'd had as many as thirty or forty dogs in there at one time in the early TUT stages, before Croase had any fix on what worked. Together, they'd dug up hundreds of dogs, pigs, monkeys, and other animals for the

154

"ultimate trip." Few of them came out of it alive. If anything survived one dose, more were administered in the research until eventually the specimen didn't come back. Neither of them knew much about what went on upstairs. Neither questioned it. They had no reason to. But now it was people.

They both hopped into the panel van and Hughes wound out to the main road from TWI. In half an hour, he turned into the Willard Funeral Home driveway and parked underneath the building in the receiving area. Willard did a legitimate business. Croase had worked out a deal with the slick funeral director: five thousand dollars a burn. Hughes knew. At least that was what Willard had boasted. It might have been more for all they knew.

Willard met them at the door. "Just two?"

Hughes jumped out. "Yeah, ten big ones tonight. That should put you in the black for the month."

Willard had short, shiny black hair and always wore a suit. He led the men into the lower cremation area. Hughes flopped Sadie onto a waiting tray while Strock opened up Bill. Both bodies were gray and hard. The two men didn't typically look long. Normally, they left them wrapped. But this time they wanted something.

Strock turned to Willard. He never liked the haircream-smelling smoothie with the soft voice. But tonight wasn't the time to deal in personality preferences. "Business been down a bit lately, eh, Dickie, old buddy?"

Willard curled his thin lips. "Just leave, Strock. I don't want any trouble."

Strock muscled a little closer, almost nose to nose. Willard stepped back. But Strock, heavy and big-bicepped moved in. "Yeah, well, the glory days seem to be gone. You must have a real drop in gross national product around here."

Willard glanced at Hughes, then moved smoothly toward the door. "They were animals, Strock, and they were cheap. This is much more dangerous. What are you suggesting?"

The heavier man smiled and looked at Hughes. "Me and Mr. Hughes here been thinkin' about a little deal. You get big money for real stiffs, humans, that is. So we were thinkin', you know, some commission-type work."

Willard looked at the two men uneasily. "I'd have to talk to Croase about this."

"You can leave Mr. Martin Croase out of this, or we might just be tempted to go down to Precinct Number Two and ask for immunity, get my drift?"

Strock could see the muscles in Willard's throat tighten. His snakelike eyes swiveled back and forth between Strock and Hughes, fixing on neither. "So what is it you want?"

"Well, we figure," Strock said, rubbing his hands, "that four or five a week should be normal for a while now that they're going for something even bigger. But say we make five the cutoff. Anything beyond that we get a slight commission. You know, like salesmen do in insurance and stuff. They have what you call a percentage figure. Anything above a certain amount they get a special kick from the financial officer. Anything below, they get nothin'."

"So what are you saying?"

"So what I'm sayin' is that every body after five per week, we get a special commission from you. You get five K for one stiff, right? So, we deliver seven, you make three-five K. Not bad for a week's work, especially since it costs you about a hundred bucks to ash one of these jobbers." Strock kicked one of the bags. "But we do all the lifting on this little deal. We should get something. Me and Mr. Hughes figure number six, seven, eight, and so on ought to get at least two K each. And anything over nine, I'd say three K. What do you say, Dickie?"

Willard started to open the door. "I'll have to think about it."

Strock grabbed him under the armpit and squeezed his thumb and fingers into his shoulder blade. Willard cried out.

"No thinkin' about it, Buster Brown. Is it a deal or not?"

"I could have Croase—"

Strock squeezed harder. "Oh, you won't tell the big boss nothin' because he might even be behind this for all you know. Furthermore, Croase don't give a rat's behind about you now that he's got you hooked, am I right?" Strock dug his thumbnail into the ligament under Willard's clavicle.

"All right. All right. Two thousand for everything over five."

"Two thousand from five to nine. Three after that." Strock brought his left hand up under Willard's chin pinching his Adam's apple.

"OK," Willard wheezed. "I'll pay you by check."

"Sorry. Cash, Dickie, honey. I'm sure you have a bank. Plus all that bragging you've been doing about your little stash in the safe upstairs." He had nearly lifted the man off the floor.

Willard cried, "OK. It's a deal."

Strock put him down and patted his right cheek with his left hand. "We knew you'd look upon it as another windfall." He let go of Willard, and the tall man gasped, falling against the door.

Hughes stood by the truck. Strock walked over while Willard hurried out.

"That was simple," Strock said as he jumped in.

Hughes laughed. "Remind me to make you my financial adviser."

They backed out and only turned on the lights when they reached the side street out onto Georgia Avenue.

2

"I don't know what to do, Ray," Andi said into the phone. "He's having terrible nightmares, and I'm getting these incredible visions at night. It's scaring me."

"Do you want me to come over?"

"Would you?" Andi breathed out noisily. Her heart was still hammering from the most recent episode, Tommy waking up in the middle of the afternoon after a nap screaming "He was here, he was here!"

"It could look bad to the seminary."

"Just one night, Ray. So you can be there when it happens. Maybe you can help. You can sleep on the couch or in the guest room." She paused, realizing the jeopardy she was putting Ray in. But she'd already talked to the staff psychologist, and he said it was normal childhood fears.

Ray answered, "I'll bring a sleeping bag. I'll stay as long as you want. Don't worry about the seminary. I'm thinking of just dropping out. This has gotten too bizarre. I'm beginning to think this whole thing is a cult of some sort."

There was a pause, then Andi said, "Whatever you do in that respect, Ray, I won't question it."

"I'll be over in several hours."

"Come for dinner."

They signed off, and Andi went back to Tommy's bedroom. The boy had curled into a ball on his bed, panting and staring blankly at a picture of a Christian rock group named Nain on the wall. She sat down on the edge of the bed and brushed at his hair. "Are you feeling any better?"

"He said he wants me to come back with him. He said some people will ask me."

"Who is this person, honey?"

"The first one. There were three. The first one I didn't like. The second one was nice. The third one is fuzzy."

Andi held him.

"Mommy, if I die, which one will get me?"

His thin body quivered and she held him tightly. His face was dark with fear, and his pupils were tiny, his voice constricted. She said, "Neither one, honey. You'll be with Jesus."

"But that's not what happened to you."

"I know, I know. We're trying to figure this all out. Just hang in there. Ray's going to come over."

"He is?" He pulled back. "I really like him, Mom. Do you think—"

She smiled and brushed the hair out of his eyes. "No, we're not getting married, honey. Ray and I hardly know each other. He just likes us and feels protective, I think."

Andi gazed into his frightened eyes, then gave him a kiss. "It'll be all right, honey. I know it will."

She let him roll over and go to sleep. Then she closed her eyes and breathed out out a brief prayer.

For the next hour she straightened up the house. Finally, there was a knock on the door. She instantly recognized Ray's precise rap. She opened it. "Thanks for coming."

He stepped in and gave her a kiss. He was wearing jeans and a flannel shirt. It made him look like he'd just stepped out of a cowboy movie. He said, "Looks like we're all basket cases."

Andi pointed to the easy chair. "Just set your things by the chair there." She called up the stairs. "Tommy, Ray's here." She turned back to Ray. "He might be asleep."

She gave Ray a worried look, then motioned her head towards the stairs. "You can go up if you want. He'll want to see you. Tell him to get ready for dinner."

"OK."

She went into the kitchen, cut up a cantaloupe, and then brought it up to Tommy's room. Ray was leaning on the dresser fingering some of Tommy's soldiers on top of it. "You been setting up any battles?" Ray was asking as she walked in.

Tommy sat on the edge of the bed, his legs dangling just short of the floor, pulling on his socks and sneakers. "Maybe we can do a battle sometime," he said.

Ray answered, "Maybe tomorrow. After school."

Andi stood in the middle of the room with the plate of cantaloupe slices. "Brought you boys a little snack before we eat."

Ray took one, threw it in the air and caught it in his mouth. Tommy looked on in wonder, and Andi laughed. She said, "Do you roll over and play dead, too?"

"Just a little trick I learned in junior high. Here, throw me one. Just get it high enough."

Andi handed a piece to Tommy. "Go ahead, kiddo."

Tommy underhanded the slice high enough to be caught. Ray bolted it out of the air with a snap of his teeth. "See. I can do nearly anything," Ray said.

"Yeah," Andi answered. "We knew that all along, Mr. Macho."

Tommy said, "Let me try it."

"Sure." Ray picked up a slice and winged it underhand to Tommy. The slice batted off his cheek as he tried to catch it, then plunked onto his bed.

"It takes a while," Ray said. "Here—"

"Wait a second, guys," Andi interrupted. "I think you should do this outside. I don't need to do any more cleaning than I already do."

159

Tommy jumped up, and soon they were wrestling in the living room. When Andi looked in, she jammed her hands on her hips and yelled, "Outside—both of you!" Ray gave her a thumbs-up and a wink, and they both went outside after some mild protests. As she started back for the kitchen to finish up, she whispered, "Lord, don't let me fall in love with this guy. I can't handle it now, all right?"

When Andi stepped outside to call them in to dinner, Tommy was laughing and talking faster than she had ever heard him. "Mom, Ray says there's a carnival up in Olney. Can we go tonight? There're rides and all sorts of stuff."

Andi looked at Ray with an amused, What-have-you-got-us-into-now smile. Ray shrugged plaintively. "Just a suggestion," he said.

"We'll see," Andi answered. "Let's see how you do with dinner."

"I'll eat every bite," Tommy said, giving Ray a confident smile. He threw an imaginary ball in the air and swung. "Home run!" he cried and ran inside.

As the boy disappeared into the house, Ray said, "What was that all about?"

Andi laughed. "He likes to play pretend baseball. Always hitting home runs."

Smiling, Ray said, "Yeah, I remember doing that."

She gave him a whimsical roll of her eyes and turned to go inside.

It was a small carnival, something put on by the fire department up Route 108 in Olney, but when they pulled in to one of the $2.00-a-shot parking spaces that night, the place was crowded, noisy, and looked like fun. Andi thought it was just what the doctor ordered. She and Ray walked and talked while Tommy scampered about, scrutinizing everything. He didn't ask to go on any rides initially. Neither Andi nor Ray

160

wanted to press him about it. But finally, he shyly suggested that they all go on a dizzying cup and saucer.

Ray bought tickets, and they plunked into one of the huge pink whirligigs and waited for the operator to get it started. The machine jolted them up and down along a wavy track about forty feet in diameter. The saucer spun, and Andi clung to the mushroom bar in the middle. Tommy leaned forward and pulled, making the saucer spin even faster. Ray simply leaned back and shouted into the wind.

Andi watched Ray as they visited here and there among the rides, games of chance, and food stalls with steaming sausages, hot ears of corn, corn dogs, elephant's ears, and greasy stuff too inviting to look at. He talked about going to carnivals as a kid growing up in Pennsauken, New Jersey. She learned he'd joined the SEALs after four years at Cornell, where he had been an engineering major.

"How come you haven't used it?" she asked casually, as they walked along, not holding hands.

"I did for a while. Before I joined the navy. I worked at Westinghouse designing a weapons system. But it got boring."

"Math always threw me."

"Maybe we can curl up on the couch sometime and go over your multiplication tables."

"That's all?" she asked, suddenly putting her arm through his. She had thought things were going too fast already, but she liked touching him, and him touching her. She wanted to get close, even if it never led to anything.

She said quietly, "I really appreciate what you're doing with Tommy."

"Just Tommy."

"I appreciate the way you treat me."

"How's that?"

"Like I'm not just some unwed mother."

He took her hand and laced his fingers in hers. "I guess you can sense what people think sometimes."

Andi reveled in his touch and noticed her heart beating more rapidly. Ray was definitely different. He didn't engage her repeatedly in heavy theological discussions as so many of the other students at the school did on dates, in the bookstore, and at the student center. She'd had her fill of that. They wanted to talk about biblical inerrancy, predestination, free will, Martin Luther, John Calvin, and hundreds of other subjects she thought were fine for a class, but she occasionally liked to talk about the price of beans. Ray didn't seem "so heavenly minded he was no earthly good," as the expression went.

She hoped, though, if they continued to be involved that he would not go into the ministry. Not that she didn't believe in doing God's work. But she knew how difficult it was living in a fishbowl, the whole congregation watching your every move. Her grandfather had been a Methodist minister, and she knew what her mother's complaints had been.

Tommy ran up to them with a slash of vanilla ice cream still clinging to his left cheek. "Ray, you've got to do this. It's a gun thing." He led them to a booth with a row of twenty-two caliber pistols lying on the front counter.

"Three shots to wipe out the birdie in the center and win!" cried the man hawking his game. He focused on Ray immediately. "You look like a marksman, friend. Try it. You can win a rifle, a Bambi, or any of these other beautiful mementoes." He pointed to several shelves of carnival junk, none of which Andi thought Ray could possibly want. Then she noticed a box of metal knights standing in their plastic wrapping on the far side.

Ray was a step ahead of her. "What's it take to win the lead soldiers?" he asked the man as the three of them stepped up to the counter.

"Two dollars, three shots, and no birdie left on the target," the man said. He had rosy cheeks, bloodshot eyes, long gray hairs coming out his ears, and he looked like he was half-soused.

"How accurate are the twenty-twos?" Ray asked, picking one up. It was a cheap six-shot Colt with a plastic pearl handle, made to look like something out of the Old West.

"I sighted them in myself," the roustabout said.

Ray gave Andi a frown, then leveled his right eye on the barrel at the target. He pulled out his wallet. "All right, here goes."

162

The man loaded the gun with three bullets. "Kicks a little, so watch it."

Ray took a shooter's stance and aimed the gun, using his right hand to grip it and his left to stabilize.

"Military, eh?" said the man.

Ray squinted along the barrel and cocked the hammer. "A little." He steadied himself, stopped, hoisted the gun, took a better stance. Repeated the procedure. Then with a small crowd looking on in silence, he fired. The lower half of the pheasant in the center was instantly cut out.

The man whistled. "You're in the money. Two more like that and you've got it."

Ray aimed again. This time he took out the right half and tail. One more steady shot and he was in. He sighted in along the barrel, adjusted his stance three times. Andi could see beads of sweat on his forehead. She wondered if he felt he had to prove something to Tommy.

Ray squeezed the trigger.

The big man hunkered over and squatted down in front of the target, then ripped it off. "Looks like you're a winner. Want to go for two?"

Ray shook his head. "One's enough. We'll take the knight set." He smiled at Tommy.

The man nodded. "Glad to see you win it." He handed over the brightly painted set to Tommy. Then Tommy said, "Can I try it, Mom?" The light glanced off his thick lenses.

"I think not, honey."

Ray clapped his hand on Tommy's shoulder. "Come on. Let's hit the Ferris wheel."

There, Andi sat down in the seat as the big wheel backed it into position. Ray directed Tommy into the middle seat, but Tommy suddenly stood aside and said to Andi, "You sit in the middle."

Ray hesitated, then smiled at Andi and helped her into the seat. Tommy sat down with a big grin on his face. As they started up, Andi looked over the crowd. Then she noticed someone familiar. She started to smile at him, but he looked away. Then she realized who it was: the security man, Hughes.

163

She stifled a gasp, then grabbed Ray's arm. "That man, David Hughes. He's watching us."

"Where?"

"Don't look now. Over by the foot-long stand."

"Don't see him."

Andi glanced back. "He's gone. He must have seen me see him."

Tommy turned to them. "Who're you looking for?"

After a nervous glance in Ray's direction, Andi patted his hand. "Just someone from school, honey."

On the way home that night, Tommy was full of talk, speaking nonstop about the guns, the toy knights, the huge sausage with piles of mustard, catsup, and sauerkraut he'd scarfed down late in the evening. He sat in the back seat of Ray's Toyota while Andi took the bucket passenger seat up front.

"I was really afraid of those rides," Tommy said. He stuck his head between the seats and looked back and forth from Andi to Ray. "Do you love each other yet?"

Andi glanced at Ray, and he smiled. She'd never seen Tommy act this enthusiastic about a man in her life. "Christians always love each other, honey."

"But are you gonna get married? I really need to know."

Andi said quietly to Ray, "This is the first time I've dated anyone that Tommy's gotten to know very well."

Tommy pattered on, "Well, are you gonna get married?"

Andi raised her hand and patted him on the head. "People don't get married after a few dates, honey. So we're not getting married, OK? We hardly know one another."

"But you really like each other, right?" Tommy had hunched forward almost directly over the shift. Andi felt increasingly embarrassed. She'd never seen Tommy act like this.

"You do, right?"

Andi sighed. Why Ray didn't come to her help, she didn't know. "We're just getting to know each other, honey. We don't know each other enough to—"

"Oh, I like Andi a lot," Ray said suddenly. "She's very pretty. She's a good mother. She's smart. A lot of guys would consider her a real catch."

164

Andi stared straight ahead, her heart suddenly hammering.

"There, that proves it. You love each other."

Ray laughed. Andi sank down into her seat and watched the lights go by. She didn't know whether Ray was joking, just defusing the situation, or speaking his real feelings. They drove along in silence for a minute.

Then she felt Ray's hand on top of hers. He gave it a squeeze and let go. She turned to look out the window, not wanting anyone to see her eyes were glimmering with sudden hot tears. She knew she was falling hard, but she had to keep her head about it.

When no one said anything, Tommy sank back happily into his seat, looking at the knights. They pulled into the driveway, and everyone got out without saying a word. Andi hustled Tommy up to the sidewalk, while Ray followed.

When they were inside, Andi took Tommy upstairs to bed. She told him to get into his pj's, but as she shut the door behind her, she said, "Tommy, you have to understand how grownups learn to like one another. Love doesn't just happen. Ray and I hardly know each other. So please don't put me on the spot like that."

"But you wouldn't, would you?"

"Would I what?"

"Get married without letting me know."

Andi's heart welled up within her. She crossed the room and hugged him as he stood there, his shirt half-off and his pants unbuttoned. "I told you, Tommy, you'll be the first to know. I promise." She held him tight, then let go. "Say your prayers. I'm going to get Ray settled."

The television was on when Andi hurried into the living room. "Ray, you've got to promise me something."

He looked up and smiled. "Anything for you!"

"I'm not joking around."

"OK." His face took on a serious look.

"Just don't lead me on, or Tommy. I've been—"

"I'm not leading you on, Andi." He stood. Across the room, the space suddenly looked to her like a hundred miles. She had to contain these feelings. It was too much. She hadn't felt like this since college.

He said again, "I swear, Andi, I'd never lead you on."

Her chin suddenly started to shake. A moment later, she was in his arms. "Please kiss me," she whispered.

After an impassioned embrace, she lay her head on his chest. "I'm just so confused about all of this, Ray. Please don't be angry."

"Why would I be angry?"

"Because I'm acting like a giddy teenager."

He pushed her back and looked into her eyes. "I like what I'm seeing, giddy teenager, so if that's what you're acting like, you have my full attention."

"But I'm afraid."

"Of what?"

She shook her head. "Of a lot of things. Rejection, I guess."

"I'm not—"

"Let me finish. And my father, Martin Croase, the things that are happening, and most of all, about Tommy."

"Maybe you should quit your job and relocate."

She shook her head. "I can't do that either."

"Why not?"

She gazed into his eyes, then blinked away. "I just can't."

"But why, Andi? Please tell me. You can be honest."

"Because I don't want to lose you."

He blinked, then pulled her to his breast. "You'll never lose me, Andi. Not now."

She began to breathe easier. After a minute of simply holding one another, she wriggled out of his arms and headed back upstairs. She got the guest room ready, patting the bed, fluffing the pillow, and straightening a small reprint of a Picasso oil over the bed. But when she came back down, Ray had set up his sleeping bag on the couch.

"It'll be more comfortable in the guest room, Ray."

"I'd better stay down here," he said quietly.

"But the couch is—"

"I'm used to camping out." He smiled. "I think we need to be careful, that's all."

166

She nodded reluctantly. "All right. That might be wise. But can we just sit for a little while and talk?" He patted the couch to his right. She said, "Let me take run back upstairs and get you a pillow."

When she returned with two pillows, she heard Tommy in the living room. She stood at the edge of the bannister and the upper wall, watching. Tommy had his right hand ready to draw an imaginary pistol. Ray said, "Draw, mister."

Tommy shouted, "BANG!"

Ray fell to the floor, clutching his belly. Tommy swaggered over. "Watch who you mess with, cowboy."

Feigning a death rattle, Ray quivered and then stopped, dead still for a moment. Andi giggled as he launched into a Three Stooges snoring routine. Suddenly, she hurled a pillow at him. A moment later, Tommy grabbed it and shot it back at her. She winged the second pillow into Tommy's teeth.

Then they were all at it. It was complete pandemonium. Ray and Tommy slugged it out with the two larger pillows while Andi bashed at both of them with two couch pillows. A moment later, all three of them went down, squalling with laughter.

When everyone had pulled themselves apart, Tommy said, "That was better than the carnival."

Ray untangled his legs from Tommy's and Andi's and sat up. "Hey, why don't we all pray, then hit the sack?"

Andi and Tommy quickly agreed and each offered a few words of thanks for the evening. Andi finished it with, "Let us all sleep well tonight, Lord."

With a playful smack on Tommy's bottom, she then sent him off to bed. For a moment, she and Ray stood in the dim light. Then without thinking, Andi kissed him again. "Thanks for giving him a great evening, Ray."

Ray stepped back. "And what about you?"

"Me too." Her eyes flickered, and she started up the stairs.

Ray called after her, "I had a great evening, too."

She paused, looked at him over the bannister. "Do you think David Hughes is really watching us?"

"I don't know." He looked into his lap. "We've got to be careful."

She started back up the stairs. "Anyway, thanks for telling me."

"For telling you what?"

"That you had a great evening."

"Well, I did."

She went into her bedroom. In the dark as she undressed she told herself not to feel what she was feeling. But it was no good. She was as good as head over heels in love.

There were no bad dreams that night. Everyone awoke the next morning refreshed.

☐ ☐ ☐

In the park late that morning, Tommy ran to and fro throwing stones at ducks and trees. Andi and Ray walked along hand in hand, quiet, enjoying the sunshine. Then Tommy ran up to them, breathing hard. "You know how to skip stones, Ray?"

Ray let go of her hand, knelt down and picked up a wrinkly, somewhat flat pebble with a brown face. "How many times you think it'll skip?"

"Six. No, eight. Yeah, eight."

They all watched as Ray sidearmed the stone across the still pond. It skipped five times before skimming flat on the surface and sinking. "Think you can beat that?"

Tommy shook his head. "I never got more than two."

"Did you do it sidearm?"

The boy's eyes widened. "No. Maybe that's it."

Ray showed him how to sidearm the stones, and soon Tommy had them skipping four, five, and six times. He went back to bombarding some ducks on the far side.

As they resumed their walk, Andi said, "I haven't seen him so happy in quite a while."

Ray jammed his hands in his pockets. "You love him, Andi. That's what makes it happen."

"So do you." She gazed at him evenly, unblinking.

"He thinks I hung the moon."

168

"And the stars, and the sun, and everything else."

They continued down the path around the pond, saying nothing. Andi's arms swayed back and forth, and Ray noticed how her body moved, fluid, an effortless grace. He wanted to offer some word of wisdom, but he sensed they needed a change of topic. He said, "Do you think it's demonic—the experience, I mean?"

Andi didn't turn to look at him. She was relieved he didn't press her. "I don't know what it is. I wonder about it all the time. What happened to me was very different from you. If it is demonic, it explains a lot. But why would God let it happen that way, if it is? Why would He give demons such a free hand, especially about something like that? And with us, making us doubt everything? That's what makes me wonder. But then what if it isn't? What if that's the way it really is, and we're all wrong?"

Ray kicked at a stone on the path and send it tumbling down the path. "That's exactly what I wonder about. Could we be all wrong? It's not like a large percentage of the world even believes like we do. Sure, a lot of people believe in some vague afterlife. But I've read some of the books—Raymond Moody, Kenneth Ring, Elizabeth Kübler-Ross. They all record these common experiences, none of which really supports the Christian world view."

Andi put her arm through his and walked along, swaying with him in stride.

He continued, "And all kinds of people out there have the same experience. How can that be? I mean, the Scriptures are clear about heaven, hell, judgment, sin, salvation, all those things. And basically the experience I had doesn't support them, especially since I saw my grandfather there—if he was really my grandfather. But if the God of the Bible is the real God, then why would He let that happen? Sometimes now I just feel like quitting. I'm definitely out of the seminary. I won't be going back. Maybe I'll finish the semester, I don't know. But Christianity—I love the Lord and all, but what is happening? Why is this happening to us? For a while now I've been thinking that God really is working out my life. Meeting you, getting to know you—you've really helped me."

"I have?"

"You have. You're the first person I've, well, felt comfortable with in a long time."

"I feel the same way."

She let go of his arm and turned to call Tommy. Then, shielding the sun from her eyes with her palm, she said, "By the way, what does Dr. Kingston say?"

"I haven't been able to talk to him for a few days," Ray said. "Right now, I don't want to. Actually, I've been spending most of my extra time with you and Tommy."

She creased her lips in a gracious smile. "I do appreciate it."

"Don't think I don't get anything out of it."

"Oh, you do?"

"You know, a salad now and then."

She punched him lightly on the shoulder. "Thanks for changing the subject."

He grinned. "That's my job."

Tommy ran up again. "I almost hit a duck."

Andi groaned. "Is this what you want to be, a duck-murderer?"

Chuckling, Ray said, "Hey, every man remembers the first time he ever hit a duck with a stone. It's an important event in his life. One of those formative things. That and pounding a drum."

They both laughed. Tommy stared at them quizzically.

"Inside joke," Ray told him. But he felt good. Bad as the situation was, he felt like he was riding the crest of a giant wave at Malibu.

3

Dr. Nakayami hovered over the still body, listening for a heartbeat. The man was dead, and this time he knew Croase was pushing things too hard. It was no use. They had to do a great deal more ground research before the TUT-B would work. He stormed into Croase's office afterwards.

"We must concentrate on the TUT, learning to keep the teams together. We—"

Croase cut him off. "We've got that under control, Doctor. What more do you want? Four teams have gone out and everyone has managed to stay together. A quarter of the campus has tried it. People are going to want to go all the way soon. They won't be satisfied with this. We've got to go after the threshold. That's the ultimate discovery. At that point, there's no more mystery."

Nakayami shook his head. "Too many people dead. Not enough groundwork. Pure stupidity."

"I want the boy," Croase said. "He's our best chance."

Nakayami blew compressed air through his tight lips. He started to turn away. "Sometimes there is a point of dividing, Martin. You are pushing my patience."

"Your patience! What about mine?" Croase hurried around the desk and stood in front of him. "We could have proceeded weeks ago if not for your insistence that we work out the problems with the TUT-B. It works on the boy. What else do we need?"

"We don't know if it works on the boy."

"It worked once. It'll work again."

"Not completely sure. I want no more dead bodies."

Croase turned his head and looked Nakayami hard in the eye. "Every precaution will be taken, Hiro. What more can we ask? Anyway, if you won't do it, there are others who will. You're not indispensable, Hiro."

Nakayami flinched. Yes, the threshold was an enigma. Why was it there? What did it mean? Yes, they had to get past it. But could the boy really understand what it meant? But could they mutilate the rules once again in the name of research?

Hiro Nakayami was a committed thanatologist and biochemist. But he didn't like seeing people die, even in the name of research and the advance of the human race. He didn't put any stock in Croase's so-called Christianity. He knew there were multitudes of sincere Christians. But Croase was just an opportunist with an eye on his wallet.

Still, what he had begun to hate was how Croase dictated to him how to do the research. What was the rush? It had taken the human race sixty centuries to get where they were now. What was another week or month?

What was worse was that he knew he couldn't leave TWI. Where would he go? What credentials could he use now? Only success would free him from this hell.

"All right. We try the boy. But only under optimum conditions."

Croase clapped him on the back. "I knew you'd see the truth." Nakayami quickly turned and hurried out. For once he found himself praying to God, if there was such a person, that He would not let the boy die on the sending table.

On the way down the hall, Nakayami bumped into Ken Strock coming around a corner. "Dr. Nakayami!" Strock said. "I'm glad I ran into you."

Nakayami gazed uneasily at the muscled security man. "Yes?"

"Just wanted to let you know we got the body problem all taken care of."

"You do?"

"Arranged it myself. Nothing to worry about anyway. Don't want you guys up there in research being bothered with this kind of thing."

"How did you arrange it?"

"Worked out a deal with a funeral home. Strictly cremation. Not a trace left."

The warm air in the corridor suddenly made him feel sticky. Nakayami gazed at Strock without flinching. Occasionally in the past Strock had taken him aside to boast about some job he'd done for Croase. Why Strock wanted him to know this, Nakayami didn't know. For some reason, Strock seemed to think it would impress him. Nakayami wasn't impressed, but he never indicated to Strock anything but being pleased at knowing about the ex-cop's exploits. "Thanks for telling me," Nakayami said.

Grinning happily, Strock lay his arm over Nakayami's shoulders. "Just want you to know I'm doin' my job, just like you're doin' yours."

"Of course. Thank you very much."

Strock walked off down the hall whistling with enthusiasm. Nakayami turned and sidled off to his office. He said to himself, "Might be good to cultivate a relationship with the man. It'll keep me informed."

A half hour after Nakayami exited, Croase picked up the phone and dialed Ken Strock's number in the security office. When Strock answered, he said, "Hughes has been watching them, right?"

"As you requested."

"All right, we have to get all three of them. I don't think they're going to cooperate about anything. So cuff them. After we perform the experiment, I'll deal with the man and woman, understand? Good. Then we can work with the boy for as long as we need."

"Easy as pie, boss."

Croase hung up and sighed heavily. If only Nakayami knew the half of it, he thought. But he'd take care of the good doctor when the time came.

He looked over the charts about the TUT-B. Autopsies were performed on each victim after they succumbed. Nothing had worked. Only the boy could seem to withstand it. What was the key?

As he reflected on it, though, Croase laughed. "What does it matter?" he asked himself. "There's nothing beyond the wall. Just more of the same. I'm getting what I want." He wasn't sure what he'd do with Ray or Andi, but at least he had the support of her father. That was probably enough for now.

If only Listra wasn't so buzzed about the TUT-B. But he had to humor her—while he took care of everything else. "One of these days," Croase muttered, "I'll be rid of all this nonsense. Two hundred thousand lousy bucks a year. They think they can keep me here for that—just because Christians aren't supposed to be wealthy. Well, I'm going to be rich, and if they won't give it to me easy, I'll take it hard."

He picked up a picture of Tommy Darcasian. "And you may be my permanent ticket to paradise, Mr. Tommy Darcasian."

173

As he gazed on the picture, he sensed that he should talk to Benreu. He smiled and went to the credenza behind his desk. Behind him the phone rang. He growled and picked it up. There was a pause as he listened to the woman at the other end of the line. "I told you not to call me here. I will picked you up later." He hung up the phone and took out one of the vials of the blue liquid. With an eyedropper he dripped a single droplet onto a piece of paper. "Just like the old days with LSD," he mused.

He was glad he didn't have to play games with the reclining chairs and all the other paraphernalia. In the last few weeks, Nakayami had perfected the drug to the point that all you needed do was place a drop on your tongue and it worked. Nakayami was working now on developing it so that you could place the drop on your skin and it would be immediately absorbed. The TUT tasted like medicinal mouthwash.

Croase picked up the piece of paper blotted with TUT, took a deep breath, and laid it on his tongue. A moment later, he slumped back and his invisible body soared away down the tunnel to meet with Benreu.

PART 2

The Boy

Behold, children are a gift of the Lord;
The fruit of the womb is a reward.

—Psalm 127

Precious in the sight of the Lord
Is the death of His godly ones.

—Psalm 116

CHAPTER EIGHT

1

Lou Miles arrived in Los Angeles from Portland on a United Airlines red-eye late evening flight. A Special Agent of the L.A. FBI office named Harry Smalls met him there and took him to Janice Koppers's house. Smalls filled Lou in on what they had. He also opened a sheaf of pictures, several ballistics reports, some close-ups of the bullets (after they were taken out of the bodies), and a diagram of what they believed happened.

"So it looks like the same guy?" Lou said.

Smalls nodded. "We found a safe and opened it. Might show the motive. Some of her girls say they know she had a load of cash. But there's nothing here. No prints, either, just Koppers's in the safe."

"Yeah, and that still doesn't explain Hasekker in Portland."

"It could be money." Smalls shrugged indifferently.

"But how could this guy know about both of these people? And those letters. He's obviously saying something."

Lou tried to be casual, searching for the slightest clue without appearing to be. Sometimes things came up off-the-cuff that you wouldn't say in report mode, but in a more casual talk it would come out. "Any other speculation as to why this guy is making these hits?"

"Lots of speculation," Smalls said. "From cultic stuff to just a random killer who's looking for notoriety."

"Why no sexual interest? Despite recent novels and stories about superintelligent serial killers, most real-life serial killers were involved in deviant sex."

"Yeah. We don't know." Smalls stared down at the blood soaked bed.

"He's probably already halfway across the country," Lou said, grimacing. "At the next hit. He definitely likes to travel."

Smalls flexed his cheek and said nothing.

"Well, let me do some looking around. Can I study this stuff?"

Smalls agreed, and they left.

2

"So did you enjoy it?" Ray said as he and Tommy stood in the living room swinging his imaginary bat and hitting home runs, singles, doubles. It was Thursday night, now near the middle of October. The three of them had just returned from a football game at the local high school. Ray thought it might be a nice way to get out and grab some air.

Halting his baseball game, Tommy pulled off the green army jacket Ray had got him that morning. He hung it up reverently on the coat rack just inside the door. "It was great," Tommy said. "I did like it. I did."

Andi crossed her legs after sinking into the easy chair. "I'm dead. I forgot how much a high school game wears you out. All that cheering. How can they stand it?"

Ray joked, "You mean you weren't a cheerleader in high school?"

"No, never could abide that crowd. I was a member of the color guard." Andi stood and feigned several moves with an imaginary rifle.

Ray and Tommy watched, then Andi suddenly shrugged and sat down again. Ray pulled out a small, red-handled knife and turned to Tommy. "Got something for you, Chief. You ever see a Swiss Army knife?"

Tommy shook his head, staring at the small knife in

Ray's hand. It was less than two and a half inches long. Ray opened it and showed him the silvery blade, then a tiny pair of scissors. "It's good for basic stuff," Ray explained. "It even has a toothpick and a pair of tweezers. I keep one on my key chain. But a friend gave me a second a while ago. Their company gives them away as a sales gift. Would you like to have it?"

Tommy's eyes were about to pop. "You'd really let me keep it?"

"Of course. Every kid your age has to have a penknife. This one is special." He placed it in Tommy's palm. Then he began to rise. "Well, gang, I hate to say it, but I really need to spend a night at my room. The fellowship of the saints will be wondering. You two will be OK without me, won't you?"

None of them had had a bad dream since he'd begun staying overnight, almost two weeks before. Whatever the problem was had vanished.

Tommy groaned, but Andi said, "We were kinda hoping you'd move in. But I guess we'll be facing an inquisition from the morals board if we continue, so we'll make out."

"Oh, Mom," Tommy said. "You can't let him go that easy."

"Easily, honey." Andi brushed the wrinkles out of her skirt and stood. "Come on, it's past ten. Time for you to go to bed." She turned to Ray. "Would you like to pray with us? Then I guess we'll have to let you go."

"Sure." Ray stuck his arms into his heavy, brown leather flight jacket. Tommy had petitioned him for one the week before, but the best Ray could do was the green army coat.

They went upstairs and prayed in Tommy's room. Then while the boy got ready for bed, Ray said, "God'll send some ministering spirits while I'm away."

"We'd rather have you," Andi said.

They both started to go, but Tommy was staring at them. Ray glanced at him. "What's up, Chief? You look like you just saw a ghost."

"I just remembered something from the place."

"Heaven?"

Ray and Andi walked over to the bed. "What?" Ray asked.

"That's what the being told me. He said he was a 'ministering spirit,' like you just said."

As the boy looked from face to face, Ray took out a pocket Bible and leafed through to Hebrews. "Here it is: 'Are not all angels ministering spirits sent to serve those who will inherit salvation?'" Ray looked up at Tommy. "He was an angel then?"

Tommy shook his head, eyes wide. "I don't know. I just remember I asked him and he said he was a ministering spirit and he told me his name." He wrinkled his brow. "I can't remember his name."

"Trell?" Ray said suddenly.

"No, something else. Bargel or something."

"Bargel?"

Tommy closed his eyes and concentrated. "He was the second one, the person after the fence."

"The wall," Ray said, glancing at Andi.

"Did he say anything else?" Andi asked.

"Lots of things. And then there was someone else."

"Same kind of person?" Ray asked.

"No, this one was stronger. Or maybe bigger or something."

"More important?" Andi asked.

"Yeah, more important."

"How did you know that?" Ray asked.

"Because the first person told me some things about him, but I can't remember what."

"And you spoke to the second one?" Andi added.

Tommy nodded vigorously. "Yes. For a long time too."

Everyone was silent, then Tommy said, "That's all I can remember. What you said reminded me."

"Maybe something else'll click off another barrage," Ray said. "Keep thinking about it, Chief."

"I will."

Andi walked Ray to the door. She smiled as he turned the handle. "I'll miss having you around."

"Not too much," Ray said.

She suddenly shrugged. "You're right. Not too much."

He laughed. "You don't give any sympathy, do you?"

She kissed him. "All an ex-navy guy needs."

He started out the door. "That's a lot, believe me." He grinned and went out into the cool air. As he walked down the sidewalk, she closed the door and sighed. "Men," she murmured and walked back to Tommy's bedroom.

Tommy lay on the bed, asleep.

She said, "Boy, he was really gone." Then she noticed his shirt was still unbuttoned. He hadn't even uncovered the bed. She stood over him and started to button it. "Tommy," she said. "Tommy? Get up."

Something was wrong. He was out. Cold. She pressed open his eyelid. His eyes were rolled back in his head. Then behind her, she heard someone move. She turned and looked, startled, her heart hammering.

A gloved hand clamped over her mouth, a white handkerchief in his hand. An acrid odor. Her mind registered the thought, "No, not—"

That was as far as she got.

□ □ □

Ray reached his dorm room at a quarter past ten. He'd been taking all his classes, trying to act as if nothing was wrong, even when he stayed the nights at Andi's. No one had questioned him about it. He had always tended to have a loose schedule, sometimes taking long runs during the night, or going off and sleeping out in the woods that surrounded the TWI complexes.

He undressed and slid between the cool white sheets. For a moment, he savored the chilly feel of the familiar bed, then he rolled over, hit a light, and fell asleep.

□ □ □

Andi awoke under hot, bright lights. Several doctors and nurses hovered over her. Two blue eyes looked into hers. "Miss Darcasian, we require your assistance." It was Martin Croase.

She blinked and jerked her head up. "Where am I? Where's Tommy?"

"You don't know?"

She paused, then sank down, her heart jolting.

"We'd like you to let your friend Ray know where you are, Andi." A black phone on a trolley table was lifted into her view. "Are you ready?"

"I don't know where I am. And I wouldn't—"

"We're in TWI, as you should know. We tried to work with you. Now you've forced us to this extreme. It was a difficult decision, but we have Tommy safe and secure, and if you give us a hard time, it may get nasty for him. Do you understand what I'm saying?" Croase's hard eyes didn't blink or twitch.

"You have no right—" She struggled and realized she was strapped down. She pushed with her arms against the tight straps. She could move only her head. "What do you want?"

"A simple phone call. We would like Ray to attend this session, and, well, we find that he is not an easy fellow to grab in the night."

"I don't know his phone number." She kept her eyes hard and unblinking, but inside she fought back rattling waves of panic.

"Don't worry, we have it." Croase's voice was sickly sweet. He scrutinized a slip of paper and dialed a number. She could hear it ringing and realized they were on an intercom.

It rang once. Ray's voice came on. "Hello."

"Ray?"

"Yes?"

"Martin Croase. We'd like to schedule a meeting with you, in half an hour. We have some friends of yours, and we'd like—"

"Andi and Tommy? Croase, I'll kill you."

"If you'd just be quiet, Ray, you will discover we're not as awful as you think we are. We have Tommy, yes, and Andi. I'm here, Listra's here. We're all ready to go. The only one missing is you."

182

Andi heard Ray shout into the receiver.

"Just in case you don't believe us, we'd like you to hear Andi's voice as a confirmation. Are you listening?"

Croase looked at Andi. "Say anything."

Andi shook her head angrily.

Croase raised his hand and clicked his fingers. Tommy screamed with sudden pain at the other end of the room.

"Don't hurt him!" Andi yelled.

With a confident smile, Croase said, "That's what I wanted." He put the phone back up to his ear. "Did you hear that, Ray?"

There was a long pause. "Yeah."

"So you will get this carefully. In fifteen minutes—at 2:32—a black Cadillac will pick you up in front of the Ad Building. Understand?"

Andi heard Ray yell as Croase put the phone down. He looked at Andi, his eyes somehow smiling. "That was easy enough. Now please, just cooperate. We're not going to hurt you."

Andi gritted her teeth and fired a ball of spittle at him. It broke up in midair and sprayed on the front of his green smock.

After wiping it off, Croase said, "Now, now, Andi, you wouldn't want us to have to restrain you even worse than you are now, would you?"

As Croase eyed her, Andi turned her head away furiously. They were going to send her out there again, and there was nothing she could do to stop it. For herself, Tommy, or Ray.

☐ ☐ ☐

Andi realized she must have fallen asleep, because when she awoke she heard rustling to her left and she turned to look. Tommy's eyes flickered open. He was now in the next recliner. Without his glasses, she knew he could barely see her. He said, "Mom, they're not going to make me go up there again, are they? Not again."

Behind Andi, Ray shouted, "Croase, leave them out of it!"

183

"Shut up," one of the doctors said, "or it'll only be more difficult. We can sedate you."

"Do it," Ray yelled. "Anything to screw up your Nazi experiments."

One of the doctors hovered over Ray. Andi could see he pressed on Ray's right eye with his thumb. "We can make you blind here, but there you'll see. Is that what you want?"

Ray jerked his head to the side, but the doctor kept on the pressure. "I won't cooperate," he bellowed. "Never."

The doctor motioned to another green-clad assistant. He said, "We can do anything we want to the boy—is that what you want?" The assistant, a woman, stood over Tommy. She laid her hand on his eyes. Tommy squealed, "Stop it!"

Ray's eyes met Andi's. She said nothing, but she could tell he knew he was beaten. "OK, just don't hurt Tommy."

"That's better," the doctor said. She noticed the slight Japanese man across on the far wall, looking very pained and angry. But Croase clapped his hands. "All right, gang, let's get moving. We don't have all night."

3

After some directives about the test to Dr. Nakayami, Martin Croase sat on the first recliner. Andi saw Listra in the fourth one, just beyond Tommy. When Listra caught Andi's eye, she said, "It'll be all right, dear. You'll understand later. It's all for the work of the ministry. You have to believe that."

"Do I?" Andi smoldered.

This time there wasn't an impressive countdown. Andi felt the cold liquid hit her arm. She closed her eyes, trying to hold onto her body.

A moment later, she was floating above it. She saw Tommy, Ray, Listra, and Croase also rise. Their bodies were like light—soft, undulant, yet recognizable. Not by features. But thoughts. She knew who they were by the thoughts that came from them. Somehow their thoughts and their spirits were one.

Listra's voice mentally called out, speaking right into Andi's mind, "Follow me. We've got to stick together."

184

Andi tried to hold herself in place, but when she saw Tommy pulled along behind Listra, she followed. Ray was behind her. Martin Croase led. Whatever was happening, Andi thought, at least she and Ray and Tommy would face it together.

☐ ☐ ☐

This time a sense of peace, warmth, and love infused her. Even as she watched Ray and Tommy stream along through the tunnel, she fought a losing inner battle. Was this real? Something about the experience made it not seem to matter. This moment mattered. A prickly, bubbly thrill infused her soul. All questions seemed to disappear in the gentle whirlpool of the beauty of the experience.

Martin and Listra led the way like Boone trailblazers through the wilderness of Kentucky. Several times Listra turned around, and though her face was ethereal, spectral, in Andi's mind it was clear and beautiful. She smiled and waved them along.

Behind her, Tommy's thoughts seemed stuck and closed in, and twice Andi turned around and cried, "It's all right." She didn't even know why.

Ray also seemed guarded in letting himself release into the joy of the experience. The sides of the tunnel were like convolutions of dark smoke, rolling under them like billows. When her spirit-body touched it, she passed through without pain or ricochet. What was it that was pulling them though? Even as the peace began to overwhelm her, she found herself able to sink back into her own thoughts and analyze, not as before when she was too confused to understand what was happening, when it had seemed like hell. But then she remembered, this was exactly what happened the previous time. Why had she thought it was hell?

Sensations rolled over her in waves. Though she had no sense of flesh, she had a real body that she moved like her earthly body. She peered at her hands as they hurtled through space at a speeds that she told herself were faster than the speed of light, though she had no reference point to understand what that might feel like. Her hands glistened with a spectral cream color. The fingernails were still defined, and the wrinkly lines across each knuckle.

She looked down at her legs. They were bare. She could wiggle the toes, and at the same time see through them to the two figures behind her. She fired a thought to Ray, having already grown used to this strange form of communication.

"Are you OK?"

"I'm watching," Ray replied. His thought spoke into her mind with the same resonance of Ray's normal muddy voice.

"Watching what?"

"Everything. I want to understand this."

"So do I."

Tommy still looked balled up, like a human bullet careening through space.

"Is Tommy OK?"

Ray didn't reply. Then, "He hasn't spoken to me. I can't seem to reach him. Something's wrong. He's afraid."

"But it's so peaceful. So beautiful."

"I know. I don't understand it."

"Understand what?"

"How it can be."

"It's wonderful."

Ray paused again. Andi realized that even though they communicated thought to thought, mind to mind, there was a way that their own thoughts remained private. It was just like speaking. If you wanted to reveal your mind in an earthly context, you verbalized. But if you didn't speak, your thoughts were your own. No one could know what ideas coursed through your mind. It was the same here. That gave Andi an even deeper sense of peace. She was still herself, even if she was really dead.

"I'm going to question whoever we meet."

Andi replied, "Do you think he'll—it, she, whatever—will answer?"

"I won't stop until they do."

The tunnel grew brighter. A moment later, the five figures wafted onto a grassy plain. Andi sensed the grass under her feet, but she could see it was not corporeal, as earthly grass was. It was some kind of spirit matter, like her body. Yet there was touch. And such a sensation to it. Like the kiss of wrinkled lips upon a cheek. Andi reveled in the magnificence of the scene. She felt overwhelmed with relief that her first experience was not being repeated. At the edge of the field stood a high wall, made of glowing rocks. *Gems?* she wondered. *Jewels?* It couldn't be.

She drew close to Tommy. "Are you all right, honey?"

"We'll all go back together, won't we? They won't leave me here?" he asked.

She gazed at Tommy, then realized he appeared adult, but with the child's thoughts and feelings. Perhaps one had to grow here too, she thought. Instinctively, she looked at Ray. He looked younger, maybe twenty-one, twenty-two. How old had he been down there? She didn't know. She'd never asked him. He had to be in his thirties. He even had a few gray hairs. But here his brown hair gleamed with a youthful brilliance.

Suddenly, she wondered if she was still a female. She had a sense of that. But for a moment, she felt embarrassed. Was she still a woman and Ray a man? Was there love in this place?

Listra bounded over, her steps lithe and sure. Andi still hadn't gotten used to standing. She felt so light, so jumpy with energy. Like she might fly wherever she wanted at the speed of thought.

Listra said, "I told you it was marvelous. I'm so excited for you."

As she rubbed her foot on the grass, Andi answered, "Will we meet someone?" All the anger seemed to have disappeared.

They had all turned to the horizon, but no light appeared.

"I hope so," Listra said. "He's usually here. Let's go toward the wall." Listra reached out with her hand.

Ray helped Tommy, and Andi moved to the other side, Tommy's left. She spoke to him again. "Are you all right?"

Tommy turned in her direction. There were no glasses. His eyes were a deep blue, but she could see the fear in them. He was still fighting it.

"They won't make me go through, will they? I will go back with you?"

"Of course," Andi said.

Then they saw in the distance the bright orb of something hurtling toward them. It slowed and stopped, then walked toward them across the field. It was a being, but not like them. He was light itself, his skin and face burning before them. Andi could see features, golden and skinlike underneath the flames. He had a kind face. His arms, long, lean but strong, burnished with a silvery sheen, flashed out toward them in welcome.

"You have come back," he said.

Andi wondered why she thought he was a he, but she had no answer. She struggled again with the feel of feminine and masculine. Had she changed in that respect too? She still didn't know.

Ray's voice broke the calm. "Who are you?"

"A friend," the person answered, calm and friendly.

"What is your name?"

"I am a guide," the being said. Andi could see a broad smile etching his face.

"Are we in heaven?" Ray asked insistently. Andi realized that if they were going to be pulled back to earth, they didn't have much time.

"Some call it that," the voice said evenly, without inflection or tremor. "Nirvana, heaven, the beatific vision. All races and peoples have their names."

"Where's Jesus?" Ray asked.

Andi was surprised that Listra and Martin had said nothing so far. But they didn't protest this cross-examination. The being seemed to welcome it.

"You have many questions," the being said. "They will all be answered. Jesus is one as you. He has found His peace."

"What's that supposed to mean?" Ray said. For the first time Andi sensed the acrimony in his voice.

"You are a Christian," the being said. "It is difficult for you here. You have such strong beliefs about the afterlife. But you will find it is the same for all. It's secure. It won't change. You will be free." He motioned toward the wall. "Soon you will see it all."

"Then what I have believed is all wrong?" Ray said.

"Right, wrong. There is no right or wrong. There only is. What is. What you are. Here, you will find true freedom."

Andi sensed Ray's fury. How could that be if they were perfect, she wondered. But the thought passed. She realized he was groping for something, some word, some argument that would pin the being.

"Are you a demon?" Ray asked.

The being laughed. It was a soft, tender laugh of identification and understanding, not a laugh at Ray but a patient laugh, willing to wait for the truth to emerge. Andi wasn't sure she liked it.

"No, I am a guide. I will lead you to the final place."

Andi sensed something at her back. A pull. A jerk.

Ray shouted, "Is Hitler here? Is Stalin here? Are murderers here, people who have never repen—"

The being motioned to his right. Suddenly, a multitude of people appeared. Some Andi vaguely recognized from pictures. Was it really Hitler? And Stalin? How could that be?

There was another tug at her back.

Andi knew now the TUT, whatever it did, was working. Something seemed to grab her at the waist. She saw Listra and Martin Croase fall back and disappear.

Then she hurtled back down the tunnel. She heard Tommy's cry, though, behind her just as she slammed into the darkness, "Don't leave me!"

□ □ □

What seemed to be only a moment later, Andi opened her eyes under the lights. A bright lamp burned onto her forehead, and she winced. She said, "Please, you must bring him back."

Doctors and nurses hovered over her. The words "Heart stabilized" were shouted out as each one of them became conscious. Andi twisted her head to her left to see what was happening at Tommy's chair. But there was no chair. She was on a bed now. Where were they? What had happened? She struggled to remember. The gate. They'd been at the gate.

Someone began wheeling her bed out of the room. She forced herself to concentrate. Surely, they'd bring Tommy back with her. She told herself to watch everything that happened, everywhere she went. Somehow they were going to get out this time, and this time they would go to someone, the FBI, someone.

The nurse pushed her out into a single room and closed the door behind her without saying anything. Andi prayed that whatever they were doing with Tommy would end and they'd be reunited.

But deep down she wondered if prayer mattered, if there was a God who answered prayer, if any of it made any sense any more. And then something else: would she really meet Hitler in that place? He possessed eternal life with no consequences for his sins?

As she thought about it, she realized Ray had hit on the right question. That was the issue, wasn't it? Did people who had orchestrated and carried out the most damnable deeds go free, without so much as a slap on the wrist? Was the only justice really in this world and if they escaped it, they escaped forever?

She couldn't believe that. It was impossible.

Yet, how could she argue with it? She'd seen it. Him. The place. He'd even said so. There was no right and wrong. And that person: had he really been Hitler?

She stared at the ceiling, an off-white color. She was still strapped down. It looked and felt like a doctor's examining room. She peered frantically around for something to use to get out. But she couldn't even move her arms.

Wanting to scream, she held it back. She had to think. She had to get out of this and get to Tommy.

"Monsters!" she screamed. "You monsters!"

The sound echoed slightly in the room, replaced instantly by silence. She knew it was useless noise. She twisted about, looking for something, anything to help. The cupboards were closed. Each one had a padlock. On the counter was a jar full of cotton, some Band-Aids, other medicinal items. The drawers underneath were also locked.

On the far wall was a picture by Norman Rockwell over a small table with a lamp on it. It was of a doctor listening with his stethoscope to a little girl's dolly. She'd seen it before in portrait catalogs. She'd always liked Rockwell. But now it all struck her as a supreme hypocrisy. Croase had to be insane.

"I'm going to get out of here," she muttered. "And this time someone's going to pay." She settled down and waited. "Just get Tommy back all right, and then we'll see what happens to you people."

4

The moment Tommy awoke he knew they wanted to question him. Everything was blurry. He wanted his glasses, and he wanted to see his mother. He knew she would be worried. Again, the whole experience was very hazy in his mind. But this time he remembered a few facts.

Martin and Listra Croase stood over him, staring down into his eyes. Tommy said, "Can I have my glasses?"

Croase motioned to someone and one of the nurses in green placed them on his head. Someone else began unstrapping him. When Listra leaned over to give him a hug, Tommy could smell her minty breath.

"What happened to you, Tommy?" Croase asked.

"I don't remember."

"I'm not trying to scare you, Tommy. What happened when you went beyond the jewel fence?"

Five faces peered down at Tommy. He felt like he was at the bottom of a pit looking up at his executioners. He struggled in his mind to remember. Images flashed through, one person, then another person, then—he still wasn't sure. It was like the last time. It was hazy in his mind.

"I don't remember real well." He was breathing hard, now that his clothing was looser. "Where's my mother?"

"She's fine, Tommy. Just tell us what happened. Were you able to move around? Did you get past the thres—, I meant the wall, the gate? Do you remember a gate?"

Tommy nodded. "There were stones in it."

191

"Did Benreu go in with you?"

Tommy gulped. He didn't remember anyone named Benreu. Was that the light being's name? They all leaned in upon him. He could hardly breathe. Their faces would crush him. He would die, and then he'd never come back. He'd be stuck there. He remembered, though, he hadn't been as afraid this time. And there was someone else. Benreu? No, that wasn't his name. Who was Benreu?

"Did Benreu take you beyond the gate, son? Was he with you the whole time?"

Tommy shook his head. "I don't know. Where's my mother?"

Croase's eyes looked big and angry to him, piercing, as though he was looking right inside Tommy's mind. He thought suddenly of the story of Little Red Riding Hood and the wolf. He shivered, wishing he could leave.

"Please, Tommy, you must tell us. What was beyond the gate? Was there a city? Did you see lights? Were there other people?"

Tommy strained to remember. A person. One person. No, two persons. No, many people. Not people. Angels? Shining. Telling him something. What was it? He couldn't remember. His name? It was Kartle. That was his name. Kartle. He was the same one from before. And then that more important person. He had done something. Touched Tommy's eyes. But with what? What had that meant? Something. Something important.

But he knew he wasn't going to tell them. Why didn't they just let him go and be with his mother?

"I want to go. Please. I want to go." He fought back the tears. Was Ray all right? Where was his mother? They didn't leave her out there, did they? Someone pulled a needle out of his arm, and a doctor said, "We have enough blood. All the other tests are recorded."

Tommy wouldn't look into Croase's eyes. Or Listra's. He didn't like them. They weren't like Ray. Or his mother. He could tell when people didn't really like him. His grandfather didn't. This man didn't. This man just wanted him to tell him a story. He thought briefly about making one up. But he knew they'd know. He wasn't a good liar. But that shining person—the important one—who was he? He'd told Tommy a name. Not Kartle. That was the first one. Tommy knew that person liked him, loved him. Was he Jesus? He wasn't sure. It all happened after he'd gone through the gate.

Croase said, "OK, take him to the room. Maybe he'll remember more as time goes on."

5

Nakayami threw the sheet of paper on Croase's desk. "I resign," he said. "You have my resignation—"

Croase laughed. "Aren't you forgetting something, my dear ethical Hiro?"

Nakayami was silent.

"Yes, you are forgetting the plagiarism, Hiro, and then what will you do when the information becomes public? Because I will make it public. You will be stripped of your degrees and never get another job."

Nakayami sucked air silently through his tight lips.

"I do not accept your resignation, Dr. Nakayami. I want you to continue with the research. And I don't want you telling me how to do my job. Sometimes I have to assist you in doing what is necessary."

"Not what is right, what is necessary."

"Yes, Hiro. Necessary. Expedient. Important. Manifest. Use what terms your limited English vocabulary can drum up. There is no right. You know that. We are. That's all. We just are, and we do what benefits the race, whatever the cost, what enables us to survive, to reach our ultimate destiny as gods."

Nakayami waved his hand before Croase finished his speech. Each had heard it a hundred times. What could he do now? He didn't have an answer. He knew they'd killed more than fifty people now trying to make the TUT-B work. But it definitely didn't harm the boy. Why?

Why did he even survive?

The researcher murmured, "You win." He left the room and walked stiffly down to his office on the same floor. His

193

life was over, he thought. It was done. He had made the mistake of his life coming here. Now what could he do?

He sank down into the chair behind his desk and put his head in his hands, closed his eyes. "Please, God, whoever You are—"

He couldn't finish the prayer. Tears burned into his eyes. He had to do something, but what?

Clearly, what had happened was beyond explanation. What was worse, Croase didn't even get it. Something incredible had happened, and Croase hadn't even awakened to it.

Still, he knew Croase would keep the boy. The others? No, just the boy. It wasn't right. None of it was right. He was through arguing with himself.

He sat there immovable. Slowly he opened a drawer and looked down at a small, yellow-covered book. He touched it, then slammed the drawer shut. All right, he couldn't resign. But he could take other action. They hadn't tied him up and gagged him.

Not yet, anyway.

CHAPTER NINE

1

Ray sat on the bed, studying a business card he'd found lying on the floor. Then the door opened and Andi staggered in, crying hoarsely, "Where's Tommy?"

For a moment she stood there, looking disheveled and broken. Ray took a step toward her. Then she was in his arms, weeping.

"Surely he came back. He's all right. Tell me he's all right."

Ray held her tightly and blinked angrily at the guard still standing in the doorway. How could her father consent to this, or did he really know? The guard closed the door, and the bolt clicked shut.

"Ray, please, we've got to find Tommy." She sobbed, then brushed angrily with her hand at the wetness. "I'm not giving them that. I won't! We're going to get him. We have to get him, Ray."

His mental processes began to harden into the patterns he'd learned as a SEAL. Be under control. Never let your emotions rule. Think clearly. Go for the objective. But something else inside him scraped and clawed to the surface, the old fear that those he loved would be taken away. Ray swallowed and fought off the rising anxiety. Then he nodded, hugged her again, and made her sit on the side of the gurney. "Let me think."

He stepped over to the door and peered out the window. He ran his finger along a metal plate screwed into the jamb on the wall next to the door lock.

"What is it?" Andi asked, still wiping her eyes on her shirt. He sensed she was calming down, maybe in the belief that he'd be able to do something. He prayed furiously that God would give him an idea.

"Mechanical combination lock," he said. "You punch in some numbers on the other side and it opens."

"No way to trigger it on this side?"

"No."

Ray listened for voices beyond the door. Ray was sure they didn't let Tommy die. But why had he not come back with them? Each time he'd stayed longer than either of them.

Then a face appeared in the window square. Someone began jabbing in the numbers on the lock. Then the door opened. It was Croase and several guards with drawn guns. Croase said, "We'd like to talk to you privately for a moment. We don't plan to hurt you or make you do it again if you don't want."

"Where's Tommy?" Andi said immediately.

"He'll be here in a minute."

"Then he's all right?"

"He's fine. I'd just like to talk to you, Andi, for a moment."

She slumped slightly, sighing with relief. Then she said, "You talk to both of us, or none of us. I include Ray in anything you say to me."

Ray didn't look at her, but her determination renewed his own. He was going to get them out of this. Somehow.

"All right, I'll make it plain then," Croase said, spreading his legs and taking a military stance. "We believe Tommy has a gift, an ability to take a form of the TUT that lasts longer than the normal dose."

Andi gasped. Ray glared at him, but his mind was on the door. As Croase talked he studied the bolt. Something blocking it would be enough, he thought.

Croase was saying, "For some reason he is the only one. We'd like to employ him as the primary test person to determine precisely what it is about his genetic makeup that ena-

196

bles him to withstand it. We will treat you all very well. No problems with studies or housing or anything else. Tommy will be given the best care. He will not be hurt. Everyone thinks the idea is fantastic."

"You want to use my son as a guinea pig for your experiments?" Andi said, her eyes wide with anger and incredulity.

"Not a guinea pig. A thananaut. He will go farther than any person before him. He will be a marvel to the world. He will see what no man has seen and come back to tell about it. He will—"

"Get out!" Andi screamed. She lunged at Croase, but Ray grabbed her at the waist.

"It won't do any good, Andi," he said, thinking he should have let her try to slam the haughty jerk.

Croase said, "You'll be a rich woman, Andi. But we will have the boy one way or another. I'd like to make it as easy as possible."

"You're a monster!" Andi yelled. "You're Dr. Mengele all over again. You're—"

"Just go," Ray said, stepping forward, sizing Croase up for the battle he knew would now come. The guard trained his gun at Ray's chest.

"Have it the way you want," Croase said. "We will not be derailed in our work." He went out.

When the door shut, Andi threw up her hands. "This is unbelievable. These people are unbelievable."

"When Tommy gets here, Andi, we shouldn't tell him about this."

She stopped and looked at him incisively. "You're right. OK." Then: "Ray, what are we going to do?"

"We're gonna get out. Just get ready." He had no idea what to do, but experience told him something would come.

A few minutes later, Croase opened the door again. This time it was Tommy. The boy looked small and afraid, and Andi crushed him in her arms. He began crying, but as she kissed him, she thanked God out loud that he was all right. The attendants stood in the doorway, blocking any exit.

Ray gripped Tommy's shoulder. "You OK, Chief?" This time Ray studied the guards, their physiques, way of walking, how concentrated they were. If he could just get out of the room . . .

Tommy wiped his eyes, "Did I do it wrong, Mom?"

Andi held him tightly. "You didn't do anything wrong, honey. What could you think was wrong?"

"I just—I don't know. I just thought I must have done something wrong."

"You did nothing wrong, honey. Nothing. Understand?"

He nodded his head, though not with any real confidence.

The guards closed the door again. When their footsteps had faded away, Ray went to the small window, looked at the lock again. Then he turned to Tommy, "Still have the Swiss Army knife, Chief?"

Tommy appeared confused a moment, then touched his pocket. "They didn't check me for anything."

Tommy handed him the knife and Ray pulled out the tiny tweezers and the toothpick in the handle. He edged the toothpick in the cleft between the bolt and the jambhole. It was too thick and stopped. He tried the tweezers. They were thinner, but not thin enough. He started to pull them apart, then an idea hit him.

"What are you doing?" Andi said, still flushed with anger.

Ray reached into his pocket and pulled out the business card. "This is what I'm doing."

He handed it to her. On the front was the name of a local appliance company. On the back was a neat, printed script. "You must escape. Croase plans to keep the boy."

Andi stared at it a moment, then handed it back to Ray, her hand shaking. Her face clouded over, but she stifled the tears. "Where did you find it?"

"It was on the floor just inside the door before you came in. I don't know whether someone pushed it under while I was waiting or what."

"Who might have done it?"

"I don't know. But the kind of printing—I've worked with Japanese people before—they print English like that."

"The Japanese doctor?"

"Maybe. I don't know."

"What is it?" Tommy asked.

"Our ticket out of here," Andi said quickly, handing the card back to Ray. "What are you thinking, Ray?"

"Give me a minute," he said striding over to the counter. Sitting on it were several canisters of cotton balls, packets of Band-Aids, sterile pads. He took out a roll of white adhesive tape, glanced at the door jamb again. It was white, close to the same color.

He walked back across the room and pulled the chair across, setting it up against the wall. He bent the tweezers open, then taped them straddling the edge of the jamb on the wall side. "When they open the door, the tweezer will push into the bolthole. The bolt won't be able to slide back in," he told them. "If they don't notice. That's why you're gonna sit here on the chair, Chief, and pretend you've fainted." He moved the chair to the back wall.

Tommy glanced at Andi, then grinned mischievously. "I feel like a spy." He sat down.

Ray said to Andi, "You stand in front of him, kneeling. It'll divert them."

"What if it doesn't work?" Tommy asked.

"It'll work. Or we'll come up with something else. But we have to try something fast. Now when I call the guard, this is what happens." He explained his plan, and Tommy and Andi listened intently.

"Let's do it," Andi said with finality.

Ray gave Tommy another hard look. "You ready, Chief?"

Tommy nodded. He leaned forward into the position. Ray rapped on the glass lightly. He waited. He rapped harder. Then harder. A moment later, he glanced back at Andi. "They're coming." He prayed that God would come through. *Just get us out of this, Lord. Don't let anyone get hurt.*

There was a sound of buttons being pushed, and the door cracked open. "We have a gun," the raspy voice said. "You get back from the door."

"The boy fainted," Ray said as he stepped back, raising his arms. "We need some orange juice. He's slightly hypoglycemic."

The man stepped in, gun drawn. There was someone else behind him also with a gun. "Watch the guy," the man said. "Step back against the wall."

Andi said, "Lift your head up, honey."

The guard bent down and looked into Tommy's eyes, while the other man kept his pistol trained on Ray. Andi placed her hand on Tommy's knee. The guard stood up. "OK, I'll get you some orange juice. Come on, Bill."

The first man ambled out, and Bill backed out behind him. As the door shut there was no click. Ray sprang to the door, looking out. The other guard swaggered off down the hall. "All right, he's going. Now we have to do this fast." He handed Andi two rolls of gauze. "When I say to hand me these, be ready. I'll take out the other guard. Soon as we get into the hall, we look for a stairway or an elevator. They might not expect an elevator."

"You're going to kill him?" Tommy said, his eyes wide.

Ray suddenly grinned. "No, Chief, this isn't the movies. I'll just bust him once and get his gun. Quick. It's an easy move, and so long as he doesn't see us coming, he won't make a sound. Remember the SEALs' main strategy: surprise. It works every time. Now get ready to move fast and catlike."

Pulling open the door to make sure the tweezer had caught the bolt, Ray stood at the window, scrutinizing the guard in the hall. Twice he pulled back from the window, waiting. Then he crept back up to the wired glass.

"OK," he whispered, "I go first. Wait here till you see I have him."

He opened the door slowly, effortlessly, without sound, palming the bolt from clicking. The guard stood with his back to them, leaning over the desk and reading something. Ray moved quietly toward him.

Ray got around the desk. Then his shoe squeaked.

The guard turned. Ray knew the move perfectly. He'd used it a hundred times in training and once in Panama. He came up under the guard's chin with his right elbow, smacking him in the jaw. The guard's head jerked back. Then Ray jabbed him in the back of the neck with his left hand, buckling him over. As the man fell, Ray grabbed the pistol handle and pulled it from the holster. Fortunately, the guard hadn't snapped the strap.

Then Ray gestured to Andi. *The gauze.*

She and Tommy scurried out, crouching. She gave him the gauze. Ray had the gun at the man's back. He jammed one roll of gauze in his mouth, then began wrapping his mouth and head with the second strip. After several wraps, he cut it with Tommy's knife and then wrapped up the man's hands behind his back. Ray sensed Andi looking at him in amazement and he said, "What?"

"You're so smooth."

Ray stood the man up. "We're not home yet." Then he said to the guard, "You're going in the room. No noise," he said low. He poked the gun barrel into the guard's back. "Andi, you and Tommy scope out the floor." He pointed the opposite way the guard had gone. "There has to be a way out."

He pushed the guard into the room, knocking him onto the floor. Then he ripped off the tweezer in the latch and closed the door. He held the gun up, one hand clutching it, another supporting, and looked in both directions. Ray saw Andi motion to a door. "An exit," she stage whispered.

"Good."

They started toward it. But then they heard someone whistling.

"Quick," Ray whispered. "Back down the hall."

They hid in an alcove in front of another office door and waited. Whoever it was didn't say anything. Down the hall to their left, something dinged. The elevator. Ray motioned to Andi to get down. The guard who went after the orange juice stepped out and went back up toward the guard station.

"Into the elevator," Ray said. They all hurried out, catching the elevator just as the doors began to close. The guard didn't seem to hear them.

The elevator doors closed. Ray looked up. The sign read "11."

"We go to eight and get off. Pray that it doesn't stop at ten or nine."

"Why eight?" Andi asked.

He chuckled. "My lucky number. We can't risk it stopping with a whole group getting on. Everyone flatten against the front wall till I look out."

The elevator stopped. The doors began sliding open. Ray saw someone in white go by, her back to them. He said, "This is the floor with the sending room. I can see it. Down to six."

He hit the button. The elevator ground again with a squeaking noise. Ray realized he was settling in now, he wasn't as nervous or afraid. It was an old feeling. Adrenaline replaced anxiety with sharp thinking and inner confidence. He just hoped it would last.

The elevator slowly creaked to a halt. The doors opened. Ray peered out. "OK. Tiptoe. Quiet now."

They stepped out. Ray turned to the left.

"The exit was that way." Andi pointed.

Ray nodded and raised his hand to calm her. "Just looking. I want to remember where we are."

He gestured to Andi and Tommy to head back down the hall. He kept looking back as they skulked down the hall in a quarter crouch. They reached the exit door with no encounter. Ray guarded their rear. Andi opened it quietly, stuck her head in.

"Clear."

They all hurried inside, closing it behind them.

"We go all the way to the basement," Ray said. "There's a loading dock down there I've seen from a distance, and I think a garage. It's our best chance. Let me lead. Quietly now."

Tommy had beads of sweat on his face, and his glasses had steamed. Andi patted his back and said, "You're all wet."

"Yeah."

They dashed down the stairs. It was a two-tier system, each floor having one turn and each length half a floor, about eight steps. The steps had metal edges and a rubber inlay. They were quieter than usual. The medicinal smell of the hallways vanished. The stairwells were cool. A mildewy smell rose from the lower floors.

They descended four flights. The exit door read "2." Andi and Tommy were already moving down the next flight,

202

but another idea hit Ray. He grabbed Andi at the shoulder. "Wait a minute."

Mother and son stopped and blinked under the stair lights.

Ray pulled open the door, and they rushed out into the dark hall. It was a row of offices. Ray said, "Find an open door. Hurry."

Ray tried several doors, but they were all locked. Then down the hall he heard Tommy. "Here!"

Ray whipped around and joined them at a door with a plaque that said "Dr. William Matthews."

"Get inside," Ray said, his gun up again, swiveling back and forth in both directions. "Let's get something, anything to smoke this place," he said. "Anything for evidence."

He told Tommy to watch the hallway with the door cracked. Inside was a secretary's office and behind it another door. Ray turned on the desk light and laid the guard's revolver on the blotter. He had Andi stand in front of the light to block it. He rifled through the papers inside the "in" and "out" boxes and glanced at them, then shoved the whole pile into Andi's hands. "Hold it for a minute," he said and tried the desk drawers. They were locked. He turned around and cranked the handle on the door behind them. It was open.

The office was dark, but a back window was lit enough by parking lot dome lights that they could see. Ray glanced out the window and saw several people scurrying around. They had dogs on leashes.

Andi gasped. "Ray, they've got German shepherds."

As he opened a gray filing cabinet, he said, "Good, take it all in. You may have to lead us out of here. We may have to hot-wire a car or something. But I don't have any tools."

"Who will do that?" Andi asked nervously, still peering down into the parking lot with the papers in her hands.

Ray looked up and chuckled. "I was counting on you for that one."

"Don't joke, Ray, please."

He returned to the filing cabinet, glad for the moment that the fear hadn't returned. There wasn't much light. "I can't read the print on the dividers," he said.

"Just take a whole sheaf of them," Andi suggested, still peering into the parking lot. "I see four armed guards, two in a guard station at the entrance gate. The whole lot is bordered by a cyclone fence. Two other guards are walking up and down along the fence with flashlights, and the dogs."

"Keep watching," Ray said.

"They don't seem to know we've escaped," she said.

"They will soon enough," Ray answered, pulling out the files. "We need something to carry them in."

Andi held up some Tyvek envelopes she found on top of a filing cabinet. "What about these?"

Ray grabbed them, stuffing files into one. Andi opened the other one and jammed her papers into it. Seconds later, Ray piled most of it into her arms, and they hurried out of the office. "Everything still clear, Chief?"

The boy was still at the door, looking out. "Nobody."

As Ray picked up the gun, Andi touched his arm. "Should we really take that?"

He thought briefly, then said, "Croase is playing for keeps, Andi. We already know too much. We have that note. What more do we need? Now we're burglars. They'll shoot to kill, I'm sure of it."

Then a fire alarm went off in the hall as Ray opened the door.

"OK, they know," he cried above the brattle of the alarm. No one appeared in the corridor, though, and they reached the stairwell again without incident. In a moment, they were running down toward the lower floors three steps at a time. Ray called to Andi and Tommy, "Move it. They don't know where we are yet."

Andi yelled to Ray, "Slow down. Someone will fall."

Ray stopped on a landing, breathing harder. It said "LL." Lower level. There were still at least two more floors. He cracked the door as Andi and Tommy made the last turn down. As they hit the landing, he closed it quietly. "It's not the parking garage. Let's keep going down."

The next floor read "G." "This has to be it." More stairs went further down, but Ray wasn't sure where they might go. He cracked open the door.

In the stairwell it was quieter, and above them there was the scrape of a door opening. At least six floors up. Several voices echoed in the stairwell.

"You go down, Pete. I'm going up."

"Up? What's up? They wouldn't go up."

"Croase says so."

Ray flattened against the wall and motioned to Andi and Tommy to do the same. Then he cautiously opened the door. There were a number of cars parked in rows. Big gray beams and girders. The stairwell had two doors and turned out to be an island in the middle of a big parking and docking area. They stayed down and moved quietly behind a blue Chevy parked just beyond the stairwell. To their left was a row of loading docks and an office, lights out. They could hear the man on the stairs. Andi whispered, "We have to hide or something."

Ray nodded. "Just let me get my bearings." He handed the rest of the papers to her and to Tommy. The boy crouched by Ray, peering at the gun in his hand. Ray didn't want to shoot anyone, but if he had to, he would. This was no time to argue war and peace. He glanced at Andi. Her face flickered rank terror and for a moment he thought of just giving themselves up. But for what?

No, they had to go all the way.

As he listened to the man moving cautiously down the stairwell, he suddenly noticed his hand shaking. He looked up, and Andi was gazing at his hand, too.

"It'll be OK," he whispered, and they went through the door into the garage. Before him a parked car had mud-spattered wheels. Brown, hard mud. Like the mud of Paitilla Runway.

Suddenly, Paitilla Airport was in Ray's mind. He could see his two friends cut down by machine gun fire. Lying there. Dead. Gone.

The mental picture riveted him in place, and he lost his breath.

Andi grabbed his arm. "Ray, are you OK?"

He felt dizzy, but he turned to her. "It's nothing. I'm—" He fought for concentration. Images rushed at him. It was all going to be taken away. He would lose Andi and Tommy just as he'd lost everything else.

"No," he murmured.

"Ray!"

Andi stood in front of him, her hands on his jacket. He was leaning back against the wall. Then her face came into focus. Ray blinked. Finally the vision was gone.

"Ray! What's going on?"

He swallowed, caught his breath. "It's all right. Just a flashback, I guess."

"We have to get going, Ray. Please, are you all right?"

He felt the concentration coming back. His mind cleared. He sucked down a long draft of air. "OK, I just—I don't know. Afraid for a second."

"We're all afraid."

"Yeah. Let's go." He started toward the cars, refusing to look again at the mud-caked wheels. But inside his mind, something was screaming that it was happening all over again. They would be taken away. God would take them away, just as He'd taken his mother, his father, his two best friends.

2

Ray told himself it was just a feeling; it was not real. He groped inside for courage, for determination, and he found something in a phrase of Christ: "I am with you always." He whispered as they stood looking down the long garage aisles, "I'm counting on that, Lord."

A loading dock stood to their left. The alarm was still blaring away. Ray motioned in the direction of the dock and said, "That way!" They hurried across the dusty floor in a crouch, keeping behind the cars as best they could. At the far end to their right was a single door, about fifty yards away. Ray pointed to several small boxes beside each door on the loading dock.

"Computer locks," he yelled. "They don't open unless you punch in the number. And the docks might be four or five feet up for tractor-trailers to back up to. I think our best chance is the far door."

Andi nodded, still watching Ray with wide, frightened eyes. He grabbed her hand. "I'm OK. It was just a sudden memory. I'm OK, I promise."

She shook her head. "I trust you," she said.

"OK, I think we're gonna have to steal a car to get out."

Tommy said, "How do we steal a car?"

"There might be one with keys in it. Or I might be able to hot-wire an older one, but I don't see anything old enough. So I'm thinkin' we'll just have to look for one with keys. That means all three of us moving fast. We'll have to split up. Think you can handle it?"

"What about the man on the stairs?" Andi said.

The alarm was so loud, Ray could hardly think. "Yeah, that's the other thing. I'm thinking I may just have to take him out. But we don't have time to worry about it. Just stay down, keep moving. He won't see us in here easily. And with this alarm screeching he won't hear us."

"OK."

Ray hurried toward the loading dock. He peered into the cars, but suddenly he noticed five body bags lying in front of one of the doors. Andi and Tommy scurried about among the other cars further in. Ray gazed at the body bags. He suddenly prayed it wasn't as bad as it looked.

He crept over and unzipped the side of the first of the blue and gray bags. Gray hair came into view, then an older man's grizzled face with several days growth of beard. A stench jabbed Ray's nostrils. He swallowed back a rush of bile into his throat. The man's complexion was green-gray with rigor mortis. "Please tell me these people weren't used in their experiments," he murmured.

He considered taking one of the bodies with them. But he knew he didn't have time. He zipped the bag back up, then moved in a crouch back among the cars. If he could get a body, that would prove it.

Ray wove in and out among the cars. They were all locked. Then Tommy popped up. "Mom!"

Ray looked in his direction. Tommy pointed to a little office, unlit, in the back that they hadn't seen. Andi motioned to Ray.

The office door was locked, but inside they could see a board with keys hanging from hooks. Each set had a tag with a license plate number and the make. "Must be some of the TWI cars," Ray said.

Then behind them a voice called out. "Hold it!"

Ray saw him in the window reflection with his gun drawn. He whispered to Andi and Tommy, "Get ready to fall to the ground."

The man yelled again, "Hands up!"

"Go!" Ray shouted. Andi and Tommy hit the deck. Ray rolled to their right, jumped up, and fired. The guard exploded backwards, his gun firing off into the air above them. Ray ran over and checked his neck pulse. The man was still alive. He grabbed the second gun. The guard's shirt turned red with blood at the shoulder.

"Don't kill me," he whimpered.

"Stay right there, and you're all right. Otherwise . . ." Ray strapped him to a bumper with the guard's gun belt. The alarm continued to screech above them.

Ray ran back to Andi and Tommy. Pointing the guard's gun at the office door, he fired into the window. Three shots. Three holes. Then with the muzzle Ray knocked it in and opened the door. With one swift motion, he grasped several sets of keys from the racks.

He threw three to Andi, two to Tommy. "First one who finds a match gets a vacation to Disney World," he said. They ran back to the lot searching for the car.

Tommy found one first. It was a Cadillac Ray remembered seeing on campus. They jumped inside, and Ray turned the ignition. The engine rolled over but didn't catch. Andi watched the stairwell island.

Two men ran out the door from the side. One pointed to the guard, the other peered down the row. Andi screamed from the back seat, "They see us."

The engine caught. Ray yelled, "Get down." He'd have to forget about taking one of the bodies now.

The Caddy squealed out of the space, backing into the main causeway to the garage door. One of the men crouched and fired. A neat hole sent glass spraying into the car. Andi and Tommy huddled in the back seat.

Ray hit the gas. The long car lurched forward toward the back door. From another stairwell on the left, three other men ran out, firing. The backseat side glass broke, pelting Andi and Tommy with more glass, but the window didn't shatter. More bullets punctured the sides of the auto. In the back, Andi clutched Tommy as they crouched on the floor.

The gray aluminum door loomed up before them like a mountain. But there was no time to wait for the switch to send it upward. Ray hoped the rollers and bearings in the rails that guided the door were thin enough to snap without destroying the car in the process. With a cry to God, he plowed the car into the big metal roll-up door, blasting it off its hinges. The door flipped up in front of them, and they slid out underneath it, cracking the front windshield further, but not breaking it.

Ray hauled the steering wheel to the right, and the car careened into the passageway to the main gate. A man with a rifle or shotgun aimed at them as they hurtled towards him. Only a lever gate stood between them and freedom. When Andi popped up behind him, Ray clapped his arm on her and pushed her down, then ducked himself.

The pellets exploded into the glass. The windshield sent small rectangles of the shatterproof window all over over them and the front seat. A third of the window was gone in the middle. Another blast cracked into the right front and a headlight went out.

Ray sat up just in time to whip the wheel to the right and avoid skidding into a field across from the entrance.

They were on the main road.

Mashing the gas again, they hurtled down in the dark. The lone headlight cut the road ahead of them with a searing beam. Past the Bible college. Past the seminary. Cold air blew through the front hole riffling Ray's hair. Bits and pieces of glass rattled away off the hood. Andi climbed into the front seat. Ray had his eyes fixed ahead, and she said, "Is everything OK?" He turned.

"I got hit a little," he said.

Andi stifled a scream. The whole left side of his face was cut and bleeding.

"Glass," he said. "Just ripped me a little." Blood dripped off his chin onto his jacket and shirt.

Tommy popped up behind them. The car sped along at nearly eighty miles an hour.

Ray said, "Watch behind us. See if any headlights come into view. Only someone after us will seem to be catching up."

As Tommy turned around, he looked in the rear mirror to see if anyone was in pursuit. Andi seemed to be looking for something next to him in the glove compartment and under the seat. He handed her one of the guns. "Can you shoot it?"

"I don't know."

"All you do is aim and pull the trigger. Just shooting it may scare anyone after us."

"What about your face?"

"Don't worry about that. Get in the back seat. It you see someone trying to catch us, let me know."

As the wind poured through the holes, Ray thought everyone had to be freezing. He hit the heater switch and a fan came on. Soon warm air began blowing over his legs.

He swerved around a bend and could no longer see TWI. The car slowed down to just under sixty miles an hour on a road whose limit was thirty-five.

Andi crawled into the back seat after handing Tommy the gun. He held it gingerly, like one might hold a fish.

"Where are we going?" Tommy asked.

"Depends if anyone follows us," Ray answered. He braked for a curve and glanced in the mirror again. No headlights had appeared. "Maybe we're really out of it," he said and pressed the accelerator up to eighty on a straightaway.

Strock and Hughes knew about the alert before the alarm bells went off. They were on first floor security and immediately began checking stairwells, elevators, offices. First, they began going up, since they knew the escapees had started out on the eleventh floor. But then Strock said, "Let's get out to the back lot."

"Why?" Hughes had his .44 Smith and Wesson semiautomatic already in his hand. "I feel a kill. Three kills."

"They want the boy, man. Cool down. No one dies. Let's get out to the lot."

"They're in the building."

Strock shook his head. "Do you ever think about anything? If they get out they'll go to the lot. If they don't, we have them anyway. But if they get out, we're gonna be there."

Hughes nodded. His lanky hair draped over his forehead. His handlebar mustache was out of line, the handlebars bent slightly. He clicked back the hammer on the .44. "Got to be ready anyway. It's two bodies for Willard. Four K this week."

Strock pushed past him. "Let's take the elevator."

When they reached the lot, the guards were in full alert, crossing the parking lot back and forth with the dogs.

"Croase is an idiot," Strock said. Croase had insisted on training the whole security force, even though Strock had been hired specifically for that task. To Strock's mind Croase had no idea how to secure a building, or keep people either from escaping or getting in. Croase wanted them to take only "special assignments"—like disposing of bodies. That took special attention, and it paid more. So Strock hadn't minded. Hughes always went along with him. Still, it irked him that Croase had to be in charge of everything.

"Let's get into your Toyota," Strock said.

Hughes had a blue Toyota Celica GT. Fairly fast. Nothing like a Nissan 300 ZX, Corvette, or anything sporty. But it held the road well. They'd been in two chases in it, and though it was beat up, Hughes knew how to handle it on a high speed run.

The Toyota was parked in the middle of the lot at the far end from the front gate. Hughes and Strock were dashing across the asphalt to it when the garage door exploded behind them.

Strock whipped around and swore. "It's them. Let's go."

211

Hughes fired twice at the careening Cadillac, but he was a good forty yards away. It skidded out from under the garage door and screeched to the right directly for the front gate. Both he and Strock could see nothing would stop them now from going through.

They ran for the Toyota. Hughes was faster and had the door open before Strock reached it, panting.

"They went to the right, up Simmering. They may be going for 108. We've got to catch them before they make the turn."

Hughes floored it backwards, then forward toward the gate. Already dogs were barking and security officers running all over the place. Hughes didn't even try to navigate through the mess. He lay on the horn and barreled out. Anyone in his way was dead. Fortunately, no one tried to argue with the wheel-squealing Toyota. They were out the front gate in less than a minute.

Ray spotted the Route 108 sign at the T of Simmerling and the main road as they came up on it, still cruising at seventy miles an hour. He slammed on the brakes and slowed quickly. It was a green highway sign with a State Route 108 insignia and two arrows above it, one pointing to the right, west, and the other left.

"Route 108 goes up into Olney and Columbia," Andi said. "Do you know anyone up there?"

"Yeah. Doc Kingston."

"Should we go to him?"

"Depends on if someone follows us or not. If we get free, it might be safe for a few hours, enough time to get some sleep and think. But—"

Ray glanced one more time in the mirror. Headlamps shone just around the last bend. He flicked off his lights. "Please don't let them have seen me," he said.

Suddenly he realized he had on his turn signal. He hit the lever and murmured, "So much for learning the rules of the road," then flung dirt and stones into the air as the Cadillac whipped around left onto 108. With the accelerator on the floor, the huge 550 cubic engine bounded up the two lane road. They sped past a small tavern on their right and a small road on the right. The speed limit was fifty, but Ray was up to eighty in twenty seconds.

He still had his headlights off, and as the road passed fields and trees, it was too hard to see. He had to turn them on. Just as he hit the lights, he saw headlamps behind him. Far back. But he knew it was them.

"Andi, get down. Both of you. They might start firing."

"But how can I shoot at them if I'm down?"

"Don't worry about it. Just stay down." He glanced back at her.

She sat on her knees and looked out the window. The left side was partly shattered, so she could stick the barrel of the .38 through it.

"Andi! Get—"

"Shut up! I'm in this too."

Ray swore, but he said, "All right, it has five shots left. Don't waste anything. Try to hit a front tire or headlamp. Wait till we're on a straightaway or something smooth. But don't shoot unless they start it."

As she looked out the back window, Tommy said, "Do you know how to shoot a gun, Mom?"

Andi answered, "Just get down, honey," and pressed his head toward the seatwell.

In the left side mirror, Ray could see the car was still a good fifty yards back, but it was obviously speeding close to what Ray was doing.

A mile clicked off. Then another. Ray swerved and slowed, keeping the car on the road. He saw Andi trying to aim the gun, keeping her head just above the back seat. He knew the sight was probably jumping all over the place. They needed a straightaway. And no bumps.

Houses appeared in Ray's lights on the right and left. Olney. "Don't let there be any cars, God," he murmured and braked, then accelerated. There was a stoplight at Route 97. It had just turned red and a truck and several cars sat idling in both lanes, both directions. The car behind them was gaining.

Ray braked as he came toward the intersection. As the car slowed to thirty he knew he couldn't go between them. He swerved right onto Georgia Avenue. "See if you guys can do that," he yelled.

The Cadillac skidded and the back came around with a squeal, but he kept it on the road. He looked at the median strip in the middle to his left. He knew he couldn't make a U-turn. But maybe . . .

He pulled the wheel left and cracked into the median strip, then hurtled over it with two heavy crunches. Over, they burst into a medical center across the road.

When he saw there was nowhere to go, Ray jammed the brakes, screeching the tires.

He looked left and right. Frantic, he searched the lot and spotted a cul-de-sac to his right into a service station. He whipped the wheel and turned into it. The big car bounced on the curb as he came around.

□ □ □

Behind Ray, Hughes fought with the wheel of the Toyota trying to keep it on the road. "I thought this guy was a minister, man!" he yelled. He turned onto Georgia Avenue thirty yards behind Ray and saw him jump the median strip.

"This is gonna tear out the transmission," he said and swore again.

Strock had his gun out and his window open. "Just give me a clear shot, and I'll blow their tires."

The Toyota bounced over the median strip. Already, the Cadillac was turning into the Mobil station.

"Where are they going?" Hughes screamed.

"Away from us, jerk!" Strock yelled back, trying to aim at the right window of the Cadillac.

□ □ □

Sweat sogged Ray's shirt. His only thought was to get away, but terror gripped him. He only hoped he would spot a policeman. But the streets were nearly deserted.

214

He veered around the Mobil station into a side street. It was straight, and the moment he turned into it, he floored the car again. With the huge Cadillac engine cranking in, it felt like the whole tread of the tire shredded off. But the car hurled itself forward. There was a Safeway shopping center down to the right and another road to the left. "Back to 108," Ray said and wrenched the wheel left. As the car came around again, for a moment he couldn't see anyone behind him.

He flicked the lights out again and shot down the little side street. Without even looking to the left, he curved onto it, careful not to stamp on the brakes and show his lights again.

After Hughes skidded around the Mobil Station, he lost the Caddie completely. He knew they had to go straight, but they must have turned. "That moron must have turned out his lights again."

"Just go straight," Strock yelled, searching the lots ahead for signs of red taillights. "They can't have gone far."

They scorched down the straightaway. To their left was a street, to their right the shopping center. "Did they go in there?" Hughes shouted, pointing to the Safeway.

Strock looked back and forth frantically. Then he roared, "Just stop!"

The car halted, skidding on the gravel, as Hughes crunched the brake.

"OK, listen."

A second later they heard the tires to their left.

"Down the street," Strock shouted, pointing the gun. "They're back on 108."

They reached it just in time to see the Cadillac disappearing under a streetlight to their right. Hughes was back on the main drag in a second.

Ray turned the lights on again as the road darkened into trees and fewer houses. Up ahead was another curve and a semi. He saw the headlights come up behind him again just as he reached the back of the rig.

He jammed the accelerator and barreled around the truck as it slowed down into a Y intersection at the Olney Theater. A flashing yellow light told Ray he had to make a fast decision, and he yelled back at Andi, "Hold on!"

The force flung her against the door as Ray came around the truck. Someone was approaching on the left, but far enough up for Ray to get around. "That'll cut them off," he yelled. He pulled back over into the right-hand lane and pressed the accelerator to gain speed around the curve.

Then he heard a horn blaring behind him. The Toyota was coming around the truck too. Then Ray saw a car coming at him in the left lane.

"Please, God, do something," Ray mumbled. "Do it!"

Ray knew it would be head on. Hughes couldn't pull back into the right lane in time. But then the approaching car careened off into the woods and came to a stop up against a tree.

"They're still behind us," Andi yelled again.

Ray swerved back and forth, trying to keep on the hilly, winding road out of Olney. He prayed for a cop to show up, but none appeared. The Toyota was still on his tail, but slowly a plan hardened in his mind. He needed a curve and something else. Maybe a bridge. The signs might show it in time for him to get ready. He was sure there was one up ahead. He'd traveled this road enough up to the Doc's.

A bullet shattered what was left of the back windshield when the Toyota got close enough, about thirty yards behind them. Andi got off one shot.

Ray shouted, "Just stay down, Andi. Don't try to shoot, it's useless."

Andi fired off another bullet. "No way, I'm nailing these jerks!" She fired twice more, and the Toyota fell back.

Ray called out of the side of his mouth, "OK, good job, that'll keep them back. But wait till they get closer. And stay lower. You've only got one bullet left. And I only have two in my .38."

They sped through Sandy Spring and Ashton with the Toyota firing off several more rounds, all thunking into the

216

dirt, sparking off the asphalt, or cracking into the rear end of the Cadillac. Ray heard one strike the trunk. He knew their only chance was a two-lane bridge or something like it, but he still wasn't sure where it was. He murmured again, "Lord, this is up to You. Please do something. Don't let me make any bad decisions. No bad decisions."

The sense of fear only heightened, and he gripped and ungripped the wheel nervously. Still, the plan looked good. But he had to get Andi and Tommy up front in time. They would have to get out of the car.

Behind him Ray heard a crash and felt something graze the top of his head. The bullet exited through the roof.

He ducked instinctively, then yelled, "That does it!"

Andi fired off her last shot. Ray called to them. "Get up front, both of you."

When she hesitated, he grabbed her arm. "Hurry."

Tommy dumped over the back into the front seat, and Andi fell into the corner a moment later when they were on patch of straight road.

"Get ready to jump out," Ray yelled above the wind. "Just throw open the door, roll out, and then run to the front of the car and keep running. Got it?"

"What are you going to do?"

"Stop these jerks once and for all."

You're going to lose both of them.

Ray swore as another bullet cracked into the rear end. Then he saw a sign. "Curve. 25 MPH." Below it was the two parallel H lines for a bridge. His heart boomed like a pile driver.

"It's gotta do it," Ray mumbled and looked into the mirror. The Toyota disappeared momentarily as Ray veered into the curve. "They may rear end us," he shouted above the wind. "But we can take a hit. They can't. Just get ready to bolt. Is the door unlocked?"

Andi hit the electronic button. There was a loud click.

You're going to lose both of them!

Ray swallowed as he slowed to sixty and the tires shrieked on the curve. "Just hold, that's all I ask," he whispered. The bridge came into his lights. He had to stop right in the middle. Andi and Tommy poised to jump out.

Then he stomped on the brakes. The Cadillac's antilocking system kept the car going straight. As the car ground to a complete stop in the middle of the concrete bridge, Ray threw the wheel left so that the rear was angled at the impact end. When he turned around, the Toyota was already deep into the curve above them, its tires squealing.

He threw open the door, jumped out, and aimed the revolver. Andi's door was already open, and she and Tommy piled out onto the road, then got up.

"Run!" Ray yelled.

She grabbed Tommy's hand and pulled him forward.

"Just get one tire," Ray told himself. He sighted down the barrel.

The Toyota lost some control then regained it.

"Please, God, just one shot."

The right front tire came into Ray's sight. He squeezed.

"Do it now!"

The gun exploded. He fired again. Then he turned and leaped forward in a tight roll. He was back on his feet as the wheels shrieked behind him.

☐ ☐ ☐

When Hughes hit the brakes, the Toyota was already in a skid. The car lurched first left, then right. But he held it, then pulled it back onto the road. They'd be OK. Then he saw the Caddy stopped in the middle of the bridge. He swore loudly.

A moment later, flame leaped out of the darkness ahead of them. There was an explosion under the wheel well. The Toyoto swerved to the right. The steering wheel spun in his hand.

"He got the tire!" Strock screamed.

All Hughes tried to do was keep the car from colliding directly with the bridge. Strock listed up against him. The right side of the concrete wall loomed up before them. For a moment, Hughes thought he saw Ray's face looking back at him.

Then they shot toward the side of the bridge. With a sickening tearing of metal they bashed into it sideways, and crashed through the trees into the creek. Hughes flew forward, his head cracking on the top of the steering wheel.

The moment Ray realized the Toyota had crashed into the creek, he yelled to Andi and Tommy, now halfway up the bridge. "Get back in! We got them." He jumped back into the Cadillac and rolled it up to them. They settled back into the front seat, breathing hard. He heard no cries for help, but he couldn't be suckered into that. The driver might be just alive enough to shoot them.

He was halfway up the hill when Tommy whooped. "You did it! You got them."

Andi peered back, then slumped forward, her hand on the dashboard, still gripping the empty .38. "Now I know why you were a SEAL," she said, looking at him sideways. Ray simply kept his eyes on the road, fighting to sketch out another plan.

His heart was hammering so hard he could barely breathe. He knew this was only the beginning. Either they had to go to the police or the FBI, or hide until they decided on a next step.

More important, what would Croase do? If anything, Croase was smart, very smart, and he knew how to take care of problems like this easily and quickly.

The FBI seemed like the best option. But was this something in their jurisdiction? He didn't know. And would they believe him? He knew the first thing was to look at the files, see what he had to prove their story. That was the problem. It was such an incredible story. What might be worse would be going to the police or the FBI with only their story, then the authorities' checking it out, finding nothing seriously wrong because Croase virtually controlled the campus and what they would say, and then everyone's writing off Ray and Andi as nut cases. He couldn't let that happen.

As Ray slowed the car down to a reasonable speed, Andi said, her voice still quavering, "Do you think Dr. Kingston can do anything?"

219

"I don't know," Ray answered sharply.

"Ray, we're out of it."

"No, we aren't. This is only the beginning."

Andi stared at him, then looked away. Ray sensed that he had hurt her. He touched her hand. It was quivering. "I'm sorry. Just still pumping adrenaline, I guess."

"It's OK." He let go and noticed his hands were sore from gripping the steering wheel.

Tommy sat between them shivering even though the heat continued pouring out below onto their legs.

"Is your face still bleeding?" Andi asked.

Ray touched his left cheek. "No. It's dry." As the night enclosed them with only the dash lights on inside, he had the feeling of passing through space at tremendous speeds. His back was soaked with sweat. But gradually, a calm came over him. His mind uttered, *Thanks,* but suddenly he didn't know whether that was a practiced reaction or a genuine feeling. He wanted to hit someone.

In the silence, he heard Andi say, "Are you OK, Ray?"

He shook his head. "Yeah." He glanced at her anxiously, then noticed a road sign for Columbia. Three miles. He felt calmer, but a voice inside him seemed to gain the momentum lost earlier. *You're going to lose both of them. That's certain.*

Ray swallowed and kept his eyes on the road. It was no time for listening to inner voices. But he knew the message couldn't long be ignored. He had to deal with it once and for all. And soon.

Strock grabbed Hughes's hair and pulled him back from the steering wheel. "You OK, man?"

The bigger man murmured, then opened his eyes. "We cracked up?"

"Yeah," Strock said, pushing open his door. "The minister got us. Come on, we've got to get out of here. I don't feel like being caught with a concealed deadly weapon and have to explain how we ended up in this creek."

Hughes's door was mashed in. They both crawled out the right side. The creek lapped cold water onto their knees.

"Let's find an empty house and call Croase," Strock said. "This really stinks."

Hughes dazedly followed him. The front of his face was matted with blood.

☐ ☐ ☐

Andi kept looking anxiously at Ray. She laid her arm over Tommy's shoulders, and he leaned against her. Her mind was a flurry of zigzagging thoughts and impressions. She didn't understand why Ray was suddenly so quiet. Finally, she said, "Ray, please tell me what you're thinking. I'm still terrified."

"I'm gonna stop and call Dr. Kingston. See what he says. How much money do you have?"

"Nothing. Everything's still back at the house."

"Neither do I. And I don't think we can risk going back there."

"Do you think Dr. Kingston can be trusted?" She wanted to be able to trust someone. But she didn't know Kingston personally. Of her friends at school, most of them already considered the TUT a great scientific and spiritual advance.

Ray answered her, "I think Doc can be trusted to help us. I don't understand why he even teaches at ATS at this point. But I know he'll help us. I really don't think he knows or understands what's happening. He is seventy years old and theoretically retired since he was sixty-five. Croase has only been around for six years, so he may not know much."

"I'll do whatever you say. Let's just go somewhere and catch our breath."

He reached over and touched her shoulder. "I just don't know who to go to beyond Doc."

"What about the police?"

"I'm not sure. What do you think?"

"I'm still so scared, my mind is a frazzle." She looked at his hand. It was almost flopping on her shoulder. "Your hand is shaking, Ray."

He pulled it away.

"I didn't mean that as an insult."

"This got me pretty bad." He glanced at her. In the light, she could see the mat of blood on the left side of his face.

"We've got to take care of your cuts."

"It's OK."

"No, it isn't."

"I'll be all right!"

She stared at him, then fixed her eyes forward. What was wrong with him? Had she done something, said something?

Then he said, "I'm sorry. I'm sorry. Forgive me."

"It's OK." She reached over and patted his knee. "You did more than I could ever ask for. You saved our lives."

"Yeah, but one mistake and we all could have been gone."

"But you didn't make one mistake, Ray."

"Yeah," he muttered with a hint of sarcasm.

She sensed he was fighting an inner battle, and she decided to wait until he wanted to talk.

After a few minutes of silence, Ray spoke again, this time more calmly. "I don't mean to snap at you."

"It's all right."

Tommy breathed quietly in sleep between them.

"It's not all right. I was just—scared."

She decided not to say anything. Ray turned onto Route 29, and she watched as he pulled into a gas station with a pay phone.

□ □ □

A sleepy voice rasped, "Hello," into the phone after Ray let it ring eight times.

"Doc. This is Ray. I'm in big trouble."

"What happened? It's past—" There was a pause. "Ray it's almost 5:00 A.M."

"I know. Doc, some strange things have happened. I need to talk, and I have Andi and her son with me. I also have a shot up Cadillac."

"A shot up Cadillac?"

222

"Doc, TWI is crawling with people who are about as Christian as earthworms."

"What do you mean, Ray?"

"Look, I'll tell you about it. It's really bad. We almost got killed tonight. I don't know exactly what they want from us, but that I think Croase thinks we know too much."

There was a long pause. "What on earth is going on?"

"Look, Doc, I'll explain in a few minutes after I get there. I'm gonna ditch this car, and we'll sneak over to your town house, come in through the back. Check outside and see if there are any familiar faces snooping around, OK?"

"Yes."

"If you see anything weird, turn your back light on and we'll disappear."

"Ray, what—"

"We'll talk in a few minutes."

"All right."

▫ ▫ ▫

They crept through the darkness past the middle school behind Dr. Kingston's town house and waited in a copse of trees. No light came on, so Ray said, "It's OK." Andi carried the files, while Ray held Tommy, still half asleep.

They hurried across an open area and opened the fence in the back into the small patio. A moment later, Ray knocked lightly on the sliding glass door. Kingston appeared in the window after throwing back the curtains. He slid the door open, and everyone stepped inside.

Kingston quickly closed the door and pulled the curtains back in place. With everyone inside, he turned on a light and looked at them.

"My word!" Kingston cried as he stared at Ray's face. "What happened? Should we call a doctor?"

Ray shook his head. "Just some glass scratches. Let me clean it up. By the way, this is Andi Darcasian and her son, Tommy." He went into the kitchen to clean up.

Andi offered her hand, and Dr. Kingston shook it and smiled. She had never talked with Dr. Kingston personally, though she'd taken one of his classes and seen him often enough on campus. Kingston said, "Ray's told me about you. Now that I see you, I remember you in . . ."

"Apologetics. Last year."

"I hope I gave you a good grade."

"B-plus."

He smiled, and Ray walked back in, dabbing a blue washcloth on his face. Tommy stood in the foyer watching. Dr. Kingston impatiently raised his eyebrows and pulled at his chin. "Well, are you going to tell me, or do I need to wait to hear about it on the six o'clock news?"

They all took seats in the living room. It was decorated with fine buff couches, an antique rolltop desk, Tudor table with a valuable-looking local artist's first edition print over it, and several tasteful floor and table lamps.

Ray poured out the story as Kingston hmmed and uh-huhed throughout. He asked pointed questions, took a quick look at the files, and glanced from Ray to Andi and back as they both added details. Tommy lay on the couch with his head on the armrest, obviously fighting off sleep. When Ray was finished, Kingston sighed and said, "I had no idea Croase would go this far. When you told me before—"

"We figured that, Doc," Ray said, shaking his head emphatically. "But how could he pull it off?"

Kingston rubbed his chin and frowned. "When Gordon Watt hired Croase, there was this big push in a lot of religious organizations to entice professional execs to come in and manage the huge hoards of money they were raking in. It was partly because of the scandals, and partly, I don't know. I was against it. But I was against a lot of things. People wouldn't listen to me. I was nearing retirement, and at the time, well, it didn't look like such a bad idea. Croase flew down and gave this terrific testimony. Watt was in his eighties. Gordon controlled virtually everything, with most of the board either being members of his family, or handpicked people who just went along with what Gordon wanted. Now it looks like this guy Croase is showing his true colors."

"Written in blood," Andi said.

Kingston winced. "Do you think we should call the police?"

Ray stood and paced. Andi was glad to see his vigor and determination had returned. "OK, Doc, but we've got a number of problems." He explained about Tommy's "gift." Kingston listened without changing expression. Ray waited for it all to sink in, then he said, "There's one more thing we have to consider, and that's whether there's any danger to the campus."

"You think Croase would use students for the experiments?" Kingston asked.

"He already is."

"But why is he doing it?" Andi said. "He's got the head job at TWI. He's fairly well off. He's got a beautiful wife. He's got everything anyone in his position could want."

Ray shook his head. "People like him always want something more. You know how much Croase gets paid per year, Doc?"

Kingston nodded. "Two hundred thousand, last I heard. Plus a nice bonus."

"Not much!" Ray said.

"Not much!" Kingston almost leaped out of the seat. "You call that—"

"By Croase's standards, not yours." Ray grinned and glanced at Andi. As she watched him talk, she felt a great pride well up within her. He not only made her feel safe, but he had humor and style. She wondered how many women had longed for him to say the magic words to them.

Ray went on, "Then it could have something to do with money. All I'm saying is whatever we do we have to take into account you, Tommy, and the people on campus. That's why we can't sashay in there with a few cops or FBI agents and think we can just arrest Croase. When it comes down to it, all we have is what we've seen and heard. And you know how preposterous it all sounds. We have no real hard evidence."

"But what about the files?" Andi said. They were lying on the table in front of her. She picked up a few and for the next few minutes, everyone examined several.

Finally, Ray said, "They look like personnel files to me. Nothing real incredible. Nothing the police can use. You can't even get a search warrant nowadays without some real evidence."

Ray looked from Andi to Kingston. "Do you both agree?"

After glancing all around at everyone, both Kingston and Andi nodded agreement. Then Andi looked down at Tommy. "Whatever keeps Tommy safe is all I'm concerned about."

"All right," Ray said. "There's one more thing." He looked at Andi. "Your father and mother."

She didn't answer, but looked into her lap.

"Do you think they would help us?" Ray asked.

There was a tense silence. Then Andi said, "So far my dad doesn't know anything. But I don't want to involve my parents. They believed in Gordon Watt and his vision."

Ray's eyes met hers, and for a moment she sensed his sympathy. Then she looked away.

"All right, then we're stuck." He sighed. "Let's get some rest then. But I want to get up at eight and watch the news—see if there's anything about what happened on it."

"Wake me, too," Andi said, yawning and feeling the cool, delicious descent of sleep onto her body.

After realizing Andi, Ray, and the boy might completely escape, Martin Croase went to his office and dialed the number of a local police captain.

"Captain Sellers," Croase said. "We've got a problem."

After hearing the story, Sellers agreed to send out several patrol cars. Then Croase got on the hook to several other parties he knew might be interested in the "burglary" as he was now calling it. When he'd finished, he rubbed his hands and decided to take a quick trip and talk with Benreu. "That should take care of that," he said, laying the piece of paper blotted with TUT on his tongue.

The next thing Andi knew was the click of the TV and Ray standing in front of her. They'd all conked out on the couch. She smelled Ray's warm, coffee-laced breath on her face. "Eight A.M., Andi."

She opened her eyes, as a prim female announcer began speaking on the screen. After reporting on a murder and a fire, the newscaster for Channel 4 zeroed in on TWI. "A local medical research foundation owned and operated by The Watt Foundation was burglarized in the early hours of the morning. Institute officials claim that two people from what they believe may be a cult infiltrated their organization and burglarized them. Police are in search of Raymond Mazaris, a student at the seminary, and Andi Darcasian, a secretary in the financial department. The couple were believed to be connected, possibly romantically involved, and using the school as a cover for cult-directed biotech thievery." The screen flashed pictures of Ray and Andi from the campus directory.

"That's us," Ray said angrily, slapping his hands on his knees and rising. He swore angrily, then stopped and looked at Andi. "Sorry."

She didn't say anything. She was too stunned to speak.

Ray said, "I thought this might happen. They've preempted us."

"Preempted us?" Andi repeated.

"Yeah," Ray said, clicking off the TV. "All tactics. Now we can't go to the police or the news, or so Croase thinks. So I think!" He banged his fist on the wall.

"It's not that bad, Ray," Kingston said.

"Oh, it isn't?" He glared at everyone, then sighed and sat down. "This really stinks."

"Clearly," Kingston said, "you've got to get away from here."

Tommy interjected, "It'll be OK, Mom. We'll be like spies or somethin'."

Andi gave him an irritated look, then turned worriedly to Ray. "Where can we go? I can't take us to one of my parents' condos." Tears welled into her eyes. For the moment, she saw her whole life crumbling. She would lose Tommy, she would end up in jail, and not even God could do a thing about it. Reading about persecution in the Bible was one thing. But having to go through it yourself was quite another. She wiped at her eyes.

Ray suddenly exclaimed, "The Cadillac!"

Everyone looked at him.

He shook his head with exasperation, then pulled on his coat. "Come on, Doc. I have to drive it to the other side of Columbia. They find it here, they'll know we connected with you."

"Good idea," Kingston said, rising. He went to the closet and got on a coat.

"What should we do?" Andi said, walking with Ray to the door.

"Just sit tight, we'll talk about it after I take care of the car and we get a few hours of sleep. We'll be worthless, dead as we are. So let's just hope nothing happens till we can figure out a plan."

When they opened the front door, the cold air made Andi shiver. She watched the two men go out to Kingston's 4x4. Then she closed the door and went back into the living room. Tommy was asleep again.

She stared at the blank TV screen, thinking and trying to pray. A hardness clotted her throat. She liked to think she was independent, tough-minded, and no crybaby. But this was all too much. But as she sat there, a taut resolve gripped her. "All right," she murmured, "whatever happens, I'm going to be a committed and fighting participant in this and not a helpless observer. We're in it together, and together we'll get out of it. All three of us."

She gazed down at Tommy and rested her hand on his side. "Please, God, make this right," she prayed. "We have no one else to turn to."

Her eyes burned slightly and she fought back the tears. "No more crying," she said. "No more tears. This time it's war."

She didn't hear Ray or Kingston come back in.

They were all back up by 2:30 and had a fast dinner of meat loaf sandwiches—one of the women from Kingston's church had given the meat loaf the previous week to the "cause," which was Kingston's way of referring to all the elderly widows in the church who regularly brought him dinners and desserts. With it, they enjoyed some heated-up macaroni and cheese, and homemade root beer, which Kingston received from another friend at church.

After the dinner, they all looked through the files they had stolen. There was nothing in them about the death studies, nothing about clandestine activities, nothing that would prove their case in court or otherwise. The files—over fifty of of them—were enclosed in green hanging file folders, all names of personnel TWI had recently hired or considered hiring. Each manila folder contained data on the person. Just job applications, letters of reference, and so on.

Then Kingston said, "Would you look at this." He handed Ray what appeared to be a question and answer form. Ray began to read. "'Question 4: Do you believe in spiritual life beyond the grave?' This person, let's see, yeah, she's applying for a nurse/counseling position, answers, 'I believe that when we die we are united with all the spiritual entities in the cosmos and have the opportunity to return to earth to do good, or to remain in the spiritual state and help others attain their divine potential.' Doc, this is right out of some of the New Age ideas I've heard."

"Worse," Doc said, "here's another one. 'Are you willing to conform to TWI's principles—monogamy, no use of illegal drugs, no drinking?'" Kingston screwed up his face. "It sounds like Croase was deliberately recruiting people who had certain mystical beliefs but were willing to embrace Christian principles until the campus and organization could be changed. That's positively demonic. It's infiltration."

Andi read from another. "This question says, 'Do you believe in the possibility of "angelic mentoring," i.e., personal contact with a spiritual being ("angel") who will guide your growth and development as a human being?' The person answers that he does not know about such things but is intrigued by the idea."

Ray put down the file. "How could Croase get away with this?"

229

"The same way he got us to take the TUT—at least with campus leaders and people who were in the Watt organization," Andi answered. "By duping them with sweet talk, and if that didn't work, then strong-arming them."

Kingston shook his head angrily. "I should have seen this coming. Do you know how many people have resigned who were originally in the upper levels of the organization? Croase didn't go after the seminary or Bible college people right away, although now I see that he has, especially the people involved in the top administration, the fund-raising, the donor contacts, and of course TWI."

"Why did they keep you then, Doc?"

Kingston sighed. "Because I'm their big-name person. They managed to keep me in the dark, I'd bowed out of a lot of campus politics and functions, and I went on the road, wowing audiences with my oratory gifts."

"You wowed me all right," Ray said.

Kingston shook his head with anger. "That's just it. Sometimes you get caught up in what you're doing for the Lord, and you forget everything else, just riding on the waves of the popularity and acclaim, being on a best-seller list. You get pulled into it. To my shame, that's part of what happened. And then Bea died . . ." Dr. Kingston's voice choked with emotion. "And"—he worked at getting his composure—"I just sort of dropped out. I didn't want to know. Lord, how I've blown it."

The professor's eyes glimmered with tears of pain, and Andi reached across to touch his hand. "It wasn't your fault, Dr. Kingston."

He shook his head with renewed anger. "It's everyone's fault. We think we can let people just go on and on and they'll change in and of themselves. Or we close our eyes to it because it's 'successful.' People are being saved. The ministry is spreading out into the world. Lots of great things are happening. So we begin to think that means God's stamp of approval is on it and anything else that's done that's questionable should just be overlooked."

"You're right, Doc," Ray said, "but what about Watt? We read in a book he didn't believe in hell."

Kingston nodded. "It was a bad period for him. He lost a teenage son—a boy whom we'd really tried to lead to Christ. But Kenneth rejected it all. Then he was killed in a motorcycle accident. It destroyed Gordon. He couldn't believe God would let that boy go to hell. So he just stopped believing in it."

Only the low sound of the television show that Tommy was watching filled the quiet as Kingston talked.

"We talked about it many times. He said to me, 'Hal, I know it's probably heretical. But I've got to tell myself God will do something to save that boy yet. And this is the only thing I can think of.' I know that's a rationalization, Ray"— Kingston looked into Ray's eyes and then blinked—"I know it's a compromise. I compromised about it. Maybe I should have left the seminary then. But at one time, Gordon Watt was a decent man. He had some strange ideas. But—well, I can't try to excuse it. I just thought I should try and help him, not hurl one more firebrand at him by resigning."

"And then?"

Ray listened patiently. He felt in some ways as if his hero was self-destructing before his eyes.

The powerful man's voice rasped with emotion. "He got old, Ray. He should have retired at seventy. But he held on. Seventy-five. Eighty. He started promoting these weird ideas about Christian experience. He had his own death experience during a heart attack. And he became obsessed with it. He said it was ultimate proof of God's existence. He felt that if everyone had that kind of experience, there would be no question about the truth of the message. It was as if Jesus' resurrection was no longer good enough. He was an old man, hurt and maimed by the battles he'd been in, and, well, I just didn't feel right to leave even though I knew what he was saying was crazy. I guess I should have."

He looked down into his hands, and his shoulders shook slightly. Ray and Andi went around the table to put their hands on his shoulders.

"Let's pray, Doc," Ray said quietly.

Dr. Kingston nodded. Ray bowed his head and said, "Lord, we mess things up so bad sometimes. But help us to find Your peace and strength in this. Turn even this debacle for good. I pray, comfort Doc, and convict Croase and those people at TWI, and help me and Andi to know what to do. Lead us, we pray, in Jesus' name. Amen."

Dr. Kingston reached up and grabbed both their hands. "He'll help us deal with this, Ray. I know it."

"So do I," Ray said.

They finished with the files. As they cleaned up dinner, Kingston said, "It seems to me there's no question about where to have you three hide out."

"We don't have much money, Doc," Ray said.

"No money necessary," Kingston said, looking from Ray to Andi. "You might even enjoy it. It's on a lake in the Poconos of Pennsylvania. My brother has a summer cabin there. Nobody around here knows about it because I kept it a secret when I went to visit—didn't want people calling me when I needed a little privacy—so you should be well concealed."

Tommy walked in and said to Kingston, "Are there boats and stuff?"

"Everything you ever dreamed of."

"We should leave now—or as soon as we can get together a few things," Ray said.

"Yeah, I'll give you directions after I call Phil and check it out."

Ray nodded. "We'll have to use the 4x4."

"I know. Start getting ready."

After calling his brother, Kingston said it was a go.

In twenty minutes, they were ready. They didn't have any real supplies, but Kingston made Ray take some cans of food and two frozen casseroles. In the guest room, he found a pair of blue jeans and several blouses his daughter kept there for when she visited and other things he kept for his grandchildren.

Ray brought the two revolvers he'd taken from the guards at TWI. Kingston gave him a box of fifty shells and a Mastercard and Visa. "I've been hoarding them for the Tribulation. You can withdraw up to $400 at a crack," Kingston said. "I can handle it till you can pay me back. There's also a whole arsenal of weapons at the cabin, which you can use. Ammo in a gray box in the doorway to the basement. I'll write down a list of places to get food and so on and where all the keys are."

He went into the kitchen and made the list, then drew a map showing how to get to the cabin on the lake. When they were ready to go, Dr. Kingston left the house first and looked around the parking lot and up and down Jett Way for any signs of strange people hanging around. He didn't see anything out of the ordinary.

When he came back into the house, everyone stood in the foyer waiting. "Let's hustle," he said.

Ray and Andi took the front seats of the 4x4 and Tommy sprawled happily in the back. After starting the engine, Kingston said, "Let's pray," but after glancing around he changed his mind. "Pray on the way. I'll pray back in the house. You've got to get out of here. Watch out for anyone tailing you."

Ray backed the boxy red 4x4 out of its slot.

CHAPTER TEN

1

Ken Strock and David Hughes stood before Martin Croase still reeling from an enraged lecture from Croase about their bumbling in letting Ray and Andi escape. Listra, seated on one of the red leather chairs, was unperturbed.

"It's no big deal," she said matter-of-factly. "What are they planning to do? You were on the news. You've got the local police nailed down. All they can do is run. We'll find them. They can't get far."

Croase pursed his thin lips. "That's why I involved them in the first place. But it still shouldn't have happened."

Listra eyed her husband craftily. "The main thing is the boy. We have all the necessary samples—blood, skin, liver, pancreas. The kid probably doesn't even know what we did while he was out beyond the threshold, thanks to your investments in the latest technology. So there's nothing to worry about. No one's caught on yet." She drew on a cigarette and blew a narrow stream of smoke out the side of her mouth. "Furthermore, I've been doing some things with Rafa that are worth hearing."

"Rafa?" Croase said, looking up through tired, red eyes.

Listra gave him her cool, thin-lipped smile. "Well, you know I've been using the TUT once a day for several weeks now. I can converse with Rafa at any time I want. The TUT is the perfect medium."

"Then what does he say?" Croase watched his wife with a look of mild toleration.

"He says first of all we're close to breaking the threshold problem permanently. Second, he says that Mazaris and Darcasian are much more confused than we thought at first, and close to giving up. Third, he assures me that we will soon hold unbelievable power as we tap the full resources of our minds. He's going to show us how to do that. And—"

Croase leaned back, waiting for her to conclude. "And?"

"And Rafa wants me to become the first disciple for the process. He will train me in all the arts of his race."

Listra spoke with cool precision and a confident detachment that Croase had not always seen in her.

"What arts?" Croase asked, finding himself still not particularly interested.

"Simple things, really," Listra said, uncrossing and then crossing her legs again. "The power to rise at will. The power to cross the boundary between the spiritual and the material with simple mental concentration. The power to know the history of the universe and its greatest secrets. The power to traverse the deepest hollows of heaven with mere meditation techniques." For the first time a genuine smile flashed onto Listra's face. "The power to become a deity now, in this life, with all the capacities and privileges of that reality."

Croase worked not to say anything sarcastic. His wife had always been ambitious. But deity? Sure, he'd heard people talk about that idea. New Age books and philosophies espoused it. But it had always seemed to him a stupid daydream. Yet, here his wife was talking about it as if it was possible in a few months. He said tersely, "It is food for thought, dear."

"Food for thought? Martin, you fool. These are the discoveries of a lifetime. Don't be so nonvisionary. The TUT is a true wonder drug."

Hughes coughed, and Croase thought he noticed him press Listra's leg. He told himself it didn't matter, but it was the first time he'd seen it even though he'd suspected for a long time.

235

"Rafa promises there is incredible power for all if I will just trust him," Listra said. "And I do. But somehow we must find a way to get beyond the threshold regularly. That TUT-B must be perfected. And if it takes bodies to do it, so be it. That's the price we must pay. It's on our conscience."

Croase knew Listra was joking in her own way. She didn't believe the conscience existed except as a hamper to every ambition of the human spirit. He stood up, feeling less apprehensive. "We'll get the boy back. I trust you'll keep me informed of any new developments with Rafa."

Listra squinted coolly. "Of course. By the way, this Ray Mazaris character is some ex-military man, right? I think you should send some security people to the house."

Croase looked at Strock. The bull-necked head of security replied, "Hughes'll handle it."

With a terse shrug, Listra walked out. Hughes followed her.

□ □ □

They didn't speak until they stepped onto the elevator. Then Listra kicked Hughes in the shin. "You fool! Don't ever touch me like that in my husband's presence again."

Hughes buckled up. "I just thought—"

"You thought! I'm sick of people who just think around here. I know how to handle Martin Croase, David. So humor me. Meanwhile, see that you can be at the house in the afternoons. That's the best time."

The tall, handlebar-mustached man smiled and suddenly pulled her to his lips. "I love you, baby."

She kissed him quickly, then drew away. "All right, just keep doing as I say, and we'll go all the way to the stars. You've been doing the TUT?"

"Yes."

"And?"

"I'm getting the hang of it."

"Who's your guide?"

"Her name is Esther."

Listra laughed. "Rather biblical of her, isn't it?"

236

Hughes smiled. The elevator stopped. He made a leering gesture at her, she guffawed, but when the doors opened, they both stared ahead as if they hadn't even known the other existed.

□　□　□

Before Ken Strock left the office, Croase said to him, "Ken, I want you to procure something."

"What's that?"

"A water cannon."

"What for? They're not easy—"

"Just get one. What if we had a riot around here? What would you do—stand around with your teeth in your mouth like you just did right now? Better yet, get two of them or three."

"They're expensive."

"TWI can afford it. We just had a four-million dollar trusteeship set up."

Strock raised his eyebrows. "You're the boss."

When he left, Croase put his hands over his head and lay nose down on the blotter on his desk. "How much longer is it going to take?" he murmured. "Something's going to come down sooner or later. How much longer will it take to get enough—three or four million at least?"

No voice answered, but Croase didn't want to use the TUT at the moment. He was too tired—of Listra, of handling difficult people, of Johnny Goge, of Strock and Hughes and Nakayami, of Christians all over the place, of all of them. He was even tired of Benreu. But soon, he knew, such problems would be a past bad dream. He had options his wife didn't even dream about. And he'd be set up—for life.

2

Johnny Goge watched the elderly prof hurry to the Louis Building where he would teach his 10:10 A.M. class. Goge sat in traffic on Winston Street in the silver gray Mitsubishi Galant he had stolen in Denver. Now in Austin, Texas, he

237

listened to Tchaikovsky's Second Piano Concerto on the car's elaborate audio system. Croase told him the prof was selling secrets from their research at the university to a local genetics firm. Apparently, he had a several hundred thousand dollar pickup at the airport that day.

Johnny chewed a piece of gum and pressed the gas as the traffic headed down toward town. He knew he had to plan this one carefully. Hammerall was supposedly a real pro, even if he did look to be a bit doddery. It would be too bold to nab him at the airport. This time, Benreu had not spelled out a plan of action. Croase said, "You're the hit man. You figure it out. I didn't have that much time to discuss it with him."

He spent the afternoon casing Professor Hammerall's home in an Austin suburb. Even for late October, the Texas heat made Johnny sweat. That was the one thing he hated about himself. He sweat too much. It had got in the way more than once with a wet hand aiming a slippery side arm.

Professor Hammerall taught genetic engineering. He was just five foot six with curly silver hair, glasses, and wide, plaintive eyes. Sixty-two years old, he was divorced and lived alone in a ranch house in Rollingwood, southwest of the city. Most of his neighbors worked during the day, and there were no children playing within three houses of his on either side of Fairview Drive. Flower gardens lined the edge of the property, with fire thorn and white roses crowding the corners of the house. At night it would be an easy entrance.

Goge went back into Austin, bought a couple of hamburgers with a coffee at a McDonalds. He whiled away the hours drinking coffee and reading the paper. He found a little blurb in the middle of the *Dallas Morning News* about the continuing investigation of the murders in Portland and L.A. and the mystery of the letters.

At seven o'clock, Johnny drove back out to Rollingwood. Hammerall's Oldsmobile Cutlass sat still hot in the driveway. Rivulets of heat streamed from the hood of the car. Hammerall was supposed to have made the pickup in the afternoon.

Goge drove off and stopped in a local fast food place, drinking another coffee with a fast dinner of meat loaf and mashed potatoes. When he went back out to the Galant, checked his Bren Ten, and screwed in the silencer.

Then he drove out again to Fairview Drive, parked two blocks away, and walked back to the house. It was past ten. Some of the lights in the houses were out. The streetlamps were spaced about fifty yards apart. Hammerall's house was right in the middle, at the point of least visibility. The light in his bedroom was on.

Dressed in a gray three-piece suit, Goge ambled casually up the street with a briefcase. He was confident he looked like a neighbor businessman returning home after a late night at the office.

When he reached Hammerall's house, he stopped, looked up and down the street, made a quick survey of the nearby houses, and scrutinized Hammerall's windows. Then he walked up to the front door and rang the bell.

Thirty seconds later, the light in the foyer came on and the front door opened. Hammerall peered out, his glasses on the tip of his nose. He wore a rumpled blue velour robe.

"I'm sorry, sir," Goge said. "My car broke down up the street, and I need to call a service station. Can I use your phone?"

Hammerall peered out to the left and right.

Goge went on. "It's another flat. I had one two days ago. I know I should change these tires. They're worn out. But I'm a salesman, and I have to drive. Pressed for time. You know. Anyway, it's a second flat in two days, and I don't have a spare. I just live over in Oak Hill. It'll just take a few minutes."

Hammerall looked him up and down. Goge put on his most carefully sculpted friendly smile. Then Hammerall said, "Sorry. Try somewhere else."

Goge's iron forearm stopped the door, slammed it backward, and knocked Hammerall over. He had the gun on his throat in an instant, and kicked the door shut behind him.

Hammerall's face was white with fear. "You can't hurt me. I'm protected."

Goge laughed. "By who?"

"I have connections."

"I know. Like GEEC, over in Dallas."

239

Hammerall flinched. "What do you want?"

"The money you got today at the airport."

"What money?"

Goge helped him rise slowly to his feet. He kept the silencer barrel right on Hammerall's heart. "No one will know, and I'll find the money, so tell me now."

"No way."

"Then I guess I'll have to maim you." Goge quickly shifted the gun from Hammerall's chest to his upper arm and fired. The bone snapped, and the arm suddenly hung loose.

The thin professor fell down and screamed.

"Where did you put it? I'll give you ten seconds."

"I tell you, I don't have it."

Goge aimed at the other arm and squeezed off a shot in the elbow. The arm shattered and flew off onto the floor. Hammerall crumpled up in pain. His screams were much weaker, though.

"Tell me where it is."

Hammerall closed his eyes. "In my bedroom closet."

Pulling Hammerall to his feet, Goge pressed him forward up the stairs. Blood spattered onto the floor. Halfway up the stairs, Hammerall suddenly stopped. "I'm . . . I'm . . ."

He fell over backwards and lay on the steps, unconscious. Goge swore. "Why do I get carried away with these things?"

He sped up the stairs. The closet was easy to find, but he couldn't locate the money. Swearing profusely, he ran downstairs again. Hammerall was clearly bleeding to death. Goge felt for a pulse on the neck. There was one, but he figured Hammerall was in shock.

Forcing himself to concentrate, he worked his mind. What to do? Then: *The TUT. Benreu'll tell me.*

Goge shot another hole through Hammerall's head and cut in the letter Croase had told him to use, another B, then left the man lying on the stairs. Goge hadn't asked about the letters, but he thought it might be someone's name or possibly a message. He didn't care about it, anyway. It was just part of the deal now.

He opened his briefcase on the small coffee table and

took out a dose of the newer version of the TUT. He lay down on the couch and placed the thin piece of paper like a wafer on his tongue.

Four minutes later he was back—with the information. He went upstairs, threw the mattress off the box spring in Hammerall's guest room and ripped off the muslin cover. There lay the box. He didn't even try to count it. He simply picked it up by the handle, strode downstairs, checked the outdoors, and left with his briefcase in the other hand.

3

Listra floated above her body on the bed in her home. David Hughes lay beside her, looking up at the ceiling and smiling. She turned and immediately sped into the tunnel. She needed time with Rafa, as much as she could get. The day would come when she might have unlimited time with him, but for now she only had the four minutes.

The tunnel trips seemed ever shorter. In moments, she stood on the lustrous turf of the "meeting place" as Rafa called it. Rafa was at her side in a moment.

"There are problems," Listra told him telepathically.

"I know. Nothing to be worried about." The being undulated before her. Each time she met him there she learned a little more about his shape, his mind. He was quick, extremely so—far wiser and more intelligent than any person she'd met on earth. Yet, he was often so secretive.

"How do you know?"

"We are watchers. We see all. One day you will see all as well." His voice reverberated clearly in her mind, like the sound of a voice in a well.

"Then you know about the escape."

"Yes."

"What are we to do?"

"They will be taken care of. You are more important."

Listra relaxed. Sometimes while in the material world she sensed a strong competition—jealousy?—with the boy, Tommy. He could go farther. But Rafa always made little of it.

"Do you know the problem with the TUT-B—why it won't work?"

There was a pause. Listra recognized the cool green eyes set in deep sockets. They reminded her almost of a skull with minimal flesh. But his skin was burnished a deep brown. Even his arms seemed to have veins through which coursed crimson fire. He was tall, far taller than her. Majestic. His nearness radiated a warmth that stirred her mind. She wanted to embrace him, to swallow him, to take him back with her.

"The problem will be solved."

"How soon?"

"Soon."

Sometimes the conversations with Rafa were frustrating like this. He did not like specifics.

"Should we continue thinking about making the TUT available to all people?"

"You should."

"What powers are you going to give me?" Listra felt impatient. He had been telling her about mysterious "powers" for the last three visits. But he had remained vague.

"Beyond anything humanity is yet capable of."

"Like what?"

"Knowledge. Knowledge is all."

"Just knowledge?"

"Knowledge about the soul. About the person. About life. Knowledge is all. With knowledge is power."

"But when will I get this knowledge?"

"You will soon begin to experience it. It cannot be imparted lightly."

"I understand. But I feel I need to understand more about it."

"You shall."

Listra felt a pull at her back. "I must return."

His voice in her head sounded suddenly shrill. "There is an enemy."

"An enemy?"

"A saboteur."

Listra sensed the pull of the return trip. There was no time. "Who? What is his name?"

242

It was too late. She felt herself slip back into her lifeless body. A moment later she opened her eyes, still slightly dizzy. As her mind cleared, she looked up into Hughes's eyes.

"How was it?" he said.

"Beatific!" she cried, sitting up. "But I will have to go up again soon."

"You really shouldn't do it more than once every twenty-four hours."

"That cannot be helped. There are serious problems."

"What kind?" Hughes crawled off the bed.

"An enemy, Rafa said. He said there is an enemy."

She began to dress.

"You mean one on his side, out there, or one down here?"

"I don't know," she said. "That's why I have to go back."

"But why didn't he tell you right away?" Hughes's blue eyes flashed with anger and, she detected, envy.

"I don't know. He had his reasons. He hasn't lied to me yet, has he?"

"I don't know he's told you enough to be caught in a lie."

Listra slid on her stockings. "Don't put me between you and him, David. I don't love him, OK?"

Hughes appeared rebuked and humbled. He went about dressing without another word.

After a few minutes, she said, "One other thing, dearest."

"Yes."

"I want that boy dead permanently when all this is over. Understood?"

Hughes shook his head. "No rivals, huh?"

Listra suddenly slapped him. He staggered back, rubbing his chin with his hand.

"Don't speak to me like that," she yelled. "I'm not a person to be toyed with. He's not a rival. Not even in the same universe. I just don't like him. I don't want him invading what is rightfully mine."

Hughes creased his eyebrows. "You didn't have to do that."

243

Listra's face was taut and twisted with anger. Then it was over. She shook her head and clucked her tongue, then touched his cheek gently. "Did I hurt you? I'm sorry. You know I love you. You're so much more gentle than Martin ever was. I don't know how I ever married him."

Hughes kissed her. "It's all right. Soon we'll be on our way."

CHAPTER ELEVEN

1

Ray, Andi, and Tommy settled into the cabin with enthusiasm. The main room served as combination living room in the front and dining room at the back. The big oak table stood below a wide picture window that opened on a majestic view of the lake, a hundred yards below down a steep trail. Three deer heads hung over a gray stone fireplace, obviously fashioned from rocks either from a local quarry or perhaps the property itself.

Andi liked the kitchen instantly, with its gas stove, Frigidaire, and sink over which another wide window overlooked a rustic ponderosa pine porch and the lake. Outside, the cabin was stained with redwood siding paint. Inside, the walls were a shellacked white pine with multitudes of brown knotholes. A chiseled length of what also looked like a whole pine tree traversed the living room from the front to the back over the picture window.

All about the cabin were the trophies of a hunting family. A moose head hung over the passageway to the kitchen and bedrooms. A fox and a wolf head graced the front of the living room, and several mallard ducks, squirrels, and a walleyed pike were scattered about. A brown horse blanket was draped over the railing at the edge of the loft where fifteen cots and beds could house a legion of people on a partying weekend.

Ray took the bedroom with twin beds on the left facing the front of the house. Tommy liked the loft, and Andi garnered one of the back bedrooms, also with twin beds. Ray fought off a few unexpected thoughts about his and Andi's sleeping together. He knew that was out of the question. He was as committed to Christ and His truth as he'd ever been. And so was she.

The cabin was comfortable, and Ray planned to make a fire the first full night. Long piles of wood—Ray estimated it must have been at least ten cord's worth—sat out in front of the house. He didn't worry about security at first, though he kept the two guns loaded and ready—one in the small flip-top desk in the living room by the television, and one in his bedroom in the drawer of the nightstand. He showed Andi and Tommy where they were and planned to give them both some shooting lessons once he'd stocked up on ammo.

Dr. Kingston's brother's gun case was filled with rifles and shotguns, even two Civil War single-shot carbines, which Ray was sure were replicas. The Doc had given Ray instructions on where to find everything, and he quickly made an inventory of what they had for protection: a double-barreled twelve-gauge shotgun; one three-shot pump shotgun, also twelve-gauge; one thirty-thirty hunting rifle with a six-shot clip; one thirty-aught-six Enfield, World War I vintage; and a .35 Remington rifle. Ray didn't look forward to shooting the Enfield. He knew the recoil would put his shoulder in permanent black and blue. So he didn't even consider using it.

There were other pistols, a thirty-two caliber automatic hunter's side arm. Another thirty-eight revolver. The .22 target pistol Kingston had mentioned, which he wanted Tommy to use. It was a semiautomatic like the .32. And an interesting silver-plated, pearl-handled pistol that looked about twenty-five caliber. It was probably something collected, because Ray knew its accuracy would probably be nil. It was the kind of gun someone might have kept in a store in case of thieves. There was plenty of ammunition in the steel gray box in the walkway to the cellar.

The refrigerator was mostly empty, though the freezer had a few items—frozen peas, a loaf of bread, and some rock-hard fish covered in plastic wrap and held together by a blue rubber band.

That first morning they went into the local town and bought food and supplies after opening an account at the bank with money they'd got from an ATM using one of Kingston's cards. Tommy had fun visiting the local "Trading Post" souvenir store with everything from rubber-tipped Indian spears to ceramic statues of rabbits and ground hogs.

Ray pushed the cart in the local supermarket while Andi picked out items. "You like cereal?" she asked him as they turned down the next aisle. Tommy was busy selecting packs of chocolate bars, some Ben and Jerry's New York Chunk ice cream, a bundle of slightly green bananas, and English muffins.

Ray pulled down a box of Mueslix and another of Captain Crunch. He explained, "I like to alternate healthy and 'definite bodily injury' during the week."

Andi smiled and didn't protest his selections.

Ray suggested they hit the clothing store after they finished with the food. Andi said, "Whose money will we use?"

"Dr. Kingston's, of course."

He liked being near her. That morning she'd found a vial of "Charlie" perfume in one of the drawers of the dresser in her room and used it. He remembered it as one of his favorites when he had dated a girl named Liz in high school.

They rang up a bill of eighty dollars. The girl at the checkout counter was friendly, with braided brown hair, a farm girl smile, and a tiny diamond engagement ring on her ring finger. "Here for a vacation?" she asked as she rang up the prices. The store didn't have any kind of automatic computer system to read the bar charts on each package.

"Kind of," Andi said. Ray could tell she was making sure the girl hit the right numbers. The girl's fingers flashed so quickly over the register that it was difficult to keep up.

"Haven't seen you before. You new?"

Andi answered, "We rented one of the cabins on the lake."

Ray raised his eyebrows, then repressed a grin, and watched the doors of the supermarket. He thought he would get her on that one.

247

"It's really nice in the summer up there. My fiancé and I grew up around here. But we don't live on the lake."

The girl said her name was Leah and gave Andi a quick rundown on all the stores in town, where to get souvenirs, ice cream cones, clothing, gas, and nearly everything else. She popped a wad of bubble gum as she talked.

When she was finished, Andi began to write out one of the new checks from the bank. Leah had it approved, then smiled as they gathered everything together. She said, "I take it you're not married," looking at Andi's left hand.

Andi said, "No, actually this is my brother, Ray. That is his son, Tommy. We just came up here to get away. My husband is a lawyer in New York. The reason I'm not wearing a ring is because . . ."

Both Tommy and Ray stared at Andi as she effortlessly spun out a story of disaster and woe that bore no resemblance to reality.

"Well I hope you all have a decent time up here. I'm sorry to hear about all the problems. But believe me, no one will bother you. It's mostly tourists and lake people around here. You probably won't even have anyone on your street, it being out of season and all. Sorry to hear about your wedding ring."

When they got out to the parking lot, Ray whistled. "Remind me never to believe a word you say."

Andi flipped her hair back out of her eyes. "I don't like lying about anything either, but this is a special case. I think we have to watch our back, OK?"

With a little chuckle, Ray said, "I agree."

Tommy, though, said, "How come you said I'm Ray's son and not your son?"

Andi gave him a quick hug. "Because you're handsome like Ray, and I think you two could pass off that way."

At the clothing store, Andi was soon outfitted in one stylish but practical wool dress, several pairs of jeans and one work shirt, a flannel shirt, and a nice blouse. She also bought some undergarments after modestly directing Ray and Tommy to mind their own business and get their own things. Ray and Tommy modeled pants and shirts for one another and gathered together the items they needed.

From there they visited the drug store where they bought much needed toiletries, including three toothbrushes. Andi selected several thriller novels and two games, Monopoly and Boggle, from the small bookstore. After that they went to the hardware store. There Ray bought two boxes of fifty .38 caliber brass-jacketed target load rounds for the pistols, one box of .38 steel tipped bullets for other than target practice, and a box of .22 shells for the gun he wanted Tommy to try, the .22 pistol. The attendant asked no questions and even seemed in a bad mood, plunking down the boxes gruffly and staring into Ray's face with hard brown eyes.

At the checkout counter, Ray asked the bald, elderly man there about any place where he might get in some target practice. The man answered, "Probably the dump is the best place. You can set up cans, and there're plenty of rats in case you're looking for something on the move."

He gave Ray directions and asked no questions, though he did give Andi a quick up and down. Ray could tell by his eyes that he found her attractive. It was a nice feeling.

On the way back up the steep road to the lake and cabin Tommy asked, "Are you going to teach me to shoot? Mom too?"

"If you want," Ray said. "I'd like you all to know how to use it."

"But what about God? Isn't He supposed to protect us?"

Andi spoke up before Ray could reel something off. "God doesn't expect people to do nothing, honey. Sometimes you have to take strong measures when you're dealing with evil people. Even King David had to cut the heads of his enemies off."

"Do you think Jesus would use a gun too?"

Andi laughed. Ray looked at her, waiting for her answer. She said, "You want to handle that one, seminary student?"

"I was kind of interested in what you would say," Ray answered.

She said to Tommy, "If God could tell David to kill Goliath, and Joshua to wipe out Jericho, and Gideon to kill off a hundred thousand Midianites, I think He could handle us keeping a gun."

Making a gesture of triumph, Tommy said, "I knew Jesus wasn't a wimp."

Ray and Andi laughed. As they talked something percolated in Ray's breast. For the time being they were a family. Just like a real family. In a way, he hoped it never ended.

That evening, Ray looked through the files he'd taken from TWI for the umpteenth time. What most intrigued him were several letters from people who hadn't been selected for working at TWI. There was one letter in response from a biochemist in Baltimore. His words roundly condemned the work and said, "No thinking Christian would ever involve himself in this kind of activity."

He stared down at the lake in the waning light. Andi came around the table and rubbed his shoulders. He leaned into her hands. "That feels great."

"I charge $42.50 an hour."

"Then what's five minutes' worth?"

"First time it's for free."

They both gazed out the window. "Be on the lookout," Ray said. His face grew somber. "Any strange characters. We don't know what they're doing to find us."

Andi kneaded his shoulders expertly. "We'll be all right. The Lord's taking care of us."

Ray laughed. "That's what I'm worried about. He took care of the early Christians by letting lions eat them."

"Yeah, but after they were digested, they woke up in heaven."

"Right. Just what I always wanted to do." He leaned into her fingers and enjoyed her nearness. Deep down, though, he wasn't joking. It still troubled him. How could you trust God when you never knew whether He was going to grant you an overwhelming victory or let you go down the sewer? By his own experience, he had no reason to trust God at all. And clearly this particular episode wasn't over. Tommy and Andi could still be snuffed out of his life like two flickering candles, and he couldn't do a thing about it.

"I know what you mean, Andi. God did protect the early Christians, even if it was through death. But sometimes I wonder if they all faced it as triumphantly as history records."

"I think we're doing pretty well at the moment."

"Yeah, for now." He went back down into his thoughts. He could marry this girl, he knew that. But he couldn't even consider that possibility till they'd completely shed all threats from Croase. And how soon might that happen? Ever?

He had no answers, and it troubled him greatly that God didn't even seem to be trying to supply a single word of hope.

She kissed him on the cheek, and his face suddenly burned. He turned to her and they were in one another's arms.

"God can't take you away from me, Andi," he said into her ear.

She replied, "He won't. I promise."

Her breath in his ear excited him, and suddenly he wished they were already married.

2

Croase, Nakayami, Listra, Strock, Hughes, and several others sat around the large walnut table in the spacious TWI conference room. "It's clear," Croase said, "that the boy and his caretakers have disappeared for the moment. Ken, you're working on that?"

Strock nodded. He and Hughes had canvassed the ATS campus and talked to a number of people about Ray and Andi. Everyone was cooperative—Croase had explained the situation in chapel that morning—but no one knew where they'd gone.

"We've hit a snag in the development of the TUT-B," Croase said after acknowledging Strock's answer. "It doesn't seem to be blood, serum, or tissue factors. We've tried"—he glanced at Nakayami—"sixteen, is it?"

Nakayami shook his head slowly up and down, keeping his eyes on the sheaf of papers in front of him. Croase noticed he was unusually pensive and uncommunicative.

"Sixteen then. We've tried numerous other matches. We believe now"— Croase looked at one of the psychiatrists

251

present—"it may be neurological. Still physically based, not mental, but neurological, something in the neurotransmitters, perhaps a cellular factor in the brain, we're not sure, maybe the hypothalamus. In short, we need the boy back. We want to get a sample of brain tissue, and also, obviously, have the boy available for more, uh, trips, for lack of a better word."

Listra's eyes were fixed on Croase's face. Everyone appeared uneasy except her.

"So." Croase laid his delicate hands on the table, rubbed the wood unconsciously, then folded them together in a waiting attitude. "What now?"

Strock said, "We're keeping a check on several professors at ATS who were friendly with Mazaris. We've also done a little surveillance on Harold Kingston. I think we'll find out where the boy is very soon."

"But you can't be sure of how soon," Croase said flatly, his eyes flashing.

"Soon."

"I want him here by next week."

Several weary sighs emitted from the members sitting around the table. But still no one offered an alternative viewpoint.

"Martin," Nakayami offered, "the TUT works fine. We have no reason to pursue—"

Croase's hand came down flat on the table. "Our mission—our vision—our life commitment is to completely break the death barrier. No more secrets. The TUT gets us far, but only so far. Is anyone here in favor of abandoning our research?"

No one moved.

Listra suddenly spoke. "Aren't we forgetting several people?"

All eyes turned to her.

"Who?" Croase asked.

"Rafa, Benreu, our spiritual mentors," Listra said with clipped precision. She looked around from face to face. Her eyes coolly paused on each pair of eyes, then moved on with calm and deft authority. "We have our equations, our research, our little jaunts, but the spiritual is the key. Rafa in particular promises to show us far more power than anything we can presently imagine. He has told me we're on the verge of a breakthrough. He has told me that the boy's brain does hold the key. I say we do everything we can to find him."

Nakayami began to rise. He glared at Listra, then looked at Croase. "What you speak of is murder! You all know what this means. We cannot take even a tiny sample of brain matter for the testing we need to do. Our best hope is the PCR. We can get a genetic fingerprint from the blood sample we already have."

The PCR referred to a powerful technology which, through what was called a polymerase chain reaction, could literally "fingerprint" the DNA in a host cell. It was used in a multitude of applications, including cancer and AIDS research. Nakayami had talked TWI into investing in a program with a local genetic engineering firm, which provided the service for a high fee. With it, Nakayami could conceivably discover what gene it was that Tommy produced that enabled him to withstand the TUT-B.

When no one answered, Nakayami continued, "Homeless street people is one thing. A twelve-year-old boy and son of one of our workers is quite another."

Listra said abruptly, "Darcasian is a renegade, a traitor. I don't see the problem."

Nakayami's eyes flared, but Croase held up his hand. "No one is talking about murder here. Certainly we can find ways to preserve the boy's life. The important thing is to get him here—on a long-term basis. And to eliminate any who might hinder that. I don't think any expense—financial, personal, or human—is too great for what we're trying to accomplish."

Nakayami sat down and stared into his lap. Listra smiled. Croase gazed around the room from face to face.

"It's decided then. We direct our efforts to finding the boy. Until then all other research will be suspended."

Strock glanced at Hughes and frowned. Their business with Willard had started, and they didn't want things to wind down.

But Croase stood. "I don't want to hear any more until the boy is in our hands."

3

Lou Miles learned of the killing in Austin by the FBI KEY. He flew in and contacted authorities, providing the ballistics tests and other materials from the previous two murders. It was confirmed in a matter of hours that the same gun and knife had been used in all three murders.

He now had three other special agents working on the case. At the university where Hammerall had been a professor, Miles began a lengthy interviewing process with everyone who would volunteer information about the deceased. It turned out to be another of the same type of story. Upstanding citizen, friend, patriot, everything good and decent, little bad. No obvious motive.

He put the team of special agents in the three cities to some hard work on the money angle with the first and third murders. They clearly had it with Janice Koppers, though they couldn't be sure there was actually money in the safe at the time of the killing.

Then he called one of his associates in Atlanta named Brent Oberlin about the letters.

"What gives on this message business, Brent?" Miles asked as he chain-smoked and paced in his motel room in Austin.

"It's unusual," Oberlin readily admitted. "But clearly psychotic and sociopathic."

"That's a lot of help. I'd think anyone like this would be."

"No, it is different. If money is the motive, and that could very well be, then the message has nothing to do with the money. But why would the guy leave a message in the first place if all he wants is money? He's broadcasting his path to the whole world, saying, 'I did this one and this one and this one.' So there's some kind of fracture in his thinking. And then there's the message itself. A-B-B could spell a lot of things I suppose, but it's an unusual way to begin a message. It sounds like he's spelling a name to me."

"What name begins with A-B-B?"

"Um, Abbe, Abbey, Abbott . . . I'm sure the phone book will yield plenty. It could also be an abbreviation, really anything. But psychopaths aren't typically prone to spelling their names on their victims."

"What could it be then?"

"Have you ever considered some religious connection? Cultic. Something like that. Frequently, people doing this kind of thing have some deep, underlying guilt that sometimes stems from a weird religious upbringing."

"But how would the word be religious?"

"One of the words Jesus used for His Father was Abba. A-B-B-A. Aramaic for 'Daddy.'"

"That's preposterous."

"Probably. Just a guess. It could really be anything. You never know with this kind of person."

"If it's religious, what's the money connection?"

"He's sending the money to a charity?" When Miles didn't laugh, Oberlin said, "Sorry, bad joke."

"This is nuts," Miles said. "He can't be spelling Abba."

"Undoubtedly that's a shot in the dark. But what else have we got? I guess we'll just have to wait and see."

"That's what I'm afraid of."

"Keep in touch, Lou."

"See you."

Miles sat back on the bed and mused. A psychotic religious fanatic who loved money and murder and wanted to get a message across. "Give me a break," he murmured and stubbed his cigarette out in the ashtray.

4

"Isn't there some reporter who went to ATS a couple years ago who works for Channel 4?" Ray asked Andi as they both sat at the dining room table going over the files one more time and looking out the picture window toward the lake.

"Yes, Lyle Hornum," Andi said. "Real nice guy. He even asked me out once."

Ray looked across the table into Andi's dark eyes. Over the last two days her playfulness had increased dramatically. She seemed to be baiting him at every corner just to get him to admit he liked her. "So did you go out with him?"

"I thought we were doing research." The upper right corner of Andi's mouth twitched up.

"You brought up the date."

"No, I didn't go out with him."

"But he's a nice guy."

"Right."

"How do you know?"

Andi gave him a stiff I-can-spar-with-you look and answered, "By how he avoided ravishing me once at the corner of Simmering and Larkspur."

"This is getting interesting. Did you get it on camera?"

"It was on the evening news. I have the video at home. Keeps the perspective on what a nice guy is like."

Tommy had been slurping down a bowl of Captain Crunch in the kitchen, but suddenly Ray was aware of him standing in the hallway looking at them. He was still in his pajamas, and his blond hair was mashed flat on the left side and billowy on the right. He sauntered into the living room and sat down. "What are you talking about?"

"It's called shadow-boxing, honey."

"People do that?"

Ray said, "Your mother is in one of her crazy moods this morning, Tommy. Don't worry about it."

Tommy scrutinized Andi's face, then Ray's. He reached into the cereal box and pulled out a few morsels, then popped them in his mouth. "You guys are weird." He went back into the kitchen.

Andi stretched her arms over her head and yawned. She sang, "'I feel good, da-da-da-da-da-dent.' James Brown. Early sixties."

"Andi, we have to make some headway here. We can't sit in this cabin the rest of our lives."

"Oh, can't we lighten up for a few minutes? We're safe. For the first time I feel like a human being again. And Lyle

Hornum is too short. He's only about five six, and he has a big head."

"Big as in pumpkin-face, or big as in proud and cocky?"

"Pumpkin-head," Andi said. "But he is definitely a nice guy, and I should have gone out with him."

Ray gave her an exasperated look, then turned back to the files.

"Just to razz you," Andi added. Her hair was still a bit disheveled and she had on no makeup. Walking around in the wooly blue man's robe and man's pajamas she'd found in a drawer, she was a real vision of the totaled woman, Ray thought. But despite that, she was powerfully attractive and alluring. A plain smile from her could get his heart hammering with excitement.

"Well, don't razz me too much," Ray said. "I may jump you at the corner of the kitchen and the rear bedroom."

Andi put her chin in her hands, gazing across at him with large, amused eyes. "Oh, is it that bad?"

Ray dropped his pencil. "Andi, we've got to make some decisions."

"Your wish is my command." She stood and cleared away their two coffee cups. "I'd better go dress in something like those old army fatigues to get you in the right mood."

"Please do."

She shuffled into the kitchen. "I'm never going to make it through this," Ray murmured and thumbed through the papers again without seeing a thing.

□ □ □

Lyle Hornum's tinny voice came onto the receiver after Ray had sat on hold for three minutes. "This is Lyle."

Ray quickly explained who he was. Lyle knew instantly all about it, having been one of the reporters at TWI the morning after the escape. "Yeah, I was thinking about tracking you down."

"Do you believe Croase?"

"Not really. But you never can tell. Even slimeballs turn out to be decent part of the time."

257

"Lyle, I have to trust you."

"I know. You can be sure I'm not going to tell Croase you contacted me."

"All right, what do you know about TWI?" Ray said, his voice a bit breathy. He was nervous and still wasn't sure how much he could trust Hornum, despite what he'd just said.

"It's part of the reason why I left the seminary. I didn't like the security they had there, and when Croase spoke in chapel, I had incredibly bad vibes. Other than that, I decided I didn't want to be a pastor."

Ray told him about the death trips, Andi and Tommy, and about the escape.

Lyle said, "This sounds big. What else can you tell me?"

Ray filled him on the rest of the information he had, the personnel records, and his discussions with Dr. Kingston.

"Sounds like something out of one of the sci-fi movies with that muscle-bound Hungarian what's-his-name," Lyle said. "By the way, Kingston was one of my favorite profs. Good man. I still keep in touch with him now and then. So what do you want to know?"

"I'd like to get some evidence on them so we can nail them. It's that simple."

"I'm glad to hear that."

"So you want me to do it?"

"Well, I don't want to impose. But I thought you might be able to help in some way—since you're apparently as un-impressed with Martin and Listra Croase as I am."

"Tell you what"—Hornum's voice suddenly had a cagey sound to it, but Ray did not find it disconcerting or decep-tive—"you keep all this info under your hat, let me handle the whole story, and I'll do everything I can for you. But you've got to promise to give me the whole story. Exclusive. No holds barred. I may want to write the best-seller."

Ray chuckled. "You reporters are all alike."

"Hey, if it was a used book sale of every theological tome in history, you'd want to be first in line, right?"

"Maybe. OK, sure, let me talk to Andi, but I'm willing to give you the whole story. Still, Lyle, you've got to understand, Croase is dangerous. I'm sure they've used a number of people in their experiments who have died in the process. I don't think they'd hesitate to whack anyone who stood in their way."

"No problem. We have some power too. This could be big. I mean real big. Once it hits headlines they won't be able to touch you without creating the *Towering Inferno* redux. So giving me your story could be protection."

"If we ever get to that point."

Andi walked back in the room, dressed in the new blue jeans and a flannel shirt. She had her hair pulled back in a pony tail. She sipped at a cup of coffee and sat down opposite Ray, listening.

Lyle continued. "OK, hang in there. When will you call me next?"

"Don't you want my number?"

"Now that would be stupid, wouldn't it? If you want to keep your whereabouts a secret."

Ray suddenly realized how much he already trusted this guy. "Yeah, thanks for the vote of confidence. OK, I'll call you back at four-thirty today sharp. That be OK?"

"Make it four. I work fast, and I like to leave the office by four-fifteen unless I have to collect a Pulitzer Prize or anything; then I'll stay till five."

Ray laughed. "Got it. Let me just tell Andi about the exclusive story business." After he told her, she quickly agreed, and Ray said good-bye and hung up.

"Sounds like you made a friend," Andi said, taking a slug of coffee and throwing her head back to shake her pony tail off her shoulder.

"He sounds like . . ."

" . . . a nice guy," Andi completed the sentence.

"No, a major stud, macho dude, heavy on the good vibrations."

Andi smiled over the edge of the coffee cup. "Hey, you *are* getting with the program."

Tommy walked in and sprawled on the sofa in front of the fireplace. He had on his new jeans and shirt as well. "So what are we doing today?" he said, lying back with his hands

259

behind his head. He kicked his feet several times, squirmed around to get comfortable, and looked up at the ceiling.

"Target practice," Ray said. "First lesson. For both of you."

Tommy jumped up. "For real?"

As Andi retrieved her jacket draped over the sofa, she said, "By the way, thanks."

"What for?"

"For asking me before you gave away the rights to the motion picture."

"I felt I should."

"Yes, you should. And you did. You make me feel like an equal."

"Is that unusual?"

She cocked her head. "With some Christian men, it is, sad to say."

"Then I apologize for all of them."

Ray placed the two .38s and the .22 into a gym bag he'd found in the basement.

5

They easily found the dump about five miles down the highway, up and around a mountain on a dirt road. They smelled it before they saw it, though ribbons of smoke rose into the air above the trees as they drove up to it. A ramshackle green truck was parked by a small shack. Ray got out of the 4x4 and went over to talk to a man standing at the edge with a pitchfork.

"I hear you're allowed to potshot rats up here for target practice."

The man turned around and smiled. He was missing four front teeth and had a lined, grizzled face with several days growth of gray beard. He took off his greasy green cap and nodded. "Many as you can kill."

"So you don't mind if we do a little shooting?"

"Nah. Hunters always up here sighting in their rifles. Kind of a tradition. I think the rats like it." He giggled, a high chirpy cackle. Already Ray spotted several gray rats sniffing garbage among the huge piles of refuse.

"Any place in particular we should shoot from?"

He gestured to the area at the top of the dump. The trash piled up on the close side of a down slope over the edge of a series of railroad ties lining the edge of the parking area. "Just shoot down into it. That's about it. I figger you know how to aim away from a human like me." He cackled again and spit out a wad of brown chewing tobacco.

"Thanks." Ray walked back to the 4x4, taking his time.

"It really stinks around here," Andi said as Ray walked over to her rolled down window. "Can't we just find a place with some targets?" Tommy had already jumped out Ray's side and come around to the front looking over the railroad ties into the slope.

"Probably. Maybe next time. We won't stay long. I just want to show you the basic moves, that's all. Plus it'll be good to try to hit some rats."

Andi reluctantly opened the door. Ray picked up the guns and the ammunition lying in the back of the 4x4. First he showed them how to hold a revolver with the cylinder open, for safety purposes. Though she'd handled it fairly well in the car during their escape, he wanted to make sure Andi understood everything. Next he demonstrated how to load and unload. "An automatic has a safety, but a double action revolver like this doesn't. Your safety is the fact that you have to pull the trigger a long way to shoot."

Tommy squeezed the trigger a few times. Andi practiced opening and closing the swing-out cylinder. Ray showed them how to pull the trigger just to the point of release, then fire. "It's not good to shoot without ammo. Ruins the action. But do it a few times anyway."

He explained about single-action and double-action revolvers. Tommy asked why it didn't have a clip, and Ray explained the difference between automatics and classic revolvers. "These thirty-eight Specials are double-action revolvers. That means you shoot it by simply pulling the trigger all the way back. Some guns you have to cock first. That's single-action. But the .38 Chief's Special is popular with cops because it's easy to hide in a shoulder holster, it's light, and and it's easy to aim. The .22 here is semiautomatic and won't have much of a kick, so I figured Tommy could try it."

He handed Tommy the gun and explained about the safety on it. Then after showing them the Weaver and Isosceles stances, how to hold it in the right hand and brace it for aiming with the left, he finally loaded the .38 with a single bullet.

"Not playing Russian roulette, I hope," Andi said.

Ray shook his head and grinned. "Don't want you accidentally firing it more than once yet."

"I emptied it the other day."

"I realize that, Andi. But this is teaching time, not escaping time."

She chuckled. "You're a born instructor. I can see it."

He rolled his eyes and aimed the first pistol, slowly traversing the dump for a moment. "See that red can—tomato on the label?" He aimed at an open garbage bag about twenty-five feet away.

Both Andi and Tommy leaned over. "Yeah."

"OK, get ready."

Ray fired. The whole pile seemed to jump, then settle. There was a neat hole in the front of the can.

"You're as good as any cop on TV," Tommy said with wide eyes.

"It always looks easier on television than it is," Ray said. "It's very easy to miss a target. And here we're shooting at stationary objects. Normally your target, if it's a person or an animal, will be moving. That makes it even harder. Usually you only get one good shot too, so you have to make it count. Close only counts in horseshoes and hand grenades."

Andi grinned. "OK, let me try."

Ray opened the cylinder and dropped the empty casing out onto the ground. Tommy picked it up, then dropped it. "It's hot!"

As Ray loaded five rounds in the Chief's Special, he said, "Let me just take a few more shots and let you get used to it. Then I'll let you both try it."

Ray plinked off five more shots at various objects and at one rat, which he missed. Most of the rats seemed to have suddenly disappeared. Andi and Tommy kept their hands over their ears. Ray noticed that the old man at the side of the dump, though, just went on with his work as if nothing unusual was happening.

He let Andi try it first. She sighted down the barrel and tried for another can. She wanted to learn to do this better, now that she realized from the escape how difficult it was to hit anything at a distance. Still, after five shots she hadn't hit the can. She said her wrist hurt from the kick, too, so she decided to take a break.

Tommy then tried the .22, but he kept closing his eyes. Ray soon realized they both had a long way to go. They shot up the first two boxes of .38 and .22 shells without once puncturing a significant target. Still, Ray was pleased. Neither of them had been afraid, and both had entered into the lessons with gusto. He thought getting some ear protectors might cut down on the noise pain, but they were expensive. When they jumped back into the 4x4, Andi suggested they buy some earplugs, like the kind people used to sleep soundly. They decided to stop at the drugstore and get some.

On the way home, Ray said, "How about a dish of ice cream, folks?"

There were no complaints about that idea. They settled down at a local dairy bar for ice cream and lunch.

That afternoon Dr. Kingston called to make sure everyone was all right. He said there hadn't been any more about TWI on the news, and he thought they might have reconsidered and decided to make less of it than it was. He didn't think anyone had been watching him.

Ray wasn't convinced. He hoped TWI wouldn't bug Kingston's telephone line. Then Kingston said, "I'm going to talk to Hal Gordon about this, Ray."

"Why?"

"He's a friend. You know him. Good man. I could have him talk to some people on the board. I know he doesn't like what's been going on at TWI. I'll be careful and won't mention your name. But I have to know what the board thinks of all this."

"All right. See what you can find out."

"I hoped you would feel that way."

Kingston signed off with a promise to keep Ray informed.

At dinner, Tommy was full of talk about the shooting and eager to do it again the next day. Ray wanted to find somewhere he could set up real targets and measure their progress. He decided to make more inquiries.

That night they all sat on the beach looking out at the still water of the lake. Ray built a fire, and they roasted marshmallows. They wore jackets they'd found in the basement. As they sat around the fire gazing in the ashes, Andi began talking about camping as a youngster with the Girl Scouts.

"We had this leader who told the greatest ghost stories. I was always so terrified by the time we got into our tents, I could hardly sleep."

Ray whittled at a stick with a knife he'd found in the cabin, and Tommy imitated him with the smaller knife Ray had given him earlier.

"You remember any?" Ray said, leaning back and lying prone on the sandy beach. Large rocks lined the edge of the water. But several beaches had obviously been raked to expose the slate gray and white sand.

"Oh, she had these stories about some being named Saparelle. She probably made him up. Nothing real stupendous."

One of Tommy's marshmallows caught fire, and he blew it out, then hungrily scarfed up the charred, creamy remnants. After a while they all lay close together against the rock with the fire between them and the beach. It threw orange and blue flaming bits of ash into the air. The fire crackled and spit, then gradually simmered down to an unearthly glow.

As they looked up at the stars, Ray began pointing out the constellations. "There's Orion, with the three stars in a row. That's his belt." Ray pointed out Pegasus on the horizon and Auriga the Charioteer, the North Star, and Cassiopeia, looking like an upside down W. Tommy picked out the Big Dipper and Little Dipper.

Ray lay between Andi and Tommy, feeling close and intimate with both of them. It was a stirring feeling, something he hadn't sensed in the years since he'd lost his dad. He'd never been close to his brother, Tim. When Ray "got religion" as Tim referred to it, they had a mutual parting of the ways. Then when their dad died in the hospital, Tim angrily confronted Ray with the words, "How can you believe in a God who lets people like Dad get mugged and then live as a vegetable for ten years?"

It was a difficult question and one Ray had never answered successfully, even with all the apologetic arguments he'd hashed out with Doc Kingston.

In the distance across the lake there was a sudden series of bangs. Andi sat up suddenly, but Ray touched her shoulder and pulled her back. "Someone setting off firecrackers."

They could see another campfire about a quarter mile across the cove from where they lay.

"Looks like we have company," Andi said. She snuggled against Ray's shoulder, laying her hand on his chest.

She whispered into his ear, "Do you have a hairy chest?" She'd noticed hairs poking out at the top of his undershirt, but she'd never seen him barechested.

He laughed. "Want to see it?"

"No. Just wondering. I've always had a hankering for men with hairy chests."

He chuckled. "Well, for your information, I do."

She patted his chest. "Good. That makes you all the more tantalizing."

A fish jumped on the lake, and Tommy sat up, looking out over the starlit waters.

"Fish," Ray said. "Don't you people know anything?"

"We like making you feel intelligent," Andi answered. She kissed him on the earlobe, then sat up. Tommy began baking another marshmallow.

"I'm not gonna let this one burn," Tommy said. "Make it a perfect brown."

Everyone watched as Tommy rotated the stick slowly. Andi rolled onto her side facing Ray. She crooked her head in her elbow. Tommy continued inspecting his marshmallow. In the firelight, orange and red danced on his glasses, and his face looked happy and fearless. She knew he was having fun, even in the midst of their trouble, and that made her feel all

265

the more in love with Ray. For the moment, she wasn't even sure if it was real love or just their circumstances that had generated these goose-bumpy feelings. She knew only she didn't want to lose it, whatever it was. She wanted it to last forever.

She nestled down under Ray's arm and a moment later she was spinning wildly down the tunnel into that red, heat-streaked darkness of her first experience on the TUT. She tried to open her mouth, but it was jammed shut. Then the grotesque creature she'd seen rose up before her out of the fire and brimstone.

"I have come for you!" it cried. "To take you."

She couldn't move. She was chained, straitjacketed in place. Something held her lips shut. All she needed to cry was "Jesus" and she'd be all right, as before. She knew it. But she couldn't get her tongue to move. It felt like a weight in her mouth. The creature stepped toward her. It's hot fetid breath made her rear back. It raised a clawed paw and touched her face.

"A pretty one," it said. "It's a pretty one this time."

It opened its jaws. The gaps between its yellow teeth wobbled eerily before her eyes.

Just scream, her mind yelled. Call for Jesus.

But she couldn't move. Why couldn't she move?

And then she heard a voice. "Andi! Andi! Wake up, it's me."

The sharp teeth touched her cheek. They cut.

"Andi!" Something shaking. An earthquake. The whole place was boiling up over them, covering them.

"ANDI!"

"Mom!"

Her eyes popped open. She was huddled on the ground, her face against a rock, sand in her mouth. The fire leaped and danced in front of her eyes.

"I thought I was there again!" she cried.

Ray helped her to her feet. "What happened? You were moaning and twitching. You fell asleep." He looked closer. "Your cheek is bleeding."

She touched it and felt the wetness.

"Sit down," Ray said. "Just relax a moment. We'll get something up at the cabin. I saw a first aid kit."

"I was there again," she murmured. "It was right in my face."

"It was just a dream, Andi," Ray said, still looking at her worriedly.

"They're here," Tommy said suddenly. "Just like before."

Ray said to Tommy, "Grab that bucket, and let's put out the fire. Let's get back up to the cabin."

CHAPTER TWELVE

1

Strock and Hughes cruised Pratt Street in the Fells Point section of Baltimore. Croase had wanted at least four people this time and they'd already found two, a young black woman, who showed immediate interest at the mention of a thousand dollars, and a teenager named Jeff who looked stoned and stressed out. The promise of free cocaine had snagged him. Already, they were both back at TWI being interviewed and prepared.

Now several ragged-looking people lounged by a bar on the corner of Pratt and Broadway, but Strock never picked up anyone attached to a group. He pulled the big green Chevy they were using that evening into a parking space facing north on Broadway and watched people walk up and down the sidewalk. As he lit a Marlboro, he said to Hughes, "D, you ever ask to try that TUT stuff they give all these people we bring in?" Typically, Strock called Hughes "D" for his first name, David, and David in turn had given Strock the nickname "Hit."

"Yeah, I know a little about it." Hughes knew plenty, but he rarely told Strock what was going on in his mind.

"It's supposed to let you die for a couple of minutes, then you come back."

"That's what I hear." Hughes began rolling a joint.

"S'posed to be better than reefer, maybe even crack."

"Yeah, I heard that."

"You want to try it?"

Hughes turned and looked at Strock with interest. "Why, you got some?"

"Possibly."

Hughes's eyes lit with interest. He flicked his little red Bic lighter under the tip of the joint and sucked in deeply, keeping his head down a moment, then sitting up. He held it out to Strock. The heavier man took it, held his hand over it, and drew on the thick roll. He handed it back to Hughes. People passed by, but no one gave them a second look.

"We might be able to go tonight. While we're still high."

Hughes laughed. "I'm not doing that while I'm high on somethin' else. Who knows what could happen?" He began watching a blue jeans-clad girl pushing a rusty supermarket cart past them up Broadway. "How about her?"

"What about the trip?" Strock said.

"Don't we have work to do?"

"Yeah, but I just want to know if you're in. Several others want to do it together. They say it's more fun."

"Who?"

Strock sucked on the passed joint again. "One of the nurses I been makin' it with upstairs, that guy in the shop who keeps the cars in shape, and one of the doctors. He's the one who got it. He asked me if I was interested."

As Hughes took the joint back. "We have to pay anything?"

"Freebie, man. One of the bennies of working for Martin Croase."

"Him!" Hughes pointed to a man strutting down the sidewalk in an Orioles cap and dirty, blue university jacket.

Strock looked up. "Nah, might put up a fight. I'm not in the mood for cracking skulls."

Hughes nodded. "Yeah, he is kinda big." He laughed. "So when's the big trip?"

"Tonight. In the garage, after we deliver two more bodies to the man. What do you say?"

Hughes shrugged. "Sure, I'm in. There's a first time for everything, right?" He squinted with a leer at Strock.

The bigger man was looking at the sidewalk again. "Hey, what about her?"

Hughes glanced at another black woman with a mammoth mane of blond hair. "Bingo," Hughes said. He rolled down his window.

2

"You had your face grinding right into that stone. That must have been what did it," Ray said as he dabbed at her cheek with a washcloth.

Andi flinched with pain. "I guess it was just a dream."

"More like a nightmare."

"It was so real. More real than a dream."

"Let's get Tommy settled. He's pretty upset. He's afraid now he'll have another bad dream."

"OK. I'll talk to him." She stretched a Band-Aid across the cut and went to his room. Ray came in and prayed with them together, then Andi let Tommy read for a while with the light on. Ray lay down on the couch while Andi plunked into one of the soft, cushioned chairs facing him and propped her legs up on the coffee table. Ray had got a fire going and was reading one of Andi's thrillers, but when she walked in he put it down.

"You sure you're OK?"

"It was just a dream, Ray." She paused. "I hope."

"Well, I know there was nothing else around."

She nodded and slumped down further into the seat, then ran her fingers through her hair. "I wonder how long we can do this. We have to make some decisions."

"Target practice went well today. You're not bad. Have you ever shot before—besides the great escape of a few days ago?"

"Once or twice. My father's a big hunter. Dad used to take us kids out to shoot skeet. I didn't get into it, but I knocked a few clay pigeons down. Maybe one in seven." She smiled. "You're a good teacher. Did you teach in the SEALs?"

270

She watched his eyes as he talked. She noticed the way his eyebrows moved when he thought deeply, and how his lips crinkled at the edges just before a smile came onto his face.

"Everyone teaches. You learn to tell your buddies everything you know and then some."

She wiggled her toes and crossed her feet. Ray noticed she had painted her nails with some clear nail polish. They glinted in the light. "What was it like in the SEALs?"

"You mean did I ever kill someone?"

"I was curious."

"Two times. At close range anyway. When I could really see the guy's face. It wasn't fun. But I was so scared at the time I didn't think about it till the whole thing was done."

"When?"

"During the invasion of Panama."

She waited for a few seconds before responding. "How do you feel about it now that you're a Christian?"

Ray gazed at the fire. "I don't think about it much. But I probably wouldn't have done anything different. I guess things happen to you in life which you can't erase, but you wonder if it could have been different."

Andi smiled wistfully. "My life hasn't exactly been the way I thought it would turn out when I was in college."

"How did you think it would turn out?"

"Oh, you know. I'd meet Mr. Right . . ."

"Not Mr. Macho?"

She laughed. "No, definitely not Mr. Macho. Mr. Sweep-Me-Off-My-Feet with a steady diet of romance—kisses, long talks in the night. I had this idea of a guy who was totally humble, who spurned money but probably never lacked for any, and who would look into my eyes and I'd feel the Holy Spirit at my elbow say, 'This is the one I prepared for you.'"

"And it never happened?"

"Oh, it happened all right."

Ray cocked his head with obvious interest. "It happened?"

"Yeah, he turned out to be this real humble but rich guy whom I was sure was the one. The Holy Spirit even whispered in my ear that he was it. But he never asked me."

"He didn't? How come?"

She crinkled up her lips and shrugged. "He couldn't deal with the reality of Tommy. Also, he wanted to be a missionary to India. I didn't want to leave the U.S. He said I was totally unspiritual. I agreed. And that was it."

"So now you've lived ever after with a huge load of regret?"

She shook her head. "No, not really. I just realized I wasn't cut out to be some super spiritual Christian who could live on mangoes and sweet potatoes for the rest of my life. I wanted the good life."

"And now you take care of a professor's house while he's on sabbatical."

She chuckled. "Yeah, well, what can I say?"

She leaned over and began kneading her toes. She groaned, gazed at them a moment, then sat back up. "Getting old."

Ray smiled. "Come here."

She didn't need a second invitation. A moment later, they were in one another's arms.

"I love you, Ray," she said and kissed him on the mouth.

"And I love you."

"What are we going to do?"

His brow knotted with consternation. "We've got to control it, Andi. We can't do the wrong thing."

She fought back a sudden urge to scream, but then she blinked and nodded. "I know. We can't compromise."

"But that doesn't mean we can't get a little romantic."

She leaned over and kissed him again. Suddenly, she realized he had stopped kissing her. She opened her eyes.

"This isn't going to help control it," he said.

"Maybe we shouldn't do it at all then," she answered, hoping he would disagree.

"I was thinking something else."

"Yes?"

"Maybe we ought to think about getting married. The idea might be enough to help us through."

She smiled. "Are you asking me to marry you?"

"To think about it, and pray. Real hard."

Her eyes fell. "I can do that."

"No," he said suddenly. "I am asking you to marry me. But I don't want your answer now. Not until we're completely out of this. But at least that will make my intentions clear."

She looked up and smiled. "I love you, Ray Mazaris."

He held her, and suddenly it felt to her as if the whole world had disappeared and it was just she and Ray Mazaris in Eden, the first two humans experiencing perfect and eternal love. She knew what her answer to him was, but she would wait, yes, until they were out of this. That was only fair.

And deep down it made her want to fight even harder to win.

3

Johnny Goge easily found Alice Chalmers's farm outside of Greenville, South Carolina. Croase had given him the address, and it was correct. Goge felt amazed once again at Benreu's precision.

Goge stopped the car forty yards down the asphalt, barely serviceable road, then proceeded on foot to the mailbox and brick walkway up to the door. It was three o'clock in the afternoon. Little traffic. He momentarily gazed across the huge peach orchards that surrounded the farm. Brown, shriveled peaches still hung on some trees, but the main harvest was over. He touched the Colt in his shoulder holster, then turned up the sidewalk.

The layout was exactly as Croase described it. White picket fence along the front of the yard. Stately southern aristocrat house with a lavish barn in the back. Orderly two-foot wide gardens along the sidewalk. How an eighty-two-year-old woman took care of it was beyond him. But Croase said she lived alone, was eccentric, and had a load of cash stashed away under some floorboards in the barn.

A gray-haired, very erect woman answered after he rang the buzzer. She opened the door wide and stared at him over steel-rimmed granny spectacles. "Yes?"

"I ran out of gas, ma'am." Goge bowed slightly. "I wondered if you might have a little gas to spare from a tractor or something, to get me to a service station."

She smiled. "Always glad to help a friend in need. Come in, and I'll get my sweater. I'll take you out to the barn."

Goge stepped into the large, paneled foyer with shiny wooden floors and thick, beautifully designed Persian throw rugs. She moved spryly, took a pink sweater off a coatrack in the corner, and pulled it on.

"I don't get a lot of visitors out here. Students from the university for meals now and then. But not much else. Nice to have a stranger."

Goge nodded.

"You know what the Bible says—'Beloved, thou doest faithfully whatsoever thou doest to the brethren, and to strangers.' So I'm always glad to do a good turn. Come this way."

Goge gazed at her, astonished. He almost choked. Why had Croase selected her? The others had been genuine dirt. He suddenly felt nervous and afraid.

She led him down the hallway and through a spotless kitchen to a porch and the backyard. When they came out, a black lab barked at him, but Goge noted he was chained and paid little attention.

"Settle down, Zipper. It's just a friend in need." She turned around and smiled. Her lips were thin and touched with a bit of red lipstick. But otherwise, her white hair was made up in a bun and she wore no other makeup.

She seemed to notice that he was looking at her lips. "I know," she said, "we're not supposed to wear it. But I just don't agree with everything the university says. And I'm not about to change my ways after eighty-four years."

"The university?" Goge said, trailing after her. They walked on a gravel path then stepped onto the dirt driveway back to the barn. He remembered Croase had said she was eighty-two. Was he wrong?

"Bob Jones's school," said the lady. "I take courses there. Working on my degree."

"That's quite an achievement, Mrs. Chalmers." Goge was sweating now. He couldn't do this.

The elderly woman suddenly whipped around. "How do you know my name?"

Goge was suddenly taken aback. Croase had told him, and she hadn't introduced herself. "Uh, I guess I saw it on the mailbox."

Her eyes flashed. "It isn't on the mailbox."

Goge swallowed. "Well, I don't know. I thought I saw it somewhere."

Mrs. Chalmers flexed the muscles in her cheek. "What do you want, young man? I have no money here."

Goge instinctively pulled out his automatic. "Just march along into the barn, lady." His voice was calm, but he glanced back at the road.

Mrs. Chalmers screamed, "Help!" She turned and started to run toward the barn, but Goge easily caught her. She kicked him, then fell to the ground. As he grappled with her, she bit his wrist. The dog was barking and howling behind him. They were in clear sight of the road. Goge knew he had to act fast.

She tried to punch him in the crotch, but he turned in time and her hand struck his thigh. Then he clipped her with the muzzle of the gun on the side of the head. She immediately slumped, unconscious.

Goge dragged her to the barn, cursing and terrified. This was all wrong, but what could he do? How could Croase do this? He hoped she wasn't dead, but he knew he couldn't just leave her. She could ID him.

He went in through a side door. The main door was pulled shut. It was a spacious barn, with many rusty farm implements, a tractor, several large bins on wheels, and a machine Goge figured must be used in picking peaches. She weighed less than ninety pounds, and he soon had her tied to the back of a tractor with rope he found lying on a work bench. Then he filled a bucket with water and threw it in her face. She revived moments later. The light was not good, but he could see her eyes flash with anger.

"What do you want, young man?"

Goge paced, holding the gun in his right hand. He didn't answer.

"Spit it out and let me go." She turned her face up to him and gave him an aristocratic, almost Roman, look.

"I hear you have a lot of money under some floorboards in here."

"That's not true."

"I have it on solid information."

"I don't have anything but my farm, my dog, my children, and my grandchildren, and they're not here."

"Where's the money, lady? I won't hurt you, if you tell me."

He began walking around the barn, kicking at floorboards. Croase had said it was in the very middle of the barn. He stooped down and tried to pull up a few boards.

"I tell you—"

Then he saw it. A loose board. He grabbed it, and it came up.

She screamed, "There's nothing in there."

But there was. It looked like the kind of box a camp stove came in. He pulled it out by the handle.

She screamed again. But Goge didn't pay attention. He opened the box. The money was all there, some of it looking old, but also many fresh bills. Several stacks of thousands. Giving a quick look-through, Goge estimated it was close to the four hundred thousand Croase had said.

She continued screaming, and he yelled, "Shut up," closed the box, and walked back over to her.

"Lady, I won't kill you if—"

Her eyes were slit, and he could see the anger glimmering in them. "What I'm going to do, young man, is start praying, and you'd best get out of here. Because I'm one good pray-er." She stared at him fiercely, then closed her eyes. "Dear Jesus, I pray that this young man would be redeemed from his sin. Convict him of the evil of his ways and open his eyes to the truth—"

Goge stood, a rush of anger and hatred burning through him. She continued on, but he smacked her on the cheek with the gun.

"Shut up, lady. Shut up!"

"Jesus, stop this man. Convict him. Make his soul writhe—"

Goge slapped her again. Her eye and cheek began to bleed. But she went on, "Jesus, forgive him. He's lost. Possessed. He's—"

Goge screamed. "Shut up!" He whacked her on the side of the head, and she stopped praying. Her head bent at an odd angle. Her mouth was still open and so were her eyes. She was dead.

Outside, the dog was still barking. Goge stared at the woman. He swore, then turned to go. But there was the letter. He went back to her. *Cut the letter into her cheek.*

He knew he couldn't do it.

Cut the letter!

Goge's hand was shaking. He pulled out the knife.

Into her cheek!

He closed his eyes. *Please, don't make me do this.*

But the insistent pushing inside him wouldn't stop. He opened his eyes and quickly cut the letter into the woman's thin tissue-like skin. It was an *E.* Then he grabbed the green box and ran.

"Just find a motel," he murmured as he gritted his teeth and turned out onto the main highway into Greenville. "I've got to talk to Croase."

□ □ □

Two hours later, he stopped and called Croase at his office. When the baritone voice answered, Goge said, "What are you trying to do to me?"

"What's wrong? Did you get the money?"

"The woman was a religious fanatic. She was praying to Jesus. Why did Benreu pick her? I'm not doing this again. The others were dirtbags. All right. But she was just a decent old lady."

"Slow down, boy. What's the matter? You got the money?"

"Yeah, I got the money." Goge stared at the cheap painting on the wall.

"Then forget it. She was worthless. Don't worry about it."

"Croase, we had a deal. Only dirtbags. This woman wasn't a dirtbag."

"Don't give me that, Johnny. You had a job to do. You did it. That's all that matters. I'm proud of you."

277

"You weren't there, man. It was awful. The woman was praying for me. Right on the spot."

"All right. So you had a run-in with a real religioso. Don't sweat it. They're a dime a dozen. You'll be all right. How much did you get?"

"I didn't count it. I'm still shaking."

"All right. Take your twelve percent and get the rest in a piece of luggage on a bus. It can be here by tonight."

"You are one heartless—"

"I don't pull the trigger, Johnny."

"Yeah. But that's about all."

"You unhappy?"

"No more of these, Croase, that's all. No more religious people."

"OK, I'll see what I can do."

Goge hung up and lay back on the bed. He was afraid to close his eyes, afraid to use the TUT, afraid to go outside. What was worse, he didn't even know why.

CHAPTER THIRTEEN

1

Strock and Hughes stood unsmiling in Martin Croase's office. The boss sat behind the desk, fixing his hard little eyes on each man with strange passivity. "So you've got it down to three people who might be helping them?"

"Yes, sir," Strock said, glancing at Hughes. "Two students, Harry Dimes and Clint Mervis, that Ray Mazaris roomed with last year. And Dr. Harold Kingston. We've got a couple bugs in place and several of the guys taking shifts. I guess we could bring them in."

"No, not Kingston. We've been trying to get rid of him for years. He's an old windbag but a big name with evangelicals. I don't want him to know anything if we can help it. How about a phone tap?"

"Too difficult and fairly easy to catch."

"Is someone tailing him?"

"As much as we can. We're a little short-handed, sir. You know we've got over fifty people patrolling the campuses and grounds night and day now."

Croase slapped his hand on the oaken desk. "I don't care what it costs. We need that kid. Hire several more people."

"Sir, it's not that easy to hire people. We have to screen them carefully, and it's always better—"

"OK, I know about that. What about using some of the nurses and doctors, other personnel?"

"They're not professionals, sir. But we can try." Strock smiled at Hughes.

"Get on it. Immediately. Nakayami is stymied, and I see no other solution." Croase looked down at his desk in his customary gesture of meeting over. Both men turned and started to walk out.

When they were outside the office, Hughes turned to Strock and said, "Got a little device the other day from the local cop supply house. Called a Rugbug. It's the perfect tracker. You can stay behind them up to five miles and still keep a fix." He handed the tiny bug to Strock. "And if you lose them, you can always try to pick them up later, even from the air."

"How many you get?"

"Six. They're not too expensive. I put it on the report."

"Good." Strock flipped it in his hand.

They swaggered down the hall and stepped onto an elevator. They were alone, and Strock punched the button to the garage.

"By the way," Hughes said, "we're not going to make our Willard quota this week."

"I know. They're winding down upstairs."

Hughes swore. "I really need the bread, man. What are we going to do?"

Strock smiled. "I've got it worked out. I'll tell you in the car."

Kent Farrell studied the headline on the layout before him. He was head editor of the campus newspaper, the *Atlantic Beacon*. Ever since he'd gone on the weekend jaunt to the conference center and tried the TUT, he'd suffered from brain-banging headaches, a sense of foreboding, strange paralyzing nightmares, and the feeling that dark forces were trying to capture his mind. He'd finally decided to do something about it despite the threatening atmosphere on campus.

Jenny Carlotti walked into the room and looked at the headline before Kent had a chance to cover it. She smiled and looked up into Kent's eyes. "About time someone decided to clobber this thing. I'm proud of you."

The headline read, "Is TWI Using the Atlantic Campus for Illegal Experimentation?"

Kent turned to her. "Jenny, if this gets me ejected, will you support me?"

"Sure will," Jenny said vehemently. "What's going on is wrong, and it all comes from that guy who runs TWI and the rest of this place—Dr. Croase. I don't like him, don't trust him, and if I'd known about him before I came here this year, I'd never have come. Every hall has a security guy on it—with a big gun on his hip."

Kent nodded. "Yeah, but this could blow the campus wide open."

"Maybe that's what it needs. Is it going out today?"

"Yeah. Be at the dorms tomorrow afternoon."

She grinned, then poked him. "This is what journalism's all about, isn't it? Taking some risks?"

"Yeah, but you never know what can happen." Kent had a sudden impulse to kiss her, but he'd never even asked her out, let alone thought she might like him. She was pretty, with long blond hair and large, brown eyes that reminded him of a girl he'd dated in high school.

Jenny leaned on the desk, then jumped up and sat on it. Her blue-jeaned legs hung down, and she scissored them back and forth. "Jefferson hasn't seen it, I take it."

"No, he's home sick. He doesn't know a thing about it."

"He might do more than eject you—us, I mean. You know, he's all gung ho for this TUT business."

"But three-quarters of the campus isn't."

"How do you know that, Kent?" She eyed him with a mixture of awe and skepticism. There had been some talk, but very little of the usual gossip was going around. People had clammed up.

"I've conducted my own little poll. It wasn't scientific, of course, but I think it could be a good indication. Eight people. And six were against it. At the meeting they had last

281

weekend—the one I went to—Dr. Croase told us everyone was all for it, it was going to push forward Christian apologetics five hundred years and offer Christians everywhere a unique spiritual and holy experience. But most of the people I saw there looked angry and terrified. Mainly terrified."

Jenny nodded, with anger in her eyes. "I think Croase has the whole campus bamboozled. Maybe we should just go to the police. Do you know anything about what happened to that ex-military guy, Mazaris?"

"People are saying he dropped out of seminary and has shacked up with one of the secretaries, Andi somebody."

"I don't believe it. It all happened shortly after they were taken on one of the weekends. Someone told me Andi's son was forced to take the TUT and nearly died. Then Croase made her and this guy Mazaris—because they refused and were going to leave—he made them take it too. Everyone I know is petrified. Two of my teachers are threatening about grades, calling parents, expulsion, everything, if any of us talks to people off campus about it. But no one seems to be worried about that kind of stuff. Just Croase and this legion of security people they've got hanging around all over the place. This place has turned into a Nazi camp."

"You don't have a car, I take it?"

Jenny shook her head.

"Neither do I, but someone told me he needed to get a special OK from the dean to even use his car now. They're taking people to the conference center in buses."

There was a sudden knock at the door, and another member of the editorial team walked in, smiling. His name was Bruce Kalimer. Both Kent and Jenny knew him to be one of the students much in favor of what Croase was doing.

Kalimer said, "Got the layout ready?" He was a tall, lanky male, who covered sports and spent more time in the weight room than writing his pieces. Kent had lobbied more than once to have him put off the staff for failing to get his facts straight.

Kent quickly folded the paper over. "Just taking it to the printer."

"Can I look at it?"

"What—the sports section?" Kent opened it up to page three, but Kalimer snatched it out of his hand.

"No, the whole thing." He scanned the headlines in the sports section, made some comments about his article.

"OK, you've seen it," Kent said, trying to take it back.

"What's the big rush? Who made the front page anyway?" He turned the sheet and looked it over.

Kent glanced at Jenny and waited.

Kalimer didn't seem to notice anything suspicious. He said, "Judd Timmerman'll like this one." He referred to an article Timmerman had done on TWI's work on computerizing the contents of the Dead Sea Scrolls.

"OK, Kalimer, let's have—"

"What's this?" Kalimer said as he spotted the headline.

"Nothing, Bruce, now—"

"This is—" Kalimer looked up. "You're saying TWI is using us as guinea pigs."

Kent swallowed. "I'm doing something I feel is right."

The bigger boy eyed Kent, then Jenny. "Maybe I'll just take this to Jefferson and see what he thinks of it." Kalimer turned and sped from the office before Kent could grab the copy work from him.

"You can't do that!" Kent yelled. He ran to the door, but Kalimer was already trotting to the main door. Kent turned to Jenny. "What are we going to do?"

"Do you have copies of everything?"

"Of course, but—"

"Then we have work to do. It's going to be one page, the front page, but we've got to get it out. You know this is wrong. I know it's wrong. And people like Kalimer and Jefferson shouldn't have the power to scare us with their tactics. Or Croase and his thugs."

Kent stared at Jenny. "I never thought—"

"Yeah, sweet little submissive Jenny Carlotti? Well, I'm getting a new name after today."

Kent gazed at her, a smile creasing his face. "What's that?"

"The Dragon-Slayer. Now come on. We don't have much time."

283

□ □ □

After dialing Hal Gordon at the dorm where he lived as resident adviser as well as professor, Dr. Kingston paced in his home office. He knew he needed to settle this one issue in his mind. Was the board completely behind Martin Croase? If that was so, then the seminary was doomed. He shook his head with anger as the phone rang. Then the phone clicked.

"This is Hal Gordon."

"Hal—Harold Kingston."

"How are you?"

"No time for formalities. I wonder if you can do me a favor?"

"Anything for you, Doc."

"Do you know about this thing Dr. Croase has going at TWI, dying and coming back to life again in a few minutes?"

"Yeah, I know about it." Kingston sensed Gordon had turned somber.

"What do you think?"

There was a long pause. "Maybe we shouldn't talk on the phone about it."

"All right. I'll meet you at Denny's down in Brinton."

"Too many profs hang out there. How about Martha's in Gaithersburg?"

"That's where we used to do our morning Bible study."

"Right," Gordon said. "It'll be like old times."

Kingston smiled. He sensed he had an ally in Hal Gordon.

Half an hour later, they sat at a booth in the well-lighted restaurant. Gordon was short, with a thick black mustache and piercing, pale, almost golden, eyes. He had been one of Kingston's prize students a decade ago, another Ray Mazaris.

Kingston briefly tested Gordon on a number of questions, and when he saw that Gordon was dismayed and completely against what was going on at TWI, he began to explain about what he thought had happened. He didn't tell Gordon about Ray and Andi.

"So what do you want me to do?" Gordon finally asked after fifteen minutes of talk and two cups of coffee.

284

"I want you to call several board members—Jed Hawkins, Glenn Pirelli, and Ford Hammond. They're the most—"

Gordon shook his head. "Doc, all three of their terms were up last year. They're gone."

"They're gone?"

"Replaced."

"With who?"

"More of Croase's cronies, I suppose. The whole board is stacked, Doc. That's how most of this has happened. Who does Croase have on it? His wife—she's worthless, I'm sorry to say. Straight out of a New Age book. Two or three other members of his family. And the others—lawyers, doctors, people he's supposedly known for years. No one objected because things were going so well, I suppose. The one thing they stood firm on was Croase's salary and bonus program. For all the money the school and TWI are taking in, we're desperately over budget and hard up for funds."

"How do you know all this?"

Gordon grinned. "I keep my ear to the rail, like you taught me."

"Guess I forgot how to do it myself," Kingston said, shaking his head sadly. "Then there's really no one we can talk to from that vantage point?"

"Nobody I know of."

They finished their coffees, and Kingston paid for them. On the way out, Gordon asked, "What can I do, Doc?"

"I don't know. But I think the first thing is find out who's with Croase and who isn't among some of the students. This could be a real inside fight, and we'll need all the support we can get."

"I've got my eye on a number of kids I can trust," Gordon said. "I'll get on it. Keep me informed."

"Of course."

2

Ray finally found Lyle Hornum by phone at 5:12 in the afternoon. He had talked with several librarians at the New

York Public Library, tracking down some leads on TWI and Martin Croase.

"I have something interesting," Ray said. "Listen to this." He began reading his uneven script. "It's from an article in the *Wall Street Journal* over seven years ago. It's titled 'Lambda Exec Joins Religious Research Firm.' I tried to get what I could, but since I don't have a fax, she had to read it to me. Anyway, this is the gist of it.

> Martin Croase, after a meteoric rise at Lambda Research, has accepted the chairmanship of a religious research firm in Brinton, Maryland, called TWI. The founder, an evangelist named Gordon Watt, has announced plans for Croase to manage their extensive research program in the unknown realms of life after death. Watt says, "My vision is for death-travelers, thananauts, to explore the outer reaches of human consciousness and destiny." Croase has long been known for his interest in the paranormal.

Lyle listened raptly without comment. When Ray finished, he said, "Pretty heavy stuff, I'd say."

"The paranormal is the occult," Ray said.

"I know. How did Watt ever get in with this guy?"

"That's what I'd like to know. But apparently Croase turned this Lambda Research place around during a recession a few years back. The article quotes Croase as saying he has a strong desire to explore Christian mysticism and supernatural experience. But listen to this. It also says, 'Before his rise at Lambda, Croase was known as the man who devised one of the first successful pyramidal financial schematics for a Libby Andrews Cosmetics that went from a home-based business to a multi-million dollar corporation.'"

"So?" Lyle said.

"But what if Croase is devising that kind of thing for the TUT?" Ray said. "It's all a big money-making scam."

"It'll never work."

"Why?"

"FDA. They'd have to approve the drug to let it be marketed. And I think this would become classified as an illegal drug but quick. Furthermore, why would real Christians lock into this? Why would they even believe in it? Look at you and Andi."

"Yeah, but what about the rest of the campus? Look at all the people Croase has talked into trying it."

Lyle was silent a moment, then said, "Ray, I think you ought to understand another reason I left that school."

"Why?"

"Because I began to think a lot of people there had no real relationship with the Lord. There were kids having illicit relationships, and the leadership just looked the other way. And there was also this obsession with experience. It was like everyone had to prove they'd had a deeper, more mystical, more incredible zap than everyone else. Look at the testimonies you heard in chapel. It was always some big miracle God had done. People were always praying that God would make this happen and that happen and He would zap the president and He would convert half of Russia in one night so everyone would know He did it. It was ridiculous. People prophesying in chapel—how much of it ever came true? Healings. Look at them. How many were authentic? It was nuts."

Ray gulped. "It made me feel like I was missing something myself."

"Me too. For a while. They offer you the Greek and Hebrew and a measure of scholarship and some big names like Dr. Kingston, and you think that automatically means God's in it. It doesn't. Not in my book."

"I know what you're saying."

"No, you don't, Ray. It's this demand for miracles, for 'big things to happen,' for personal experiences that has led to this. A lot of Christians can't seem to deal with the fact that Christ called for faith, following Him to death, and obeying Him even when it hurts, even when it doesn't make sense, even when He doesn't do some miracle to make everything right again. A lot of the Christian life is just plain trekking along day by day, doing good, praying, giving, sharing, encouraging. A lot of it is tough and painful. God sometimes does heavy things here and there. But most of the time, He expects us to grow up and get off the chocolate bar fix and start eating real meals—which involves blood, tears, toil, and sweat. That's the only way I can put it."

"You don't know how good it makes me feel to hear you say that."

Lyle chuckled. "That's how I feel, Ray. That's why I left. I began to realize all this pyrotechnic nonsense wasn't real Christianity. I suspect that most of the people on that campus are searching for something that doesn't exist—that's why they've gotten sucked into this TUT deal."

"It makes a lot of sense."

"I'm glad you think so."

"But we still haven't figured out what Croase is trying to do."

The reporter paused, and there was a lengthy silence. "I'm not sure. But I think we're going to have to understand this experience a little better. What exactly is happening and why? I mean, the Bible says when we die we go to be with Christ, right? But obviously that's not what happened to you. Exactly, I mean."

"That's true. I hadn't thought about it. You know, though, there was an article in *Christianity Today* or one of those magazines about a guy out in Oregon who had a theory. A Christian, I mean."

"You remember when?"

"A year, two years ago."

"Try to dig it up. Meanwhile, I'm going to do some snooping at TWI. I'll see if I can find anything out about this Lambda Research too. Anything I ought to look for?"

Ray considered a moment. Then he said, "Remember the body bags I told you we saw? Maybe they were people they'd already experimented on. They died in the process. So where could they be getting the people without being caught?"

"Lots of places. Homeless people. Vagrants. Hookers. Alkies. People no one cares about. They disappear all the time. There's always someone in here with a report about someone on the street who's vanished. But who cares about them? You got bucks, they care. You got nothin', forget it."

Ray thought about it and felt the anger churning his stomach.

288

"All right," Lyle continued, "what about where they're taking the bodies after they're dead? We get some of that on camera, we've got murder one, man. They're probably shipping them to some place to be buried, maybe a big garbage pit. No, that might be too much of a pain. They have to get rid of them completely."

"Cremation," Ray said.

Lyle was silent. "Then that means they have some way of burning them."

"Maybe they own some place with their own setup."

"Somewhere nondescript. Nearby, in the country probably."

"Could be." Ray looked out the window at Andi and Tommy sitting on the patio talking and having Cokes. Tommy was throwing peanuts to several of the chipmunks and squirrels that lived in the woods beyond the patio wall. "I just don't want any of us ending up in a body bag."

"Don't worry. I think we can pull it off. But you'll probably have to come down here to do it with me. Frankly, I don't know who I can trust in the station with something like this. They might consider it crazy religious stuff. Not many of the brethren or sisteren around here. But I can scope the place out in some unmarked vehicle, try to get a fix on the kind of truck they might be using, and follow it. Then just get the material on a little video camera I have. It shouldn't be too hard. Following the right truck will be the hard part."

"I remember seeing a white van outside when we checked out the garage that time. That might be our best bet."

"Could be. I don't think it'll be that hard, brother. How soon can you come down?"

"Let me think about it and discuss it with Andi and Tommy. It'll be difficult to talk them into staying here alone."

"I understand."

"I'll give you a call tomorrow. Four-fifteen. Be available. I don't want to run up Doc's brother's bill too bad."

"Gotcha."

Ray went outside and sat down on the patio with Andi. They had unearthed several green and white chaises in the basement. Andi had started a talk session with Tommy each afternoon. They discussed whatever was on his mind, read some Bible, and prayed. Ray usually joined them, but today he wanted to get through to Lyle before he left the television station office.

"Get through?" Andi asked as he came down the back stairs off the raised porch.

"Yeah, he had some ideas about what to do."

Tommy stopped pitching peanuts and turned around.

"It means he wants me to come down and help."

"Leave here?" Andi exclaimed. "No way. Not until these guys are dealt with."

"But how are they going to be dealt with unless we do it?" Ray said, staring back into her flashing eyes. "No one is investigating them. We're the ones they're after. We've got to get something to blow this whole operation sky high."

"Dr. Kingston will do it."

"He's a professor, Andi. Not a PI. And—"

"Neither are you."

"I'm an ex-SEAL, and Lyle's done investigative reporting before. We can handle ourselves. It'll be OK. It's what we need to get enough evidence to get the police to get a search warrant and bust the thing wide open."

Andi folded her arms. "Then we're coming with you."

"Oh no. You're not leaving here. I'm sure that—" Ray stopped, realizing Tommy did not know TWI wanted him for experimentation.

"Sure of what?" Andi said, glancing at Tommy.

The boy's eyes behind the thick glasses were fixed on Ray's face. "That they want me," Tommy said.

Both Andi and Ray turned to face him. Ray said, "Now Tommy, I didn't say that."

"But you know it, and so do I."

"How do you know that?" Andi asked.

"Because they told me. When I was alone."

"What did they tell you?" Ray leaned forward.

The boy's eyes flickered, and he wouldn't look directly at Ray.

"That I was the only one ever to go beyond." Tommy looked down into his lap. His hands were tightly wound together.

"Beyond what?" Andi asked.

"Something out there. Something when you die."

"The wall," Andi said. "Remember the wall, Ray? That was what Croase meant by the special gift. We just made it to that wall, then we came back. But because Tommy was up there longer—" She turned back to him. "Did you go beyond the wall? I think they called it 'the threshold.'"

"I think so. I'm not sure. I don't remember so good. They asked me if I met with him."

"Who?" Andi said. Her face was white with fear.

"That person. They said his name was Benreu."

"Benreu?" Andi looked at Ray. "Did he—it—give you a name?"

"No," Ray answered.

Tommy looked from Ray to Andi. "You won't let them do it to me again, will you?"

Andi came over and sat next to him on his chaise. "No, never, honey. Never. Tommy, why didn't you tell us this before?"

"I was afraid. I was afraid you might think I had done it wrong. They stuck needles in me and everything. When I was dead. I could see them."

Andi glanced at Ray, her eyes brimming with tears. "Call Dr. Kingston, Ray. I want him to come up here this weekend."

Ray said, "I think we can handle this, Andi."

"I don't want him to come up to counsel Tommy. I want him here so we can go down and help Lyle."

"We?"

"You and me. We're going to get Croase. I don't care what it takes." Her face was red, and Ray could see it took all her self-control to keep from swearing.

"I think we should discuss this later."

"No discussion. I'm going. Tommy'll be safe with Dr. Kingston. It'll do him good to be around a grandfather. You'd like that, wouldn't you, honey?"

Tommy suddenly smiled. "Yeah, I'd like that." He paused, then shifted his feet back and forth. "He won't ask me a lot of Bible questions, will he?"

Ray laughed. "Probably demand that you explain dispensationalism to him."

Tommy grinned. "Oh, I know about that. I had one of them when I was younger."

Staring at him uncomprehendingly, Andi said, "What?"

"A disk spin. Remember, you gave it to me for Christmas."

Andi and Ray laughed. "Disk spin-sationalism, huh?"

"Right," Tommy said, nodding heartily. "People who really spin well."

"Like you?"

"I was pretty good at it."

Ray tousled his hair. Andi crushed him with another hug, and Ray put his arms around both of them. Ray said, "Let's get some dinner."

Tommy shouted, "Yeah, some dinner!"

Andi looked from Tommy to Ray, then shook her head with exasperation. "We have this heavy discussion, and then all you think about is your stomach."

"That's the best way to feel better I know of."

"One of these days I'm going to make you cook the whole day. It'll be the miracle of the Fall."

Tommy wriggled out from her grasp. "I'll set the table," he called behind him as he ran up the stairs.

Ray and Andi walked over to the redwood-stained siding on the back of the house. At the bottom of the stairs, Ray said to her, "He's a resilient kid, Andi. This'll soon be way behind him. We're seeing flashes of his humor already."

"I know, though I'm not sure he even realizes it."

He pulled her to his chest. "That's the best kind."

She kissed him, and he said as they pulled apart, "We'll get this all worked out. I'm sure we'll get the evidence we need."

She blinked. "I know." She moved out of his arms and started up the stairs.

He touched her shoulder. "Thanks for making me feel a part of the family."

She turned around, and he could feel her breath on his face. "That's because you are." She suddenly kissed him again on the lips, then quickly hurried up the steps.

3

Martin Croase stood with Ken Strock at the huge underground piping system that controlled all the water flow at TWI and the Atlantic campuses. "What I want is some way of feeding a special chemical into the water system, Ken."

Strock stood on a stool and rapped on the pipe. "Should be easy. Just put in couple of valves to control it and some way of filtering it in. What kind of chemical, sir?"

Croase shrugged offhandedly. "Just a project I have in mind. Sort of like putting fluoride in water to help your teeth."

"Whatever you say." Strock told himself whatever it was he wasn't planning to be around to drink any of that water when Croase gave the word to inject it into the supply.

"I want something else, Ken."

Strock climbed down from the stool. "What?"

"A mechanism for releasing the chemical and then having the whole sprinkler system on campus start up at the same time. I want it all to happen at the push of a switch. Maybe one of those electronic radio devices. Think you can organize that?"

"Shouldn't be too much of a problem. You mean the fire sprinkler system in the rooms and halls?"

"Right."

Strock tried not to stare at Croase with any obvious bewilderment or fear. He looked away and pretended to be concerned about moving the stool.

"Any reason you have for doing this, boss?" he said casually. "Pretty expensive operation."

"I just want it done. That's all. Let me know when it's all completed."

"You got it, boss. By the way, the latest course is set up in the barn for you."

"Great. I was hoping you'd be done."

□ □ □

Later that afternoon, Croase went out to the barn ready for a good shoot-'em-up. But somehow the usual excitement didn't accompany all the blasting of the Uzi and a perfect score on the dummies.

When he was through, he stood in the doorway as the acrid gunpowder smoke still formed small puffs in the air. *I wonder what it's like to really kill someone*, he mused.

He raised the Uzi and squeezed off a few rounds at the last dummy, now hanging sideways out of its bin where it had popped up only a few minutes before. *Someone like Mazaris. One-on-one. That would be the ultimate.*

With a quick, deft motion, he pulled another thirty-two-round clip from his belt, dropped out the empty, and pushed it into the slot. He looked around the room, then up at the long beam that went along the ceiling. Gritting his teeth, he leaped to the floor, rolled, lay flat, and began raking the beam. Chips of wood clattered down around him. The smoke was intense. All thirty-two shell casings spit out and pinged on the concrete.

When the smoke cleared, Croase looked at his handiwork. A long neat line of holes appeared on the beam.

"Yeah, someone like Mazaris."

4

In the morning Ray kept Andi and Tommy to a stiff regimen of fifty shots each with the .38 and the .22 respectively. Both soon learned to be accurate enough at twenty feet to stop anyone coming at them. Tommy began calling it the "GI Joe Session." He added after one workout, as he and Ray walked together and Andi was getting a picnic basket out of the 4x4, "Pretty soon I'll be like the good Terminator."

"You see the movie?"

"Yeah, it was cool," Tommy answered.

"How come?" Ray was curious what kind of answer Tommy might give. It seemed he learned something new every day about a child's perspective on life.

"Because he liked the boy and his mom. I could tell. He really liked them even though he was a robot."

Ray wondered if Tommy thought of him that way. But Tommy immediately seemed to sense his question and said, "But I know you're not a robot, Mr. Ray."

"Oh, you do? How do you know that?"

"Because you make jokes. And you don't talk like the Terminator does."

"How's that?"

"Like he has the inside of a peanut butter and jelly sandwich stuck to his tongue."

Ray laughed and gave Tommy a little shove. "That's what we're having for lunch."

"No, we aren't. Fried chicken. I saw."

"Oh, how come fried chicken?" Ray had begun to enjoy bantering with Tommy considerably.

"Because you're always s'posed to have chicken on a picnic. Didn't you know that?" The boy squinted at him in the sunlight, a red Phillies cap he'd found in the loft perched almost on top of his glasses.

"No, why's that?"

Tommy answered with teacherly frustration, "Because of Kentucky Fried Chicken. They started it hundreds of years ago. Like a tradition."

Ray batted the back of his head and knocked the cap off. "You're nuts."

"And you're updock." Tommy gazed at him hard and unblinking, obviously waiting for the joke to register.

"What's updock?"

"Who do you think you are—Bugs Bunny?"

Ray couldn't stop it. He nearly roared, then recovered and said, "You're silly."

"Yeah." He smiled sheepishly. "Uh-oh, here comes Mom. We have to be serious now, so she doesn't think we're talking about her."

After one of Andi's masterful picnic lunches, Ray spent each afternoon trying to get information about Watt, TWI, Martin Croase, and the NDE. He found an assistant at the New York Library who was willing to do the digging for the professor's article about a Christian interpretation of the near death experience. That Friday the assistant found the article, but it was four years old and was actually a review of a book on another subject. But it had several paragraphs in which the author, Thomas Summerville, had spoken of the classic NDE research and his theory about its meaning. Ray decided to call him at a seminary in Oregon.

When Ray finally got through, Summerville was eager to talk. He sounded young, a theologian on the way up. It felt good to do some theological shop talk, something he'd missed. But then Ray asked him about the NDEs he'd studied.

"I've been studying it ever since seminary," Summerville said, "and frankly, I think it's one of the greatest deceptions the devil's come up with yet. If people become convinced scientifically that death holds nothing but joy, peace, and love for all eternity with no consequences for their past life, virtually all religions fly out the proverbial window. There's nothing to hold the Christian in his convictions because he now has so-called scientific proof of what happens, and there's no need to believe in judgment, hell, sin, or any of the other elements of Christianity—including salvation, the cross, bodily resurrection, a last judgment, you name it."

Summerville tended to speak in long-winded run-on sentences, but Ray did not find him hard to follow.

"How do you think these demons operate?"

Summerville paused, then began slowly but emphatically. "Of course, this is just my own theory, Ray. I have no clear evidence about it from the Bible, but I think there is some kind of middle ground out there between death and the actual entrance into the eternal state. Or should I say, the spiritual state before bodily resurrection. What I mean is that there definitely is that tunnel you experienced, that place, and that 'being of light,' as some of the other researchers call it. It's all part and parcel of 'getting there,' getting from your body here on earth to heaven, Paradise, or whatever you want to call it. But that middle place is like a temporary state just before entrance into the real thing. It's like C. S. Lewis's 'wood between the worlds' in his book *The Magician's Nephew.* Do you know it?"

"One of the Narnia books?"

"Yes."

"Read them several years ago."

"Good, well, this place is an in-between place and state. I'm certain of that because most people who report extensive out of the body experiences say they reached some kind of point of no return, a threshold, a dividing line which they knew they couldn't cross without being dead for good. Of course, some people claim to have crossed it and actually gone into heaven, met relatives, and so on, but frankly I still think they were in that middle point between the earthly and the eternal."

"So this place is like the doctor's waiting room."

Summerville laughed. "Good illustration. I'll remember that."

"But people report that while there they reviewed their whole lives, the light being they talked to assured them any sins didn't matter, and so on. Why would that happen?"

"It's all part of the deception," Summerville said. "I believe God has given Satan and his cohorts authority over that middle ground. Up until that point, they're free to deceive and roam about as they wish."

Ray was stunned. "You think God gave them permission to do this?"

"Not permission to deceive but authority over the temporary stopping place. They have chosen to use it to deceive people."

"But why would God do that?"

"Do you know what it says in Second Thessalonians two about deception?"

"Sort of."

"Let me quote it." There was a pause, and Summerville read, "'For this reason God will send upon them a deluding influence so that they might believe what is false, in order that they all may be judged who did not believe the truth, but took pleasure in wickedness.'"

297

"Yeah, I've studied that one before. So you think God's enemies are using this middle ground place as a means of deceiving the world."

"One of many such deceptions," Summerville said, "but a particularly effective one."

Ray rubbed his knees, thinking. Then he said, "Do you have any proof of this theory of yours?"

Summerville laughed. "Not much, except that I believe the Bible and therefore must try to come up with some explanation in light of it. Satan can appear as an angel of light, God is allowing deception to go on in order to seal unbelievers in their wicked state, and there are demons at work in the world. Also, the NDE is virtually a twentieth-century phenomenon. There are very few reported instances before the rise of modern resuscitation methods. Finally, there are many horror stories besides all the flighty, positive ones you hear on the talk show circuit. People have claimed to have experienced hell and demonic torture during an NDE, and many cannot substantiate the claims of the researchers. I honestly feel most researchers focus in on the positive cases and put that forth as the truth. I'm afraid it's just more of the great deception."

"Why aren't we doing anything about this?"

"I am."

Ray laughed. "Yeah, but there aren't any big bucks from Christians being used to finance scientific research into the truth—at least not—" Ray decided not to say anything to Summerville about TWI.

Summerville answered, "Why should they? The enemy has the burden of proof on this issue, and to my mind he hasn't proved a thing. Deception is always like that. It throws out some preposterous claim, and then all the little Christians are scrambling to disprove it. By the time they get their grits together on it, the deceiver has already shoved five other issues out there that require just as massive an effort. It happened with evolution, so-called Bible contradictions, nearly every area of hard theology, and more ethical issues like abortion and euthanasia. Just think of how hard it is to prove a case in court today. Any case. Divorce. Murder. Even the most clear-cut cases often have just the right mix of truth and error to make you wonder. Don't you think it would be even more so with a metaphysical, mystical issue like this?"

"So why do you think God is doing this?"

"Why does God do anything, Ray?"

Ray waited.

"Because it's God's prerogative to do it any way He chooses, within the parameters of His own attributes."

Ray nodded agreement as he listened. Finally he said, "I guess He has His reasons which, if we had the same wisdom, omniscience, and perfection, we'd agree with."

"Yes, you're a seminary student all right."

"Well, Dr. Summerville, you've been a great help. Thanks."

That afternoon, Ray told Andi about the conversation. She commented that it made sense, but was more interested in any progress made with Lyle. Ray didn't have any.

That night, he called up Dr. Kingston. "Doc, it's me. Think you could come up this weekend?"

Dr. Kingston's voice was gruff, as if he'd just awakened. "I don't have plans, but do you think it's safe?"

Ray sat at the window phone. Andi and Tommy stood by the back door, listening to what was said. He knew they were both for it now, even though Tommy was nervous about being alone with Dr. Kingston. He kept asking if the good doctor would lecture him in "Bible stuff." Ray had assured him over and over he wouldn't.

"We've got some ideas we want to discuss with you, and it's necessary for you to be here."

Kingston coughed. "OK, I understand. Let me make arrangements. But I'm a little wary. I've seen some strange people around."

"You think they might be trying to follow you?"

"Possibly. I'm not sure. I've been a little paranoid ever since you called me up that first night with news of a murder plot against you. But I'll be careful. I can pull a few evasive maneuvers I've learned about in those crime novels I read. Friday night OK? Probably late. I have a 4:30 class."

"I know. I'm supposed to be in it."

Kingston chuckled. "Don't worry. I'll give you the test over the weekend."

"Just what I need." He put the receiver against his chest and nodded to Andi, mouthing, "He says yes." She opened the door, saying to Tommy, "Come on, hon, let's go down to the lake."

Ray put the receiver back to his ear. "All right. We'll be looking for you. You need directions?"

"Right," Kingston said with another chuckle. "By the way, I talked to Hal Gordon about the board situation."

"And?"

"Pretty grim. Looks like the whole board is just a Croase rubber stamp."

Watching Andi and Tommy walk down to the lake, Ray said, "That's what I figured."

"I'll see you soon. Sorry about the bad news." Kingston hung up.

Ray went out the back door and down the stairs. He caught up with Andi and Tommy as they meandered down the wood chip covered path. Putting his arms over both their shoulders, he said, "I think we're actually going to do it this time."

When they reached the lake, Andi climbed up onto the dock, pulled high up on the beach for the winter, and dangled her legs over the edge. Ray went down to the water with Tommy. "Want to skip some stones?"

Tommy bent down to pick up several round stones and began throwing them in the air and trying to hit them with his stick. He missed several times, but each time he said, "Home run!"

Ray sidearmed some flat stones out across the water, skipping them ten times or so. "Still hitting home runs, Chief?"

"Definitely," Tommy said with a determined look in his eyes. The stick suddenly cracked with the sound of stone striking wood, and the stone flew over the water, plopping about thirty feet out. "Now there's a double."

Ray threw several more before speaking. As Tommy hit more stones over the water, Ray said, "You really feel OK about this, Chief?"

Tommy ripped another liner over the lake. It stung the water, skipped, then sank. He turned and squinted at Ray through the thick glasses. "I guess I don't have much of a choice."

"You have a choice. Do you feel like you can handle it?"

Tommy nodded. "I have to stop being scared sometime, don't I?"

"Being scared doesn't mean anything, Tommy. It's what you do when you're scared that counts."

The boy hit another stone. "I know," he said. "I think it'll be OK. He can even talk about disk-spin-sationalism."

Ray smiled. "Still into toyology, huh?"

"Toyology?"

"The study of toys."

Staring at him quizzically, Tommy suddenly smiled. "Maybe that's what I'll be when I grow up: a toyologist. You'll study theology. Mom'll study nurseology. And I'll study toyology. We'll be the genius family." He beamed as if he'd just discovered the ultimate family glue.

They threw stones for a minute, then Ray said again, "You sure you'll feel comfortable with Dr. Kingston?"

They both watched another stone skim the water gracefully and arc to the right at the end. "You think he's good, don't you?"

"Sure. But that's me."

"Then I think he's good, too." Tommy kept his eyes on the water.

Ray touched his shoulder, suddenly feeling somber and moved. "Tommy, you have to understand. I don't even want your mother to go, but I can't order her around. Still, I think it's safer for you here. And if we don't go, if we don't get this cleared away, we'll never be able to go home."

"I know."

Ray gripped his shoulder.

"Just as long as you're coming back."

"We'd never desert the likes of you." Ray looked back at Andi swinging her legs on the edge of the dock and combing her hair. He sensed that she had been watching him with Tommy and approved. It made him feel good.

He looked at the setting sun, shading his eyes with his hand. It would soon be dusk and time for dinner. The air smelled of pine, and slightly of dead fish. Ray noticed a perch lying belly up a few yards downwind. "Be thinking about you, Chief," he said and walked over to Andi, letting Tommy continue hitting stones into the lake.

She scissored her legs from the dock above him. He lay his hand on her jogging shoe and said, "He's a good kid."

"Think he'll be all right?" she whispered.

He nodded. "Yeah, he'll do OK."

He looked up into her eyes. In the dimming light, her face looked dark and mysterious. "Andi," he said, "you're a very beautiful woman to me."

She threw back her hair, exposing a fine, white neck. "That's what all my lovers say."

Ray coughed. His heart had begun to pound. He ignored her joke. He didn't want to joke. "I mean, this is all going to be over soon. You don't think last night was just—"

She waited. Why didn't she say something? Ray growled in his mind.

"Just?"

"You know—the passion of the moment?"

"Do you want out of your question?"

He tried to read her face, but suddenly it was utterly un-readable. He wondered why women could be so up front one minute and so secretive and inscrutable the next. Again he realized how much he loved her, and he realized it was her differences from him that made him desire her. If she had been more like him, he probably wouldn't even be attracted to her.

Looking evenly into her dark eyes, he said, "No, I don't ever want out of that question."

She raised her eyebrows whimsically. "Well, what's the matter—cat got your tongue?"

He breathed deeply, trying to control the hammering in his chest. Why was it all suddenly so difficult. Last night had been so easy. "It's just—" he murmured. He couldn't get it out.

Suddenly, she leaned down and looked into his eyes.

"Ray, I'll make this a little easier on you. First of all, I love you. Second, I never want to be without you. And third, if we survive all this and you suddenly decide you want out of your question, I'll let you out, and then I will personally kill you."

The unease evaporated. "You make me feel so good, Andi. I can't stand the thought of not being with you. And Tommy, too."

He kissed her gently, warmly, his finger raising her chin slightly.

Afterwards, she said, "I've never met anyone like you, Ray."

"Lucky for me."

"Seriously."

"Maybe we're a perfect match."

"Maybe." She smiled, then jumped down off the dock and planted a fierce kiss on his lips, hugging him tightly. "Now let's go eat dinner before I swoon."

Ray turned and held her happily, then looked around at Tommy, wondering if he'd seen what was going on. But the boy was still skipping stones, totally absorbed in selecting the right stones for maximum skips. *Yeah, he's a good kid,* Ray thought, *and this woman is incredible.*

CHAPTER FOURTEEN

1

Ken Strock walked into Harvey Konopka's office and stood, waiting. Konopka stepped inside and shut the door. Konopka was a short, wiry man with a weather-beaten face and hard brown eyes. He was the head bookkeeper, nothing special, but ultimately all the numbers came down to his computer entry system. Strock had worked out a few rather sticky deals with him before that involved some number finagling that was profitable for both of them. Konopka didn't make a lot of money as a bookkeeper, had seven kids, and a nasty wife on top of it all. "All right, what's this about extra dead bodies?" Konopka said.

"You know Willard?"

"Of course. I worked out the deal."

"Well, we've got something a little better going."

The short man sat down and lit a cigarette. "Yeah."

"Nakayami's not killing them off fast enough."

"So?"

"But TWI will still pay five thousand per body, right?"

"Correct."

"So we're thinking about an increased body count that goes around Nakayami."

"I'm not interested in the details. Just where do I fit in?"

"You approve the pay slips. Just pay Willard for how

ever many bodies we sign for. Any extras, you get four hundred a crack."

"What do you mean extras?"

Strock rubbed his chin. "It's like this. Say Nakayami delivers three to cold storage."

"You mean people who die because of these experiments?"

"Right. That's fifteen thou, all Willard's."

"I'm following."

"But what if Hughesie and I go out and make three more stiffs."

Konopka's eyes got big. "You guys would do that?"

"Look, don't worry about us. Just imagine. So now there's six. But Nakayami has only accounted for three. Still, if we turn in six, and you OK it, Willard gets thirty thou. Now the way I see it, we should get a big cut of that. It only costs him a hundred or so to incinerate them."

Konopka dribbled smoke out of his mouth and drew it back in through his nose. "So I get four hundred for each one I approve above the Nakayami number?"

Strock smiled craftily. "Let's make it five hundred."

The dark little man shrugged. "Sounds good to me. But I want to know the precise numbers. No cheating."

"Of course not."

The two men shook hands, and Strock left for a meeting with Croase.

2

Listra gestured angrily at her husband as both Strock and Hughes stood at the door, waiting for the argument to finish. "I think this obsession with Tommy Darcasian has got to stop," she seethed. "I don't want to hear any more about him. Just get him and find out how it works."

Croase stared at her incredulously. "There's no reason for you to feel in competition with him, my dear."

Listra screeched, "I don't feel in competition! Next thing you'll say is that I'm jealous."

"You are, Listra dear. There's no other explanation."

305

Listra swore furiously. "It has nothing to do with jealousy. It's rightful position. I don't want anyone thinking this boy has an edge or something."

"He doesn't have an edge." Croase looked helplessly at the two security men. Listra's sudden rages had increased, and it was making problems for all of them. "It's just that he's—"

"The only one who can tolerate the TUT-B! That's it! Well, I can too. Rafa has assured me that we are only a few steps away from a breakthrough. And once it's perfected, I want to be the first and only one using it on a regular basis. Is that understood?"

"Listra, this is contrary to all the principles of our plan and research in general. Yes, you are good at this. And you may be the primary trainer and guide for thanatravel. But you can't go dictating every little thing."

Listra's face was a searing twist of anger and revulsion. "If it wasn't for me, you would know nothing about it!" she yelled. "Or have you forgotten that?"

Croase stilled his anger and looked down at his desk. "I haven't forgotten anything. Please control yourself, honey."

"I am controlled. And don't tell me what to do. I'm tired of taking orders around here. I should be giving them."

Hughes moved closer to her, but he was wary of touching her or trying to stop her. Croase moved out from around the protection of the desk. "Perhaps we should all just have a drink. That will settle our stomachs."

"I don't have an upset stomach. I want to get past that threshold, Martin. I want you to do whatever it takes. That's all I'm concerned about. All we have is failure, failure, failure."

"And if we get the boy, we'll have success, success, success!" he gestured plaintively and smiled at Hughes and Strock.

Listra was still not ready for a joke. "I told you, I don't want to hear about the boy. Just get him, find out what makes it work, and make it work for me. You are planning to be rid of him when that's accomplished? And the other two?"

"Of course. We certainly can't keep any of them around after all that has happened. It'll be taken care of. Now please, calm down." Croase stood at the bar and waved a crystal decanter of scotch. "Chivas Regal, anyone?"

Hughes nodded with a frustrated look on his face. "Mrs. Croase, please." He laid his hand on her shoulder. She shook him off, but then nodded. Her husband poured the drinks.

As they sipped at the biting scotch, Croase noticed she seemed a little more subdued. "Believe me, dearest, we only need the boy for a few tests. You are and always will be the primary thananaut."

Eyeing him over her glass, Listra said, "I'm not a little girl to be coaxed and pacified, Martin. I just want things done properly. Don't patronize me."

Croase swallowed, realizing once again Listra's tantrums were never easily overcome. "Then tell me about what Rafa is saying? You haven't been filling me in like before."

Taking another sip, Listra said, "Rafa is concerned that TWI seems so disorganized, and he is convinced Nakayami is a bad choice for chief research engineer. He believes he is a traitor, and you will run into problems down the road."

"Dr. Nakayami is—"

"The best. Yes. But Rafa has grave doubts. Believe me, Rafa knows. Rafa knows a great deal, Martin. More than Benreu. More than any of the others. You'd be surprised. He is teaching me great things."

All three of the men watched her. "What things?" Croase said nervously. This was one part of Listra and Rafa's relationship he did not especially appreciate—their apparent sense of privacy and of having something over on the rest of them.

"I'm not prepared to show them yet," Listra said. "But we must heed his words. He has great power. I believe now that he may be able to pulverize whole buildings, move large inanimate objects, raise the dead, at a mere word."

Croase stared at her. "This is some kind of psychic power?"

"In a way. But more. The power of a divine master. He is convinced that humans can become divine masters while still on earth. They may never die once they have attained it.

They may—well, I've already said too much. He is teaching me each time we meet."

"How often is this?" Croase held the drink at his lips to still their sudden quivering. He wondered if Rafa was observing them at that moment and preparing to inform Listra of other events or problems she shouldn't know about.

"At least once a day, usually the morning." She gave Hughes a sudden hard-eyed stare. Croase felt even more uncomfortable.

"You mean sometimes more than once a day?"

Listra shook her head. "Rarely." She kept her eyes off Hughes. He didn't flinch. But Croase was sure she was not telling the truth. Still, he told himself she really didn't know what Benreu had been telling him, and that was enough. He briefly wondered what the effect would be on the body and brain with too many doses of TUT. Was it like an addictive drug? But he told himself not to worry. So far it had done nothing but good for him.

When they were finished with their drinks, Croase sat back down in the chair at the desk, and Listra excused herself. The two security men and he were alone.

"Tell me the truth, Ken. Is she doing it more than once a day?"

Strock shifted his feet but remained impassive. He didn't even look at Hughes. "She says she is doing it only as often as she and Rafa agree upon. She's your wife, Mart."

"I am aware of that. But it's more than once a day?"

"I don't know." He glanced at Hughes.

"Cut the bull and tell me."

"Occasionally I believe she does it more than once a day. Rarely, though, I think."

Croase swore. "Ken, I'm paying you to watch her. I'm concerned about her attitude. She has this sudden sense of power I hadn't seen before."

"There is nothing to worry about."

Croase eyed him levelly, then motioned him to go. "Keep me informed, both of you. I don't want our primary thananaut and my wife going off the deep end."

The two men went out.

Croase sat at his desk smiling to himself. He murmured, "I have you right where I want you, babe."

□　□　□

"Hiro," Croase said into the phone. "Come up here, I have something I want to discuss."

Nakayami was in Croase's office in less than ten minutes.

"I understand the TUT and, I suppose, the TUT-B can be taken in water now."

"Yes," Nakayami said. "One gulp and boom."

"What I'm wondering is what happens if you put the water with the TUT on your skin."

"Same thing," said Nakayami. "It's absorbed right through the skin. It takes a little longer, though."

"How long?"

"Without the apparatus, ten, fifteen seconds."

"So theoretically, you could sprinkle it on yourself and not even have to taste it?"

"Sprinkle one drop," Nakayami said with a smile.

"What happens with any more?"

Nakayami eyed him suspiciously but said, "That would not be healthy."

"You mean, you'd be dead."

"Yes."

"All right. I'd like you to do something. I want a whole gallon of unmixed TUT-B made up."

Nakayami dropped his mouth. "A gallon? That would cost a hundred thousand dollars."

"I want a gallon, Hiro."

The Japanese researcher didn't respond for almost half a minute. Then he said, "May I ask why?"

"We're thinking of making it available to other research facilities."

"To try to perfect it?"

"That's right."

"That would not be possible, Martin. It's—"

Croase's hand slapped onto the desk. "Don't tell me what's possible! We've got to develop it, and you're hopeless-

309

ly behind. I've decided to involve whoever I can talk into working with us on it. That's final. I want the gallon in two days."

Nakayami swallowed, but nodded. "It will require working around the clock."

"Then do it."

It was past 8:00 P.M., and Croase was still in his office. The building was quiet. There was a knock at the door.

"Come in."

A leggy blonde walked in with a birthday cake.

Croase smiled. "Jillie—what is this?"

"Our anniversary."

"Anniversary?"

"Three months to the day. Remember? I thought I'd bring you a couple of presents."

Croase rose and rushed around the edge of the desk. After she put the cake down, he took her in his arms and kissed her. "And what might these two presents be?"

"The cake, first of all."

"And?"

"The second one is me."

Croase's eyes lit and he smiled. "We're going to be in the clear real soon, baby."

When Kent Farrell and Jenny Carlotti's headline hit the campus Friday afternoon several things happened immediately. Hugh Jefferson, the faculty adviser to the newspaper staff, contacted Martin Croase and informed him of everything. Croase didn't seem to be perturbed.

"This was bound to happen," he said. "Round up the students who did it. We'll have them confined to their dorms over the weekend until I decide what to do with them."

Hugh Jefferson was a thin, gaunt man with hollow cheeks and a roving eye when it came to female students.

310

"Can we hold them there? Isn't there the risk of some students calling home and informing their parents of our actions?"

"I control the phones around here," Croase said. "Call the security office and have them send over two people to take care of the editor and the other traitor. Then I want a Saturday edition of the paper put out immediately. I'll give you the copy. I want this thing nipped, or it's your head, Jefferson. Understand?"

"Yes, sir."

"Then get on it. Any more defections from your staff and I'll personally deal with you."

"Yes, sir."

"Most of the papers have been held then?"

"Only one dorm got them."

"I'll come over and talk to the students tonight. Have the dorm captain call a meeting."

3

Strock knew within seconds that the lethal injection had worked. Both of the homeless derelicts they'd picked up that afternoon got drunk quickly enough and were subdued without a fight. Willard would get nine bodies that night, even though only four of them came from TWI. The deal with Konopka was already in motion, and it was only twenty-four hours old.

"Tell me again how no one finds out," Hughes said as he zipped up the body bags.

"Croase doesn't check this stuff," Strock said. "Nakayami doesn't look at it either. I keep the tabs on the bodies and make the report. Security is oblivious about counts. Konopka turns in the figures. If there's any difference in numbers, it's between us and Willard and Konopka, and that can't happen. TWI just pays it without asking questions. The biggies are so loaded with money that they don't think about it. You'd be amazed at how many donors they have. Anyway, TWI can't afford to make a big stink about it at this point. They're in too deep, and they know it. If Willard had any

311

sense, he'd know he had them over a barrel, but all he cares about is his measly five grand per body."

"I can't believe Croase is that stupid."

"I can't believe," Strock answered, "that we haven't been doing this before. Ten K for a few hours' work. By the way, how was your trip with the nurse?"

Hughes said with a grin, "Great. Really something." He wasn't about to tell Strock it was really with Listra Croase. "She likes it too. We're doing it again tonight." He looked at the blue body bag, then hefted it and threw it onto the floor of the white Ford van. "It does bother me, though. Just killin' these people. At least before it wasn't us."

"Hey," Strock said. "What's it matter? You've had that spirit thing out there tell you. Ha-ha and all that. There's nothing to worry about here or hereafter."

"Yeah, I guess so." Hughes threw the last body into the van. Five lay in the heap. They had delivered five others a few hours before. "I am getting kind of interested in that person out there, though."

"Who's that?"

"You know, the person you meet. Don't you meet someone each time you go out?"

Strock scratched his head. "Yeah, but I don't really talk to him too much."

Hughes laughed. "Well, you should. I'm going to try to find out his name one of these times."

"How many times are you doing it a week now?"

"I've done it five times. I like it."

Strock stared at him. "I didn't know you were that into it."

Hughes laughed again. "I guess I didn't either. Until now."

Strock hopped into the van as Hughes stepped in the passenger door. They said no more as they headed down toward the gate. When they drove out, though, they didn't notice Lyle Hornum's car pull out from a hidden ditch and follow them at a distance down Simmering Road to the intersection into Gaithersburg.

Lyle Hornum kept well behind them for the half-hour drive through the country. He saw them finally pull into the Willard Funeral Home. When they disappeared into the lower garage, he took a quick video of the front of the home and the garage just as the door closed on the van. A stirring excitement pulsed in his veins. Somehow he and Ray would have to get inside. But he figured they would work that out together. It shouldn't be too hard.

As the rear wheels spun dirt and rocks into the air, he headed back toward the Channel 4 office in northwest D.C.

Ray called that evening about 4:15. Lyle immediately gave him the news. "All we have to do is get them on video with the bodies, show it to the fibbies, and I think they'll do something quick."

Ray was skeptical, but said, "I think it can be done—but you're handling the camera."

"Right, and you keep me covered."

"That's what I'm good at. We should do some recon as soon as we get down there."

"Always be prepared."

"Right."

Andi was out in the kitchen cooking an early dinner. Ray looked out the window and spotted Tommy in the woods looking at different trees. He'd found a book on trees the day before and had set out a project to ID all the trees in the yard before Dr. Kingston arrived.

"It's not going to be easy," Ray mused.

"Nothing ever is. Anyway, we've got them. Just have to get into that funeral home and find the basement shortly after these punks arrive with the bodies. How hard can that be?"

"Hard, when people have something to conceal."

"Hey, God's in this, Ray. He probably has some tricks up His sleeve."

"Yeah. But what if He decides to let us get cleaned as part of His 'testing' program?"

Lyle laughed. "You don't trust the Lord too much, do you?"

"Yeah, well, it's become a struggle. I have a lot of questions—especially about the issue of God's sovereignty."

"I understand, but forget the theological brainteasers. Just tell me what your itinerary is. It may take a few days before these guys make another trip."

"Tonight Dr. Kingston's coming up for the weekend. Probably late. Andi and I will drive down on Saturday or Sunday, depending on how things go. I may take Andi out to dinner somewhere." As he said it, Andi walked out of the kitchen with plates and utensils.

He winked at her as she placed a plate in front of him. She returned the wink, then headed back for the kitchen.

Lyle continued, "By the way, have you read anything about these murders where the killer is cutting letters into his victims?"

"I've seen it in the papers and on the news."

"What do you make of it?"

"Strange," Ray said. "Real strange."

"I'm collecting clippings and watching the AP wire service. Do you know what the letters say so far?"

"No."

"A-B-B-E."

"Strange way to start a message. What could it mean?"

"There're only a few words in the dictionary that start with those letters, amazingly enough."

"What are they?"

"Abbe, abbess, and abbey—all religion-related words. And another word about a period in early human history."

"So?"

"So maybe there's a religious connection."

"You think some abbess is doing this?"

Lyle laughed. "Yeah, it's interesting, though. Whoever's doing it definitely has my attention."

"That's morbid, Lyle."

The reporter laughed. "I learned to be morbid after going to ATS for two years. Sorry, but that's the way I feel."

Ray paused for a moment. He was sure now he could trust Lyle, and he had to be able to get in touch with him or Andi if he learned something important. Lyle hadn't probed him about the phone number, didn't even seem miffed that Ray hadn't given it to him. Ray figured if he had been working for TWI or was sympathetic in any way, he probably would have pressed the issue by now.

"Lyle," Ray said, "I want to give you our phone number."

There was a long pause. "You sure?"

"I have to." Ray noticed his heart suddenly pounding and his palms wet.

"OK, but I won't write it down anywhere. I'll have to memorize it. I don't want anyone else knowing."

"All right. Here goes." Ray gave him the number.

Lyle asked him to repeat it twice. Then he said, "OK, got it. I'm glad you trust me. That makes me feel good."

"Let me know if you get anything else important."

When Ray hung up, he told Andi what Lyle had said. Then he told her he'd given Lyle the phone number. She closed her eyes and breathed out tightly. "You're sure about that."

"It's too late now."

She sighed. "I think it's OK. We've got to trust somebody."

Ray smiled with relief that she wasn't angry.

4

Bill Linton, the man Strock had assigned to watch Kingston, saw the tall, white-haired professor throw a suitcase into the truck of his gold New Yorker sedan. When he pulled out onto Proust Way, Linton began to roll. After radioing Strock that Kingston was off on a trip, Strock told him, "Just don't get made, that's all." Strock was using PI vernacular for being discovered. He continued, "Keep as far back as you can. Is the beeper still working?"

Linton held the CB microphone up to the receiver on the electronic tracker set.

"Good. Try not to lose him, but he may be watching for you. Croase says the old coot is pretty cagey."

"I know how to tail somebody."

"All right. Let me know immediately if there's a problem."

Linton let several cars get between him and Kingston on Route 108. But when the seminary prof turned onto the ramp out onto Route 29 north, Linton settled down. On major highways it would be much easier. The beeper was strong. He figured he had nothing to worry about. The ten thousand in cash Strock had promised for learning the whereabouts of the boy would come in handy.

☐ ☐ ☐

Dr. Kingston watched the road behind him constantly as he drove up Route 29 and reached Interstate 70 to the beltway around Baltimore. He had never had to run an escape maneuver, but he figured he'd better take no chances. Years reading crime novels and mysteries gave him several creative ideas that he thought he might try, even if he didn't spot someone in particular.

There was no apparent sign of anyone following, but he knew on the big roads it was much easier than on back streets. He glanced in the mirror repeatedly but did not notice the same car over a period of time.

As he thought through a plan, he began to relax. He had considered renting a car, but realized that might not do much good if he was followed.

He put in a music tape of Handel's *Messiah* and soon the melodies filled and refreshed his tired mind. Usually he listened to the whole oratorio from beginning to end on a trip to "the lake" as he called it. Now the first strains of the opening overture lanced some burning boil in his mind and he suddenly felt relieved, confident, happy. It would be good to see Ray and Andi. He sensed from Ray's conversation that he was probably in love with the girl. That was good, he thought. He needed someone, and she seemed right.

At the end of Interstate 70, instead of turning onto the superhighway, Kingston suddenly hit the gas and veered off on a back street towards Baltimore. He turned off and on several main arteries till he came back out onto the Beltway at a higher exit. The whole time he kept his eye on the mirror, convinced no one could have tailed him.

But he decided to do it one more time before he settled down.

The moment Linton saw the big Chrysler hit the gas at the end of Interstate 70, he knew he'd either been made or it was a diversionary tactic. When the car turned left, he saw it in time to make it to the light and peer up the street. The New Yorker was gone.

Linton swore. He had no idea which way Kingston might be going on the Interstate, but he sensed it was probably north. He quickly turned around and burned back to the main road. For a moment, he found himself praying, "Just don't let me miss him," even though he had no particular beliefs about an Almighty.

He pulled off just ahead of the next exit praying that Kingston's New Yorker would slip into view.

Kingston decided to drive further on through town. He knew he could catch Liberty Road further up, or perhaps Reisterstown Road. There was no reason to hurry back onto the Interstate. He sang along with *The Messiah* and watched the mirror. If anyone had been following, he could not have kept up with this manic pace, not in town.

He settled down and reentered the Interstate at Reisterstown.

After an hour, Linton sat wet with sweat and fear. Strock would kill him. But he had to call it in. At least they still had the beeper. But unless you were within five miles of it, nothing happened. And even then you could not be sure where the person was, just that he was within that five-mile radius.

The beep had quickly weakened in the first fifteen minutes, and now it was gone. Even when Linton sped down the Interstate, there was no sound on his radio.

He finally called Strock on the CB and turned around.

□ □ □

Kingston arrived at 11:00 P.M. They were all waiting for him, and when he stepped out there were hugs and handshakes all around. He was elated to see them all looking so exuberant and healthy.

He said, "So you want me to marry you tonight, or wait till the license?"

Ray and Andi laughed and exchanged a secret look. Kingston could tell his joke was only a hair shy of their feelings for one another, and he wondered if they'd already decided to do it.

They were soon settled into the house, talking and reminiscing, confident that all was well and Ray, Andi, and Lyle would soon have the evidence to blow the whole TWI situation to smithereens.

5

Listra Croase kissed David Hughes, then wriggled out of his embrace. "There's a serious problem in the heavenly places. Rafa says there's a murderous enemy, mentors who have rebelled and gone to the other side."

"I thought that was Satan."

"Oh, forget the Satan baloney. That's all Christian garbage. This is a real war among the mentors."

"What does it mean?" Hughes had been summoned to Listra's house on the ruse of checking the security system, though it was getting to be a shopworn purpose for his visits. Listra, however, was convinced her husband knew nothing about them. But what worried her was what these enemies might be able to reveal. Already, she had discovered that Martin's mentor, Benreu, was supplying him with confidential information about donors involved with TWI. It was fine

318

with her if Rafa or any of them revealed secrets to her. But what about the secrets others might reveal about her?

Rafa had assured her there was no breach of confidence between him and Benreu.

"I don't know yet," Listra said. "Rafa said he and Benreu are working on a way to destroy the credibility of these two enemies."

"Who are they?"

"He said one was named Cardle or Cartell or something. I didn't really get it right. He didn't give me the name of the other one."

"What should we do?" Hughes adjusted his shoulder holster and pulled on his navy blue sports jacket.

"I think we should prepare for some move in the near future. I know Martin has at least one safe crammed with money. I may be able to get access to it."

Hughes' eyes lit with interest. "How much?"

"Several hundred thousand at least."

"That could set us up. I've also got some sources."

Listra stared at him, incredulous. "You? You spend every cent you get."

"But not every cent others get."

"Tell me!"

Hughes grinned. "It'll be taken care of. With close to a million or so, we could be set up."

"I want more than money, David."

"I understand that. But with the formula for the TUT and right handling, you'll be in the spotlight where you belong. You'll be at the top of the ministry."

Listra smiled and cuddled with him. "You know how to keep me happy, honeybunch."

Martin Croase had just finished his talk before the students at Rolley Williams Memorial Hall, named after the man who donated the money over ten years before to build it. The room was spare, with several orange and brown plaid couches, and a fireplace on the far wall. Croase looked out over the group of over a hundred students, half women and half men.

One of the young men raised his hand. Croase motioned to him to speak.

"We understand that Jenny Carlotti and Kent Farrell are being confined in their rooms. Is that true?"

Croase nodded. "You all understand what kind of pressure a school like this gets from the outside. Doing the work of God is no simple task. We're criticized from every quarter. To have an incendiary headline go out like this, and without the adviser's approval, is unconscionable. It could ruin our work here, your work here, and your future. I'm sure none of you want that. So we have had to take firm disciplinary measures."

Another student raised her hand. "Dr. Croase, we understand that nearly half the campus has tried the TUT. What kind of reaction are you getting?"

"Overwhelmingly positive. Until now, we've had no one complain. If someone does have a complaint, certainly they should go directly to the person responsible or at least to one of the staff. You know what Jesus told His disciples—'If your brother sins, go to him in private, and if he repents, you have won your brother.' To go public without even talking to those responsible and laying out your intentions is the worst sort of worldly tactic. This campus is not operating according to the principles of the world. This is the kind of thing that creates scandals like the ones that rocked the Christian world several years ago. Does anyone here want that?"

Students all over the room were shaking their heads.

A third student raised his hand. "We have heard that several people have left campus as a result of the experience. Ray Mazaris, a seminary student, is said to be in hiding."

"Do any of you realize who and what Ray Mazaris is?"

No one answered.

Croase shook his head with sadness. "It'll all be coming out in the paper tomorrow. Mazaris and a secretary in the finance office were planted here, as you know from the original burglary, by an undercover CIA operation bent on finding some dirt on people here at Atlantic and TWI. Yes, the CIA, believe it or not. With all the changes in the world situation, the Soviet Union turning into a virtual democracy and all, the CIA has turned to working against the United States's own people. There's a tremendous conspiracy out there, young people. We here at the Bible college have tried to prevent you from having to deal with it by providing a healthy, growing environment. But you can understand our new concern for security. The U.S. government is literally trying to destroy us."

A buzz went up in the room, and Croase was satisfied he'd effectively silenced any further defectors. Another hand went up, and Croase answered three or four more questions.

Then Hal Gordon, Harold Kingston's friend, said, "The original newspaper report said you thought Mazaris and Darcasian were from a local cult."

"We couldn't very well say they were CIA, could we now?" Croase answered with a wry smile. He looked piercingly around the room. "Understand, young people, we are in a spiritual war. The devil will do anything to rip us to pieces. This is part of the reason we have worked to develop the TUT—to get direct contact with angels involved in the war and so engage in it more effectively ourselves."

Gordon said again, "How do you know the angels you're talking to aren't something very different from what you think they are?"

"You mean demons?" Croase gazed firmly and fiercely into Gordon's eyes.

"I had considered that."

"If you had tried the TUT, Professor Gordon, you would know the kinds of beings we're meeting out there. You haven't tried it yet, have you, professor?"

Gordon shuffled his feet. Many of the students turned around to look at him. He answered quietly, "No, I haven't."

"I suggest, then, before you criticize it you experience it." Croase looked back at the group. "As you may suspect, young people, there are some people who have not yet tried the TUT for mostly specious reasons. We suspect that these people are some of our harshest critics."

Someone said, "Kent Farrell tried it and didn't like it."

321

Croase shook his head. "Kent Farrell had no problem with the TUT itself. He believed—wrongly—that we are using you people as guinea pigs like it's some mass experiment. But is that reasonable? Come on! We don't operate that way. You know what The Watt Institute has accomplished over the last decade. We're not a fly by night organization. Anyway, Kent Farrell has already admitted his mistake. "Furthermore" —Croase glanced at two of the other professors present, Jefferson and Coombs, both firmly on his side—"I guess I'll just have to reveal this. Kent Farrell has been undergoing psychiatric treatment at the medical center for severe depression and extreme anxiety. Some of you know that. We believe that's really at the bottom of this, and we also know that this has been happening for several years in Kent's life."

"Jenny Carlotti hasn't had any problems like that," someone else said.

"Jenny wants to support Kent," Croase said quickly, turning to the student, a girl with long, brown hair and glasses. "It's plain she has more than an editorial interest in him." Croase coughed and leered slightly at the audience. Several of the female students nodded in agreement.

"Well," Croase concluded, "we can go on all night like this. I'm sorry this has happened. But you have to understand what we're up against. Now it's necessary that everyone here stay firm on one thing—this: we keep this all in the family of God. We deal with it internally. We do not want to involve the world in God's work. Can I count on your loyalty on that issue?"

There were a number of amens and students nodding their heads. Croase smiled and waved on his way out. "I knew I could count on you."

Once outside, he said to Strock, "Watch Gordon. I don't want him going off campus."

"Got it, boss."

□ □ □

The next morning, the paper came out with a full explanation. Several faculty members offered strong positive testi-

322

monies about the TUT. Evidence was offered about Ray Mazaris's complicity with the CIA.

By Saturday night, the seminary, Bible college, and TWI were ready for battle with the world. The campus buzzed with rumors about imminent attack from outside. Everyone was encouraged to stay in the dorms except when going to classes, and to spend time in prayer, both alone and in groups. Each dorm's head personnel organized a twenty-four-hour schedule of prayer, Bible study, and snap courses in spiritual warfare for the weekend and the coming week.

6

In the mountains, while Atlantic Seminary and College dug in, Ray, Andi and Tommy, and Dr. Kingston all took a hike up the beach to "the point," a jutting of land at the top edge of the cove on which the cabin was situated. Ray carried a pack full of hot dogs and rolls, apples, pears, and some Cokes for lunch. Dr. Kingston stepped out ahead of them with a thick walking stick he kept in his broom closet. Tommy scampered about, joyously hurling driftwood and rocks into the water. Andi and Ray walked hand in hand, finding their way over the rocks with deft precision.

"You're a real mountain goat," Andi said as Ray navigated a way between several huge rocks and pieces of gnarled driftwood.

"I don't see you tripping up," Ray answered, holding his hand out to her as he stood on top of the tiered rocks.

"It's because I have the perfect shepherd."

"I thought I was a mountain goat."

"Mountain goat shepherd." She laughed. "Though maybe mountain goat is better. They are kind of hairy."

Ray laughed. "I never know what's going to come out of your mouth."

Kingston and Tommy were examining something on the beach far ahead of them. A moment later, Tommy held aloft something. It was a water snake.

"Ugh, let's slow down," Andi said.

"You afraid of snakes or something?"

"No. But that doesn't mean I want to be friends with one."

They wove around the docks pulled up along the beach and the big and small rocks that dotted it everywhere. Ray felt as if he were walking on a cushion of air. He told himself to enjoy it while it lasted.

Andi asked, "By the way, what ever happened to that kid who hit you, when you had your near death experience as a boy?"

"John Godwin?" Ray cocked his head and sighed. "Sad story. Had to go to reform school for a while. His dad started this big vendetta against my family, and the community began bringing pressure to get the whole Godwin family to move. No one really liked them. Kind of a closed-in, nasty group. Although John was different."

"How so?" She brushed her hair across her forehead and covered her eyes from the sun, looking down the beach.

"I could never get a fix on it. Real cool. Like he never felt anything inside. I don't know. Even with his car, he just seemed to me to be too cool, even for a man. Like he didn't really care about anything or anyone. Strange I should think of that."

"He sounds like a weird guy."

"Yeah, he was."

When they reached the point, Kingston and Tommy began exploring a trail into the woods. In a few minutes they returned with some wood for a campfire. Ray and Andi joined them in a kindling and log-hunting trip. Soon they had enough for a roaring afternoon fire. The air was crisp. Windbreakers were not quite enough in the cool breeze. Ray stoked up a fire. Andi put the Cokes in the cool water lapping the sandy beach at the point. Remnants of other fires, charred sticks, and razed logs lay in different places on the beach.

Kingston cut some lengthy green sticks for roasting the hot dogs. They all sat around the fire, hugging their legs and talking about the history of the lake. Soon Kingston turned them to the subject of TWI for the hundredth time.

"So what have you learned from Gordon Watt's books, Ray?" the professor asked.

"He does have an interesting theory about death in his book *Final Destination.*"

Kingston nodded unhappily. "That's one of the ideas he became obsessed with in his last years. He became theologically—well, it was downright heretical. That's all there is to it."

"You didn't tell me about this," Andi said.

"I just read it this morning while you were all having your second cup of coffee."

"Not me," Tommy interjected.

"Right, Chief. You were playing with your gun." Tommy had carved a fair version of one of Ray's pistols out of driftwood.

"Not playing with it," Tommy said with a twinkle in his eye, "cleaning it. Like you do with the regular guns."

"Oh, excuse me," Ray said smiling.

"Well," Andi interrupted, "what's the scoop?"

Ray turned to her. "Well, it seems he believed that death was the real problem of humanity. If we could rid ourselves of the fear of it, we'd become good, honest, and loving people. Actually, the case histories he gave support that theory, I suppose, and so does some of the stuff the secular researchers have posed. But it seems to me they were being very selective about whom they chose to talk. He did coin an interesting line, though."

Before Ray could answer, Kingston said, "The fear of death is the root of all evil."

"Right," Ray said. "You know it."

Kingston shook his head. "He thought he'd happened on some earth-shattering truth. If you ask me it's hogwash. It's the fear of death that in many ways drives us to Christ—who then takes that fear away as we learn of Him. But Gordon turned it around. It was a fateful move for him."

Everyone waited for his next comment.

"How so?" Andi finally said.

"That was when he began moving TWI in the direction of which we are seeing the results now. Watt had come perilously close to promulgating classic occultic ideas."

"But how could that happen to a born-again Christian, Doc?" Ray asked.

325

"I don't know. Right now I'm inclined to suspect Gordon developed an incredible root of bitterness about the loss of his son, and later the loss of his wife. He was so strong on God's sovereignty at one point that he could not understand how God could ever let anything bad happen to him personally. A lot of Christians fall into the same trap."

Ray gulped.

Kingston eyed him mercilessly. "Prime example sitting in our midst."

"I'm working on it, Doc."

"I know. It's a difficult concept to get into balance. But you can never let personal experience dictate what you believe about the universe, God, life, death, anything. Personal experience, in whatever form, is always subjective, changeable, and open to deception."

Jabbing his stick into the ground, Ray said, "But what if your experiences contradict completely what the Bible says, Doc? Are we just supposed to believe blindly, without any corroborating evidence?"

"Of course not!" Kingston shook his head with emphasis. "But look at your own experiences. Some are positive, some negative. Some are good. Some are evil. If something goes wrong in your life—say you lose a son like I did—do you automatically give up believing in God because of it? No, the sensible thing to do is try to be realistic. The Christian knows we live in a world rife with evil. God never promised to eliminate evil from our lives. He promises to see us through it, and get us to His heavenly kingdom safely. In that place, God has judged and destroyed evil forever. But coming back to the point, experience is never a good barometer of truth."

"Then how does God expect us to trust Him at all?" Ray said. He glanced at Andi, but she was looking at Doc raptly.

"On the basis of His Word."

"And if experience contradicts His Word?"

"Then you still hang onto His Word."

"But that doesn't make sense, Doc." Ray punched his stick angrily into the ground.

"Of course it does. Look at it this way. Say you have a friend who's completely trustworthy and reliable. He says he'll come over to your house at 6:00 P.M. You get all dressed up, 6:00 P.M. comes, and no friend. What do you do—throw out all you know about your friend—he's reliable, and so on, and has suddenly become a complete liar—or do you give him the benefit of the doubt and tell yourself something else has happened?"

"Give him the benefit of the doubt."

"And that's how we deal with the problems of life. We can't just take one little promise or verse of Scripture like Romans 8:28 and apply it rigorously in every situation, demanding that God come through now, right away, immediately. We have to study many truths and try to see how they intersect. In fact, I'm convinced one reason God allows us to have experiences that seem to contradict His Word is because He wants us to dig deeper into it. As you really get into Scripture and understand it, you begin to see that hundreds of truths may impinge on one experience, and somehow you have to hold them all in balance."

"Sounds pretty tough to me," Andi said.

"That's why you can't base any doctrine or principle on personal experience!" Kingston said triumphantly.

Tommy said, holding up the just broken tip of his stick, "Or on your hot dog stick."

Everyone laughed, and Kingston handed him the knife to make a new tip, but Tommy took out the knife Ray had given him. "I got my own hardware here," he said. Ray caught Andi watching her son admiringly. He suddenly realized how far Tommy had come in a few short months. He wondered what the reason was, and it suddenly occurred to him that perhaps he had something to do with it. It gave him a warm, joyous feeling deep in his bones.

Everyone began sticking the hot dogs onto the forks of the branches Kingston had cut down. They held them over the fire. Soon the frankfurters were sizzling in the heat.

As the tantalizing odor of beef and fat laced the air, Ray said, "A lot of this makes sense to me now, Doc, but what do you think this NDE thing is all about? I mean, I know some of it's demonic and some of it involves God, maybe angels.

Summerville had some good ideas. But I still haven't put it all together. We still have to deal with it."

Everyone was silent. Andi methodically turned her hot dog and told Tommy his was getting burned. He was obviously listening to Ray and Dr. Kingston. Ray waved his own hot dog back and forth and noticed his hand was getting cramped. He switched hands.

"Consider several thoughts," Kingston asked. "First of all, demons are deceivers, murderers, and haters of God. Their purpose is to destroy God's kingdom, and short of that, to confuse the people in it, lead them astray, and guide them into sin so they become useless to the work of God."

Ray nodded. "Yes, I know all that. But what could they do? For instance, do you think a demon could supply someone with secret information?"

"Of course. Laced with lies."

"Not lies, though. Real info. Like, say you were a guy on Wall Street and you wanted to know if someone at some big firm was going to start a buy-out of some company. The classic 'insider information.' Do you think demons could give a Wall Street exec that kind of info to make him rich."

"Depends," Kingston said.

"On what?"

Tommy and Andi roasted their hot dogs and looked from Ray to Kingston as the two men talked. Ray could tell they were almost mesmerized.

Kingston cleared his throat. "What's in it for the demon, for Satan's kingdom? He's not just going to give this Wall Street guy this information for nothing. He'll want something in return."

"The guy's soul."

"No, that will be at the bottom of it. But your Wall Street powerhouse won't even be aware of the fact that he's selling his soul, and selling it short. No, the demon will want more. Perhaps something that will advance him personally, or at least the work of Satan. Their purpose is not to enrich mankind, but to destroy it. If the demon saw that this Wall Street magnate's actions would further corrupt and lead astray others, he'd probably be willing to do it. But he'd do it in a very cagey way, to keep the person hooked until he was finally brought in."

"Dead, you mean?"

"Safely entombed in hell. Yes."

"How would this demon know these things?"

"They're organized. They know how to cooperate, work as a team. They can certainly observe what's going on in the world of men and keep records. They're supposedly far more intelligent than any of us."

"If that's the case, then why haven't people—Satanists, mediums, demon-possessed people—done this before?"

"Maybe they have. Maybe some of the insider traders have been in league with demons. I don't know. But if they haven't, maybe it's just a new thing for them, something demons have never done before. They're not perfect, or omniscient, you know. They have to learn, too."

Ray looked at Andi and Tommy. "You two following this?"

They both nodded. Andi said, "It's fascinating."

Tommy said, "Easy as toyology."

When Kingston gazed at him questioningly, Ray said, "Tommy's a toyologist."

The old man nodded. "Used to be one myself. Still am a lot of the time. Maybe we'll do some this week, what do you say, Tom?"

The boy looked up. "Teach you all I know."

Andi gave him a quick clip at the back of the head, saying, "Don't be smart," but Ray and Kingston laughed.

"Good joke," Kingston said.

Ray turned back to the Doc. "What if you were a senator? Do you think these demons could supply you with inside political information?"

"Of course. But it would have to be in line with the demon's purpose. He doesn't want to help these people. In fact, the demon hates said senator. He'll do whatever he thinks is necessary to get that person in hell. If it's cards, he'll get you with cards. If it's the fear of death, he'll get you with a near death experience that keeps you from believing the truth. He doesn't much care what it takes, so long as his victim ends up in hell."

Ray began eating his hot dog and thinking about Dr. Kingston's words.

Andi said, "What about the near death experience itself? What do you think the demons are trying to do?"

"It's obvious," Kingston said. "Once they have you believing everything is OK when you die, there's no sin, no judgment, all that—Christianity is unnecessary. It's that simple."

"Sure, but why did they bring out Ray's grandfather?"

"All part of the deception," Kingston answered. "It wasn't really Ray's grandfather, I don't think, otherwise Christianity really is untrue—if he was an unbeliever. But I suspect these demons, being spiritual and highly intelligent, probably have the capacity either to change their form, or to influence your mind so that you see what they want you to see. They knew Ray was going to undergo an NDE, so they got ready."

Andi screwed up her face and shook her head. "Yeah, but why did I have that hellish experience the first time? What was the point of that?"

Kingston blew rings out into the air. "I suspect that the demons involved in this particular deception—and you can be sure that there are probably a group of them who are now specializing in it—have not learned complete control over it. God is still in charge. Perhaps He allowed you to have that experience for another purpose. The demons can't do anything unless God actually lets them do it."

Ray leaned forward. "And that's why the idea of demons supplying confidential or secret information to governments, Wall Street people, and so on, probably hasn't been done right now—though who knows what intrigues in history have occurred because of demonic influence? Still, God isn't letting people get such information from demons on a regular basis. Otherwise, mediums would be the richest people alive."

Kingston smiled. "Good thought."

Tommy suddenly said, "The one I talked to even made a mistake."

Everyone looked at him.

Tommy nodded vigorously. "I just remembered. He was supposed to be my great-grandfather, and he asked me how his granddaughters were doing? But Mom has no sisters, just two brothers."

"He said that?" Andi asked.

"Yeah, and he even looked like the picture you have of great-grandpa. Kind of. But maybe his nose was a bit outa whack."

Tommy looked around at everyone brightly till they burst out laughing, but Ray shook his head with open-mouthed wonder, realizing that was precisely what had happened to him. He interjected, "So you think this was a demon posing as Tommy's great-granddad?"

"Why not?" Kingston asked. "And probably he caught flak for making that mistake, too."

Everyone laughed again. Then Tommy said, "And what about that wall that I went past? What's that? I just wish I could remember everything that happened there."

"That's the beginning of the real death experience," Kingston said. "I think you were at the very fringe of what it's all about for the Christian. Like Dr. Summerville told Ray, there's this interim place where demons may have sovereignty for reasons known only to God, possibly the ultimate deceptions of the last days. But beyond it there's a real heaven waiting for us to enter."

"So that's exactly what they were trying to do with me," Ray said, "convince me Christianity was wrong and that I had no reason to believe it."

Everyone agreed. Andi remarked, "It's really incredible what can happen."

"Yeah, and I think we're going to find it gets a lot worse," Ray said.

Andi asked, "That brings up something else: why haven't the demons told Croase and the others where we are—if they're still after us."

Ray's face went white. "I never thought of that."

Kingston shook his head. "Comes back to God's sovereignty. He hasn't allowed them to. They can't do anything He doesn't choose to let them do."

"It makes sense," Ray answered. "It does fit together. But it's pretty complicated. Takes some rather creative leaps of the theological imagination." Ray turned to Andi. "This is why he's the most popular professor at ATS—because he's always leaping around in his classes."

Kingston laughed, and looked at Andi. "And tell me, lovely lady, are you sure you want to continue hanging around with this theological tape machine? Are you ready for a life of talking about the ramifications of theological inquiry?"

Andi put her arm through Ray's. "Oh, he's much more than a theological dictionary. Right, Mr. Macho?"

Ray grinned ruefully. "I can't shake this 'macho' image they've got of me on the campus."

"Don't knock it," Kingston said. "It's better than being a ministerial wimp."

They all laughed.

Tommy suddenly stood up. "There's somebody standing on the beach."

Everyone turned around. It was at least a half-mile away, but he looked like he was standing in front of the dock on Kingston's property. A moment later, he disappeared into the woods behind it.

"Who could that be?" Andi said hugging her arms. "This is all we need now."

"You're sure you weren't followed?" Ray said to Kingston.

"It could actually be a lot of people. Did you see what he was wearing, Tommy?"

"It looked like a suit."

"You're sure?" Kingston asked again.

"No, it might just have been the sunlight."

"Would anyone normally be around, Doc?" Ray asked.

"There is the public road to the beach right by my cabin. It could have been one of the residents coming down to the beach. But let's get back to the house. I'd like to check things out."

They quickly gathered everything up, then hurried back down the shoreline toward the docks. When they reached the trail up to house, there were no telltale footprints in the sand. They followed the winding path up the hill. The house was undisturbed.

332

"Maybe it was just the meter man," Kingston said with a grin. "He might have seen the cars here and stopped by. My brother asked him before to keep an eye on the place. I've talked with him myself. I'll give him a call."

Andi said to Ray, "Do you think we should leave?"

Kingston put his big hand on her shoulder. "I know how to use pistols, rifles, every weapon in this place. And you taught Tommy some tricks too. We'll be all right. You can't keep on the run much longer."

Ray added, "It could have been anyone, Andi. It didn't have to be people from TWI or anything sinister at all."

"OK," Andi said, "but let's all take a ride around the block in the 4x4. Just see if anything unusual is about."

But after a quick trip through the neighborhood, everyone admitted there was nothing out of order. There were cars only at houses they'd normally be at.

Kingston called Jim Higgins, the meter man, and he did say he had been at the house a week or so before, but not since then. He hadn't known anyone had been staying at the cabin.

Kingston said afterwards, "We'll get to the bottom of this. Don't worry."

They played Monopoly that afternoon. Andi jumped at every strange sound, but Ray was able to calm her by sitting next to her and giving her occasional shoulder massages. Kingston and Tommy were still dueling it out when dinnertime came. Nothing unusual happened.

"Could have been someone taking a look at the lake," Kingston told them. "People are always buying and selling around here, and the house next door is on the market."

Then that night someone did come to the door. It was a man in a suit. He said he was a local realtor, gave them a card, and said his office had a number of people looking for places on the lake. He said he'd been by that afternoon with some people and they'd walked down to the lake.

That settled the issue for everyone, but Andi continued to be concerned. She thought they should all go together to Gaithersburg, but both Ray and Kingston were against it. They won in the end.

"What about your classes, Doc?" Ray asked before bed on Sunday night.

"Don't have any next week. You know my schedule's very flexible. I'm only doing one course on Mondays and Fridays, and this week I have several guest speakers from the evangelism and Bible departments. I arranged it before I left for up here. I figured, well—"

"I appreciate it. It takes the pressure off."

Doc coughed with emotion. "Just get that evidence. I sense that the whole campus is breaking apart because of what Croase is doing."

The night was quiet, starry, with only crickets twittering. Everyone slept fitfully, but Sunday morning came without a mishap.

CHAPTER FIFTEEN

1

Strock talked quietly to Martin Croase in the hall. "We're certain it's Kingston who's hiding them."

"So you've been watching the house."

"He left yesterday. Hasn't been back. We have a beeper in the car. But we may have to take other measures to locate the exact place."

"You let him get away?"

Strock shook his head. "He made our man and avoided him. By the time we recovered it was too late. But we know what to do."

"OK, I don't care to hear the details. Just do it."

"Just making sure you approve." Strock went in the opposite direction down the hall, cursing Hughes and Linton. Hughes had put Linton on the case against Strock's better judgment. Now they had to pull off a burglary to get the right info. But he wouldn't do it with Hughes this time. His indifference to details had antagonized Strock for the last time.

2

Johnny Goge passed the huge octagonal building in Lexington, Massachusetts, noting the sign out front. "Kemm, Lincoln, and Vesser, CPAs." One of the associates, Harris

Simmons, was supposedly the associate who handled the dump. Apparently the office was a front for a major Mafia money laundering operation. The cash came into the CPAs' office, and Simmons flew with it in the corporate jet to the Cayman Islands where the cash was dumped into a bank under the name of a dummy corporation set up specifically to launder the money and make it available for use back in the U.S.

Goge knew that messing with the Mafia was not a wise choice. But his experience with people like Carlos Giotto gave him the confidence that he would not get caught, even with the notoriety he was getting in the news. He smiled faintly. At least this person definitely had nothing to do with the church or religion. Croase had promised he wouldn't let that happen again.

Goge cruised around the neighborhood, then headed out onto the main drag and got a hamburger at a local joint. He'd found a coupon in the paper that morning. He enjoyed a freebie when he could, though he was far from a coupon clipper.

He knew Simmons's wife was on a week's trip to Cincinnati to help her daughter, who had just given birth to a baby. "Too bad Grandpa ain't gonna be around too much longer," Goge said as he slouched back in the Chevy Nova he'd stolen in Philadelphia. This hit would get an N, and then it was on to somewhere in New Jersey. Then Croase wanted him to stop off at TWI for a few days.

He wasn't worried. He had nearly a quarter million stashed away at this point, and this hit would haul in over 2 million if everything went right. Croase was not a bad boss, giving him a fair cut and all. But Goge had plans about that matter too. The spirit he'd been meeting on the TUT excursions had offered him a special "deal" that could do an end run on Croase and still gain the ultimate power Goge craved.

3

Kingston turned to the ABC news on the little portable television he had in the cabin. They had all finished a delicious meal of linguine in shrimp sauce Andi made and were sitting in the living room around a warm fire.

No one was paying much attention to the rendition of events in the Middle East, Europe, and the American economy, and then a clip came on about the latest murder, this time in Boston. A reporter named Tim Noone was speaking live. He had interviewed one of the FBI agents investigating the "alphabet killer." Noone said, "An FBI Special Agent named Lou Miles has headed up the work on the alphabet killings, which have occurred in four states, all the way from the West Coast in Portland, Oregon, and Los Angeles, then Austin, Texas, and Greenville, South Carolina. Now a fifth has been perpetrated here in Lexington, Massachusetts. Mr. Miles has checked extensively on the backgrounds of four of the people killed, and the FBI has been unable to find a precise motive, though they think it may be money. Beyond that, though, is the message angle. The killer is obviously saying something through the grisly process of actually carving a letter of the alphabet into the victim's face. What are some of the conclusions you've come to, Mr. Miles?"

Miles sat alone at a desk in a rumpled shirt and tie. "The letters are A-B-B-E-N. We've been working on the possibility of an actual name, which, of course, could be anything. It's obviously a message. Clearly esoteric, maybe something that has meaning only for the killer. Of course, we've had a lot of suggestions about what it could mean—from the idea of an Arab terrorist to the KGB. So far nothing has made sense."

"Do you have anything on the killer?"

"Very little. He uses a 10 mm semiautomatic pistol, probably with a silencer. He's quick, catches his victims off guard. He may have ways of getting into houses just by being friendly. Obviously, he's not afraid of being caught, or he wouldn't be giving off such a clear message of his itinerary."

As they listened, Kingston was writing on a notepad. When he looked up, Ray stole a glance at him, wondering what was going on. He thought about the letters. He thought about the languages he knew something about—Greek, Hebrew, Japanese. Then it hit him.

337

The newscast continued, but Ray got up and looked at Kingston's notepad. He said, "It can't be that, Doc."

"Why not?"

Then Andi was standing, looking down at the pad.

"What is that?" she asked.

"In Hebrew, AB means 'father,'" Ray said. "Also in Hebrew, BEN means 'son.'"

Andi whistled eerily. "You think it's right?"

"Let's listen." They all turned back to the broadcast.

Noone was saying, "What about the money motive?"

Miles answered, "If it is money, this person is going after people who are not known to have it, though we are certain the madam in Los Angeles had close to a half million dollars in a safe—which was empty when we made our search. We were also told by relatives of the elderly woman killed in South Carolina that she was believed to have hidden a large amount of money somewhere on her farm. We did find a place in the barn she might have used, but it was also empty."

"How is this person getting the information to know about such people?"

Miles answered, "That's the big question we're asking ourselves."

Noone asked, "Anything the FBI wants to say to our viewers?"

Kingston, Andi, and Ray all leaned forward to listen.

Miles shook his head. "Don't allow any strangers into your house. Report anyone suspicious to the police immediately. If you have a hoard of money stashed somewhere, get it out and into a bank where it will be safe. If the motive is money, he will presumably know that you no longer have the money and will not go after you."

Noone turned to the camera. "This is Tim Noone in Boston. If you can offer any enlightening information on this subject, please call the number on the screen."

Immediately, Andi wrote it down on Dr. Kingston's pad.

Ray said, "Doc, it's too incredible. Do you really think that's the message?"

Kingston gave him a skeptical look. "The next few letters will tell."

"What do you think they could be?"

"If it's an R—God forbid that this person should kill someone else—but if he's not caught and it's an R, then we could be onto something."

Ray pronounced the letter over in his mind. Then: "Father, son, spirit! RUACH."

"Right," Kingston said.

"What is it?" Andi asked.

"R-U-A-C-H. The Hebrew word for Spirit."

"This is giving me the creeps," Andi said.

"Yeah, five more bodies, too," Ray answered.

"Wow, and if it happens," Tommy said. "that would really be something. Then you figured it out, you and Dr. Kingston."

Kingston sniffed unhappily. "Not the kind of thing I like to figure out. But it comes from forty years of doing crossword puzzles."

"If the next letter is an R, I'm going to ask to have my body freeze-dried and auctioned off to the highest bidder," Andi suddenly said.

She went into the kitchen and brought out an apple pie she'd made that afternoon. "All right, gentlemen, here's my first major effort at complete domestication."

They all dug in with relish.

4

Early Sunday morning, Tommy gave Andi and Ray a tearful hug in the little parking lot in front of Dr. Kingston's cabin. Kingston assured Ray and Andi, "We'll be all right. Just be careful in Gaithersburg."

Tommy said, "I promise I'll take good care of Dr. Kingston." Everyone chuckled, and it relieved some of the pain of the parting. Ray was glad the boy and the prof had melded so well. They were on the way to becoming close friends, like a grandfather and grandson. Ray honestly felt they were close to their goal and in a matter of days would be permanently free of the Croase problem.

He had one of the .38 Chief's Specials with a box of fifty shells sitting under each seat in the front, the pump action shotgun from the gun case in the back, and Doc's Smith and Wesson 9 mm DA Luger equipped with a 15 round clip. He had three extra clips filled with shells and another whole box of ammunition. He left the other .38 with Kingston. They also had a toolbox from Kingston's basement, which held a number of tools, including a pair of wire cutters.

He and Andi climbed into the 4x4 with Ray in the driver's seat. As they drove out of the parking lot Kingston and Tommy waved, then turned to go back into the house.

It was a misty morning, cold at 6:45 A.M. The trees had turned color, and most of the leaves were brown. Leaves trickled down from the trees as the 4x4 roared up the hard-packed dirt road. Ray gripped Andi's hand.

"I love you, Andi Darcasian."

"I know you do. I love you. I just hope—" She blinked back tears.

"Nothing will happen. No one knows Tommy's there. It's the safest place we've got for him. Furthermore, Doc's a tough dude. He'll protect the place. Don't worry, OK? We've got to get our minds on what we're doing here. We can't have a lot of loose ends dragging at us. Believe me, we can't go into this with our hearts shot out."

She wiped at her eyes. "I know. I'll be all right. It's just the first few minutes of leaving. He's such a vulnerable kid. I just hope we get the video and can get on with our lives after Croase and his gangsters are dealt with."

Ray kept the 4x4 right on the speed limit as they came around the big bend by the Wallenpaupack dam and the main route out. The sun beamed directly behind them. Andi gazed at the forest around them. She said, "With all the beauty in the world, it's hard to believe there're places like TWI and people like Croase running them, especially when they're supported by Christians."

Ray kept his eyes ahead, following the winding Route 590 toward the intersection with Interstate 81 for the haul down to D.C. He said, "I guess you really have to take that proverb to heart."

She looked back at him. "What one?"

"About trusting God with all your heart and not relying on your own understanding of things."

"Yeah, I memorized that one last year."

"Good one to know. Hard one to apply."

She was silent, watching the road ahead. "I just hope this guy Lyle turns out to be on the up-and-up," she finally said with a sigh as she placed her feet up against the dashboard and slumped down in the seat. She let her hand rest on Ray's lap.

"He is." After driving a mile with no further exchange, Ray said cautiously, "Think we should pray about all this?"

She bowed her head and closed her eyes. "You pray," she said. "I'll listen. By the way, in case you didn't know, you don't have to bow your head or close your eyes when you're driving. The Lord understands. It's much healthier too."

He threw his head back and laughed. "Thanks for the spiritual instruction." Then he began, "Lord, we're trusting You to—"

5

Dr. Kingston and Tommy had an early breakfast, then planned to take a jaunt around the lake in Kingston's car after going to church. They headed out onto the road around the lake at 1:30. Kingston planned to have a late lunch at a restaurant on the way. He put the .32 automatic under the seat in the car but said nothing to Tommy about it.

The first place they went to was the Wallenpaupack dam, east of them at the base of the lake where it had originally stopped up the Wallenpaupack River and created a thirteen-mile-long haven for water-skiers, sailers, and swimmers. When they parked at the dam, Tommy was full of questions and seemed more relaxed than earlier.

Kingston led them out onto the top of the dam. The water was low. Each fall the authorities let a lot of water out of the lake in preparation for winter and the spring thaw when it would fill up again. As they stared down into the water, Tommy said, "Do you think my mom and Mr. Ray will really get married?"

341

Kingston put his arm over the boy's shoulder. "If I ever saw two people in love, it's them. I think they want to get past all this, though, before they make that kind of decision."

Tommy kicked a stone off the edge of the dam into the water. "I hope they do," he said. "I want to be just like Mr. Ray."

Kingston laughed and placed his hand on Tommy's shoulder. "That's a good goal to aspire to."

They walked along, throwing stones, laughing and talking. Kingston thought about what Ray and Andi were trying to do and prayed several times about it. Somehow, though, he felt at peace that God really would fulfill their grandest dreams. More than anything else, that was what he wished for them.

□ □ □

Nakayami called Martin Croase on Sunday morning. He had been up most of the weekend getting the gallon of TUT-B ready, and Croase had demanded it be done by Sunday. Nakayami just wanted to be done with it.

When Croase answered, Nakayami said, "The TUT-B is ready."

"The whole gallon?"

"Yes."

"Where is it?"

"In the lab."

"Take it to my office. I'll handle it personally."

"It's very dangerous—"

"I know that, Hiro. It's packed safely, correct?"

"Yes."

"It can be handled with rubber gloves?"

"Yes."

"Then no problem. Good work, Hiro. Take a day off."

Nakayami hung up, trying to think of what Croase could be doing. He was certain it had nothing to do with offering the B strain to other research firms. A whole gallon, he knew, could kill off half a city. But Croase surely wasn't planning some kind of blackmail operation of a whole city such as Washington, D.C.

342

Nakayami chewed his lip. He knew he had to find out what Croase was up to. But how, and where?

6

Ray and Andi arrived at Channel 4 headquarters on Nebraska Avenue in Washington at noon. They quickly found Lyle's desk and offered to share some of the takeout food they'd got at a drive-in restaurant. Lyle said he had gone to an early service at his church in Silver Spring.

When Lyle was finished, both Ray and Andi agreed his plan was worth trying. Lyle had been watching TWI and noticed the white truck usually went to the funeral home in the evening about eight o'clock. But he hadn't had time to pick up any pattern.

"We just watch for it as much as we can," he said.

"What about the funeral home—what have you noticed?" Ray asked.

After a quick description, Lyle said, "I think we just go in the front door. I have the video camera, just a regular Panasonic that fits in my briefcase. I've also got a set of three walkie-talkies. One for each of us. You and Andi go in and pretend you're looking for a funeral place for, say, your grandmother, who is very old—you know the patter—and you case it. See how many people are around. If there's another viewing or something going on, so much the better. Then when you've got them diverted, you somehow signal me to come in and look around for a doorway into the basement."

"This sounds too risky, Lyle," Ray said. "If there's anything I learned in the SEALs, it's the power of surprise. I think we'll have to try something else, maybe something with that underneath garage."

"You're the SEAL."

"All right," Ray said. "I want to go out there tonight. Let me see what we're up against, and then we can go for it."

"I feel confident," Lyle said, looking at Andi.

Ray put his arm over her shoulder. "You feel OK about this?"

343

"You're the SEAL," she said with a smile.

Rolling his eyes, Ray answered both of them, "This is a team, people. Another thing about SEALs is that they recognize there are no Lone Rangers, except the kind that end up dead. We're going in as a team, and we'll function as a team."

Both Andi and Lyle grinned knowingly, but Ray knew they were looking to him as the leader. It made him feel good in a way, but also nervous. Panama flitted into his mind momentarily, and he murmured to himself, "No bad decisions," on the way out.

7

Dr. Kingston and Tommy enjoyed a dinner of New York strip steaks, peas, and baked potatoes. He told Tommy that after his wife died, he'd learned to prepare a variety of delicious dinners.

Tommy told him, "This is almost as good as my mom's."

They cleaned up together in the kitchen with Kingston washing and Tommy drying. The woods out the kitchen window were lit by two spotlights off the porch, so they could see partway down the path. Spotlights across the lake sent rippling lines of warm yellow light on the water. As Kingston passed plates and bowls to the boy, Tommy asked, "Dr. Kingston, what are demons?"

"They're fallen angels."

"How did they fall?" Tommy had decided he liked the way Dr. Kingston talked about things like that. A lot of it made sense to him, and somehow it was exciting. He'd played Dungeons and Dragons a few times, and though he'd stopped, the idea of supernatural beings intrigued him. In light of his own recent experiences, his interest was obviously stronger. As Kingston talked, Tommy concentrated on the ideas.

"God's highest angel, Lucifer, didn't like the way God ran things. So he decided to start a rebellion with some of the other angels who didn't like God's methods either. When a third of the angels God had created followed Lucifer, God took action. He drew a line or something in heaven beyond which the rebellious angels couldn't go. Then He gathered the rest of the angels and started a program to show them He was worthy of their loyalty."

"How come?"

Kingston worked at a bit of burned-on steak in the frying pan. "Lucifer was telling everyone what a wretch God was. So God had to show them He really was loving, good, righteous, holy, and all that."

"Why didn't He just kill them all?"

Kingston smiled. "Is this an examination?"

Before Tommy could think of an answer, he put a wet hand on Tommy's hand. "Just kidding. Think of it this way. If God killed the rebels off, all He would have proved was that He was a tyrant who could get rid of the opposition. Later on, some of the loyal angels might get the same idea Lucifer had. So God had to do it another way. He had to let Lucifer go out and show everyone how he would run things. In the meantime, God would also work around Lucifer and keep things under control. In other words, God'd work His own plan and eventually all the angels would see whether Lucifer's or His way was best."

"But what about us? How are we in there?"

Tommy looked at him with squinty eyes. He wondered if Dr. Kingston was one of the smartest men in the whole world.

"That was part of the reason God created the world and people and everything else. That was where Lucifer—who became Satan—would get to test out his theories. In effect, right now, and ever since history began, Satan has been trying every way he can to show his way is the wise, good, and worthwhile course. By the end of time, he'll have exhausted every possible way to live except, of course, God's way. In the meantime, the people of God all through history have shown how God's way goes too. So right now we see both Satan and God working."

"Can Satan win?"

Kingston looked upward and sighed. "It looks like he is at times. Like right now with your mother and Ray and you. But God is always working behind the scenes to make sure His real purpose gets accom—I mean, done."

"I know that word. Accomplished." Tommy grinned. He wondered if Dr. Kingston thought he was smart too.

Kingston laughed, "Good. Then I know I'm talking to a fellow theologian."

"You think I'm a theologian?"

"Sure, son." Kingston clapped a dry hand on his shoulder. "Anyone who asks questions as deftly as you has to be. That's all theology is—asking questions and finding out what the Bible says about them."

Tommy cocked his head. "So that's why you think the person we met out there was a demon?" He thought about the experience again and tried to picture it all in his mind. He remembered the first being, then the wall. Then things got hazy.

Kingston hung the wet dish towel inside the cabinet under the sink. "I'm not sure where those creatures fit into Satan's scheme, Tommy. But I'm certain neither an angel or Jesus Christ would ever lie to someone about the truth."

"So you think Jesus is the truth?"

"Yes, Tommy, I not only think He's the truth, I know He is. I'm as certain of it as I am of the wrinkles on my hand." He held out his hand and looked at it. Tommy looked down, then turned his face back up to Kingston.

"But how do you know, really know?"

Kingston led Tommy back into the living room. As Tommy stretched out comfortably on the couch, Kingston piled several logs in the fireplace, rolled up some newspapers, and lit them. When he sat down, he said, "There's a vast difference between believing and knowing. You can believe something is true, but not be absolutely sure. On the other hand, you can *know* something is true and nothing could make you change your mind—because you know it. It's like math. If you ask me how much two times two is, I say four. I know it. There's no question, no argument. But if you say to me, Do you believe the Russians are being honest about the latest treaty? I might believe yes, might believe no. But it's not something you can completely know absolutely.

"A lot of people come at religion like that. They feel it's a matter of opinion and everyone gets to choose what they believe, as if a thing is true because someone believes it. But believing something is true doesn't make it true. And believing something is false doesn't make it false. But you asked me how I know Christianity is true, right?"

Tommy nodded. He had his hands behind his head propped up on two colorful pillows. It was a position Mr. Ray liked to stretch out in, and it made him feel a little like Mr. Ray. He told himself if Ray ever became his father, he would never be a coward again. He'd do everything right. Ever and always. He watched Kingston's face as the old man talked.

"I know it's true for only one reason, son. Because God has given me a gift called faith. You know what it says in the Bible, 'By faith we understand that the worlds were created by the word of God.' The same chapter says, 'Faith is the assurance of things hoped for, the conviction of things not seen.' That's what it means to know—to have an assurance, a conviction. You're convinced because God has put it in you to be convinced. Faith is like a sixth sense. With it we see things that are unseen. With it we hear the voice of God that can't be heard any other way."

"That's what happened to me," Tommy said suddenly. The image that crackled into his mind was so strong that he almost rolled off the couch. His heart began pounding.

Kingston gazed at him. "What happened?"

"I just remembered it." Tommy sat up and looked at Kingston, a fresh excitement burning in his chest. "When I was dead. That's what happened. I met this person, a very powerful, kind person. He told me to believe the truth."

"And what did he say the truth was?" Kingston said, staring at him with amazement.

"That was it. He said I'd know the truth because it would be in my heart. I would hear it and know it was the truth. He said, 'My sheep hear my voice.'"

"He said 'my sheep'?"

Tommy nodded his head fervently.

For a moment, Kingston looked lost in wonder.

Tommy said, "Is there something wrong with that?"

The old man shook his head. "It's remarkable, that's all. I would never have believed it, but—" He looked back at Tommy. "And what conclusion have you come to?"

347

"That Jesus is the truth," Tommy said, nodding his head. He felt so light and full he wanted to scream for joy. "Because of Ray and my mom and you. I knew it before, but I forgot. Because I was scared."

Kingston leaned forward. "Scared of what, Tommy?"

"Of the other person."

"What other person?"

"The first one. Before the gate. When I died. There was the gate. And before I went through, there was one person there. And he told me to believe in him. But I couldn't. Then I went through and there was a second person. He told me his name, and he said—"

"What was his name?"

Tommy shook his head, wrinkling his face with thought. The name just wouldn't come. "I still can't remember. But he told me he would protect me."

"And he told you to believe the truth?"

"Yes."

"Why didn't you tell your mother and Ray this?"

Tommy looked down at his hands. "I don't know. I kind of just remembered now. When you started telling me about Satan and all. And then there was the third person."

"The one who told you, 'My sheep hear my voice'?"

"Right."

"Do you know who he was, Tommy?" Kingston's eyes were big and surprised, and Tommy wondered if the old man was going to be sick.

"No."

Kingston shook his head. "It just can't be that simple," he said. Then he looked up at Tommy. "I think you met Jesus, Tommy."

"I did?" Tommy sat back on the couch, suddenly very afraid. He remembered how they'd learned in Sunday school that when people looked on God's face, they died instantly.

"It's all right. It's wonderful!" Kingston suddenly exclaimed. "It's glorious."

Tommy sat back, watching the old man. Kingston stood up and began to pace. "This is incredible. I've never seen it quite this way. Not like this. So the war rages right up to the door of heaven."

Tommy looked up at him. "The war?"

Kingston nodded excitedly. "The war between God and Satan. It's like this, Tommy. Satan not only wants to prove God is wrong and unworthy of our love but also to get as many people on his side as he can. Or at least not to believe God. So he deceives people. Constantly. Every moment he has his legions of demons out there whispering taunts and lies and falsehoods and boasts into the minds of people—God's people, unbelieving people, everyone. He'll do anything to keep a person from believing in God. But this near death experience—this could prove to be one of the greatest deceptions in history. It has to be."

Tommy stared at the barrel-chested man. "How could it be one of the greatest deceptions in history?"

"You see, Satan's only real weapon is deception. All he can do is twist or deny the truth. So he's using this near death experience in the lives of multitudes of people to convince them of a whole new religion of 'it's all OK.' I'd call it the 'OK religion.'"

Tommy laughed.

"It's not funny, son." But Kingston did chuckle. "I guess it sounds funny. But the point is this. If you can convince people that the future world is all right and there's nothing to worry about, no debt to pay, no judgment to face, it really doesn't matter what you do in this life. Sure, you can pay lip service—"

"What's lip service?"

"Saying you believe something but not really ever doing anything about it."

"Yeah, I've heard my mom say it sometimes. But she tells me not to give her any 'lip.' But I give it to her anyway." Tommy smiled and waited for Kingston to get the joke.

The prof chuckled. "Lip service is actually a biblical expression. From Isaiah. But listen. People can pay lip service to morality and being decent, and even believing in some kind of reincarnation, but ultimately if you think when you die all that will happen is you'll meet this friendly being of light who assures you whatever you did is OK, then you'll have no reason to trust Christ, receive His forgiveness, and accept His salvation. It's the final destruction of Christianity."

Tommy gazed at Kingston with amazement. Then he said, "That's why Ray asked the being if Hitler was there."

"What's that?"

"When he was up there, he asked the first being if Hitler was up there and it was all OK. The being didn't give an answer, but I guess he didn't have to."

"Because he'd already assured Ray that his own sins didn't matter."

"I guess." Tommy sat on the edge of the couch.

Kingston suddenly laughed. "You know, I'd almost like to go on one of these excursions myself, just to see what it's like."

"I don't think you'd like it."

"How come?"

"Because you'd want to argue with everybody."

Kingston leaned against the mantel and roared. "That's a joke, I take it."

Tommy smiled. He felt proud. Dr. Kingston really liked him. And so did Mr. Ray. It was great. Now he had at least two people besides his mother who liked him. A lot. Maybe even loved him. He nestled on the couch and felt this huge smile coming onto his face. He wanted to jump and hug Dr. Kingston and tell everyone he loved them, but he simply sat there and watched and prayed that they'd all be back together soon.

8

Ray, Andi, and Lyle crept up a side street by the Willard Funeral Home on Sunday evening about 7:00 P.M. It was dark down the street where they had parked Lyle's car. The back of the home was well lit, but once under the overhang of the underneath garage they wouldn't be easily seen.

Ray scrutinized the four windows along the second and third floors of the funeral home, then when he was sure no one was looking, he whispered, "Go."

The three of them scurried down the asphalt into the depression in front of the garage doors. It was dark inside.

The main doors were the roll-up variety, run by an electric motor inside. A door to the left had four windows, and they could see a short hallway inside. Ray knew they could easily cut a hole in the window with a glass knife and suction cup. The dead bolt probably had a turn handle on the inside.

They stood out of the light and spoke quietly about how and when to get in. Suddenly the lights went on inside. They heard footsteps on the pavement inside the garage.

"Two of them," Ray whispered.

Through the door a man's voice said, "You can just lay them here till I get here and can take care of it. They usually come in around 8:30."

A second voice answered, "No problem."

There was a whirring noise, and the garage doors began to rise.

Ray whispered, "Over to the far wall—up next to it."

They crossed in front of the doors and hurried back up the garage driveway, then turned sharply to their right and crawled behind the brick wall that rose to the left of the garage doors. They were out of the light, but if anyone came to a back door immediately to the left of the wall, they'd be caught.

Ray and Lyle peered over the wall, while Andi lay with her back against it. Two men stepped onto the driveway just outside the garage. One was tall and wore a three-piece suit. He smoked a cigarette. The other was short with a black-and-gray-flecked beard. He had on workclothes and a green baseball hat.

The tall man spoke with a dry raspy voice. "Just hose it out and keep the place neat and clean. You have to be available at all times on call."

"I understand, Mr. Willard."

"You need to get into the habit of just doing as they say, though I'll probably be here. But there's no need to ask any questions. For your own information, they're from one of the local medical schools, you know, the cadavers they use to learn on."

"All cut up, huh?"

"A little. But they'll be in body bags. No need to open them, just lay them out on the floor here. I'll always let you know well in advance when they'll be here, but it's usually around 8:00 P.M. Second shift people, you know. You should leave the garage open until they get here. They like to come right in."

"Whatever you say, Mr. Willard."

Willard flicked his cigarette into the driveway. "All right, the main thing is cleaning up before and after. Thanks for coming out on such short notice. I know they won't be here tonight as I thought. Sorry to inconvenience you."

"Anything for a few extra bucks, Mr. Willard."

"Well, just keep it quiet. I'm giving you the extra two hundred to remind you of that."

"No problem, Mr. Willard."

They both walked back into the garage. When Ray heard a door shut and the garage become quiet, he said, "Come on. They're making it easy on us."

Andi grabbed his arm. "What are you going to do?"

"Go down in there now and find a place for Lyle to position his camera. You stay right here."

She shook her head. "I'm coming with you."

The lights were still on. They found several closets, an elevator, a stairway, and two other doors that were locked. At the far end was a pile of furniture with drop cloths thrown over it. Ray lifted one and looked under. There were two couches, a table, and several stacks of chairs.

Lyle said, "Just what the doctor ordered."

"You can do it?" Ray said.

"If it's still here whatever night they come out. This is almost too good to be true. Either these people are fools or so cocksure of themselves they're not thinking straight."

"Then we'll have to get out here each night well before eight o'clock," Ray said. "If this clean-up guy follows through, we may get an opening when he goes inside or something."

They ran up the driveway to the sidewalk. A few minutes later, they were back in the Malibu, all three in the front seat with Andi in the middle. Lyle started it up and drove up the street past the funeral home, then made a right on Georgia Avenue.

Lyle followed Georgia Avenue south where he would catch the beltway and back down through Chevy Chase where he had an apartment. Andi and Ray had decided to stay there since he had a guest room for Andi and a rollaway bed in his small living room for Ray.

"I can't believe how messed up things get," Andi suddenly said. "How did we ever get into the fix we're in now?"

Lyle laughed. "Paul said anyone who desires to live like Jesus will be persecuted. Maybe you're just living like Jesus."

"Yeah, right," Andi said.

But Ray answered, "If God's in this, He'll work out the details. And if He's not, it doesn't matter what we do."

Lyle smiled. "Oh, He's in this all right. Smack in the middle. Regardless of what Croase is up to, I know the Lord's doing something far more important. What, I'm not sure. But He's grinding it out yard by yard. So let's just keep plugging away. I'm going down to City Hall tomorrow too. My day off. Going to see what I can drum up by way of records on Martin Croase."

"What are you planning to do?" Ray asked.

"A little investigative reporting. You know, there's a lot of public information out there. You can get all sorts of stuff at the MVA just from license information. Then there's the public library—city directory, which'll give you info about property and so on. City Hall is loaded with stuff, the tax assessor's office, voter registration. Then the courthouse, at the county recorder's office you can get marriage and birth info, stuff on any lawsuits he might have been in, and, of course, criminal activity. I don't know why I didn't do it before. Just didn't think of it I guess."

"So that's what you do for a living?" Andi said, sounding a bit awestruck.

"No, that's what I want to do. For a living, I just interview people about whether they like the bug spraying on Route 29 or what the local aerobics club is doing for kicks."

Ray grinned. "So that's where a seminary education got you?"

"No, that's where a journalism degree at Northwestern got me. Seminary got me nowhere except angry. At least this seminary. I'm willing to give another one a chance."

Andi laughed. "I ought to do a study about how many of our grads actually stay in the ministry."

Lyle nodded with saddened conviction. "Not as many as you'd think. I know several from my class selling life insurance now and one doing color tile in a store. And they weren't even disgruntled or anything. It's a tough marketplace, even for the average minister."

Lyle directed the big Malibu onto the ramp to 495, the beltway. "River Road here we come," he said. Soon they were zipping down the highway at seventy mph, which both Ray and Andi soon came to realize was slow for Lyle.

9

On Monday morning, Dr. Nakayami waited nervously in Ken Strock's office. He had several questions, and he thought Strock might be able to impart the information. He didn't want Croase to know he and Strock had been talking. Strock's desk was a mess, but on the top was a blueprint layout of the water piping in the pump room. Nakayami looked it over and then picked up a small black device lying by the blueprints that looked like a cordless telephone. There were two lights at the top and a number pad underneath. The lights read, "Prime" and "Detonation." Each was a push button. A small silver antenna could be telescoped out the top, but the device had no mouthpiece or receiver. Nakayami turned it over in his hands.

Then the door opened.

Strock walked in. "Looking over my latest invention, doctor?" He smiled and did not seem perturbed that Nakayami was looking at the strange equipment.

"I was wondering what it was," Nakayami said, placing the device back on the desk and putting his hands behind his back.

Strock walked around the desk and picked up the device. "It's a radio detonator, like they use in demolition work.

I programmed it myself. See, you press this button—'Prime'—and it sends a computer message to a receiver. That sets in motion the process. Then you push 'Detonate' and *ka-boom*—you can blow a building to bits."

Nakayami eyed the detonator cautiously. "What's it for?"

Strock shook his head. "Some harebrained thing Croase has going. He wanted me to set up some special equipment in the pump room so some chemical can be fed into the water system. At the same time, all the sprinklers go on and everybody gets wet." Strock laughed. "He says it's a special surprise for everyone on campus. Ask me, I think it's nuts. But you know Croase." Strock grinned at the slight doctor as if extremely pleased that he was imparting this knowledge.

"You have this all set up?"

"Just about. Got the chemicals yesterday."

Nakayami gulped but kept his face impassive.

"Croase is being real secretive about it. But I think it has something to do with the TUT business. Probably Croase wants to do a mass NDE or something. You know how Listra Croase is always talking about such stuff."

"Could be," Nakayami said casually, looking at the detonator again. "What's the code?"

Strock smiled slyly. "Now I told you that, Mr. Croase might not like it too much, would he?"

Nakayami nodded. "I suppose."

"By the way, what are you here for, doctor?"

Nakayami smiled tightly. "Just thought I'd come by to say hello, see how things are going."

Strock smiled. "Well, this is a pleasure. Why don't we have a cup of coffee and talk?"

"Of course." Nakayami sat down and waited as Strock prepared two cups from the coffeemaker behind his desk. Nakayami's mind was a blur of thought. But one question kept ringing in his mind, *Is Croase really going to try to kill off the campus in one huge shot of TUT-B?*

CHAPTER SIXTEEN

1

That afternoon, Dr. Kingston took Tommy to Carbondale to show him some of the coal mines in the area. Kingston also took him into several fishing supply stores and explained to Tommy various techniques of catching fish on the lake and as far north as Canada, where Kingston's brother had landed the twenty-nine-inch walleyed pike hanging on the front wall of the cabin.

Kingston was pleased the boy continued to be talkative. Tommy asked question after question about hunting and fishing adventures, and Kingston, being a renowned raconteur, regaled him with his adventures.

After having dinner at a small restaurant called The Local Dive that featured a scuba-diving motif, they returned to the cabin at 7:30, tired but on ever-friendlier terms.

2

Lyle Hornum spent the whole morning at the library and courthouse digging up information on Martin and Listra Croase. By the afternoon, he had several pages of mind-numbing notes. Nothing stupendous, except that Croase had sold several properties recently in the Maryland area.

Lyle had also looked through the personnel files Ray had heisted from TWI. He began sketching out a theory about what TWI was up to. The picture up to that point looked like an organization bent on a kind of "scientific ecumenism" that would unite all religions under one banner through the use of the near death experience. With similar beliefs about morality and eternity, everything else would fall into line. He found one letter to a United Methodist leader that hinted at this ecumenism, which the leader responded to with fervor.

3

Lou Miles swore as he looked at the three notices in the FBI KEY. Between Sunday morning and Monday afternoon, there had been three more murders in New Jersey and Pennsylvania—the first in Newark, the second in Trenton, and a third in Philadelphia. A manhunt was on in both states, with roadblocks set up at various places. Miles didn't give it much hope. No one had discovered the first body until early Monday morning. All three were drug people known to be moneyrunners. The money motive was clear now. But the three letters, R to the first, E to the second, and U to the third made no sense to him.

Miles picked up the phone and talked to an agent in Baltimore named Clyde Harrison. Before dialing, he knew it would be a vain effort. This murderer was very creative—and cagey.

He put down the phone and swore again. "I need a piece of luck," he said. "Just one piece of luck."

4

Ken Strock hurried into Martin Croase's office. He laid a telephone number on the desk and a tape recorder. "We think we have them," he said.

"What's this?"

"Some place in northern Pennsy that Kingston goes to. We broke into Kingston's town house last night and ransacked the place. Luckily we found one of his latest phone bills. Several calls there. We called the number, and a kid answered. Listen to this."

Strock hit the forward button. There was musical sound of a phone number being punched in. Then after three rings a boy's voice came on. "Hello?"

Strock's voice answered, slightly disguised. "We're offering a special this week on porterhouse steaks. Is the lady or the man of the house in?"

"I don't think we're interested. But I'll ask."

Croase smiled. "It's him. I recognize the voice."

"Keep listening."

Kingston's voice came on. "Who is this?"

Strock's voice came on again. "Leed's market. We're having a special on porterhouse steaks this week. A box of twelve retails for—"

"Sorry, we're not in the market." The phone clicked off.

"Where are they?"

"We're working on a trace. The phone company is not cooperating. But it's a Bucks County prefix. We're looking in Kingston's house now for an address. Might be able to get a crisscross directory for the area."

"How soon can you get there?"

"By helicopter?"

"Yes."

"Two hours at the most."

"Do it. But be careful. Mazaris is an ex-commando, and Kingston was a war hero marine. They're both tough. But I want them all alive."

Strock snickered. "We can take them."

5

Lyle stopped his Malibu two blocks from the Willard Funeral Home on Georgia Avenue. It was just past 7:30 Monday evening. As he gathered the video equipment, Ray checked the two revolvers and the 9 mm automatic. They also had the shotgun in the trunk, but Ray didn't want to use it. Stalking up

358

Georgia Avenue with a loaded twelve-guage was a bit on the loony side.

Ray handed one of the revolvers to Lyle. "You know how to use one?"

"Of course." Lyle glanced at Andi. "Somewhat."

Ray gave him an exasperated look. "Have you ever fired one?"

Raising his eyebrows with revealing surrender, Lyle answered, "No."

Ray took the gun back and gave it to Andi. "Better not to have one than have one that can be used against you."

"That a SEALs principle?" Lyle said with a grin, but looking relieved that he didn't have to carry the weapon.

"No, just common sense. A SEAL would know how to use just about anything anyone could shoot at you, as well as how to get it away from the enemy. Don't worry about it. Nothing's going to happen." Ray put the 9 mm automatic in his pocket with the other two clips and left the extra pistol under the seat.

Lyle grabbed the video camera in his palm and shielded it next to his dark sweatshirt. All three hurried up the sidewalk. As they came up from the back end of the side street the funeral home stood on, they quickly saw the back lights were already on. Ray stopped them.

"I've got an idea," he said. When he'd spelled it out, Lyle dropped the keys into Andi's hand and she hurried back to the car. Ray grabbed him at the shoulder, just as he was about to leave. "Let me also give you some hand signals. Key way to communicate and still be silent."

Lyle scurried across the street to the back lot of the funeral home and came up behind the out-building. Ray walked up the sidewalk, and after scrutinizing the garage and windows above it, hid in the bushes.

He listened for several minutes, then peeked over the brick wall down into the garage well. The doors were still closed. It was 7:38. He hoped if anyone was coming, the handyman would open the doors ahead of time. But there was no noise inside. Half-brick-sized openings lay in the wall, and Ray was able to look through one of the chinks at the door.

After several silent minutes, Ray came around the wall, keeping to the inside, and flitted down to the door, sticking to the right of it. No noises sounded within. He took a quick look in the one of the four windows on the door, but there was no light on in that hall, and the door just inside it was closed. However, light shown in the crack along the base of the inside door. The lights were on in the garage.

Ray hurried back up to the wall, signaled an OK to Lyle watching him across the way, and hid again among the bushes. He felt along the ground and found a pebble. Biting his lip, he poked his head again above the wall, then lightly pitched the stone at the garage door. It ricocheted off with a tick, then plunked to the ground. Ray waited.

A moment later, the whirring noise came on and the garage door started to open. Ray ducked down and waited. He peered through one of the chinks in the wall and saw the handyman step out into the driveway with a flashlight in his left hand and a gun in the right.

"Bingo," Ray whispered and hoped Lyle was sitting tight.

□ □ □

Andi drove the car around the two blocks and parked down the street from the funeral home. She set the gun in her lap and watched the street for signs of activity. She couldn't see Ray, but she sensed that the white panel truck had not yet arrived, if it was going to come at all.

She stilled her heart by breathing easily and steadily. She stroked the handle of the gun and prayed she wouldn't have to try and use it.

She noticed a vague ache in her bladder, but she told herself now was no time to have to use the bathroom. She fought back an urge to start up, hit the gas, and careen out of there with Ray and Lyle. But she told herself to be calm. It would work out. Ray knew what he was doing.

The handyman walked up the driveway, shone the flashlight around the yard, then muttered, "Some truck musta kicked up a stone. Where are they, anyway?"

He walked back down the driveway to the doors. This time he didn't close them. He sat down on a green upright lawn chair in the middle of the garage area with the gun in his lap and the flashlight on the ground next to him. A pile of papers lay on the floor. He picked up one lying in front of the chair and continued reading.

Ray crept noiselessly out from behind the bushes and hurried to the end of the wall. Looking across the way, he saw Lyle just out of the light from the outbuilding. He knew Lyle could see him. He signaled "sit tight," then scrambled back behind the bushes, leaning up against the wall and listening. He figured the truck would show up tonight. He only hoped they got something on film.

☐ ☐ ☐

David Hughes turned off his headlights as he turned onto the lane by the funeral home. He stopped just past the driveway, then put it in reverse and began backing in. "He just better have the cash this time," he murmured as he watched the edges of the driveway through the mirrors. Moments later, he stopped underneath the fluorescent lights of the garage and opened the door.

Before he was out, the handyman stood at the door to greet him. "You Strock?"

"Hughes. Strock isn't here this time."

"Mr. Willard wants me to take the delivery."

Hughes swore. "Did he give you the money?"

"In there. In a bag, like you asked."

"OK, let's get this done."

Hughes slammed the door and walked around the vehicle. He opened up the back doors and they both looked in.

"Four?" the handyman said.

"Yeah, and one of them's a kid."

"That's awful."

□ □ □

Ray stood and signaled Lyle frantically. It had to be fast. But Lyle had already seen what was happening. Moving in a crouch, he hurried to the edge of the wall. He clicked on the video camera and aimed it at the front of the truck. He panned the area, then tried to get a fix on the bodies through the front window. But he couldn't get anything. The headrests on the seats were too high.

He glanced at Ray, then moved in.

The gravel was slippery. He knew he had to be sound-less. The camera was still whirring, and he aimed it in the general direction. Bending down and grunting slightly, he hurried to the front of the truck. He could see Ray looking at him over the edge of the wall. Then Ray ducked down.

Lyle looked up into the windshield. The two men pulled the body bags out. Lyle held the camera above his head against the windshield, hoping he was getting something. Something in his mind told him he might be seen too easily doing it this way. Lyle breathed out and prayed.

After taking twenty seconds of film, he stopped and squatted in front of the van. He wanted to get in closer. His heart seemed to be pounding through the top of his head.

He peered down under the chassis. It was high enough to crawl under, and the four bodies were piled right on the ground.

Lyle lay down on the ground and peered through the camera, adjusting the zoom lens for a close-up.

Two pairs of feet moved back and forth in front of them. With his elbows and knees, Lyle pushed himself forward under the van. Then he heard something behind him. He looked back. A pair of feet stood directly behind him. It was Ray.

Lyle groped forward.

The driver of the truck said, "Just give me the money."

The handyman answered, "Can I see one? I ain't never seen a dead body before they fixed him up."

"What are you, some kind of jerk? You can look at it after I leave."

Lyle saw the man's hands on a zipper. "It'll just take a second."

"Do it," Lyle whispered to himself, the camera trained right on the hands.

The big man swore several times, but the handyman was already unzipping the bag. He pulled it open and Lyle got an across the face shot of a gray old man with a growth of beard. The face looked twisted in a contortion of pain.

"You want to see something'll make you puke, look at this." The big man seemed to have changed his mind.

He opened up a smaller bag. Lyle winced. A boy's face—he couldn't even have been in his teens—looked out gaunt and cold, the eyes still open.

"It's just a kid," the handyman said.

"Yeah, I told you. Now you've seen it, give me the money. I'm outa here."

Lyle crawled forward a little closer. One more shot of that face and he'd be ready. Then, if he could, something of the two men.

Shoes clicked on the concrete, and the two men headed to a back door. Lyle moved closer, panning the whole room, getting close-ups of all four body bags, then turning back to the door. As the two men came through, he leveled the camera on both their faces.

Lyle didn't even think that they might see him under the truck.

Both men saw him at once. "What the—" screamed the big man, opening his jacket and pulling out a gun.

Lyle jerked up, smashing the back of his head into the gas pan.

□ □ □

The moment Ray heard the men yell, he knew it was over. He jumped around the van and shot two rounds into the ceiling above the heads of both of them.

363

They both hit the ground. Ray aimed at the fluorescent light and with two more shots put it out. He could hear Lyle backing up. "Roll out the left side," Ray yelled.

The big man returned the fire, and Ray leaped back in front of the van. He clicked on the walkie-talkie. "Andi— move!"

A bullet blasted through the truck windshield above his head. Lyle shot out past him on the left. The two men were still on the right. Ray heard tires squealing down the street. He looked above his head, aimed, and shot out the lone light over the driveway.

Everything in the garage plunged immediately into darkness. Lyle fled up the driveway. Ray stuck his hand out the side of the van and two bullets ripped by. He had more than ten rounds left in the fifteen-round magazine. He fired several shots, still above the men, forcing them to stay on the ground.

With a single word of prayer—"Help!"—he sprinted forward in a half crouch, trying to keep the van between him and the men. A bullet splatted into the asphalt next to his feet and two more crackled by above his head and over a shoulder. Andi screeched to a stop in the street by the driveway.

Ray turned and fired several more rounds into the van, trying for the front tire. The angle was bad, though, and he couldn't hit it.

Andi yelled, "Get out of there!"

Lyle threw the back door open. "Get pumping, Ray!" he shouted.

Ray sprinted up the slope. At least Andi and Lyle were all right. That was all he cared about. Then the big man jumped up and ran past the van, stood, and aimed. Ray saw him in time to leap, roll, and fire the last rounds at him.

They missed, but he wasn't trying to kill him. The man hit the ground.

The car door was open wide in front of him. Two explosions cracked out behind him. Ray dove for the open seat, and slid in. As Andi mashed the gas, Ray pulled his feet in. The door slammed shut against the bottoms of his feet as he scrunched up inside.

"Where to?" Andi cried.

"Anywhere but here," Lyle answered, ducking nervously.

Realizing the door wasn't tight, Ray opened and reshut it. For the first time, he noticed he was sweating again. But he didn't feel fearful. Knowing Andi and Lyle were no longer in danger helped. But he hoped the pain and fears of Panama were behind him. Maybe God had really freed him from it.

Andi whipped the wheel right onto Georgia Avenue. The tires never seemed to stop screeching.

"What did you get?" Ray cried.

"Everything," Lyle said. "It couldn't have been better if it was rehearsed eight times."

6

As Ray and Lyle watched the video on Lyle's television at his apartment, they were jubilant. They did indeed have everything. Andi was plainly impressed. Ray confessed, though, that he should have tried to wound the big man with the gun. "They could have winged me," he lamented. "I held back. SEALs principle number one: once you're in it, you're in it all the way; never pull a punch."

"Well, you survived, and they didn't hit you," Lyle said, ever optimistic. "Let's get this to the newsroom, show it to my boss. They'll be there now. They'll know if there's any chance of blowing this thing into orbit."

"Let's call Tommy and Dr. Kingston," Andi said. She dialed the phone and waited. A moment later, Dr. Kingston's voice came on.

"Yes?"

"It's Andi. We got the video."

"Bravo. What happened?"

She described the whole scene.

"Do you want to talk to Tommy?"

"Put him on."

Tommy was obviously excited about the video. "I knew Ray could do it."

"Well, you all sit tight up there. We'll be out of this in a few days."

365

"I'm glad. I'm beating Dr. Kingston in Scrabble. Best out of three."

"Win one for me, honey."

She hung up. "I'm ready to take a long bath. You mind, Lyle?"

"Go right ahead," Lyle answered. "I'll go to the station. Be back in a couple of hours."

Ray lay down on the couch feeling exhausted, but happy. He smiled to himself and said, "Thanks, God. You really came through." He was confident now they were on their way home.

7

It was past ten o'clock when Dr. Kingston closed up the Scrabble game he and Tommy had been playing. Tommy sensed that his new friend had let him win, but he didn't mind. He told himself, *Friends should do that sometimes. Not all the time. But sometimes.* He wondered if Ray did that kind of thing.

Suddenly, Kingston cocked his head. "What's that?"

Tommy gazed at the professor. "I didn't hear anything."

The big man listened again, then shrugged. "Just the wind, I guess. Let me close the doors downstairs, and we'll get on to bed."

"I'll put the game upstairs."

Tommy followed Dr. Kingston to the door of the cellar. He flicked on the light and started down the steep stairs. Tommy went to the refrigerator to get a last piece of his Mom's apple pie. Then he heard it. Voices downstairs.

He froze.

Then Kingston yelled, "Tommy, run!"

Tommy dropped the plate and ran to the door. "Dr. Kingston!"

A man he'd never seen leaped at him from the darkness. A moment later he was down and the man had his hand over Tommy's mouth. He tried to scream, then to bite the man's finger, but the pressure was too great.

Then the man clapped a rag over his face with a pungent-smelling odor in it. It was wet. Tommy told himself not to breathe, but his last words were "Please, Jesus, don't let—"

8

At 11:10 Strock called Croase at the latter's home. Croase answered and Strock said immediately, "We got the boy and the old man."

"What about the other two?"

"Gone."

"What?"

"We don't know where they are. We just found out their hideout a few hours ago, boss. What do you want?"

"Could they just be out somewhere?"

"It's Monday night," Strock said. "Past eleven and no one has showed up. Neither the old man or the kid will talk. Maybe they're out having dinner or a movie or something."

Croase swore. "All right, stick around till twelve, then bring them down here. By the helicopter. We'll have to do what we can to contain this."

9

Lyle came back in at 11:40. "They love it," he told Andi and Ray. "But we'll have to do a little more work before it can go on the air. We don't even know who any of these people are at this point."

"We can still use it for the FBI in any event," Ray said.

Lyle nodded. "Did you hear on the news?"

Ray said no. He was still in his street clothes, but Andi was wearing a robe, with her hair still wet from the bath.

"Three more alphabet murders. You were wrong. The letters weren't R-U-A. It's not RUACH, like Dr. Kingston thought."

"What was it?" Andi asked, running the other letters over in her mind.

367

"R-E-U. No one can make anything of it."

"I wonder what the Doc would think," Ray said. He looked at Andi skeptically, but she was thinking about the whole word.

"Why don't you call him again?" she said absently. "He won't mind."

Ray agreed and went to the phone. As he dialed, Andi wrote on a sheet of paper the letter sequence as she remembered it and looked at it. She looked up when Ray still hadn't spoken.

He frowned. "Nobody's picking up."

Andi looked up from the sheet of paper. "They're probably really conked. They were playing a mean game of Scrabble. Try it again."

She studied the sheet and turned to Lyle. "Would you look at this for a moment?"

Ray let it ring even longer. "No one's picking up."

Andi looked up at him, suddenly feeling panic surge through her abdomen. "They have to be there! We just talked to them this evening." She hurried over to the kitchen where Ray stood with the phone in his hand. "Try it one more time."

Now her heart was booming inside her, so loud she couldn't think. A sinking nausea came over her. *They didn't get him*, she cried in her mind. *Please, dear Jesus, don't let them have gotten them.*

Ray hung up and tried again. Then twice more. "Something's wrong. Doc is not that heavy a sleeper."

"They found out! I know they found out, Ray!"

"OK," Ray said, grabbing her arm. "Let's calm down. Remember that heater man the Doc spoke about?"

Andi searched her memory frantically. "Riggins. Something Riggins. John Riggins."

"He supposedly didn't live far away. I'll call him. He's a friend of Doc's brother. Maybe he'll help out."

Ray called information in the northern Pennsylvania area and got the number of the only Riggins in Hawley. Andi listened as Ray dialed, then explained who he was to the person on the other end. Ray said, "Could you go out to the house and check it out? It's really important."

When he was done, he told Andi, "He's going out to the house."

"No, no, no!" Andi said. She clenched and unclenched her fist, beating her sides with them. "I knew we should never have left." She looked back at Ray, fighting the tears she knew would come. But something else was inside her, an anger so hot and furious she knew that if Tommy had been taken she was going to get Croase once and for all. Forget the video. Forget the police. They were going down to TWI and get Tommy back and rid the world of Martin and Listra Croase once and for all.

Half an hour later, Riggins called. "I'm here now," he said when Ray answered. "It doesn't look good. The car's out front, but the front door was open and the place is a mess, like there was a fight here. The electricity's cut. No one's here. What's going on?"

Ray put his hand over the receiver and told Lyle and Andi. She looked more controlled now, though Ray knew she was fighting it. Lyle stood next to her as Ray continued talking.

"Any idea what time it could have happened?"

"Can't tell," Riggins answered.

"If the electricity's cut, an electric clock will tell the time it was cut. There's a regular wall clock in the kitchen."

"Gotcha, give me a minute."

Riggins came back on. "Ten-oh-five it says. But that could be morning or night."

"We talked to them just a few hours ago, so they had to be hit at ten tonight." He looked at Andi. Her eyes were closed, and she was shaking her head, pacing back and forth. Suddenly, Panama was back in Ray's mind, and he felt as if the floor were quaking underneath him. God wouldn't let it all be taken away now. Not after this.

He roped in his thoughts as Riggins offered to call the police. Ray told him to go ahead and have them check it out. He gave Riggins the number where they could be reached and said to keep them informed. When Ray hung up, he went to Andi. Her face was a picture of terror and anger. "He was supposed to be safe there!"

"We thought he was, Andi!"

"Well, obviously he wasn't."

"We'll find him, we will. I swear it."

"Yeah, in a body bag."

She pushed Ray away and put her face in her hands. Lyle stood back, and Ray quietly touched her arm. The words *Bad decision!* were in his mind, and he knew it was all his fault again. He groped for the right words, even as the inner recriminations began to scorch through his mind. "Andi, please. We can't lose it now. The Lord's brought us this far, He'll take us all the way. I'm convinced."

She turned and buried her face in his shoulder. "They'll eat him alive, Ray. They'll destroy him. They'll send him up into that death place and put him in the hands of that demon!"

Ray held her tight and looked over her head at Lyle. The reporter's face was etched with lines of despair.

As he held her, though, he fought to still his emotions. "All right," he said, "we made a bad decision. But we can still make some right ones."

She slowly stopped crying. As he searched her eyes, he prayed in his mind, *God, You've got to come through. If You don't—*

He didn't finish the sentence.

He said to Lyle, "It takes five hours to get back here by car. They must still be on the road."

Lyle nodded. "You think we can head them off?"

"If they're coming in by car."

"How else could they come?"

"That helicopter."

"How long would that take?"

"Hour, hour and a half at the most. Maybe two." Ray gazed into Andi's streaked face and eyes. "OK, are you committed to this?"

"To getting Tommy back—absolutely."

"Not just to that. To getting Tommy and Dr. Kingston, exposing Croase, possibly us having to face everything all alone?"

She nodded furiously. "Whatever it takes."

"All right, we may be able to do something before they get Tommy into that death room. We're going to have to make no more mistakes and pray like mad that God will help. But we have the guns, we have the tools we need. I think we can do it."

Andi took a long breath. "All right. Whatever you say."

For a moment, Ray fought another battle with inner doubt, but then Andi said, "You didn't make a bad decision, Ray. This isn't Panama."

He sighed. "I wish I could believe that."

"I trust you. Like you said, it's no time to start crying and wailing. God's going to do what He will do. In the meantime, we have to do our best."

Her sudden confidence ignited him. "All right."

Lyle interjected, "What if we go to the FBI, get a search warrant or something? Show them the video?"

"That's the first step—for you, Lyle," Ray said. "You think that'll be enough evidence to get them to search TWI?"

"The funeral home, anyway. Maybe the whole campus. I don't know. If we could just get enough FBI people to believe us."

Andi suddenly looked down at the piece of paper still in her hand. "Maybe this will be enough," she said and handed Ray the piece of paper.

Ray looked at it. The word spelled was ABBENREU. He stared at Andi.

"Benreu, Ray. The word that alphabet killer has been spelling. Tommy said the demon's name was Benreu. If I understand what you were talking about the other night, the murderer has written, 'Benreu is father.' Look at it. Whoever is doing these killings must be connected to Martin Croase or at least this demon!"

Ray read the sheet again. A cry of triumph infused him. This would be more than enough. He said, "Let's call that FBI man doing the investigation. Now. What was his name?"

Lyle grabbed a little notebook and flipped through. "Miles." Andi ran to her pocketbook. "And here's the number they gave a few days ago from Boston."

Andi added with rising fury, "If Croase does anything to my son, I'll kill him. I swear, I'll take that gun you taught me to shoot and kill him."

PART 3

The Guardian

Do not forget to entertain strangers, for by so doing some people have entertained angels without knowing it.

—The Letter to the Hebrews

Millions of angels are at God's command.

—Billy Graham

I don't know why it is that the religious never ascribe common sense to God.

—W. Somerset Maugham

CHAPTER SEVENTEEN

1

A weary special agent named Doug Stecher answered the FBI phone in Boston when Ray called. Ray gave his name and asked to speak to Lou Miles.

"I'm afraid he's in New Jersey."

"I have some interesting information that might be pertinent to the alphabet killer case."

Stecher said with genuine weariness, "Give it to me and I'll convey it to Special Agent Miles."

Ray explained about what happened to him, Andi, and Tommy during the past month. Stecher slowed him down to take notes, but he was tired and Ray was talking very fast. Then Ray told him about Benreu.

"Yeah, we've thought of that one," Stecher said. "But no one knows anyone by that name."

"We do," Ray said emphatically.

There was a long pause. Then Stecher said skeptically, "All right, who?"

Ray took a long breath. "We believe Benreu is a spirit being, an evil spirit."

On the other end, Ray heard Stecher roar, and then say after coughing into the phone, "Now I've heard everything. John, pick up on line two."

"Sir, if you will just hear me out." Ray heard a click and

a second agent came on who introduced himself as John Denton.

"All right, I want to hear this one. Go ahead." Stecher laughed again.

Groping for some point of reference, Ray said, "Let me try it from another angle. You've heard about channeling?"

"Shirley MacLaine stuff? Yeah. Malarkey, if you ask—"

"Look, sir, I'm not going to argue theology with you. But what if something like that is really possible? What if there are really spirit beings out there who can communicate? What have you got so far—a person who's killing people and writing out a morbid message and you don't have a clue as to why? You think there's a money motive. How does this person know about these diverse people in different parts of the country, totally different occupations and backgrounds? How does he know where the money is?"

"Tell me that."

"What if this person has actually contacted some spiritual being who gives him the information about who has the money, where, and how to get it?"

Ray sensed that Stecher began to listen more intently, even if his normal response probably would have been raucous laughter. His friend John on the other line didn't speak. Ray said, "If I was simply talking about theory, that would be one thing. But both I and several others met this being during several near death experiences and believe me, none of this was voluntary."

"They forced you to do it?"

"Yes."

Stecher laughed again.

Ray said, "Look, what have you got to lose just by hearing me out?" Ray felt his heart sinking and realized the whole rendition might be pointless. He could think of nothing that would convince the man. He said, "Have you ever watched Donahue or Oprah or one of those talk shows when they featured someone who had had an NDE?"

"NDE?"

"Near death experience. When you are clinically dead for a few minutes or more and then are resuscitated."

"Yeah, I've seen them on occasion."

"Good. What if a company developed a drug that induces NDEs? It would be the ultimate street drug, right?"

"Pretty heavy, I'd say."

"All right, then—what I'm saying is that we have a medical research institute here that has done it. Probably several hundred people have tried it now. The people in charge are—"

"You're saying someone has actually developed a drug that does this?"

"Exactly."

Ray heard Stecher whistle. "What proof have you got?"

"Just myself and my girlfriend here. Plus her ten-year-old son, and I could probably get other people." Ray looked at Andi, and she dug her hands into her pockets, looking at him hopefully.

"All right, let me hear your girl's spiel. By the way, how old are you?"

"Thirty-three."

"What kind of work?"

"Right now, a student at this school. But I was in the navy for ten years."

"What was your rank?"

"Captain. I was in the SEALs."

There was a sudden silence, and Stecher obviously covered the phone with his hand. Then he said, "Those are some pretty impressive credentials. How long were you in?"

"The navy? Ten years. Seals for the last six."

"In any engagements?"

"Panama."

"The guys who took Paidilla?"

"Right."

"My brother was there—in Panama City, not the SEALs." Stecher chuckled. "That's a tough outfit. Well, let me talk to the girl."

Andi got on the phone and gave Stecher the same information. Then she handed the phone back to Ray. She looked nervous and still afraid.

"OK," Stecher said. "Give this to me straight. How are these people doing this?"

Ray calmly explained, "We don't know exactly how the drug works, but somehow it transports you spiritually into the realm of death and eternity. It literally kills you for a few minutes, then automatically revives you. Sort of like a jump start. The people behind it are using the whole campus as a testing ground for the drug. I'm convinced the leaders have manipulated all sorts of people into going along with it. Up until now. And they may be doing more."

As Ray talked, Stecher seemed far more subdued. Ray began offering some history on Martin and Listra Croase and what he knew of the purpose of the TUT. Then he said, "In order to develop these drugs, we believe they've abducted people, homeless people, runaways, and used them in the experiments. Some people have died. We have a video of them delivering several bodies to a local funeral home where we think they cremate them."

"A video? Of everything?"

"As much as we could get."

Stecher was silent, then said to John, "Maybe these people—" Then he covered the phone. A moment later, he asked, "Why didn't you tell me this before?"

Ray grinned at Andi. "It was my ace in the hole."

"You always come at them with your main firepower first, you know that."

"Yeah," Ray said, giving Andi a sheepish look. "But you kind of got me off the track."

"All right, you say there's a definite connection to this TWI place?"

"Not on the video. But the man in the van was the same one as the one who shot at us from the car during our escape."

"You're sure?"

Stecher said to the other agent, "John, this might fly." Then to Ray, "You're sure this Croase person has the boy at the headquarters? And this spirit thing definitely was named Benreu?"

"That's where they do most of the medical procedures. Yeah, that's the name that we've always understood."

"All right," Stecher said to Ray, "I'm going to call Lou

378

Miles in Phillie. I want him to get in touch with you immediately. Can you give me your number?"

Ray gave him Lyle's phone number. Stecher said, "I don't know how soon we can get through, but I'll put a rush on it. Just stay put."

☐ ☐ ☐

The phone rang in Lou's room where he was going over all the files for the umpteenth time that night. He picked it up and instantly recognized Doug Stecher's voice.

"I've got something for you, Lou. Sounds a bit iffy, but also bizarre enough to be a real lead."

"Go ahead," Miles said.

Stecher gave him a run-through on the whole conversation with Ray Mazaris. It took him a good ten minutes, but Miles let him talk without interruption.

"He doesn't sound nutty?"

"Not at all, Lou. They saw you on TV. The only reason they haven't come to us before is because this TWI place apparently got the police to put out a warrant on them. I didn't tell him about the possibility of declaration against penal interest. They felt some problems they had with antiabortion work could maul them, too. And they didn't have any real evidence until now. I don't know what they have or if this is really anything, but it sounds more substantial than any other leads we have. The guy was a SEAL, too, so probably not some nut case. You think there really could be a spiritual connection?"

Lou answered, "I grew up under preaching that talked about the war between good and evil all the time and that made Satan out to be a real person. I'm not sure what I believe now about it, but I know plenty of sane people who wouldn't flinch at the idea."

"So you think it could be something?"

"Like you said, what else have we got? I can talk to them anyway."

Stecher gave him the number.

Miles talked to Andi and Ray for another thirty minutes.

379

Miles wasn't sure they had anything that related to the alphabet murders, and it looked like a long shot, but the kidnapping and the idea of a whole campus saturated with a drug like this worried him immensely. He had to drive to Quantico anyway, the FBI training center, so he said, "I'll get on the road to Washington as soon as I can. Where can you meet me? It'll take two and a half, three hours. It's past 1:00 A.M. now. If it looks substantial enough, I'll go for a search warrant."

Ray answered, "OK. Why don't you meet us at Channel 4 News?" He handed the phone to Lyle to give Miles the address in D.C.

□ □ □

After finishing with Miles, Ray grabbed Andi's hand, pulling her up off the couch. "Come on, we're going down to TWI."

"I was hoping you'd say that," she said, still clearly upset. She ran for the guest room to get her coat.

Ray turned to Lyle. "If we're not back in time, you meet Miles at the station." He handed Lyle one of the walkie-talkies. "We'll be down on the campus somewhere. I just feel we have to get moving now. I know this Miles guy won't like it, but I can't just sit here and let them fry Tommy. Think you can handle it?"

"Sure. I'd do the same thing."

They gathered their parkas, some dark gloves and hats that Lyle had in his closet, and Ray checked his pockets for the Swiss Army knife and some other small tools he'd brought from the cabin. Then Ray and Andi went down in the elevator and climbed into the 4x4. She had her arms folded. She stared straight ahead, and Ray instinctively took her hand. "He'll be OK," he said fervently, hoping he was right.

She didn't look at him. "If Martin Croase knows what's good for him, Tommy will not only be OK, but unharmed and undrugged." Her jaw flexed and unflexed in the light behind the apartments.

Ray still had the two .38s, the 9 mm, the shotgun, and plenty of ammunition. Surveillance and secret abductions were a SEALs specialty. He headed out, and in thirty minutes they drove up Georgia Avenue. Ray prayed silently, then with Andi as they drove. She gripped his hand the whole way. When they finally turned onto Simmering Road, it was past 3:00 A.M.

□ □ □

The helicopter touched down at the campus at 3:05. Strock and his henchmen moved Kingston and Tommy, both gagged, into the TWI building.

"I'll call Croase soon as I see what's going on," he said to Linton and the others. "Just take them up to the eighth floor lock room."

Linton grunted acknowledgment, and Strock headed to the security station on the second floor.

2

Hal Gordon sat on Kent Farrell's bed in the semidark. A small penlight lay on the floor, giving them some illumination. It was just past 3:00 in the morning. "How many people do you think you can trust?" Hal asked Kent.

"Ten I know of. Maybe fifteen."

"You can give me their names?"

"Why should I trust you, Prof? You might be one of them."

Hal shook his head, fervent with understanding. "I realize that. But they won't let you past the guard station downstairs. I have to do it. I think Croase is completely flipped out. And I think you're right about him using the students as lab rats for his grisly experiments. We've got to get the campus moving, maybe just leave. They can't shoot all of us."

"But what if there's a real battle out there?"

"Kent, we have to go for it. Something terrible has happened to this campus in the last few years, and most of us haven't been aware of it because we were so caught up in the great results we were seeing in other areas. I take the blame as much as anyone."

Kent stood and paced a moment, then went to his door and looked out. When he turned around, he said, "All right,

381

I'll give you their names. And they probably know others who will help. I'll give you a note from me to each of them."

"Good. Amazing the level of trust on this campus."

Ken nodded grimly. "It's what's happened since people began using this TUT stuff. Everybody thinking they know secrets no one else knows."

"It's all a satanic deception."

"You're dead right on that."

"All right," Hal said. "This is what I'm going to do. Go around to these rooms, talk to these people, see if I can get something going by morning. Maybe a demonstration, I don't know. Maybe we should just get on the road and leave."

"That might be the best thing."

Kent took out a number of index cards and began writing on them. Hal stood and looked out the window at the campfire across the way where several of the security guards were stationed. Suddenly, he saw the underlights of a helicopter as it touched down. In the bright headlamps, he saw several people get off. He recognized Strock, but no one else.

"What is this?" he asked.

Kent got up and crouched down in front of the window with Gordon. "Probably more weird stuff going on."

Hal said, "This campus has gone completely nuts."

Kent went back to his cards. Watching the helicopter out of the corner of his eye, he murmured, "None of this ever should have happened. But maybe it's God's way of waking us up."

3

David Hughes stood before Ken Strock in the security office. Strock was already angry. Hughes said, "They had a video camera, that's all I know, boss."

"It was this Mazaris guy?"

"And someone else I haven't ever seen."

Strock swore. He was wet with sweat and nervous. He sensed that Croase was bringing everything to a dark conclusion, and he wanted to move while the moving was good. He said, "All right. I'll talk to Croase. We may have to do something about Willard."

"Sure."

"One other thing, Hughes. After this, you get on a plane and get out of here. You're a fool. Go to the Bahamas and forget you ever worked here because I've already forgotten it myself."

Hughes stared at Strock with cold anger, then turned around. "Consider it done."

☐ ☐ ☐

Strock immediately called Croase at home. After a few sleepy questions, Croase listened intently. Then he said, "All right, call Nakayami. I want him at the facility by 6:00 A.M. Get the boy and the old man to the safe room."

"We have them in a locked room now, sir."

"All right, that's good enough for now. What else am I not thinking of?"

Listra Croase stirred beside her husband and sat up. "What's going on?"

Martin covered the phone with his hand. "Your boyfriend has screwed things up but good."

"My boyfriend?"

"You know who I'm talking about."

Listra threw off the covers and got off the bed. "I don't know what you're talking about."

Croase spoke again to Strock. "What about Willard?"

"I'm on it already."

"Good."

"What else? The water system. Have you got the chemical set up for injection into the campus water system?"

"All ready to go, sir. The radio detonator is on board the helicopter now."

"Good work. All right. I think we've got it all covered. I'll be at TWI in less than an hour."

"I'll be handling some other things, sir, so I probably won't see you."

"No problem."

Croase hung up. Listra was already dressed. "Where are you going, my dear?"

"Wherever you're going, honeybunch."

"No you're not."

"Don't order me around. You have the boy. I'm not going to lose my chance. I want to go up with him as soon as possible and see what we can do about that wall. I want to get on with the work of TWI. Or have you forgotten that? What is this you're doing with the water system?"

"Nothing you need to worry your little head about."

"Don't patronize me. What is it?"

"I have to make some calls. I'm going downstairs. We'll be leaving in about twenty minutes."

Listra swore. "Hurry up then, I want to deal with that kid and get it over with."

□ □ □

Strock called Nakayami at the researcher's home about ten miles from TWI. When Nakayami answered with a sleepy croak, Strock said, "Good morning, Dr. Nakayami."

"Who is this?"

"Ken Strock."

"Why are you calling?"

"We got the boy, doctor. Croase wants you at TWI by 6:00 A.M. You should have seen it. Everyone performed perfectly."

"I'm sure they did," Nakayami said, not wanting to antagonize Strock. "Why does Dr. Croase want me?"

"Don't know, doctor. Just be there. He was very insistent."

Nakayami hung up and stared at the wall. His wife, Toshiko, was still asleep. He decided not to wake her. But whatever Croase planned to do with the boy, this time he would not agree. Not one more time. There was only one reason to obey Croase this time, and that was to try to redeem a shred of dignity from the whole sordid situation.

384

4

Johnny Goge poised another TUT-paper blot over his tongue, then laid it carefully on the tip. He lay on a hotel bed in Baltimore. The last three murders completed the last of Croase's requests, netting nearly another million dollars. He still had it in the trunk of his car. In addition to the money, Croase promised to personally take him to meet Benreu so he could get the power that Carlos Giotto and so many others had had. He lay back comfortably, waiting for the drug to hit.

His body suddenly tensed, rigid. A rushing noise filled his ears. The moment of separation—something he'd now experienced over fifty times—struck. Moments later he saw his body lying still and dead on the bed. He floated up over it, turned, and looked over his shoulder. The tunnel was there. The rush of euphoria poured over him.

He made a swimming motion with his arms, a movement he'd discovered long ago speeded him on his way to his exit. He reached the tunnel. The jerk of the pull forward snapped him, then filled him with the wonder of the colors, the free effervescing joy that gushed through him.

He whooshed through the tunnel, barely paying attention to the whorls of dusky gray that enveloped him. He saw the light far ahead, then closer, then he was there.

He alit and looked around. On other excursions, he had talked to different "light beings," but none had ever given him a name. Twice they'd told him that he would be in contact with Benreu when the time was right.

As always his eyes had that special distant vision that enabled him to see things that must have been thousands of miles—maybe even light-years—away.

He waited quietly, hoping Benreu might even appear without Croase. But nothing happened.

A glowing object to his left moved.

Goge waited, noticing his sense of anticipation mounting.

It came closer. He recognized a form underneath the pulsations of light. The being mentally spoke. "You have completed the work."

"Yes."

"The master Benreu will see you with your human guide Martin Croase. You are going to him?"

"Yes."

"You have done well. You have done all that you have been asked."

"Yes."

"You will soon experience the great power you desire."

The figure began to recede. Goge tried to touch the being, to grasp him, to hold him back. His arm was, as always, translucent, almost aflame. He felt the tug of the TUT.

The figure turned. Goge sensed that he was staring through him, into him. With others of these light beings the feeling was always one of power, of ruthless strength, the ability to do anything the mind could think. This being radiated something else. Goge tried to get a fix on it. What was it? Malice? Anger? Disgust?

It couldn't be. Wasn't this another divine one? An ascended one?

Something pulled at his back. The TUT was drawing him.

He called, "Who are you?"

There was no answer. Goge awoke a moment later, his mind dizzy and nauseated. He opened his eyes. There was vomit on his face and chest. He was shivering.

He went to the bathroom and turned on the shower. He noticed his heart palpitating hard as the hot water cleansed him.

"Soon I will have it." Goge lifted his face up to the shower. A powerful inner joy gushed through him. "Soon I will have it, and then I won't have to step-'n-fetch-it for this Croase dude anymore."

A moment later, he heard his phone ringing. He looked at his watch. It was almost past 3:30 A.M.

"Yeah?"

"This is Martin Croase."

"Figured that."

"Get down here immediately with the money."

386

Goge swore. "I was just getting into the shower, and I'm tired."

"Don't tell me your problems. Take your shower, get in your car, and get down here. Before 6:00 A.M."

"We're still going to meet with Benreu?"

"Definitely. We've got plenty of TUT, and he's ready to meet with you."

"All right, I'll be there."

5

The orange and black fences that formed a roadblock a mile down Simmering Road reflected in Ray's headlights. Two men turned in his direction. Both had shotguns over their shoulders.

"What are they doing?" Andi asked, letting go of his hand and bracing herself against the dashboard as Ray hit the brakes.

"They've either shut down the campus, or they're checking everyone that's going in. Probably both. We can't risk being caught."

The 4x4 grated on the gravel. Ray backed up into the weeds and turned around. The men at the roadblock didn't move, and Ray headed down the road around a curve. Before he stopped, he turned off his lights, then cut the wheel left and climbed up a slight hill into an open field, turned the headlights back on and barreled across it. He stopped the 4x4 in the woods on the other side.

"We're about two miles from the school," Ray said. "You up for a hike?"

"Whatever it takes," Andi said, getting out.

Ray handed her a walkie-talkie. He didn't like the idea of Andi's getting involved in a possible gun battle, but Tommy was her son and she knew how to handle the weapon well enough to defend herself. He figured as long as she acted as backup, they'd be all right. He said, "If we get separated, we can keep in contact with this." She put the .38 in her parka pocket. Ray gave her a handful of extra shells. She stuffed them into the pocket on the other side. He also opened the

387

box of tools in the back of the 4x4 and took out the wire cutters and a set of binoculars, then jammed them into different pockets.

"Now don't try to take anyone on, OK?"

She nodded her head. "I'm not here to kill anybody, much as I'd like to."

"Good. We're just going to scope it out, see if we can find out where they have him."

"I know where they have him."

"But not what floor. Not what room."

"All right. What do we do?"

Ray looked into her eyes, then kissed her. "Remember, I love you, God loves you and Tommy, and we're going to get out of this alive and kicking. Can you focus on that?"

Her eyes shimmered, and he felt his heart quake with the pain in her eyes. But she nodded assent.

Then he explained the necessity of quiet and stealth. "We don't know what we're up against yet. So don't do anything you're not ready to fight for." He took out a lighter, picked up a piece of wood, and held the flame under it until it was char. When it had cooled off, he began rubbing the charcoal on his face and hands.

"Put some on every white place you got, lady."

For the first time Andi grinned and shook her head. "So men do use makeup."

"Estée Lauder!"

"Oh, you know about that stuff?"

He grinned, but he saw for all the sudden joking, her dark eyes and face were grim with determination.

"There's one other thing, Andi."

"Yes?"

"We don't try to rescue Tommy unless I say so."

She paused, looked away and coughed, then said, "All right. I'll follow your orders, Captain."

"I'm not a captain here, Andi. But this is the kind of thing I was trained to do. I don't want you, or Tommy, or Dr. Kingston to get hurt. There's a time and a place to go for an objective, a time and place to make a stand. But you also have to know when to cut and run. We can't risk either being

388

caught or getting shot. That won't do Tommy or anyone else any good. Miles will be here in a few hours, and by morning we should have the warrant—if we're going to get one. So don't do anything without my order, even if it looks to you like a sure thing." As he spoke, his mind prayed, *Please let me be right about this, Lord. No bad decisions.*

"OK. Let's just go." She set her jaw and returned Ray's steady gaze.

"I want to get onto the campus first. See what's going on. There's a prof in my dorm who might be willing to help."

"Who's that?"

"Name's Hal Gordon. The guy Doc talked to about the board."

"I remember. OK. Lead on, Captain Mazaris."

Ray pulled her into his arms again and hugged her hard. "I love you, Andi. God's with us."

"I know, and I love you too, Ray." Her charcoaled face didn't show any sign of tearing, and Ray was confident she was ready.

They both began moving down the edge of the field toward the school.

6

After the call to Johnny Goge, Croase told Listra he wanted to take a shower. He locked the bathroom door and turned on the water. Then he took out an eyedropper and squeezed a droplet of TUT into a glass of water. He went into the steaming shower and leaned against the wall.

"Bottom's up," he said gleefully.

Moments later he and Benreu stood in the field at the meeting place. "There's trouble," Croase said immediately.

"I know."

"What am I to do?"

"I must be with you always."

"What do you mean?"

The spirit being moved closer. Croase felt the gentle pulsations of his power and presence. "I will go back with you. I will be inside you. I will instruct you."

"You can do that?" Croase said, astonished.

"Yes."

"But why haven't we done it before?"

"It was not necessary."

"Then we will go back together, and you will communicate to me directly?"

"Yes."

"Have others done this?"

"Of course."

"Who?"

"Listra and Rafa."

Croase paused. "Listra said Rafa told her there was an enemy."

"There is."

"Is it another mentor?"

"No."

"Who is it?"

"One is named Kartle. Another is Trell. There are others."

"Who are they?"

"Renegades, rebels, killers. Now we must go."

There was a sudden flash of light, and Croase felt a change, an inner power, a strength he'd never had before. The voice spoke directly inside his mind. "We go back."

"Yes."

There was a pull and a moment later, Croase opened his eyes in the shower.

"I will be with you always," the voice said.

Croase rose as the water sprayed into his face. "I feel very strong," he said. He smiled. "This is great. Why didn't we do this before?"

The voice said, "You weren't ready."

"Well, I am now."

He turned off the water and stepped out to towel off. All the worry and fear began to fall away. He was truly omnipotent. He could do anything. Now he would not be daunted, and anyone who opposed him would pay.

While her husband was in the shower, Listra quickly dialed David Hughes's number from the home office downstairs. "Something's happening, David. What?"

Hughes told her about the video. Listra swore.

"I've got it taken care of," Hughes answered before she could say anything else.

"But what about us?" Listra gripped the phone as though it were alive.

"Don't worry about it. I'll work that out, too."

"But I have to go to TWI with Martin, David. And he knows about you."

"All right, that's probably good. Then we can take him by surprise."

"But how?" Her breath came in little, taut bursts.

"After you get to TWI, if anything strange happens, leave a note in the security office or in your office. Under the blotter."

"OK."

"We're on our way, babe."

"I'm nervous about this, but Rafa has assured me that glory awaits."

Hughes chuckled. "We're going to get what we want, babe. So just be cool about it. Go along with Martin and leave me a note."

"I love you, David."

"I love you too."

7

The fields were separated by wooded areas. Ray and Andi hurried along, silent, catlike. Ray noticed how smooth she was. *She would make a good SEAL,* he thought, and smiled. In the moonlight, it wasn't hard to see the beaten trails through the woods that some called the "passion paths" lovers from the school traveled to be alone.

Finally, they saw a few lights on in the dorms of the seminary, at the far northern section of the complex. A baseball diamond and several soccer fields sat behind the campus on

Ray and Andi's side. At the corner of one of the fields, a campfire sent sparks and ashes into the air. Ray made out two men sitting by it. He grabbed Andi's shoulder and pulled her down as they stepped out of the woods. He noticed his heart drumming, but he felt a deep inner calm within. His mind echoed, *No bad decisions.*

"More guards," he whispered to Andi. "They've turned the place into an armed camp."

Listening in different directions for signs of other guards, they crouched in the bushes opposite the entrance to TWI. It was still dark, and since daylight saving time had not started, it would remain dark, Ray figured, for at least another hour and a half. The dorm Ray wanted to reach sat across the soccer field. There were two fires, each separated by over a hundred yards. It would be difficult going.

"We're gonna have to crawl," he whispered to Andi. "But I want to get to the dorm. Hal Gordon's room is on the first floor."

"Why him?" Andi asked.

"Our best chance to find out what's going on around campus. I don't think he'd get sucked into this too easily. Doc seemed to think he was totally against it."

"What if he turns us in?"

"We'll have to take that chance. I don't see what else we can do."

"All right. You're the captain."

Ray knelt in front of a tree. "It's surprisingly hard to crawl a hundred yards on the ground. Maybe I should go alone."

"No, I can handle it."

In the moonlight, he could see her eyes set and etched with confidence. "All right, let's move."

Ray led the way, squirming and snaking across the field. The ground was cold and damp. In a short time, they were both wet and muddy. The dorm was dark, but several lamps burned around the small parking lot behind it. Fortunately, a row of bushes around the rim would hide them once they reached the dorm. Ray just prayed that Gordon would be there and not an enemy.

While Ray and Andi crawled across the field, Hal Gordon moved stealthily from room to room inside the dorm. He'd already informed six other students from Kent Farrell's list, and they were all eager to help. He told them to meet in his room at 6:00 A.M. Two told him there were others who opposed what Croase was doing. Gordon said, "Tell them to stay in their rooms. We'll come up with a battle plan and spread it by the grapevine."

The rosebushes around the edge of the dorm scratched Ray's face as he stood under Hal Gordon's window. "Here goes," he whispered to Andi. "Pray we're not making a mistake."

Andi crouched below him, the .38 in her hand.

Ray tapped on the window. The room was dark. He couldn't see anyone inside, but the bed was out of his view. Ray tapped a little harder.

"No one's here," he said to Andi.

"What should we do?"

Ray sank down next to her. "Maybe . . ." He hadn't expected to find an empty room. Maybe a sleepy resident, maybe a skeptic, or even an enemy. But at least someone.

Then above him a light shone from the hallway into the bedroom. The door had opened. Ray looked up. "Someone's coming."

He stood and watched in the dim light as several young men filed into Hal Gordon's room. "Looks like a prayer meeting. He used to sponsor one on Saturdays," he said to Andi. "But this is Tuesday."

"Just tap."

Ray plinked the window with his index finger. Immediately, the door closed, and he saw everyone crouch. He tapped again. Hal Gordon's face appeared in the window, looking out. He pushed it open.

"Dr. Gordon, it's Ray Mazaris."

Blinking down at Ray, Gordon said to those behind him, "It's Ray Mazaris."

Everyone crowded around the window. Gordon said, "It's really bad, Ray. What's going on? There're a million rumors about you and one of the girls in—"

"Andi Darcasian. Right here," Ray said.

Gordon leaned out, and Andi smiled up at him.

"Watch it, one of the guards might spot you."

"What on earth is going on?" Gordon said, pulling back in and peering just over the sill.

"You tell me," Ray said. Andi stood next to him, both of them still covered by the bushes.

"Martin Croase told us you're working for the CIA."

Ray shook his head with amazement. "Right, and Andi here is in cahoots with the KGB."

Gordon laughed, and several of the men behind him snickered. "Well, what's going on then?"

Ray quickly explained what he knew. When he was done, he said, "I think the whole campus could be in danger. You've got to get everyone out and away. Or at least warn them to get off campus."

There was a sudden whispering of voices behind him, and Hal turned. When he looked back at Ray, Gordon said, "We're not jumping ship. There're too many kids here who are just scared. We've got to rouse the whole campus."

"What will you do?" Ray asked.

"Demonstrate. We're going over to TWI and tell Croase what we think of him."

"All right." Ray glanced at Andi. "They kidnapped Andi's son, Tommy."

Gordon winced and relayed the message to the others. "All the more reason to confront Croase," Hal said.

"Good," Ray answered. "It might provide some decent cover. Look, we're going over to TWI now to see if we can get inside. The FBI will be here, possibly in a few hours, hopefully with a search warrant."

"Be careful," Hal said. "We'll have half the campus at the gate by 8:00 A.M."

"Pray," Ray said as he moved away.

394

"We're already doing that," Hal answered and shut the window.

Ray and Andi kept to the darkest areas as they moved from building to building. His anxiety rose, and he felt more fearful about Andi's safety and ability to deal with any frontal danger. But he knew she was committed and gritty; that might be enough to get them both through unscathed.

The fence around TWI was another hundred yards across a playing field. Ray peered through the binoculars. As he did, a car went through the gate and parked in the back lot. Ray watched as a man got out, opened the trunk, and took out a suitcase. Ray handed the binoculars to Andi. "Know who that is?"

She focused in on the dark-haired man with the suitcase. "Never saw him before."

"All right, we go for the fence. We'll have to open a hole with the wire cutters."

"I'm right behind you."

They both crawled rapidly across the open field. The first grays of dawn stretched across the horizon. It was still cold and damp, and the grass there seemed even wetter. Ray felt the chill reaching through his parka to his chest and abdomen.

At the two ends of the fence, the guards were still hunched over their fires, not paying attention to the campus or much of anything else.

Dr. Kingston jerked the handcuffs up the pipe to get into a more comfortable position in the small room Strock had dumped him and Tommy in. He knew it was on the eighth floor. It looked to him like a storage room of some sort. To his right sat a folded-up bed, some shelving with medical gowns and green scrubs on them, two large metal cabinets that appeared to house medical supplies, and several piles of towels, washcloths, and soaps. Several occasionally clanging pipes grew out of the floor and wound through to the ceiling. Kingston leaned against the cinder block wall and did some figuring.

No one had mentioned anything about Tommy's taking the TUT. The boy appeared unworried at the moment, with his eyes closed and obviously asleep, even though he would certainly wake up with a major neck crick judging from the tilt of his head onto his left shoulder.

Kingston struggled with the handcuffs, wishing he'd learned something from his years of reading crime and mystery novels about how to pick a lock. His watch read 6:15. His neck ached, and the spot where Strock had rapped him on the head was matted with blood.

After another rattle of the handcuffs and a long sigh, Kingston closed his eyes and prayed that if anyone got hurt it would be him. As he spoke out loud, his eyes teared. "I'm sorry, Lord. I should never have gone along with Gordon about Martin Croase. Forgive me."

He leaned against the metal pole. It felt cold against his forehead. Whatever happened, he knew he had to try to save Tommy. That was all that was important. If he died trying, perhaps that was the price he had to pay for his willingness to overlook Gordon Watt's eccentricities.

□ □ □

Ray reached the fence and peered left and right at the guard stations by the two corners. No one had spotted them yet. He said to Andi, "I'm going to cut a hole. Be on the lookout."

She huddled behind him, watching. She wasn't holding the gun anymore, having tucked it into a pocket.

As Ray began to cut, another car sped into the lot. He dropped to the ground. But the garage doors opened, and the car screeched down into the underground area. Ray whispered, "That's Croase's car. I recognize it."

"Looks like everybody's having a prayer meeting this morning."

"Yeah."

He pressed the cutters, and the first link in the cyclone fence snapped. In a few minutes, he'd cut a two-foot-wide rectangular doorway into it. "Keep down," Ray said as he crawled through.

396

Then another car pulled into the lot. Ray pressed Andi to the ground, and they both lay flat and still as the headlamps passed over them. The car stopped outside about thirty yards away.

Hiro Nakayami opened his car door and mentally swore in Japanese. "What can I do now?" he murmured. For the second time in a month, he prayed to the God he wasn't even sure existed. Then he slipped out, closed the door, and went to the trunk to get his briefcase.

Ray whispered to Andi, "Wait here. It's that Japanese researcher that does all the experiments. I might be able to get some information out of him."

Andi gripped his hand. "Should I cover you?"

Ray smiled. "Thinking like a real SEAL. But keep your gun holstered."

"OK. Be careful."

He jumped up and hurried in a crouch across the parking lot. Nakayami had parked in the midst of several cars. It would provide some cover. Ray's feet made scrabbling sounds on the gravel, but the researcher didn't seem to notice as he bent over his trunk. Ray came up behind him, then reached around and covered his mouth, at the same time jamming the 9 mm into Nakayami's back.

"Don't say a word," Ray breathed into Nakayami's ear.

The man struggled a moment, then stopped.

"Where do they have Tommy?" Ray whispered. "You try to shout for help, I'll hurt you. Answer through my fingers."

Ray parted his fingers over Nakayami's mouth. The man's lips twisted in his hand trying to enunciate. "I don't know where they have him now. Dr. Croase called me this morning."

"What are you going to do?"

"I don't know."

Ray tightened his grip slightly. "I'm sorry, but I'm going to have to put you in your trunk."

Nakayami suddenly said, "I want to help you."

For a second, Ray froze. Maybe this was the gift of grace they needed. For a moment, he thought about not believing the man, but as Nakayami stood there still and obviously submissive in Ray's grasp, Ray decided to chance it. Both men breathed hard in the cold air. Then Ray said, "How?"

"Croase is planning something terrible. You must stop it."

"What?"

"I don't know. But he has a way of putting the TUT-B into the water system. I think he wants to kill everyone on the whole campus and the offices."

Ray tensed. "How do you know?"

"I've seen how he will do it—with a radio detonator. But maybe you can disconnect it at the pump room."

Ray glanced across to the pump room briefly through the early morning mist, then said to Nakayami, "Why should I believe you?"

"I want to help," he said. "Croase is a madman, and his wife is worse. I fear them, and I hate them. But I can find out where the boy is and help. I swear."

Ray relaxed his grip. "What is this thing in the pump room?"

"I don't know. I just know Ken Strock made it and it's there. But you have to let me go into TWI. I'm already late."

Looking back to where Andi still lay, Ray could see her face now in the increasing light. "All right. I'm trusting you. I'll check out the pump room. The FBI will be here soon, too."

Nakayami nodded. "Good. I will try to meet you when they get here. I can lead you."

"All right." Ray let go of the slender man. Nakayami turned around and extended his hand.

"I'm only sorry that I have been a participant in any of this."

To his right, Ray saw Andi jump up and run toward them. When she reached the two men, she said, "What's going on?" She glanced at Nakayami suspiciously, then looked directly at Ray.

"He's a friend," Ray said. "He's going to help us."

Andi looked at Nakayami. "Thank God," she said suddenly.

"All right, we'll meet you," Ray said, relieved that Andi was willing to trust Nakayami too. "Just get Tommy safe. I'll do what I can about the pump room."

To their right, two cars turned into the parking lot. Nakayami said, "Workers are arriving." Then he pulled out his briefcase and said, "Your God will help us."

As Nakayami walked toward TWI, Ray and Andi scrambled around the cars and hurried to the pump room. With workers arriving and in the early light, they might not be suspected as easily. Ray hoped anyone who saw them now would think them regular employees of TWI. They stopped behind the last car in the lot before the pump room. Ray told her what Nakayami had said about what Croase had done to the water supply.

"He could set it off anytime?" she asked with a horrified look.

"Presumably when he's got himself and his wife to safety."

"This could turn into Jonestown," Andi answered, looking back towards the campus.

"That's why we've got to get to the source—either stop it at the pump room or get the radio detonator."

"And Tommy's right in the middle of it. And Dr. Kingston."

"Right." Ray squinted at the guard station once more, then looked at Andi again and shook his head. Her clothing was stained with brown and green smudges of mud and grass. Her charcoal covered face was streaked with lines of sweat. He winced and looked at his jacket. "Do I look like you?"

"Yeah, but I don't think we have time to worry about whether we're in style or not."

"We should get the charcoal off."

"Right."

He grimaced, then said, "Pray," and they both sped for the pump room.

8

Lou Miles arrived at Channel 4 News just past 6:00 A.M. Lyle Hornum was waiting for him in the foyer. He immediately explained Ray and Andi's absence. Miles swore. "They could get killed."

"So could Andi's son," Lyle said. "They had to do something."

"OK," Miles said with a grim nod. "Let's see this video."

Lyle took him upstairs and after viewing it, Miles said, "It's solid evidence. I'm sure we can get a judge to sign a warrant for the funeral home. Now what about this Benreu thing?"

Lyle told him about the letters and how Andi had figured it out. "We suspect this serial killer or Croase or both of them are in contact with a spirit being, a demon, who is feeding them information about these people. That's the best we can figure. But both Ray and Andi have really met this spirit being. I know it sounds—"

"I know, nuts," Miles said. "I agree, but the whole world has gone nuts, if you ask me. It's the best lead we've got at this point, and I'm willing to roll with it, but a judge won't give us a warrant on TWI without Mr. Mazaris and his girl there. I don't think he will, anyway."

"Let's try for what we can get," Lyle answered. "That's all I know to do." He pulled out the walkie-talkie. "When we get to TWI, we can call Ray on this and link up with him."

Miles smiled. "You guys know your stuff."

"Ray's done everything right so far."

Miles shook his head. "Got a couple of friends in the Bureau who are ex-SEALs, so I know what they're like. I want to meet him. Let's get to the judge, and let me call my office and get some other agents lined up. We can't go into this without some major backup."

"Let me take you to a room where you can be private then."

9

At 6:25 A.M. Hiro Nakayami stepped into Martin Croase's office. "What is this all about?" he said.

Both Listra and Martin were present. She stood at the window smoking. Martin was hunched over his desk. "The boy is upstairs now," Croase said, looking up at Nakayami. His face was drawn, etched with weariness. But Nakayami noticed a large green canvas bag on the desk. He thought it might be Croase's Uzi. Croase continued, "They're in a medical supplies room, locked in. Listra wants the boy to be readied for some thanatravel right away on the TUT-B."

Nakayami shook his head. "Impossible. We're not ready, and he may die."

"Then he dies," Listra said, turning around. She looked fresh and eager. Nakayami wondered what the rush was. Listra said, "He's the only one who can do it. And I want to get beyond the wall. Today."

Nakayami blinked. "Impossible. We don't know why it works on the boy. I do not want the boy to die. I do not think the boy's ability is biological, genetic, or even psychological or mental."

"Then what is it?" She blew smoke furiously out the side of her mouth and stared hard and unblinking at Nakayami. He couldn't look her in the eye. Something about her eyes was overpowering, terrifying to him. When he looked at her directly, she could almost hold him motionless, unable to disagree. He didn't like the feeling.

"I don't know," Nakayami said, but he had an idea, a supernatural explanation that he wasn't about to tell them. It was completely unscientific, and they would never accept it. But he knew there was no scientific basis for the boy's survival, or if there was, he had no clue as to what it was.

Listra snorted with exasperation. "You and your tests. I should just try the TUT-B and see if it works. For all we know it will work fine on me."

For a second, Nakayami detected a twitch of a smile on Martin Croase's lips, but it quickly vanished.

"The boy could die," Nakayami said again.

"If it comes to that," Listra said, "then so be it. We can do an autopsy. Everything has been prepared, Hiro. He won't die, I assure you."

The Japanese couldn't prevent the sudden surge of anger through his gut. For a moment, he looked into Listra's eyes. "Assure! Assure? You assure? What do you assure? That a hundred people died in the last two months. That you assure!"

Croase interrupted, "Let me do the talking, dear." He put on his sympathetic, fatherly face. "Hiro, you know this is what we have been working toward for over twenty years. Now that it's in our hands, why are you suddenly choking?"

"Choking? Not choking. Ethics. Killing boys, men, women. It's wrong. Anywhere—Japan, Russia, America—it is very wrong."

"And I suppose plagiarism is ethical."

Nakayami glared at him, started to say something, then looked down at his desk. Air sizzled out of the tight lips.

"Sometimes I wish . . ." Nakayami didn't finish the sentence.

"Wish you'd never gotten involved in this? Is that it, Hiro?" Croase smiled toothily. "This is your life's work. This is what you will be known the world over for. This is what the prizes will be offered for. Bodies will not matter in the new world, Hiro. A few bodies for the whole of humanity? For world peace? For all of us living in unity and harmony? A few bodies for that, Hiro?"

Nakayami shook his head again, resigned to acquiescence, at least for the moment. He murmured, "What kind of ethics will there be in this new world? Ethics of killing anyone for science?"

"Of course not, Hiro. This was only necessary to get there. Need I remind you that you went along with it at first."

"Accidents at first."

"And then, after that?"

Nakayami bowed his head. He refused to look up.

Croase walked across the room, stood behind the slight man, and put his hands on Nakayami's shoulders, kneading them. Listra glared at both of them, but didn't move. "Remember, Hiro," Croase said. "If we go down, you go down. TWI goes down, you go down. I go down, you go down. But I assure you, no one's going down. We will finish the job, the

402

boy may become the toast of the world, being the only one who can explore death at will. Think of it that way, will you? You're not sending him into death. You're sending him into fame and glory. He'll be the great path-maker of humanity. He'll be—"

Listra's shriek was immediate and insistent. "Never! Never! He will never be that! Shut up, you fool!" She kicked Croase in the leg and raked at him with her hand, but Croase was quicker. Jumping back, he cried, "Listra, get hold of yourself. This is not—"

She glared at him. "I don't want to hear any more about this. I want that wall. Now let's do it."

Nakayami glanced at Listra, then at her husband. He said tersely, "I want to talk to the boy." But he sensed something was deeply wrong between them, and he tried to think of a way to exploit it.

"First agree to the test," Listra snarled.

"It will take some preparations." He worked at stilling the thrumming in his chest.

"We realize that," Martin Croase answered. "Get yourself ready. You can talk to the boy."

"He is in the safe room?"

"On the way. I'll take you up there."

Listra stepped around the desk. "No, I'll take him up there, Martin. I want to hear this conversation."

Croase shrugged. "That's fine with me."

When his wife and Nakayami were gone, Croase stood behind the desk thinking. In his mind, the voice reverberated, *You must get the money.*

"Johnny!" Croase almost shouted. "I forgot."

He is downstairs, in the security office.

"Good."

Croase hurried across the office to the van Gogh reproduction, lifted it off its hanger, and placed a key in a small, almost invisible, hole in the paneling. The paneling screaked as it opened. Inside was a safe. Croase dialed the numbers, then pulled the heavy metal door wide open. Inside, stacked in neat packets of a hundred, each were row upon row of thousand, ten thousand, and one hundred dollar bills. At last

403

count it equaled at least $6 million. Johnny Goge had another million downstairs.

Croase went to a closet on the other side of the room and drew out a large silver briefcase. He began piling the bills into it. After almost filling it, he realized he had far too much for one briefcase. He swore, then stopped to think of where he might have another briefcase.

What about the helicopter?

"I almost forgot." He swore again and called Bill Patton, the pilot, at his TWI-provided apartment on the campus. When Patton answered, Croase said, "Get the helicopter ready. I'll let you know when."

"It's all gassed up, Mr. Croase."

"Good. We'll meet you at the pad. I'll let you know the time."

He hung up and dialed another number. "Jillie?"

"Martin!"

"You ready to roll?"

"I just got up."

"We're flying this morning."

"This is the big exit?"

"Yes. Patton's getting the helicopter ready. Johnny Goge is here, and we've got nearly seven million."

"I have all the ID, honey, and the tickets. All we have to do is get there."

"You're beautiful. Get to the helicopter pad and meet Patton. I'll be in touch."

"I'm there, darling." She made a kissing noise.

Croase scurried around the office, looking into two closets and the credenza for something to carry the money in. He figured Listra would be with the boy getting her kicks, and everything else was a go. But he still needed another briefcase. Then there was a knock at the door.

His heart hammering suddenly, Croase said, "Wait a minute." Then he said, "What am I to do now?"

Just think.

Croase closed his eyes, took a deep breath, then put the briefcase in the leg area under his desk, shut the wall safe, and covered it with the picture. He went to the door. When he opened it, Ken Strock stood there. "What's going on, Ken?" Croase pumped himself up to look his most confident. "I hope it's not bad news."

"Some of those kids on the campus, boss. Actually, a lot of them. And some faculty. Apparently, your talk the other night and the newspaper article didn't convince them."

Croase swung around. "What, are they sending a little entourage up or something?"

"It looks like a demonstration. They're gathering on the quad now."

"How many of these renegades?" Croase was in no mood for more pep talks.

"We don't know. But there's definitely enough to make some noise, sir."

Croase cursed and went to the credenza to get the bottle of scotch. "All right," he said quickly. "Keep me informed. Just contain it, that's all. Long as it doesn't get off campus, we should be all right."

"I think you may have to talk to them, boss. What I seen of this kind of thing, it gets out of hand real easy."

"I'll attend to it." Croase said as he poured the scotch.

As Strock left, the voice inside Croase's mind spoke again, *I will tell you what to say.*

"You sure better," Croase said and shot the hot liquid to the back of his throat. He noticed his hand was shaking, and he didn't like the feeling.

CHAPTER EIGHTEEN

1

Lou Miles gave Judge William Schneider at his home near the Montgomery County Courthouse in Rockville a sworn statement-affidavit on the kidnapping. The FBI team, along with several policemen and Lyle Hornum, waited in the small alcove outside the judge's house. No one on the assembled FBI team knew Schneider personally, and it made Miles nervous. They had heard he was a somewhat crotchety, old-time corporate lawyer who became a judge back in the sixties in the days of Governor Spiro Agnew.

Miles never liked to come before a judge without plenty of information about his policies, reputation, and habits. But Schneider was the only one available at the moment.

As Miles stood alone before him, Schneider looked up from behind a stately walnut desk. He was still dressed in a blue bathrobe and deerskin slippers, had dry sallow skin, and looked like an artifact from the Ichabod Crane Chronicles.

"You think this is probable cause?" Schneider asked Miles, looking at him skeptically over silver frame glasses.

"Your honor, the witnesses involved were abducted with the boy mentioned in the affidavit. We believe they have the boy inside. I'm certain their testimony is reliable. Yes, I think it's probable cause." In the report Miles had purposely steered away from revealing details about the nature of TWI's activities, especially the spiritual and mystical elements.

"Nothing is completely certain, Mr. Miles. You do realize this is a respected organization in Maryland with no previous record of crime of any sort."

Miles shifted his weight nervously. He wanted to avoid questioning, if possible. The sworn statement had been drafted quickly at the news station. Miles had tried to include all the facts they knew, but he realized that on paper it was sketchy. They had no definite connection to TWI except Ray and Andi's testimony, which should have been sufficient, but they weren't even present.

"All right, I'd like to talk to these witnesses of yours," Schneider said.

With a barely disguised exhale of frustration, Miles said, "There's only one present, the news reporter."

"I thought you said you had two witnesses."

"They're not available at the moment, sir."

Schneider shook his head with exasperation and waved to Miles to bring in Hornum.

Lyle walked in and stood behind Miles.

After an introduction, Miles said, "Your honor, I think there's more than probable cause here. The video includes a clear picture of one of the men who works at TWI. The video reveals the van parked there, and this reporter saw the body bags on the loading dock."

"What are they doing that is producing all these dead bodies?"

Miles took a deep breath. "We believe they're developing drugs that can be used to produce NDEs—near death experiences. You've probably read about or seen in recent movies the great speculation going on in the country now about what happens following death. This organization seems to have decided to pursue a more scientific approach to it. We believe there may even be a connection to the serial murders—the 'Alphabet Murders' as the press is now calling them."

Schneider looked back down at the document. Then he turned his yellow-eyed gaze on Lyle. "This boy is a relative of yours?"

"Not mine. Andi Darcasian's, your honor. One of the witnesses."

"How did you get involved in this?"

Lyle began to explain about Ray's first call. The judge shook his head with irritation. "I know about that. If all these people have supposedly died as a result of this company's rather bizarre research practices, why didn't these three others die?"

"I don't know. We believe—" Lyle paused and glanced at Miles. He tried to motion with his eyes, but he wondered how it could be explained otherwise.

Miles stared straight ahead and gave him no indication of what to say.

"We believe there's a lot of occultic activity going on," Lyle said. "You know, demonism, possible satanic ritualism, that kind of thing."

"How do you know that?" Schneider spoke in clipped hard-edged sentences, belying an obvious boredom with the whole proceeding.

"Your honor," Miles interrupted, "this research facility has some rather strange beliefs motivating them. We really didn't want to get into it."

"They're fanatics then?" Schneider said.

Lyle started to answer, but Miles cut him off. "We don't know all the details at this point. We believe a kidnapping has taken place, TWI and Martin Croase are the kidnappers, and we want to search the premises."

"Don't get curt with me, Mr. Miles," Schneider said, looking at the warrant. He looked up at the two men again. "Is there anything I should know that compels me to sign this which you're not telling me?"

With a quick glance in Lyle's direction, Miles shook his head. "Your honor, we've told you everything we think is pertinent."

Schneider sighed noisily through brown-tinted teeth. "All right, I think you have probable cause for the funeral home. I'll grant a search warrant for that. As for TWI, I'm sorry, but I think the connection is not as strong as I'd like. When we see what comes up at the funeral home, then we'll consider TWI. This had better not be a wild goose chase, Mr. Miles."

"Your honor, if we go to the funeral home first, they might alert TWI and allow them time—"

Schneider set his thin lips, handed him the paper, and folded his hands. "I think that will be all."

Miles sighed, looked helplessly at Lyle, then thanked the judge and went out. When they reached the parking lot, Miles said with intense frustration, "I'm sorry, but I thought this might happen."

Lyle said, "Can we do anything else?"

"Plan B," Miles said gruffly. "Bluff them. Come on, we've got more than a search to do."

Outside, Miles divided the men into two teams, three to go to the Willard Funeral Home and three to go with them to TWI. Miles clambered in on the driver's side and started the black Ford Taurus. "All right, Lyle, lead me to TWI."

2

"Willard is not expecting us?" Hughes said to Strock as they cruised up New Hampshire Avenue toward the turnoff. Hughes drove a battered Pontiac Grand Prix he'd got after the smashup of his Toyota. He hadn't told Strock it was part of a deal in which he had also procured a Mitsubishi 3000GT sports car with some of the reward money they'd received for capturing Tommy Darcasian. It was the top-of-the-line VR4 and cost over $35,000.

"I talked to him," Strock said, still fuming after learning about the video episode. "Croase wants us to make sure the fool's taken care of everything. He thinks there may be a visit from the police." Strock flicked a cigarette out of the window. "I want you to go in and check it out. I'll sit in the car in case we have to wind out of here."

Hughes kept both hands on the wheel. "Got it. You think it's coming down?"

"I don't know. All I know is me and my little nest egg are outa here if so much as a cop shows up."

"How much you got?"

"Over a hundred K."

"In the bank?"

Strock gazed at him severely. "You think I'm going to tell you that?"

"Just making conversation."

Strock lit another Marlboro and kept his eyes on the highway. He knew the best thing to do was probably to whack Hughes as soon as possible and then take care of Willard. Then fly. But Hughes was a pro. He would probably be very cautious. Still, Strock was sure Hughes hadn't saved a penny of what they'd made from TWI, the stiffs, or anything else.

Turning right onto Georgia Avenue, Hughes gunned the engine and headed west toward the funeral home. Strock fingered the silencer in his right-hand pocket. He mentally formed a picture of his plan of action.

3

Lee Greeber, the leader of Miles's team of agents driving out to search the funeral home, turned the Chevrolet rental car onto Georgia Avenue, trying to spot a house number to be sure which side the Willard Funeral Home was on. Clem Lofton and Tom "Whit" Whitaker were in the car with him.

"The first place we go to is the basement," Lee said. "That was where the bodies were left."

Clem and Tom nodded.

"You do that, Whit," Lee said. "Clem, you gather together any employees and get them into one safe place. I'll go through the first floor and find the crematorium. If this guy Willard is around, Clem, keep him with you, but don't ask him any questions."

"I know how to do a search," Clem answered.

"I know. I'm just nervous," Lee said. "Check your side arms before we go in. We don't want any problems, but who knows what these people are all about."

Both men pulled their 9 mm Berettas out of their shoulder holsters and checked them.

A moment later, Lee spotted a number and said, "Man, it must be up several miles." He pressed the accelerator. "Clem, after you get all the employees in one room, I want you to go for the records room or office or whatever they have. Anything linking them to TWI will be sufficient."

Up ahead traffic was slowing down, and a long line of red taillights was on. It was rush hour.

"Just what we need," Greeber exploded. "A backup."

4

Hughes turned the Grand Prix into the Willard driveway to the underneath garage.

Strock said, "All right, I'll sit here. Go in and get Willard." Strock opened his door. "Kind of warm," he said. The garage door was up.

Hughes stepped out. As he started toward the door, Strock took the silencer out of his pocket, laid the 9 mm Colt in his lap, and screwed it in. Hughes was almost to the door inside the garage.

Strock eased out of the car. He stood behind the car door with the gun in his hand below the window. "Hughes," he called. "Wait a minute."

Hughes stopped and turned around.

"I forgot. There's something here from Croase." He waved a letter in his left hand.

Hughes began walking toward him. At fifteen feet, Strock raised the gun. "And something here from me."

He squeezed off a shot that struck Hughes in the chest, knocking him down. As the big man sat dazed on the floor, Strock fired two more shots into his chest. Hughes pitched backward and lay still.

Strock shut the car door quietly and walked across the pavement to Hughes. He stepped over Hughes's legs and pointed the Colt at his forehead. "'Bye, Hughes," he said.

Hughes's foot caught Strock in the crotch. The bullet ricocheted off the pavement into the wall. Strock crumpled, grasping his crotch. Bending down to the floor, he braced himself with his right hand. Hughes had his own gun out in a moment, the silencer already affixed. He shot Strock in the chest twice. As blood pooled from the wound, Hughes stood and looked into the eyes of the dying man.

"You think I'm dumb, don't you?" He pulled open his shirt. "Should always wear a vest when you play with people like me." He placed the silencer muzzle on Strock's forehead. "And I know where your money is too."

Blinking with pain, Strock moved his lips but couldn't speak.

"You shouldn't have put it in the briefcase. That's what tipped me off. You really thought you were the smart one, didn't you, Strock? Plus I got a friend in Paradise."

Strock wheezed. Blood streamed from his wounds onto the floor.

Hughes shook his head and smiled, his handlebar mustache still neatly curled at the corners. "Yeah. That person I been meeting out there in Paradise. He told me what you were going to do. Can you figure that? I'm invincible, Strock. Invincible. That's what he told me. Both me and Listra. We're going places. Could you guess that one? Me and that little bimbo Listra Croase. So I suppose I'm going have to do Willard too, huh?"

He squeezed the trigger. Strock's head jerked backwards.

Hughes picked up Strock's Colt and put it into his pocket. He walked catlike toward the door into the funeral home, listening intently. "Now that did feel good," he murmured as he quietly pushed open the door.

5

Lee Greeber and the two other agents sat morosely in traffic waiting for a policeman to clear the area where a truck and a fortunately empty school bus had collided at an intersection. Lee drummed his fingers on the steering wheel and silently cursed their luck. Finally, traffic began moving.

"About ten blocks, Lee," Whit said behind him. "We can walk if it comes down to it."

A policeman directed traffic around the bus, lying on its side. When they were by it, Lee accelerated around the slow moving traffic.

"I see the sign," Clem said.

Lee barreled past a Volkswagon Jetta and flicked the signal to turn left.

□ □ □

It didn't take Hughes long to find Dick Willard, sitting in the plush office in the back of the building, going over paperwork. As Hughes jammed the Beretta into Willard's jaw, he told him to stand up. "Go to the safe, big boy."

Without protest, Willard, white and trembling, edged over to the wall safe behind the Gainsborough reproduction of a fox hunt.

"Just open it real quick, and there won't be any problem," Hughes said. "I'll just sashay out of here, and you will continue a respectable business in the community like you always wanted."

As he turned the dial, Willard's fingers shook violently. "There's not much in here."

"I'll be the judge of that," Hughes said, his back to the door. His friend in Paradise had also told him how much there should be. The office was in the back, and no one else had been out front. He knew from their long-term relationship that Willard employed as few people as possible and often had them working at odd hours. The early morning was down time, and since there was no funeral that day the funeral parlor was deserted.

The safe clicked open. Willard began pulling out the inch-thick piles of hundreds, twenties, and fifties that he had boasted about to Strock and Hughes on occasion. He never said how much it was, but Hughes always figured on at least $50,000. His "friend" said there was at least $200,000, probably more.

Willard laid the money on the desk.

Hughes looked past him into the safe. "What else is in there?"

"Some valuable coins. Not much—"

Hughes jammed the barrel of the silencer into Willard's bony rib cage. "What else is in there, Buckwheat?"

Willard sighed. "Some jewels."

"Oh, you didn't brag about them. Put them on top. My lady digs jewels."

Still shaking, Willard took out a number of small, labeled manila envelopes secured with a rubber band. Hughes peered again over Willard's shoulder. Satisfied that the safe was empty, he picked up a gallon-size trash can by the desk, dumped it on the floor, and then set it on the desk. "Fill it up."

The trembling man hurriedly stuffed the bills, jewels, and coins into the trash can until it nearly overflowed.

Hughes nudged him with the gun again. "Now, you won't talk to anyone about this, right? You won't become state's witness or anything like that, right?"

Willard shook his head vigorously. "I'll never tell anyone."

"That's right. You won't." Hughes raised the gun quickly and aimed it at the bridge of Willard's nose. "You're very right. You'll never talk."

When the bullet hit him, the thin man collapsed backwards in a heap.

Hughes opened the door. He was about to whistle a catchy tune when he heard someone ding the little bell on the table in the foyer. He cursed, turned right outside Willard's door, and hurried down the hall. He stepped down the back stairwell into the basement.

Strock lay on the floor in a still shimmering pool of blood. The car sat quiet in the driveway, both doors open. Hughes walked toward it, slammed the passenger door shut. He hurried around the front. Just as he reached the driver's side, a man he didn't know came around the corner.

The man called, "Are you with the funeral home?"

Hughes didn't answer. He raised the gun.

☐ ☐ ☐

Whitaker was fast. He leaped to his left. Hughes fired three quick rounds, one catching Whitaker in the shin. The

414

agent dragged himself to the wall and pulled out his Beretta. But before he could get a shot off, he heard the car roar in the driveway. As it came up the slight hill in reverse, he tried to stand and aim into the windshield.

But the car careened backwards into the alley, then screeched forward. Whitaker pulled off two rounds as the Grand Prix squealed on the asphalt, flinging gravel behind it. He memorized the thirty-day temporary license number as the car skidded around the corner. Then he staggered back up to the front of the funeral home. Lee Greeber and Clem Lofton dashed out the front door with guns drawn as Whitaker rounded the corner.

"There's a dead man in the garage downstairs," Whitaker yelled. "Better get an alert on the radio. I got the number and make of car."

After getting the information, Lofton ran back inside to make the call. Greeber was already examining the wound.

"There's another dead man in the back office," Greeber told Whit. "We think it's the owner, and the safe was open. Empty."

The agent lay on the lawn, groaning. Greeber tore off his tie and wrapped it around the wound.

When Lofton returned, two police sirens were already wailing in the distance.

"Let's get you to the hospital," Greeber said.

A light rain began to fall and in the distance there was a sudden crash of lightning.

□ □ □

"I'm invincible," Hughes yelled as he wheeled the car onto a side street off Georgia Avenue. "Invincible." He caressed the pile of money on the front seat.

"But I got to do Konopka now," he said to himself. "He's the only one who knows about the extra murders. Then me and Listra are gone."

He parked the car behind the Mitsubishi VR4 he'd bought two days before. It was less than a mile from the funeral

415

home. "I thought I'd be seeing you again today," he said as he got out.

He climbed into the VR4. "This should keep me invisible while I go about becoming completely invincible," Hughes said with a grin as the engine roared.

He drove under the speed limit back out to Georgia Avenue. When he passed the funeral home on the far side, already two white Montgomery County squad cars were there, and several men were on the front lawn.

Hughes laughed and kept under the speed limit up to the intersection of 108 and Georgia. They couldn't know about the switch this soon. And by the time they found the Grand Prix, he would be done at TWI and on the way to paradise on earth.

"The fear of death is the root of all evil," Hughes said and roared, banging the steering wheel and jostling merrily in the seat. "What a joke."

CHAPTER NINETEEN

1

Ray and Andi stood at the door of the pump room. From a small puddle of water, he washed off his face and Andi finished off the job with a shirttail. Then he cleaned her up. Behind them on the campus the drone of a crowd, the voices of several hundred students, began to rise. Ray looked in that direction and said, "Looks like Hal Gordon is getting some real support. It could provide a good diversion. Plus it gets them out of the buildings."

He grabbed the handle and said, "Here goes nothing."

It turned slightly, then caught. Ray said, "Rats," and looked at Andi. "One more thing might work."

Andi said, "Please hurry, Ray. Croase could do it anytime."

"I know." He opened his wallet and took out the plastic card, cut in an L shape. Ray slid it into the space between the jamb and the lock. He moved it up and down and jiggled the door. In his mind he prayed, *God, You've got to—* Suddenly the door released. He sighed with relief and pushed the door open, half expecting a Doberman to charge out at them.

Inside, a maze of pipes all led to the pump station in the back.

Andi was right behind him. "Hurry."

Ray dashed through, checking everything for something that might look like a chemical injection device. On the far wall were a number of circular valve handles. Each was marked—"TWI." "Weems." " Lincoln." All the dorms, offices, and buildings. Each handle was locked in place by a link chain and padlock.

"We can't turn off the water," Ray said. He looked up and spotted one of the automatic smoke nozzles, set to spray water the moment heat touched it. But there was no danger of that happening.

Pointing, he said, "Croase must have them set to open up when he hits the radio detonator." His heart was jumping in his chest now.

Andi pushed him forward and pointed to the large electric machine in the back. "What about that thing?"

Ray's eyes followed her finger down the line of pipes to the huge pump. "That's the pump. It might be in the apparatus somewhere."

He rushed to it, leaned in, looked over the huge motor. In his mind he followed the different lines in the main pipe. Then he saw what had to be the injection cylinder. It was a square box around the main pipe leading out to the different lines. Fastened and welded around it, the face had a green double door latched in the middle with a padlock.

Ray felt along the top above his vision.

"What are you feeling for?" Andi asked. She kept glancing back at the door. "What if someone finds us here?"

Ray said, "That's the least of our worries. There it is."

"What?"

"An antenna." His hand touched a light piece of metal that bent under his pressure. He let go, grabbed the pipe and hoisted himself up. "That's it. Hold my legs. I want to break it off."

Andi laced her fingers together and provided a step for Ray's right foot. "Will that stop them?"

"I can't be sure. The nub could still pick up any signal, but it's worth a try. It's fairly primitive. I don't think it could have an auto detonator."

"You mean we could detonate it?" Her eyes were wide with panic.

Ray took a deep breath. "There would probably be a keyhole or something to turn it off if there was an auto detonator."

418

"Ray!"

He looked down at her. *No mistakes!* resounded in his mind. His heart hammered. He couldn't take that chance. How could he even have thought that? He told himself to be calm, though—that was why Andi was with him. *Trust God. Just trust God and listen to Andi.* The thought struck him again. He looked at her in a strange way, then said, "All right. We'll have to try something else."

Ray let himself down and surveyed the piping again. "I'm not an electronics expert. We're just going to have to stop Croase."

"I think you're right," she said.

He looked at her with renewed amazement. Was that part of it—that he was not alone? God was with him. Andi was with him. That was the thing he'd missed. All along. All the team lectures in the SEALs—he'd always felt the loner, the one in charge, the one who had to make the decisions. But it wasn't that way. It had never been that way.

She stared at him, searching his face. "What is it?"

"I'll tell you later. Just something."

Their walkie-talkies crackled, and she turned away, but he looked at her back and her hair with renewed love and commitment. How could he have missed it? Then, the walkie-talkie crackled again. "Ray! Ray, Andi, are you there?"

It was Lyle's voice.

Ray pulled the walkie-talkie out of his jeans pocket. "Lyle?"

"You're here. Praise God. Where are you?"

"In the pump room. Croase really is trying to do the whole campus in."

There was a brief silence. Then, "Can you shut it down?"

"I've tried, but I'm not sure it'll work. I thought of breaking off the receiving antenna, but it might have some kind of detonation device. I don't think so, but I can't take that chance. And breaking it off might not help anyway. What about Croase? And where are you?"

"Coming down Simmering with Miles and two other FBI people."

"Three FBI people altogether!"

"That's all we could get. I'm—"

Ray shouted, "This whole campus is becoming Jonestown Two, and all we could get—"

Miles came on. "Calm down, Ray. I'm working on getting more people on the way. But this is the best we could do. We didn't get a search warrant."

Feeling Andi's eyes on him, he turned to her. He could barely breathe, and he felt the old fears coming back.

Then Andi grabbed his shoulder. "Come on," she said. "This is what we have to work with. No use arguing about it."

Fighting the sinking feeling, he said into the walkie-talkie, "All right, Croase is here somewhere. There's a demonstration starting up at the school against what he's doing, and their main researcher, Dr. Nakayami, is helping us. He's in the building now trying to locate Tommy."

"Good," Miles said. "One more thing. The funeral home was hit. There's two dead men—the funeral director and another that was ID'd as Ken Strock. Lyle thinks he's head of security. You know who he is?"

"No."

"Someone else got away. We think he did the hits. Also, one of the FBI men got wounded."

"Bad?"

"In the leg. He's all right. Just get to the front of the building. We'll need you to ID people and so on."

Ray nodded and looked at Andi, his mind still a flurry of emotion. "All right," he rasped. "Croase can't do anything while he's in the building—he'd be committing suicide. The main thing is Tommy at this point and protecting the campus. But so long as Croase is inside, we're all right. Otherwise, we have to get that radio detonator."

There was another silence. Lyle came back on, "All right, no one knows we're coming. Wait a minute—OK, I see the TWI tower now. We're going in. There's a roadblock up ahead. But that won't stop us. Better get moving, Ray."

"Got it."

He grabbed Andi's hand and pulled out the 9 mm Smith and Wesson. *No mistakes!* echoed in his mind again, and his stomach churned. Then: *Trust.* As they ran to the door, he

420

knew more than just Andi, Lyle, and several FBI agents were with him. He cried to Andi, "It's gonna be OK." She followed but seemed unaware of the new calm inside of him.

He threw open the door. To his left the campus was alive with students chanting, "Stop unlawful drugs!" Some had signs, and they were moving toward the fence.

"At least they're out of the buildings." Ray jerked Andi out toward the front of TWI.

Listra Croase scribbled a note for David Hughes and tucked it under his blotter in the security office. She prayed that Rafa would not allow things to go haywire, but if they did she was confident he would lead her through unscathed. She hurried out of the office to the elevators. Getting the boy was the main issue now, and if Nakayami wasn't going to cooperate then she could do it herself. She decided to go up to the eighth floor, grab a supply of TUT and TUT-B, and then get the hostages to the safe room.

2

The men guarding the roadblock did not try to stop anyone when Miles showed them his FBI ID. Miles radioed to the police to get some county officers up there and cuff the two guards.

They reached the main gate without incident. There, a security guard tried to stop them, but Miles flashed his FBI badge again and barely waited for the trestle gate to rise. He floored it to the left toward the front parking lot.

As Ray and Andi raced back toward the front of TWI, she suddenly grabbed his arm.

"They're pulling something out," she said. "Looks like fire hoses."

Ray stopped and watched as several security people dragged three large water cannons across the parking lot.

He knew now there was no turning back. Croase was really planning to do it. "We've got to move," he shouted and bolted toward the front of the building.

Andi was right behind him. "What are they doing?" Her words came in sharp huffs.

"Going to use the water cannons against the crowd. And if Croase hits that detonator, several hundred students could be dead in a few minutes."

They swerved around the edge of the building. As they came around the corner, a guard suddenly jumped up with a shotgun in his hand. "Hold it there, buddio."

Ray and Andi stopped up short.

Behind the guard, Miles's siren screamed and his car zoomed into the parking lot. The guard turned. That was all Ray needed. He clipped him in the head with the butt of the Smith and Wesson. The man crumpled. Ray grabbed the shotgun, quickly pumped out all six cartridges, and then slammed the barrel against the brick wall.

He dropped the shotgun and grabbed Andi's hand, as she stood staring. "What's the matter?"

"I thought it was all over for a second."

"Yeah, I know."

Miles and Lyle Hornum were just getting out of the car when the pair ran up to him. Miles said, "You're the two missing witnesses."

"Right," Ray answered, panting. "What can we do?"

Ray saw Miles looking at the gun in his right hand. He quickly jammed it back into his pocket. "You guys are in charge. I'm just here to take orders."

Miles nodded. "Good, but I'll have to ask you to leave the gun in the car."

Ray wished he hadn't had the pistol out, but he decided not to argue. He didn't say anything about Andi's .38.

The two other agents stood by, and Miles introduced them as Rod Tower and Phil Debuss.

He laid the gun and the three extra clips on the front seat of the car. For a moment he thought about slipping it back into his pocket, but he couldn't risk doing that with FBI people.

The group stalked up the sidewalk to the front of the building. It was nearly 7:30 A.M. Inside, standing before the guard station in the foyer, Miles laid his wallet badge on the desk. Two security officers examined it; then the first asked to call down one of the company officers.

Miles answered, "We'll give you two minutes."

Looking over Miles and the other two agents, Ray noticed that they were all sturdily built. Each was affecting a nonchalant position, but he sensed they were making numerous observations of the building, room, and people. Ray thought that up against Croase it shouldn't be much of a match. But he wasn't sure if Croase had access to weapons and, if he did, could use them. It was one fact he suddenly wished he knew an answer to.

3

After discovering two more aluminum briefcases in a supply closet, Martin Croase packed the last of the $6 million. Hefting the first one with his right arm for the third time, he realized he'd need a cart to get them to the safe room. He thought briefly about heisting more money from another safe in Harvey Konopka's office, the primary emergency fund. But it was only several hundred thousand. *Small potatoes,* Croase decided. And too risky.

He was about to rush out to find a cart when the phone rang.

Swearing, Croase picked it up. "Martin Croase here," he said with controlled anger.

It was the security guard at the front desk. "Dr. Croase, there's an FBI Special Agent here name of Lou Miles. Two other agents and three other people, including a reporter. They want to have a look at TWI."

Croase swore again. "Tell them to wait there. This is completely illegal. I'll be there in a minute."

He slammed the phone down and closed his eyes. The inner voice spoke. *Everything is in hand. Go down and tell them what they're doing is unlawful. It's that simple. They're men of law.*

Croase breathed out slowly, looked at the canvas bag containing the Uzi and several extra clips still lying on the desk, and calmed himself. As he headed toward the elevator, a light and bell signaled that the car had just stopped on his floor.

A moment later, Bill Linton stepped off. "Dr. Croase, I've—"

"What do you want?"

"Those kids, sir. They're really stirring it up. Shouting and everything."

"Are the water cannons in place?"

"Yes, sir."

"All right. Get out there with a bullhorn and tell them to disperse. Tell them it's illegal and non-Christian and whatever else you can think of." He paused, tapping his foot impatienty. "All right, tell them I'll come out and talk to them in a little while—but in the main quad. Get them away from the fence."

Linton shifted his weight nervously. "Bill Patton also said to tell you the helicopter's ready."

"Good." Croase stopped, then swore again. "How big is this demonstration?"

"You go out there, sir, they'll maul you. They're a mad bunch of people."

"I guess I couldn't walk over to the helicopter pad then."

"No way, sir."

Croase snorted and peered down the hallway. His mind said to the inner voice, *What is going on?*

The voice answered, *Nothing to worry about.*

"All right, I'll take care of it," he said, turning back to Linton. "Make sure those water cannons are ready. But try to disperse them. Tell them to get back to their rooms and pray about what they're doing."

"I've got it, sir."

They stepped onto the elevator. When they reached the first floor Croase got off, while Linton went on to the lower-level garage.

When he saw the police cars drive into the front parking lot, Hiro Nakayami immediately left his front office and hurried downstairs by the stairwell. His heart was hammering wildly, but he knew he had to take this action. Nothing else would save the boy, or the campus.

Listra Croase led Tommy and Dr. Kingston at gunpoint out of the supply room down the hallway to the elevator. They got off at the fifteenth fllor. There, she opened a door to another storage room. The boy and professor were handcuffed together, and Listra had a security officer with her to make sure there was no trouble. She shoved Tommy ahead of her. "Are you crippled, boy?" she said as he tried to slow down. She had a small semiautomatic that looked to Kingston like a .32.

"No, I'm not crippled."

"Then move."

Dr. Kingston said, "Just obey them, Tommy. It's all right."

They all stepped inside the storage room, and Listra shut the door. While the guard watched Tommy and Kingston, she marched to the back of the room and began feeling along the concrete between the cinder blocks.

Tommy watched closely. From what had been said, he figured that there was some kind of secret room they were taking him and Dr. Kingston to. But why? He knew he had to do something quickly, but he wasn't sure what. Maybe Ray and his mother had managed to get in. He glanced at Dr. Kingston apprehensively. The big professor signaled with his eyes that Tommy should watch closely.

Tommy decided he had to somehow let Ray and his mom know where he was. As Listra continued feeling along the wall and the guard stood behind Dr. Kingston with a gun jammed into his back, Tommy ran through a mental list of the things he still had. The little Swiss Army knife, which

425

they'd never taken away because they'd never found it on him so far. His glasses. His shoes.

That was it. His shoes. His mother would recognize them.

He kept his eyes on Listra while he worked on the heel of his right shoe, holding it down with the toe of his left foot. The guard seemed to be concentrating on Dr. Kingston, so Tommy made as little movement as possible, clinching down the heel with his toe.

Suddenly, the guard said to Tommy, "What's the matter, boy?"

He quickly answered, "I have to go to the bathroom." He got the heel of the sneaker down in the noise of the question and the answer. Fortunately the laces were a little loose.

"You'll have to wait," the guard said curtly. "Don't do anything stupid."

The shoe was loose enough now. He could step out of it as they walked forward. Hopefully no one would notice. He considered whether he should discard one or two shoes. He decided one would be better. Two might not make them think anything but that the shoes were thrown there. One would indicate he'd been there and had left a sign.

Maybe they would think that.

Tommy prayed in his mind that someone would notice.

Listra suddenly said, "I've got it." She pushed a key into the concrete, and instantly a motor whirred somewhere in the side wall, and the whole cinder block wall scraped slowly to the left. It opened about two feet, then stopped. It was dark in the room, but Listra stepped in. A moment later a light came on.

The guard poked Tommy's back with the barrel of the gun. "Move, kid."

As Dr. Kingston and Tommy lurched forward, Tommy stepped out of the sneaker. He walked on tiptoe toward the door, praying that no one noticed him leaving the white and black striped Nike in the middle of the floor.

The guard said nothing. Kingston, then Tommy, stepped through the aperture.

When they were all inside, Listra said, "Handcuff the professor to the legs of the cabinet there, then get one of the other pairs for the boy and just cuff his hands. Then you can go."

The guard nodded and unlocked the cuff on Tommy's hand, then told Kingston to lie on the floor by a large gray metal cabinet. He placed the chain around a leg, then cinched it onto Kingston's other hand. Listra told Tommy to sit on a small sofa on the other side.

It was a small room with two doors in the back. Listra smiled as she sat down, waving the gun in front of her. She said, "Rafa is watching. He's here with us now."

The guard placed a second pair of handcuffs on Tommy, then said, "Dr. Nakayami will be coming up?"

"Yes."

"Should I leave it open?"

"No. I'll open it when he signals. Just put some gauze in the old man's mouth. I don't want him to start bellowing at an inopportune moment." She glared at Kingston, then looked back at the guard and smiled primly.

The guard jammed a wad of gauze into Kingston's mouth, then wrapped tape over it and around the back of his head. A moment later, he left.

Listra crossed her legs as she sat on the couch opposite Tommy. She lit a cigarette and gazed at Tommy with a nasty leer on her face. "Well, well, the famous professor and the famous death-traveler both in the room with little old me. What a pleasure this must be for both of you." She opened her purse and took out a semiautomatic pistol.

Tommy noticed Kingston's eyes were darting about, but he looked at Listra calmly and sat still. He didn't feel afraid now. He was sure both God, Kartle, Trell, and all the others were far more powerful than Rafa. But he wasn't going to say that to Listra.

4

His heels clicking on the linoleum, Martin Croase strode down the hall and into the large foyer of TWI. Miles motioned to Rod Tower and said, "You do the talking. See if you can divert him."

Croase didn't even stop at the guard station. He swaggered confidently up to the group of men. He held out his hand, but Tower simply opened his FBI badge and ID. Croase didn't even look at Andi and Ray, though they stood near the group. "FBI. All right, I see the ID," Croase said offhandedly. "What do you want?"

Tower said, "We have information that you're detaining a boy named Tommy Darcasian and an older man named Dr. Harold Kingston here against their will."

The perfect actor, Croase wrinkled his brow. "We are a medical research institution, not a terrorist organization, sir."

As the security guard at the desk in the foyer watched the discussion between Tower and Croase, Lou Miles edged to the left and motioned Andi and Ray to move with him. Tower stepped around to the desk in front of Croase and leaned on it, so that Croase's back was to the others.

Miles whispered to Ray and Andi, "If we can get to an elevator without him stopping us, we may be home free."

As Croase argued with Tower, Miles started for the elevator. A second later, the security guard called out, "Wait a minute there!"

Immediately Croase whipped around. His visage changed. "Unless you have a search warrant, sirs, I'll have to ask you to leave."

"We'd just like to take a look around, that's all," Miles said, a rising stridency in his voice.

Ray sensed it was over. There was nothing more they could do. He glanced up at the ceiling and noticed two of the brass sprinkler fixtures. Every room probably had them, he thought, and made a mental calculation of how many people might be in the building now. The number 100 came into his mind.

Croase stepped in front of Miles and the others, blocking the route to the elevators. "I'd like you to leave. Now. You have no business here."

"What are you afraid of?" Miles asked hotly into Croase's face.

"Nothing. But if you don't have a search warrant, you have no right to look around. That's final. I know my rights."

To their left, Ray heard a door open. He looked but could see nothing. Croase grabbed Miles's arm. "I'd like you out, sir. Now."

He pushed Miles to the door, and everyone began filing out sheepishly. Croase glowered at Ray and Andi, but when Ray's eyes met his, he looked away. Getting them outside, Croase said to the security guard, "Escort these people to the gate, please." He turned and hurried back inside, then disappeared into an elevator.

5

When Croase was gone, Hiro Nakayami stepped soundlessly out the stairwell door by the elevators. He hurried outside and called to the security guard herding Miles, Ray, Andi, and the others to the parked cars. The security guard stopped and turned.

Still dressed in a white lab jacket and pants, Nakayami called out, "I'll take care of this, Bill. Get on up to the eighth floor immediately. We need some help up there."

The security guard stared at Dr. Nakayami. "But Dr. Croase—"

Nakayami smiled toothily. "It's all right. I know what to do. Just do as I say."

The guard shrugged. "You're the boss."

When he was gone, Nakayami turned around. "Please hurry. Follow me."

Ray said, "I wasn't sure you'd come through, Doc."

"I have not yet seen the boy," Nakayami answered, glancing at Andi.

Her eyes didn't blink, and Ray could tell she was bracing herself for the worst.

Nakayami continued. "I think I know where he is, though. We must hurry. Dr. Croase is desperate. He will take drastic measures."

Andi grabbed his arm. "Have they done anything with the TUT and Tommy?"

429

Nakayami shook his head.

Andi glanced at Ray with obvious relief in her eyes, but everyone was clearly tense.

Turning to Miles, Ray said, "This is Dr. Nakayami, the head of the research team. He has offered to help us."

Miles looked Nakayami up and down, then turned to the two other special agents. "All right, let's move in." Lyle, Ray, and Andi followed them inside.

At the elevators, Nakayami said, "I don't know what can be done, but the boy's life and the professor's are in danger. I do not think Dr. Croase is really interested in doing any testing today. His wife, though, has become extremely unstable, in my opinion."

Miles looked apprehensively at Ray and Andi. "Where are they?"

"In what we call the safe room. But I do not know how to get in or where precisely it is. I have only heard talk about it."

"Leave that to us," Miles said. Before stepping into the elevator, Miles called local FBI Dispatch through the radio he carried. After defining the situation to the person that answered, he said to the others, "Police and backup should arrive soon."

"We should have come in with more people," Ray said.

"It couldn't be helped," Miles snapped. Then he looked down at the elevator buttons. "I'm sorry. We're doing the best we can."

No mistakes! echoed in Ray's mind again. He glanced at Andi, but her eyes were set forward. He could tell she was storming inside, but they had to cooperate. They couldn't pull this off alone.

They stepped grimly into the elevator, and Nakayami punched the button to the fifteenth floor.

He gripped Andi's hand. She gazed at him again wonderingly. "What is it?"

He smiled. "I think it's going to be OK, that's all."

Her lips twitched, then she said, "I wish I had your confidence."

"You do," he said.

Her eyes flickered with emotion, then she squeezed his hand, and they both looked up at the flashing numbers above them.

6

Ten minutes after they reached the safe room, the phone inside rang. Listra picked it up.

"Listra Croase," she said. "Yes . . . OK. Where's Nakayami? . . . You don't have to come. . . . All right."

Tommy wondered who she could be talking to, but Listra hung up abruptly.

"That was my husband," she told them. "He's gotten rid of your FBI people and your mother and her friend." She glared at Tommy. "So we just sit tight until everything is clear." She leaned back against the desk and laid the gun down on the blotter, then began to file her fingernails.

Dr. Kingston tried to move into a more comfortable position by the cabinets. Tommy glanced worriedly at him, but the old man again shook his head, indicating that Tommy not talk.

Listra began to pace and smoke, the gun again in her right hand.

Tommy took in his surroundings. In a corner was a desk with two phones on it, each with several line buttons. On the wall was a contraption that looked like a walkie-talkie. Tommy recognized it as a CB radio. The room was about ten feet wide and twelve feet long. There was nothing of the plushness of the other offices. The walls were bare Sheetrock. Spackling was still visible.

After several minutes, Listra opened one of the cabinets. It was filled with weapons, side arms, and two rifles that looked like the type Tommy had seen in war movies. She shoved another side arm and several filled clips into her purse.

As Listra watched Kingston and Tommy, her anger grew. Above all, she did not want her husband interfering with the project now that she had the boy. But she knew something had gone wrong. If only Hughes got her message. She searched in her mind for the voice of Rafa, then sat down on the chair and closed her eyes. "Rafa," she said, moving her lips but not speaking audibly. "Please speak."

Instantly, the voice was there. *I am with you.*

"What is going on?"

It is all well in hand.

"What about David?"

He is coming.

"I'm scared."

I am with you always.

She opened her eyes at a sudden buzzing sound from one of the fluorescent lamps overheard, then closed them again. "What will happen?"

Do not fear. I am with you. Relax in my power.

7

Martin Croase picked up a briefcase in each hand. Another was tucked under his arm. He knew his only chance now was the safe room. Listra would already be there, but he knew he could deal with her. The Uzi and pack were slung around his back.

The briefcases weighed about twenty pounds each. He staggered into the hall under the weight, gave a quick look around, then hobbled to the elevator. Once aboard, he hit the button to the fifteenth floor. When the door opened, the floor was silent. He went directly to the storage room, fumbled for the key, placed it in the crack, and turned. The wall rumbled back.

He dumped the briefcases through the opening, then stepped over them and turned the key again to shut the wall.

"What are you doing?" Listra yelled, jumping off the desk. "Where's Nakayami, and what are those briefcases?"

"Our salvation, my dear."

"What do you mean?" She bent over one and tried to open it.

432

"It's $6 million, dearest. We're rich." But his mind said, *Jillie and I, that is.*

She gasped and stood up. "Six million? How—"

"I have my ways. Now I have to count on you, dearest. This is not going to be easy." He unstrapped the Uzi and began checking it, then slid a round into the chamber.

She stared at him wide-eyed. "What's going on?"

Croase explained about the student demonstration, the FBI, the helicopter.

"But what about the TUT-B? And the boy?"

"We'll take him with us, dearest, a little fire insurance. Mazaris and the others won't shoot at us as long as we have him. You'll have plenty of time to do your own experiments." He looked down at the Uzi, then grinned at Tommy, said, "Ratta-tatta-tatta," and swung the gun around the room. "Your friends are in big trouble, sonny boy."

Tommy winced, but Croase turned away, grinning and mentally working out a quick operational plan. He wasn't sure precisely when he'd deal with Listra, but it wouldn't be until they were in the clear.

After she had looked her husband over several times, Listra's mouth finally dropped with amazement. "How did you think of all this, dear?"

"With my own little mind. Now, please, let me get things in order here."

The phone rang. Croase swore. Listra ran to get it, but when she answered it was security. She handed the phone to her husband.

"Yeah . . . Yeah . . . Oh . . ." Croase began swearing. "That little Japanese traitor! All right, just contain it. I'll handle myself up here. Stall them. Do anything you can. Do your job." He slammed down the phone.

"Nakayami's leading them around the building."

Listra swore this time.

"It's all right. He doesn't know where this room is, even if he knows about it. I've got it handled."

"What are we doing to do?"

"I'll have Patton land the helicopter on the roof. I had it prepared long ago just in case, and we can get to it from here."

433

Listra looked about her. There were those two small doors in the back. She'd been here only once. "How?"

"It's all handled, dear. Just let me do my job." He picked up the phone and dialed the number for the helicopter station. The Uzi hung from his shoulder menacingly. He hardly looked at Tommy and Kingston and then began speaking heatedly into the phone.

When he was through, he called Linton at the security station near the demonstration. "Hit them with the water cannons . . . All right, take the ten minutes, but get it going."

8

"It's somewhere on the fifteenth floor, top one," Nakayami said. "But I don't know where the safe room is exactly, or how to access it."

"Let's just spread out and move fast," Miles said. They all tramped off the elevator at the fifteenth.

Nakayami pointed left.

"Start checking rooms," Miles ordered. The hand-held radio coughed and sizzled again and a voice came on.

"Miles?"

"Miles here."

"Howard County Police on the way. Two backup teams also dispatched."

"Thanks." He nodded. "That should do it."

9

Andi opened the door of the storage room and flicked on the light switch. Everything looked in order. Then she spotted Tommy's sneaker. "Ray!" she screamed. "Ray! Mr. Miles! Here!"

A few moments later, everyone stood around looking at the sneaker. Andi hadn't disturbed it. The back end was pushed in, as though it had been slipped off in typical childish fashion. Miles scrutinized it.

Ray said, "Tommy left this on purpose."

"How can you tell?" Miles asked.

434

"The heel. He loosened it, then stepped out of it when they weren't looking. That's why there's only one."

Nakayami looked up at the wall. "I heard talk of the safe room behind a concrete wall," he said.

They all marched over to the wall and looked at it closely. Ray ran his finger along the edge of a corner. "It definitely slides," he said. "See the crack. It's not sealed. They have to be in there."

Andi started to shout, "Tom—"

Ray clapped his hand over her mouth. "We can't alert them!" he whispered.

She nodded, her eyes darting. "I'm just petrified."

Everyone stopped and listened. No sound emitted from the room.

Miles inspected the wall. "Let's see what we can do to open it up." He looked at Nakayami. "Is there any other way out or in?"

"I don't know," Nakayami said. "This is the top floor of the building." He squinted thoughtfully. "No, wait. There's something else. On the roof is a maintenance building where all the elevator motors and air conditioning and heating equipment are. And something else."

Everyone stared at him.

Nakayami said, "Recently, Mr. Croase had the very top capped off with a flat piece of concrete and a ladder from the top equipment room. I don't know—"

"They could land the helicopter on top of it, Lou," Debuss said, wrinkling his brow.

Miles nodded. "Yeah. That may be how they're planning to escape." He turned to Rod Tower. "You guard this entrance. When the police arrive, get them working on it. Meanwhile, we'll see what we can do to get into the maintenance shack on top. If they haven't already escaped to the roof, we might be able to seal them in."

The group ran toward the stairwell.

Croase spoke into the phone. "Patton? Where is Patton? Get him." His fingers drummed on the desk.

"Change of plans, Patton—is Johnny there? Good. I want you to get the helicopter and land it on the roof of TWI. Yes, the roof . . . Don't argue with me. That's what I had it concreted for . . . I don't care if it's getting windy. Get it up there. Be ready to go in ten minutes."

Croase stopped and swore. "All right, twenty minutes. No more." He slammed down the phone. "Years of work and nobody functions when it's critical." He swore again.

Listra said, "What is Nakayami doing?"

"Leading them everywhere, I suppose. I don't know what's got into him. I should have seen it coming. He's been edgy for months. But I think we're OK. We get on the helicopter, we should be all right. We'll get to one of our properties in western Maryland, then disappear."

"But what about the boy? And the TUT-B?"

"It's taken care of, dear. We'll take the boy with us. As I said, fire insurance."

Tommy stirred uncomfortably.

Listra lit a cigarette and sucked deeply on it. She leaned back and exhaled smoke towards the ceiling. She looked at Tommy with slit eyes, then turned away.

As Listra and her husband talked, Tommy began thinking about some way to divert them. He said suddenly, "I think I know why the TUT-B works on me."

Listra swung around. Croase stopped and stared. "What do you mean?" Listra said suddenly.

"I think I know," Tommy said. "It's where it goes into your body."

The woman stood and leaned closer. "What do you mean where it goes?"

"Where the TUT-B touches your skin. There's a special nerve."

Listra laughed. "Give me a break."

"A nerve in your arm," Tommy said, thinking fast. "When Jesse did it the first time, he pressed it just above my elbow. That's where the nerve is. It causes a special effect. Then once you've done it once, it happens like that always. Like a medicine."

"This is ridiculous," Martin Croase said.

"Shut up!" Listra suddenly yelled. "You always were a fool." She gazed with hard eyes into the Tommy's face. "You're not lying to me, boy, are you?"

He shook his head. He felt Kingston's eyes on his face, but he didn't look at the professor.

"What's the name of this nerve?"

"I don't know."

"How do you know this is the reason?"

"Kartle told me."

Listra's eyes almost popped. "Kartle! You said Kartle?"

"Yes." Tommy nodded vigorously. "That was the spirit's name. Kartle. He said he protected me by having it go in at that nerve."

Listra looked at her husband. "Kartle is the one Rafa told me about, the one who is an enemy."

Croase rolled his eyes.

She looked at him with contempt, then turned back to Tommy. "Rafa told me about this Kartle. Who is he?"

"An angel, I guess."

She snorted. "What does he do?"

"He protects people."

"So he told you about the nerve?"

"Yes."

"Why didn't you tell us before?"

"I didn't know that was what you wanted."

Tommy glanced at Kingston, but the professor kept a straight face.

Listra sucked her cheek, then said, "So this Kartle person really exists?" She looked at her husband in triumph. "Well, well, well. And how am I supposed to access this nerve if I want to use the TUT-B, little boy?"

"I don't know."

"Show me your arm."

Tommy held out his arm, and she inspected it around the elbow.

437

Croase said, "Listra, this is all garbage. It's a big lie."

"Shut up!" She continued feeling the muscles and looking at his arm. "Where did it go in?"

Tommy gestured toward his arm with his head. "Just above my elbow."

"Are you lying to me?" Listra glared at him with angry, slit eyes.

Feeling a cold vise grip his chest, Tommy said, "No. But I'm afraid."

Listra leaned forward again, pressing the flesh on his arm. "What are you afraid of?"

"Something else Kartle said."

"About what?"

"Things he didn't want Rafa to know."

Listra's face darkened, and she glared at Tommy. "There's nothing Rafa doesn't know. What are you talking about?"

"No," Tommy shook his head. "There are many things. Rafa is a demon, a fallen angel. Not a—" He searched for the right word. What was correct? What was best? He had it. "Not a prince. Kartle said he was a prince. And Jesus was there too."

Listra suddenly slapped Tommy on the cheek.

Kingston jerked on the handcuffs and tried to yell through the gauze. But Listra said, "He said no such thing, you little twerp. You're lying. There are no demons, no angels."

This time Croase waved her off and knelt in front of Tommy. "What did this prince being say, Tommy? No one here is going to hurt you for anything you say."

Tommy looked from Listra to Martin Croase. He knew now he'd gone too far. But he had to keep going. "I don't remember everything he said. Just those things."

The phone rang again. Croase jumped up and answered. "Croase." He listened. "All right, do whatever diversions you can think of. Just make sure . . . No, don't worry. I'll take care of it."

He eyed Listra, placing his hand over the receiver. "They've found the storage room. Our little friend Tommy

438

here left a sneaker in it." He looked at Tommy with a flicker of respect. "Not such a dumb bunny after all."

Listra said without emotion, "It doesn't matter. Rafa will take care of this."

"Rafa, Rafa, Rafa. What has Rafa done?" Croase asked incredulously. Then he turned back to the phone. "All right, don't worry about it. Just get on with the diversion activities. Are all the files stowed? . . . All right. Nothing to worry about. They won't find anything important."

Hunching deeper into his seat, Tommy watched apprehensively. He wondered if they believed him, if it was doing any good. He wondered where his mother and Ray were now. What if they did take him in the helicopter? Would he ever see them again? And what about Kartle? Was he here with them? Now?

He searched in his mind for some piece of hope and surety. But nothing held him. He watched Martin Croase shift the Uzi back and forth on his hip. He hoped Ray had his gun. If Croase tried to get Ray, Tommy was sure Ray would win. But he knew Ray only had a pistol. He kept swallowing, telling himself to be calm.

Listra hopped off the desk. As Tommy watched, she closed her eyes, nodded, and moved her lips as if speaking. Then she opened them quickly and glared at Tommy. "What do you want, boy?"

Tommy didn't answer.

She stood and stalked toward him, then stopped, went back to her pocketbook and pulled out the gun. She waved it at him. "Would your ascended prince Kartle be able to do anything to stop a bullet?"

Tommy curled tighter in his seat. Kingston tried to rise, but the handcuffs held him. Tommy's lone sneaker had dropped off onto the floor in front of him.

Croase grabbed his wife's wrist. "Put that away," he said. "This is no time for games."

Listra shook him off and strolled over to Tommy, still waving the gun. "Oh, it's not loaded." She raised it to Tommy's head. "Does your heavenly friend know how to stop a bullet, boy?"

Croase hung up the phone. "Listra, calm down."

She pointed the barrel at Tommy's forehead. "You need a part, don't you? Right down the middle would be nice."

Croase stepped toward her. "Listra, I demand that you put down that gun."

Listra shifted the barrel up and down in front of Tommy's forehead.

He breathed quietly, praying and blinking, steeling himself for whatever came.

"He protects me, he protects me not. Repeat after me. He protects me, he protects me not. Say it, you little twerp."

Croase said, "Listra, stop it."

Listra turned to face him. "Look, fool. I'll do as I please. Stay out of this, or I'll part your hair too."

Croase didn't move.

"Say it," Listra said. "He protects me, he protects me not." She pointed the barrel between his eyebrows.

As he wrestled against the handcuffs, Kingston's muffled voice bellowed from the floor.

Listra trained the gun on Kingston's head. "Watch it, old man, or I'll make you do it too. Does Kartle protect him, too, little boy?" With the tip of the barrel she drew a cross on his forehead.

Tommy looked from Listra to Kingston to Croase and back. "H-He protects me. He—"

"Faster, moron." She pressed the barrel hard against his forehead, forcing his head back against the couch. It hurt. He began to wriggle, but she said, "Don't move, you little idiot. Say it. He protects me, he protects me not. He protects me, he protects me not."

"H-He protects me—us—he p-p-p-protects me not."

"No stuttering, moron."

Tommy took a breath. His eyes wouldn't seem to focus. He looked pleadingly at Croase. "Pl-please—"

"Say it, hero-boy, boy wonder!" Listra yelled. "Say it. No stuttering."

Croase spoke again, this time firm and low. "Listra, please calm down. There's no reason—"

"Shut up!" she yelled. "Whose side are you on?" She turned back to Tommy. "He protects me. Say it."

Slowly, Tommy told himself. Slowly. "He protects me."

"He protects me not."

"He protects me not."

"He protects me." The gun went up and down in front of his eyes.

"He—protects—me."

"Faster. He protects me not."

"H-H-He—"

"Stop stuttering!" She jerked the trigger as the gun came up over his head. The blast and heat singed Tommy's hair. He fell to the side, momentarily deafened. But he knew he was alive.

Croase screamed, "Listra!" He grabbed the gun out of her hand. "Stop it!"

"Must I?" she said, glaring. She turned around. "Just wanted to see if he'd puke. Brave little kid. The type I need."

Kingston struggled to rise. It was a useless effort. Listra kicked him twice with her pointy cream-colored high heels. Kingston buckled up, groaning. The wad of gauze was still in his mouth.

Croase said, "Tie his feet. He's only more trouble."

"We have to take both of them," Listra suddenly said.

"Why?"

"Because Rafa commands it!" Her face was hard and set.

Croase still had her gun, but Tommy could see there were others in the cabinet.

The blast was still ringing in Tommy's ears. He tried to focus on Croase's face, but he felt confused. It all looked black, dark.

Croase said to Listra, "Sit down, dear. No more of this."

Listra sat down and lit a cigarette. "Oh, this is just the beginning of birth pangs."

Tommy suddenly felt as if he were falling into the darkness of a deep tunnel.

CHAPTER TWENTY

1

David Hughes roared down Simmering Road in the sleek Mitsubishi sports car. When he saw the first roadblock with two of his TWI security men standing around listlessly, he said, "What's going on, guys?"

The first answered, "Lots of weird things going on down there, Dave. Some FBI agent just stopped in, and I've heard the cops put out a bulletin to get down here. Expect them to be showing up anytime."

"All right," Hughes said. "Just stick here till it's over."

"You got it."

Hughes turned off into the campus well before TWI. He parked in front of one of the dorms and got out. He saw the crowd of students in front of the main gate, obviously demonstrating. He ran around behind the dorm and went by the helicopter pad where he saw Bill Patton running towards the helicopter, grumbling and pulling on his flight jacket.

"Where are you going?" Hughes said, trying to be friendly.

"The whole place is nuts," Patton said. "Croase wants me to land the helicopter on the roof."

"What for?" Hughes was suddenly intrigued.

"FBI are here, man," Patton said, hurrying by. "Got to move. He wants me up there in twenty minutes."

Hughes stared at Patton scurrying across the parking lot to the helicopter pad behind the dorm. Why would Croase want to land it on the roof? Whatever it was, he thought, it didn't matter. After Konopka was dead, David Hughes was truly invincible. He and Listra together.

2

Phil Tower heard the shot as he rechecked the wall into the safe room. He radioed to Miles, already on his way to the maintenance room on the roof, that something was happening. Miles replied, "Do what you can to get inside."

Tower examined the wall. "Probably steel behind the cinder blocks," he muttered. "Need a jackhammer and a torch." He looked around in the room. There wasn't even anything he could use to pry at the cinder blocks. He couldn't leave his station, so he decided to get ready in case the wall began to open. He started to pull a cabinet out so he could hide behind it.

3

Miles, Phil Debuss, Lyle, Hiro Nakayami, and Ray and Andi stopped in front of the sealed-off door at the south end of the air conditioner room. Nakayami explained the layout.

"It's in two tiers, with different equipment on each. The first level has the cooling tower for the air conditioners and a lot of piping when we first go in. You have to circle around the middle, which encases the elevator cables. As you go around, you pass the heating units, then come to the second tier stairwell. I don't really know what's up there."

"So we can only go in one direction?" Miles asked.

"Right. Like a circle." Nakayami motioned with his hand.

"And they could ambush us at any point along the way?"

Nakayami nodded vigorously. "You do know about Dr. Croase's hobby?"

"No," Miles said. "What's that?"

The researcher looked anxiously about at the two FBI men. "Antiterrorist games. He is an expert with an Uzi and also handguns."

443

For a moment, Ray's heart seemed to stop, then it boomed so loud in his chest he had to catch his breath. Miles gaped, then swore, glanced at Ray and sucked his lip. He said to Nakayami, "You think he's got that Uzi up there with him—if he's up there?"

"I don't know." Nakayami swallowed and waited.

Miles shifted nervously on his feet. "We've got to get some backup here, possibly a SWAT team."

Ray was already shaking his head. Glancing up at the ceiling, he immediately spotted another fire spigot. "Soon as Croase is out of the building, he could hit the radio detonator. We have to go after him now." He resisted the impulse to say, "I told you so." But he did wish he had the Smith and Wesson. The word *Trust* echoed again in his mind, and he fought back the flak of fear that was starting to hit him again.

"How many clips you got?" Miles asked Debuss.

"Three."

"Me too. One of those Uzis spits out 900 or so rounds a minute." He swore again and squinted at the brass sprinkler. "We have to go. Now."

Ray said, "I shouldn't have left my gun down—"

"Yes, you should have," Miles said angrily. "You have to let us handle this." He talked into the radio for another twenty seconds, demanding backup and an update, but the dispatcher only said several patrol cars were on the way. Miles said, "We'll go in first. Dr. Nakayami, you'll have to tell us where to go."

Miles tried the door handle, but it was locked. On the door hung a yellow and black DANGER sign warning them of the electrical power within. Nakayami said, "The only people with keys are maintenance men and security in the basement."

"It's not dead bolted, though," Andi added. She looked at Ray. "Still got your emergency exit card?"

Ray pulled out his wallet. Miles waved him off. "Phil, you got the tap set?"

Debuss took out two small pieces of metal from his pocket. One looked like a paper clip bent on the end, and the other was a thin, jagged piece. He put the first on the lower part of the lock and the other in the top, then began jiggling it back and forth. There was a click, and the handle turned.

Everyone sighed with relief.

"All right," Miles said, "Phil, you lead. Nakayami right behind telling him where to go. Ray, you're behind me. But I don't want you getting involved, OK?"

Ray nodded uneasily and caught Andi chewing her lip and fingering the gun still in her jacket pocket. He signaled to her not to draw it out. Miles looked at Lyle and Andi. "You two stay in the back."

Lyle agreed. But Andi shook her head and said, "I'm sticking right behind Ray. I'm not staying here. That's my son, and if it comes to it—" Ray quickly knocked her foot. *Don't mention the gun!* She said, "I'll do what I can to get him safe and alive."

Miles eyed her skeptically. "All right. But we've got to move fast. They may already be on their way." Debuss drew his gun, then stepped inside the doorway, affecting a shooter's stance up the stairs. "All right," he barked, "let's move."

Debuss bounded up the stairs with the others behind him.

☐ ☐ ☐

As Andi followed Ray up the stairs, she tried to swallow away a flurry of knots in her stomach. She believed God wouldn't let anything happen to Tommy, but deep down she knew she couldn't be sure. If God really was in charge of the world, then plenty of children had died by all sorts of foul means without a word from God or anyone else in protest— or so it seemed.

She wasn't sure what to say or do, but she knew she had little choice. She had to believe and at the same time take what action she could. That was the only way to make sense of it.

Her heart was thundering as they reached the top of the stairs. Still, she knew whatever happened, she would fight. And no matter what Lou Miles said, if it came down to it, she'd use the .38 too. Something inside her wanted to go faster, much faster. She took several deep breaths, then as the others started into the room, she touched Ray's back. He turned around.

She wasn't even sure why, but she suddenly said, "Yes."

"Yes?"

"If anything happens to me or you, I want you to know, I will marry you."

"Andi, this—"

"Just shut up and tell me you heard me say it."

"OK. But we're going to be all ri—"

"I know. I hope that. I just wanted you to know."

He gripped her hard. "Thanks."

Suddenly, the noise of the room resounded around them as Debuss cracked open the door at the top of the stairs. As Ray turned away she watched his face and his eyes harden with calm determination. She prayed if someone had to die that it would be her. But she knew that she didn't want that. She wanted Ray and Tommy and herself together, safe, without a Croase or anyone else hounding them. Strangely, she was almost reluctant to ask for it. But then she did. "Lord, make that happen. You're the only one who can."

4

People scurried and rushed about on every floor Hughes passed. He caught a glimpse of two men he figured for fibbies, but he was looking for Konopka. He hoped he would either be in the accounting section or in his own office on the sixth floor.

He was in luck. He found Konopka stashing a pile of books in a wall safe in the accounting office. Konopka was alone.

Hughes strode in, shutting the door behind him. "Harvey, old pal, I got a problem," Hughes said as he set down his briefcase. The gun butt lay in his palm, reversed so that the barrel and silencer were encased up his sleeve.

Konopka was a dark, Indian-looking man with thick lips and a flat nose. "You know the FBI is here?"

"So I have learned."

446

Konopka jammed the files into the hidden safe. "When it rains, it pours," he mumbled, and Hughes waited patiently.

"Say, I was wondering about that safe you have access to, where Croase used to keep several hundred thou in small bills. For emergencies and whatnot."

Konopka stopped and stared at him. "I don't have access to that."

"Yes, you do."

"I don't. I swear."

"You used to brag about it. It's right over in the next room, isn't it?"

"Yes, but—"

"And you're head of the accounting office, correct?"

"But I don't—"

"Come on, Harvey, you know we're in big trouble. What do you say you and I make a little deal?"

Konopka wiped beads of sweat off his upper lip. He took off the thin, steel glasses. "I'm married, David. I have seven kids. I can't—"

"You could take Strock's and my five hundred a cadaver."

"That was a mistake, and I'll give it back."

"I'm not an Indian giver, Harvey. I just want a little of that money. For old times' sake. Look, from what I hear the fibbies are going to crack this place wide open. They're not onto us yet, but they will be. Way I figure it, we should get what we can while the gettin's good."

Konopka breathed noisily. "You think the FBI has Croase for good?"

"Definitely. No question. This place is ready to go up in smoke. So what do you say, just let me look in, take some of the bread—no one will miss it in all the confusion—and you and I part complete friends."

Konopka rubbed his eyebrows. "You think it's really coming down."

Hughes nodded. "Absolutely."

"All right. I'll show you. But you have to promise you won't—"

"I promise. Let's go." Hughes grabbed the suitcase and Konopka led him into the small, vice president's office. Kon-

447

opka went to a picture, took it off its hook, and exposed a wall safe. In two minutes' time he had it opened.

"See, I knew you could do it."

Hughes opened the briefcase. When Konopka saw the contents, he gasped. "Where did all that come from?"

"Inheritance from my grandpa. He was a funeral director too. Like Willard."

Konopka stepped back as Hughes began grabbing the bills out of the safe and lining them neatly in the briefcase. Konopka said, "Just take a few piles. Not more than—."

Scowling, Hughes leaned closer to Konopka, and the diminutive man stepped back. "That's good," Hughes said. He continued to keep his left hand concealed at his side. Finishing, Hughes smiled and said, "Now, Harvey, you and I go way back. You know I wouldn't want to have to do anything hurtful to you. But I always hated a haggling woman. Or man, as the case may be."

Hughes closed the briefcase, not latching it. Then he flipped out the gun. Konopka fell back, tripping over a chair, then catching himself on the credenza.

"Now, David, you know we had a deal. I won't talk about anything."

"I realize that. Just one last question. You know where Listra Croase is?"

"You'll leave if I tell you?"

"Of course."

"She's up in the safe room with Dr. Croase and the boy and someone else."

"Thanks. Now as I promised, I'm going to leave. But only after—"

Two claps erupted from the gun. As the bullets slammed into Konopka's chest, he was thrown back, then lay crumpled against a wall.

"I finish every bit of business," Hughes said, latching the briefcase. He went to the door and looked out. "Still alone." He whistled. "Ah, to be invincible." He chuckled and walked to the outside door after jamming the pistol into his belt.

The hall was alive with people moving back and forth with books, files, papers. No one seemed sure of what they were doing, even though Hughes knew they'd drilled it more than a few times. The elevator bells pinged across the hall, and Hughes quickly shut the accounting room door, leaving it open just a slit. Two workers stepped off and hurried down the hallway. Hughes listened intently. One said to the other, "There're more FBI people on the way supposedly. And cops."

Hughes leaned up against the wall and cursed. "It really is coming down." He rushed to the window and, stepping over Konopka's blood-soaked body, looked out into the parking lot. Two cop cars screeched through the back entrance, their lights on and sirens blaring. Hughes swore again. Then he looked across the field to the factory and beyond. The helicopter's rotors were just beginning to turn. He gazed at it a moment, thinking.

"So that's what Croase is doing?" He smiled. "Well, I might just be able to beat them all to the exit door." He grabbed the briefcase and hurried out the door, this time oblivious to anyone who might see him.

5

Martin Croase stood in the small safe room, mopped at his head with a white handkerchief, and said, "Let's get going." He had already released Kingston, but the handcuffs were still on his wrists.

Croase opened a door at the back of the room. Inside, Tommy saw the first steps of a spiral staircase, straight up and around a pole. Listra waved her gun at Tommy and Kingston. "Get up. We're going for a ride."

One of the briefcases in his left hand, Croase climbed the stairway with the Uzi pointed up. Tommy could see nothing above them. When Croase stopped, there was a scraping noise, then the whir and whoosh of electrical equipment. Fluorescent light shone down through the hole. Croase threw the first briefcase through the hole, then returned for the second and third. Still holding the Uzi out in front of him, he

449

called down to Listra, "Have them come up. You come up behind them. You'll have to carry one of these briefcases up here."

Listra said, "I've got enough to do without—"

"Shut up!" Croase yelled. "You want two million dollars or not?"

She sniffed royally, then prodded Tommy with her semi-automatic.

6

From where Debuss stood, the noisy blast of air at the top of the stairs seemed to fill everything. The room was eerily alive with the sounds of fans, electrical motors, and numerous noises too mingled to separate. The whole building vibrated under the power of the upper fans. The reason they hadn't noticed it before was because the door had been soundproofed with a thick layer of fiberglass cushion. Ray whispered to Andi, "Are you sure you want to go in? There may be gunfire."

"I'm not afraid," she answered. "If I can get Tommy unhurt, that's all I care about." Her jaw was set. Ray wasn't about to argue with her. He figured she had a right to be there, and she knew how to handle a .38, if it came to that.

Debuss stepped out onto the main floor and Nakayami said, "This way."

Before them straight ahead was a maze of pipes, twisted and at odd angles, covered with thick, white insulation. Debuss and Nakayami were parallel, striding ahead of everyone.

To their right was a long cinder block wall. It closed off the area at the top of the elevators, concealing the cables and protecting them. They had to go down the aisleway through the piping and then around. As the two FBI agents and Nakayami cautiously stepped into the piping area, Ray crouched and looked ahead through the piping. He signaled to Andi to get down. Lyle stooped behind them.

Ray watched as Debuss ducked to get under the pipes. It was foolhardy. He was an open target. Why weren't they

450

clinging to the walls, keeping down? They were too confident. Ray waited. "Let them get to the corner," he said to Andi, watching behind a latticework of pipes.

☐ ☐ ☐

Listra prodded Kingston and Tommy down the corridor. Martin Croase stood low by the stairwell hole listening. He heard voices, and he crouched behind a pipe, peering through the maze. He cocked the Uzi.

Then he saw Nakayami with a tall man Croase recognized as one of the special agents. Croase raised the Uzi, hesitated, then mumbled, "This is what it's been all about."

He jerked the trigger.

☐ ☐ ☐

The moment the gunfire resounded in the noisy room, Ray knocked Andi and Lyle back behind him. "Down!"

He saw Nakayami lifted backwards, blood already staining his shirt. Debuss dropped too. Miles fired three shots, but obviously had no target.

"Stay down," Ray yelled, and dove forward behind a thick brass tube. Nakayami lay moaning. Ten more bullets ripped through the air, pinging on pipes and splattering bits of white pipe insulation all over the floor. Miles got off two more shots.

"He's at the corner," Miles shouted back to Ray. Two more rounds slammed into the door, leaving neat holes. Another shot caught Nakayami in the side. The small man seemed to be unconscious.

"Pull him out," Miles yelled to Ray.

Ray waited, then groped forward and grabbed Nakayami at the armpits. There was shouting on the other side of the pipes, and Ray saw Croase hurry to the left with two silver briefcases in his hands. Miles fired several more shots, then dropped his first clip and rammed in a second. He stood and scurried to the corner, then stuck out a piece of wood.

A flurry of rounds erupted, shattering the wood and spewing chunks of concrete, Sheetrock, and cinder block.

Ray, Andi, and Lyle hovered over Nakayami and Debuss. Both were still alive. Nakayami had been hit in the chest, side, and leg, but he opened his eyes and said, "I'll be OK. Stop Croase."

Debuss had two in the shoulder.

Ray said to Lyle, "Go back downstairs and call 911 for an ambulance."

Lyle stood and ran out the door.

"Get out your .38," Ray said to Andi, wrapping Nakayami's wounds in his jacket. Debuss pushed himself up into a sitting position. He flipped his Beretta to Ray and pulled out the three clips with his good hand. "Do it," he said.

Ray answered, "You're sure."

"Yeah. You got to. I'm out of this one."

Nodding, Ray took the gun and clips. Miles crouched behind a twist of piping and radioed for the backup. The dispatcher said policemen were already at TWI. "We've got two men down. Get an ambulance on the way."

The radio crackled with static. "Already on the way."

Ray stood at the corner with Miles, then turned to Andi. "Give me your jacket."

She pulled it off.

Ray jammed Miles's stick into the arm and held it out. Nothing happened.

He looked across the aisleway. There were three chillers—long, heavy tubes that cooled the air for the air conditioning equipment. He figured he could kneel behind one and get a fix on what Croase was doing. "Here goes nothing," he said. He leaped across the aisle behind the first chiller. No more shots boomed in the hallway.

"He's gone around the corner," Ray shouted. As he stood, Andi leaped over behind him.

"Let me go first," he said. "You wait for Miles and some backup."

She shook her head.

"Wait, please, Andi. This is too dangerous."

452

She shook her head again. Her face was wet with sweat. Miles signaled with his gun he'd go down the aisle, but Ray said, "Let me cover you." He darted down the hallway behind the chillers, keeping his head down. Andi was right behind him.

As they crouched, panting, behind the chiller, Ray said, "All right, you're in this. At least keep your gun pointed up, not down. Like I taught you."

She nodded, mute with determination.

"But you've got to stay behind me. You can back me up. As I move, you cover." He could see the fear in her eyes, but he knew her greater fear was for Tommy's safety, and that drove out any terror she might have of Croase's Uzi. He sensed, though, that he'd have to keep her back. She was too on edge, too willing to take the risks. He had to be the one to do that.

He signaled to Miles to move down the aisle.

A moment later, all three stood at the next corner. They'd completed half of the circle around the cinder block center of the room. Around the next corner should be the stairs. On the perimeter of the space stood three huge heating units. More cover. But also perfect for an ambush.

"Behind the heaters," Ray said.

Andi didn't wait. She was out ahead of both Ray and Miles. The FBI man swore, and just as she reached the open air, more shots rang out and electric sparks showered behind her. She fell down and blood began to ooze from the top of her shoulder.

Ray shouted, "Stay down."

She grabbed her shoulder. "It just grazed me. He's in the next doorway."

A dozen more bullets thudded into the walls and heaters. But no one was hit. Ray sensed that Croase was shooting wild. Whatever gaming Croase had trained himself in, he knew nothing about the real thing. And that was something Ray knew plenty about—a primary advantage.

"No mistakes," Ray said again, as he dove for Andi behind the heater.

□ □ □

Croase knew the layout of the maintenance tower. They had to go around the main elevator enclosure, up another flight of stairs, and then around again to reach the spiral stair to the roof. Beyond the piping and the chillers were three large heating units on the side. He stood in the stairwell, watching, hoping to take out one more of his pursuers before he ran up the stairs. Getting Nakayami was a particular pleasure, but he wanted Mazaris even more than the Japanese. Mazaris would be a virtual medal.

As he thought about it, though, he quickly pictured the best way to stop them. It had to be in the maze on the second floor.

They were slow in their pursuit, but he knew he could not just go to the roof and set off the radio detonator. The helicopter might not yet be there. More important, this was the real fun of it. For a moment, he realized this was what he'd wanted more than anything else in life. Even the money somehow took second place. Blowing a man away—several away—he'd envied Goge about that. But now was his chance, and he wasn't going to lose it.

He had already taken the two briefcases he was carrying to the top; Listra had the third, and she was well out ahead of them. Now he waited at the bottom of the stairwell trying to nail Mazaris and the woman behind the heating unit.

He stepped down to the floor and rose.

Instantly, two shots whizzed by his head. Miles.

Croase fell back. They were operating as a team. He knew now he'd have to be more careful.

"Come any closer and I blow away the boy," Croase yelled, starting back up the stairs. He wondered how much ammunition they had. It couldn't be much. But they weren't wasting shells either.

Andi called out, "Tommy! Tommy! Are you there?"

There was no answer.

He saw Ray lean out from the right side of the heating unit and fire. Croase backed up one more stair. Then he saw the woman creeping closer to the stairwell behind the heating units. She was well concealed. She might just pull off a good shot. Croase couldn't get a clear aim. He waited and counted five more seconds. Then he emptied his Uzi at the heating unit she was behind, hoping one would go through. Mazaris cut loose with two more rounds into the stairwell behind him. But he wasn't even close.

Croase knew now he couldn't afford to let the girl get closer. He pulled the door shut and sprang up the stairs. At the top, he released the empty clip and jammed another into the Uzi.

7

Listra prodded Tommy out of the second stairwell. She knew they had to get all the way around the circle to the back where the spiral stairs went up to the roof. Immediately past the stairs was an air handler, filled with filters tilted toward the ceiling and gray with dust. They came around the end of the air handler, completing the top of the last circle. She headed up the final corridor by a fan room. Inside was a fan with blades the size of a ship's propeller. Twice, Kingston stopped and made protests, having pulled the tape off his face and spit out the gauze that muffled him.

But Listra jammed the gun against Tommy's temple. "Do you want the boy dead?"

Kingston kept moving, though as slowly as he thought he could afford. He heard the repeated gunfire below and prayed that whoever was following would not get shot.

After another long burst, Croase came up behind them, holding his Uzi up. When the group reached the corridor between the elevators and the fan room, Croase called to Listra. "I have a plan. Shut off the fan and open the door to the fan room."

Listra gazed in confusion at the three gray throw switch boxes on the wall. Croase caught up to her. "Forget it. Get on the roof. I'll take care of this."

Shoving Kingston and Tommy once more, Croase pushed the two into the room with the stairs to the roof.

Listening intently, Croase pulled the left arm on the switch box to the left. A moment later, the shaking stopped

455

and the fan slowed down, then ground to a stop. The whole building suddenly settled into a tense quiet. The walls ceased to vibrate with the power of the fan. Croase cocked his ear toward the hallway, panting and focusing on the footsteps of his pursuers. Then he opened the steel-covered door to the fan and left it open at an angle. His heart hammering, he hid behind the wall of the last ladder well, signaling to Listra to go up the ladder.

"I want Mazaris," he murmured.

As Kingston mounted the stairs with Tommy and Listra behind him, Croase looked up and to his surprise saw that the hatch was already open. But he didn't have time to worry. He listened for any sounds down the corridor.

8

Ray, Miles, and Andi stood outside the door to the second stairwell. "You throw it open," Ray said to Andi. "Lou, cover me from behind the heater."

Ray checked the clip in his Beretta, then took it out and placed it in his pocket. "Always better to be sure," he said as he slid the third clip into the brown handle. He had one clip left. Andi had already reloaded her .38. He nodded to her. "Ready."

She jerked back the door, and lay back against the wall. Miles aimed up over the edge of the top of the door. "Do it," he said.

With a quick, deft swivel Ray stepped in, crouching, the gun straight out ahead of him.

No one was there. He ascended the stairs slowly, the gun still out ahead of him. When he reached the top, he signaled to Miles and Andi. Abruptly, the whole building stopped shaking. The noise level went down to a dull roar. Everyone froze. Ray stepped around the corner.

"No mistakes," Ray murmured again as he pressed forward, his shirt rubbing against the wall.

Miles and Andi were behind him. Ray moved slowly past the bank of air filters, then came around the corner. A silver metal door stood open ahead of him. Was that the way to the stairwell?

He told himself to go slow, be careful. His heart seemed to deafen him, and as he advanced, he signaled to Andi and Miles to stop. He crept forward along the wall, the door in front of him. He couldn't see beyond it down the corridor. If they had gone in there, why had they left the door open?

He approached the doorway cautiously. Andi stood at the corner and waited, her gun up.

Ray had to make his move. He edged up to the frame of the doorway, his automatic up, both hands on the handle. Then he pivoted and came around into the doorway, crouching low, pointing the gun every way, ready for the slightest movement.

Again, there was none. It was a huge fan, silent. Through the blades he could see more concrete space. He peered past the blades, looking for a sign of someone, or at least a stairwell.

Andi came up behind him. She whispered, "What is it?"

Suddenly, the door slammed behind her and threw her against Ray. At the same moment, the fan started up. In a second, a wild, horrible suction was pulling them both toward the fan blades.

As his face crunched against the safety bars that shielded the face of the fan, Ray heard the stutter of the Uzi. But he felt weak, and the noise was so great, it drowned out all thought. The blades whirled with a deadly vibrato and the wind sucked at him. At the same time, Andi rolled down and backward against the bars spaced a foot apart before the face of the fan. Her head tilted back through the metal slats, and her hair strung out straight toward the blades. Ray realized if her hair caught in the fan, her neck would be broken instantly.

Ray screamed, "Andi!" He leaned down to grab her head, dropping his gun. Instantly the pistol was sucked into the fan and out the other side.

A moment later he realized she had fainted. The big blades whirred, and he felt his whole body flattening under the pressure.

"Help us! Somebody!" he screamed. "Help!"

The moment Croase hit the switch and the fan started up, the door slammed shut. He caught Miles by surprise. Croase dropped him with a burst from the Uzi. He thought about opening the fan door and nailing Mazaris once and for all, but he knew that would be impossible with the fan on. Once he was on the roof, all of his enemies were finished anyway.

He turned around and sped through the last door. The briefcases sat waiting on the floor. He had done it. Now all he had to do was deal with his dear wife, and he was on his way.

Turning into the room, he saw Listra halfway up the stairwell, prodding Tommy. Kingston was out of sight, obviously already on top. "Get through!" he yelled.

But Listra looked down at him, her face dark with menace. He couldn't read it, but he thought he detected a smile on her face as she looked away.

Something was up. He could feel it. He reached the stairwell just as her shoes disappeared through the trap door.

10

Hughes knew it would be close, but he hoped he could get there before the others. He lucked out. He already had a universal key to the maintenance door on the fifteenth floor, and after stepping inside, he shut it and made sure it was still locked.

He passed the hatch to what he knew was the safe room. It was still closed. He made it up to the roof just as the helicopter began making its descent for pickup. Below, he heard the shooting and waited. Patton was taking his time centering the helicopter on the small concrete pad, slowly descending and wheeling. As the cold prop wash battered Hughes's face, he waved to Patton confidently. He couldn't see Patton's face. The old Huey that TWI purchased at an Army auction at Croase's insistence hovered, its wide side doors already open. The long runners underneath the helo touched down.

Hughes watched as first old professor Kingston came through the hatch. Then the boy. Finally, Listra. She ran to Hughes just as the helicopter rotors began to idle.

Finally Croase poked his head through the metal opening in the concrete.

Hughes smiled as he aimed his .45 at Croase's chest. He said, "Imagine meeting you here." *I am invincible, and smart, too.*

Croase looked stricken as he turned from Hughes to Listra. "So you really think you're going to get away with this?"

"Sure I do," Hughes said, grinning. "Me and Listy go way back."

"I should have known."

"Because you're a fool, Martin," Listra said. She patted the briefcase. "All of four million, honey." She said to Hughes, "Take the other two from him, dear."

Hughes stepped toward Croase, the .45 still trained on his chest.

"One thing you didn't reckon with, though, David," Croase said, his eyes suddenly bright with renewed confidence.

"What's that?" Hughes answered as he grabbed one of the briefcases.

"Johnny Goge."

Hughes's face went white, and he wheeled around. Goge stood in the bay of the helicopter with his pistol trained on Hughes's forehead. Listra screamed. Hughes tried to get his own gun up on Goge. He wasn't fast enough. The bullet blew his brains all over the roof. Hughes's pistol clattered onto the concrete as he pitched backwards, sprawling.

"No!" Listra screamed. She gesticulated at her husband, then bent down to touch Hughes's hand. "You murderer!"

"And what was he going to do to me, dearest?" Croase stalked by her, threw the three briefcases onto the helicopter, then added Hughes's satchel to the pile. Jillie appeared at Goge's side in the bay and stepped out onto the roof with Croase.

"Oh, Listy, dear," Croase said. Listra looked up. "You didn't know about Jillie here. I wanted you to know—just in case you thought you were putting anything over on me."

He helped Jillie back into the helicopter and glanced up at Goge. "Where's the radio detonator?" He looked over the edge of the building and saw the water cannons hurling their discharge at the gathering of students. "It'll be only a second now," Croase said, grinning. This was truly a day of glory.

The fan's powerful suction was overwhelming. Andi's head swayed nearer to the blades, caught between two of the bars. Ray wedged his foot between the slats and held her shoulder with his foot, blocking her from sinking closer. But he couldn't hold her for long. Her long hair whipped and lashed in the suction, streaming closer to the blades as she sagged down.

"Andi!" he screamed. "Andi!"

Her eyes were closed. The floor vibrated, and the metal bars buzzed under his flesh. He pulled at her collar, trying to get a firm hold. Then her eyes suddenly opened.

"Andi!"

Immediately, she moved and he lost his hold with his foot. The fan jerked her inward.

"*Andi!*"

She looked up, her eyes darting about in fear. As she rolled closer to the blades, he lunged and grabbed her belt. "Get hold of a bar!" he shouted.

She reached up and gripped the bar.

As she moved, the .38 clattered to the floor and slid toward the fan, then blew out the backdraft. The pull of the air tugged at her hair and threw her head back.

"It's too strong," she yelled, trying to push back through the bars.

The suction deepened as the blades accelerated. Ray knew he had to get to the switch box. "Hold on!" he shouted, then reached toward the door. There was a small handle, but not much to grab onto. Andi seemed to be holding tight, but he knew she was weakening. The blower only seemed to be accelerating. Sooner or later, Ray knew, something would get caught and break a neck or pull them into the blades.

Ray held her around the waist with one hand, his foot against the bars, bracing him. His shirt ripped free from his pants. The suction tugged at it and whipped it back and forth in the wind.

"What can we do?" Andi screamed above the noise, getting herself into a better position.

Ray made sure she was safe outside the bars, then leaned against the suction and reached for the door. With a last surge of strength he lashed out toward the door, trying for the handle.

He missed, and fell back against the bars.

"The radio detonator!" Andi screamed. "He'll get it."

Ray lunged once more at the door and caught the handle. It turned, but pushing it open would take several men in this suction. He leaned against it, then pushed with all his strength. It cracked slightly. His strength was going. His whole body felt like sodden cereal. He pushed at the door again, and his feet slid out from him, whopping him face down onto the concrete.

Andi crawled on the floor, bracing a foot against the bars. Together they pushed against the door.

It wouldn't budge.

☐ ☐ ☐

Miles knew he was hit bad. Blood pooled under him, but he wasn't dead, and somehow he had the feeling he wouldn't die. Not yet.

Through the glaze in his mind, he sensed that something had happened to Ray and Andi. He lay face down and listened. It was a fan. A big fan.

In a moment, the realization came to him. He had to get to the switch boxes.

Blood surged into his throat, but he spit it out onto the floor. He pushed himself up with his hands. His Beretta lay in front of him. The door Croase had gone through was closed.

He raked at the cinder block wall with his fingers. *Get the switch,* he told himself. *Just get the switch.*

His breath came in knotty gasps. The fan roared inside the room. He could hear Andi screaming.

Just get the switch, he told himself. The pain in his side erupted. He closed his eyes, then lunged one last time at the box. His fingers reached the gray throw lever. As he fell forward it came down.

□ □ □

The sound of the fan engine stopped immediately, though the fan was still running. Ray and Andi relaxed instinctively as the pressure lessened. The fan slowed, then stopped. Ray got to his knees and pulled Andi to her feet. He was cold and weak. His arms shook. "You OK?"

She nodded and pointed to one of the sprinklers above. "We've got to get going."

"Thank God you're OK," Ray said, pushing gingerly at the door. He prayed Croase was not waiting for them. Their weapons were gone out through the latticework behind the fan exhaust. Something was blocking the door though.

He leaned against it and shoved the door open a foot. He knew instantly that the gray pants were Miles's. He pushed through the opening. "Lou!"

A moment later, Andi stood next to him.

Miles lay on the floor, face up. "Through there," he whispered. He crooked his finger at the door. "I'll make it." Ray picked up the Baretta. Miles held up his last full clip.

"Take that," he rasped. "Get Croase."

When Ray opened the door, he could hear the helicopter through the hole. He saw a single sprinkler directly above him. He prayed one more time as he ran for the ladder.

11

As Ray climbed the staircase, he told himself to be ready and prayed that his aim would be straight. As Andi climbed the ladder behind him, he poked his head through the hole.

Listra knelt to his left next to a body, looking at the Vietnam-era Huey helicopter. Tommy and Kingston were behind her, also gaping at the chopper. Ray immediately brought his gun up. Croase sat in the doorway, one foot on a runner. He had something in his hand and was beginning to press some buttons. The helicopter started to lift off.

Ray leaped through the hole, stood, and aimed for Croase's chest. Just as he squeezed the trigger, the CEO looked up and began to grin. Ray fired once, twice. Croase tumbled backward into the helicopter, his facial expression reflecting total surprise. The thing in his hand fell out onto the concrete. The Huey was in the air now.

Another man appeared in the doorway, pulling Croase in, and for a moment Ray stared at him, a stab of recollection gripping him. But there was no time to think of who the man was. It was just an image of something from long ago.

Firing at the doorway two more time times, Ray watched helplessly as the helo veered away from the building in the direction of the pump room. Then as it moved off the edge of the TWI tower, Ray aimed at the tail rotor, close to the center. "Just hit once," he murmured and squeezed off the remaining rounds. On the fifth shot there was a sharp ping. The helicopter suddenly stopped its ascent and hovered a moment, then began to revolve slowly over the pump house, making no forward progress. Ray watched as it rotated more and more swiftly, descending. Out from the other side, he thought he saw someone plummet to the ground in a flash of silver, then the helicopter struck the side of the building and exploded.

Ray fell back as a fireball ascended. Then, jumping to his feet, he turned and stooped to pick up the radio detonator. *Safe,* he thought.

Then he heard Listra scream. "Get back!"

☐ ☐ ☐

As Andi advanced, Listra stood shivering, the gun on Tommy's temple. The angry woman led him backwards to the edge of the concrete pad. Andi stood panting, the .38 still in her hand, telling herself to be calm, to think, to speak directly and honestly. Kingston was next to her.

Tommy said, "Mrs. Croase, you should give up. It's—"

"Shut up!"

She leveled her gun at Andi. "You want to meet Rafa?"

Tommy tried to wriggle free, but Listra cuffed him with the gun on the ear. "Stop it, boy! Stop now, or I shoot all of them."

Behind her, Andi heard Lyle say to Ray, "Miles, Debuss, and Nakayami are on the way to the hospital." An elation filled her that the others were all right. *Now just solve this last problem,* she thought, *and we're home free.* She watched Listra's face, trying to decide if she should try to reason with her. But what else was there to do? She fought back a desire to rush her, grab Tommy, and topple her over the edge. But she knew Tommy could easily be pulled along.

Trying to speak low, Andi said to Ray, "She's talking about Rafa. I think she's lost it."

"I haven't lost anything!" Listra screamed.

Andi stood straight, stilling a sudden shaking in her abdomen.

"I have your precious boy, don't I?" Listra said. "What will you give me in exchange for him?"

As Ray stepped forward, Andi waved him off. "Let me talk to her," she said.

As Andi moved closer, Rod Tower came through the hole. After looking around, he spoke into the radio. She heard him say, "Get the SWAT team on the ground on the south side of the building. There's a crazy woman up here."

Listra eyed everyone fiercely and said, "I'm not afraid of you. Rafa can take care of all of you."

Tommy called to his mother, "I'm OK, Mom. I'm all right." Andi could see the fear in his eyes, but she sensed Tommy was far from panic. A strange pride filled her that her son could be so controlled under such circumstances.

Andi moved forward cautiously. "Listra, you can still get out of this."

"No, I can't. It's over. The only thing to do is the big one. That's all that's left."

464

"The big one?"

"Complete resurrection."

"Listra, you're talking craziness!"

Listra waved the gun at Andi. "No, you're the ones who are crazy. No one would listen to me. They all went their own way. Well, now Rafa and I are leading things. From now on."

Andi moved to within ten feet of Listra and Tommy. With Ray and the others behind her, she felt strangely quiet. Listra's eyes were wild and agitated, and as Andi moved closer, they narrowed. A confident gleam shone in them. "Come no closer," she said, bending Tommy to the right under the press of the gun.

Andi said, "Listra, your husband is dead—"

"Gone with Rafa," Listra seethed. "I know where he is."

"Rafa is not who you think he is," Andi answered. She spoke methodically, carefully, each word precisely enunciated. Tommy still didn't appear to be afraid, but she couldn't take the chance he might do something radical. He wriggled a little, and the handcuffs were still on his hands. Andi said, "Tommy, just be still."

He nodded. "I'm all right, Mom."

Andi looked back to Listra. "Rafa is not almighty. He is not God, Listra. He has deceived you, completely deceived you."

Listra's lips were trembling, but she said fiercely, "You are the one who was deceived." She waved the gun momentarily, then jammed it back against Tommy's head. "Rafa can protect me. Us. All of us. He'll raise me from the dead. He'll show the world his power, my power. The world will know what we have done, Rafa and I." Listra stepped up onto the ledge. Tommy was still in front of her, on the main concrete pad. But one backward move and Tommy could pitch over the side with her.

Andi swallowed. Now her heart was thundering. She shook her head. Her voice rattled on with a hard-edged quaver. "Rafa is a demon, Listra. He's a demon who has deceived you and tried to deceive all of us. You know the truth. You know what Jesus did. Only one Person has been raised from the dead. Rafa cannot help you."

"He can!" Listra looked down the side of the building to her right and stepped back to the edge of the concrete pad. "My husband thought the boy was unique. The research team thought the boy had a gift. But no, it is I who have the gift. It is I who will overcome. It is I who will show the world. Rafa will do far more than what the TUT or any drug can do. Rafa will raise the dead. He will raise me. And the boy will die. I will prove it once and for all."

She's not going over! Andi's mind screamed. *Not that.* Panic surged through her, and she glanced at Ray, fighting off nausea. The woman was crazy. Forcing control into her voice, though, Andi said, "What are you going to do, Listra—jump? Do you want to die?"

"Yes!" The woman's face was a mask of darkness. The lips twisted with malevolence. "I want to go all the way into death and then come back and tell about it. That is what I want." She gesticulated with the gun, then brought it back to the side of Tommy's jaw.

Ray suddenly said, "There's a SWAT team in position, Listra. Do you want them to shoot you? Can Rafa patch up an obliterated head?"

"Yes!" Listra screamed. "Rafa can do anything!"

Andi said evenly, "Rafa is a demon, Listra. He can't do anything!"

But the woman wasn't listening anymore. She babbled, "I was the one who went first. I was to be the guide. Then my husband let this moron become the important one. He has destroyed everything. But Rafa will deal with my husband too."

Listra fixed her stare on Andi. "And you—I will show you all. The whole world. I will prove once and for all what is there, beyond the grave. I will be the one to come back and tell. I will tell the world."

A slight wind whipped at her hair. Her face was streaked with dark makeup. As Andi watched, a terrible helplessness gripped her. This woman was in the grip of forces totally beyond all of them. *Please, God,* her mind uttered, *please show us the way out of this.*

Swallowing hard, she moved closer. "I'm going to drop the gun, Listra. No harm to you. Just release Tommy." She dropped the .38, and the gun clunked and bounced on concrete. Andi said forcing control over her voice, though something in her screamed that she had to leap now. "There is no reason to prove anything, Listra. Jesus has already proved it. Now just step back and put the gun—"

"Jesus! Always Jesus," Listra yelled. "Jesus is nothing. Rafa knows. He has told me. Jesus means nothing. He can do nothing. Rafa alone can raise the dead."

Andi glanced at Ray behind her. He was closer now, the gun still in his hand. He started to move it up, but Andi shook her head. "Listra," she said, "let Tommy go. We'll let you prove whatever—"

"No! The boy is the contra-proof. They thought the boy could do miracles. They thought the boy was special. Now they will see he also is mortal."

"Give me the gun, Listra. You will be taken care of. There are people who can help you now." A terror broke inside of Andi. Listra was really going to do it. No one could stop her. She had to get closer. Maybe if she could grab Tommy at the last moment—

Listra laughed chillingly. "You think I'm insane. That's it. You think I belong in an institution. You think I've lost my mind. Well, it is you who have lost your minds, with your petty religion and your petty beliefs and your petty prayers and games and words. None of it amounts to anything next to what I will accomplish."

"What will you accomplish, Listra?" Andi tried to move without looking like she was moving, edging forward as she emphasized different words. She was less than five feet from Tommy now. The dizzying height off the edge of the fifteen-story building made her feel nauseous. But she had to get Tommy before—

Then Ray, behind her, said, "Listra, look at all that has happened. What has Rafa led TWI to do? To kill homeless people? To murder children? To conduct experiments on people like Nazi doctors? Think about what this Rafa—and

467

Benreu too—has led you all to do. How can that kind of person rule the world? How can he raise the dead? Why didn't he raise those others, if he could do that?"

Listra's face twitched, but she shook her head. "You all refuse to believe. I'll just have to show you."

She leveled the gun at Andi. "You first, Christian!"

Tommy screamed, knocking her arm upward. The gun went off into the air. Andi ducked instinctively. Listra stepped back to get her balance. But there was nothing to step onto. She twisted, her arm around Tommy's neck. Then she was falling over backwards.

Andi leaped at them. Tommy flung out his cuffed hands. "Mom!"

They touched.

But Listra's left arm had him tight. Tommy jerked backward with her.

Andi screamed. Ray leaped forward.

"Mom!"

Instantly, light flashed and a violent wind blasted everyone back. There was another flash of light, like an explosion in a cave and the sound of breaking glass. Listra screamed something incomprehensible.

Then all was silence.

Ray reached the wall and looked over. Andi crumpled to the ground behind him. "No! No!"

□ □ □

Ray searched the ground for Tommy. But he saw only Listra, spread-eagle, obviously dead. The others crowded behind him. He leaned way out to look at the building. Then he saw it. Two stories below—a shattered window. He whipped around and knelt down by Andi. "Come on!"

She looked up at him with teary eyes. "He's not—?"

"Something has happened."

He pulled her up.

Kyle shouted, "Where are you going?"

"Down to the fourteenth floor," Ray yelled as they ran past everyone to the hatch.

468

12

Tommy lay dazed on a brown carpet by a desk. As he turned to the window, he noticed his glasses lying broken on the floor. But the shattered glass had not cut him. He stared out at the two shining beings standing in the window like two suns. Strangely, their faces were clear to his myopic eyes.

"Who are you?" he said. But he knew one was Kartle. The other had dark hair and looked almost Indian. The second being started to speak, but suddenly there were shouts outside the door. Then Ray and his mother and some others burst into the room. His mother was crying, Ray was hugging both of them, and everyone was cheering and yelling.

"What happened?" Ray yelled above the din.

Tommy tried to focus his eyes. Without the glasses, he could make out only a fuzzy, funny face. A surge of joy like the roar of water in a tunnel filled him. "Kartle," he said. He turned and pointed. "They broke the window and threw me in here. I don't know how it happened. It just happened."

□ □ □

Ray turned to look at the broken window. There in the light stood Trell and the being Tommy called Kartle. Trell looked exactly as he had that day over twenty-five years ago when eight-year-old Ray Mazaris survived the impact of John Godwin's car.

Ray started to speak, but Trell raised his arm and smiled. Then they were both gone.

Stunned, Ray stood still only a moment. Then he ran to the window and peered out. Tears seared his eyes as he looked up into the sky. He shook his head with wonder and a sense of gratitude filled his chest. "He really was an angel," he whispered and shook his head again. "And after all these years I've—"

His throat knotted, and he turned and hugged Andi and Tommy again. "We're going out for ice cream every night for a week," he said suddenly.

Andi wiped at the tears on her cheeks and refused to let go of Tommy, even as someone cut off his handcuffs. "I was so afraid," she said.

Tommy nodded. "I was, but then I wasn't anymore. It was like—" He looked at Ray, at Dr. Kingston, and then at his mother. "It was like I knew God was there the whole time. I just knew it. Like Dr. Kingston told me."

Below them only the sounds of the burning helicopter and the gathering crowd reached their ears. After Tommy told the story three more times, everyone settled down and filed out of the room. Lyle began trying to get interviews, and the whole building suddenly seemed to be alive with police, special agents, and paramedics.

Reaching the main floor, they headed out of the building. Andi walked between Ray and Tommy, gripping their hands. "I'm never letting either of you out of my sight again," she said.

Ray grinned.

Tommy said, "Do you think it was really them, the angels? Kartle and Trell?" He looked from Ray to Andi and back.

Ray answered, "If it wasn't angels, it was God and Jesus in angel disguises."

"Wow!" Tommy said. "Wait till I tell this one to Grandpa Darcasian."

"Only after you've had a good hot meal," Andi said, hugging him again. For a moment, they all stood in the parking lot together, then Andi said, "Ray, what happened up there? When we were going in, you got this funny look and you said you'd tell me later. What was that?"

Ray sighed. "Something I should have learned long ago."

"Well, what?"

"That I'm not alone. It doesn't all depend on me. Just to trust that God knows what He's doing and all I have to do is do the best I can."

She suddenly poked him. "That's all it was?"

He rolled his eyes and shrugged. "For me that was quite a revelation."

She smiled meekly. "It is. I guess we're all just learning it." Her deep brown eyes flashed in the morning light, and

470

the sunlight gave her hair a soft glow that seemed to come from the inside. He knew he was more in love with her than ever, and he knew now they could start really living. He felt Tommy studying his face and Andi smiling at him with fervent love reflected in her eyes. Fighting off a tightness in his throat, Ray said, "Let's thank God for a minute."

"Let me go first," Tommy said enthusiastically as they bowed their heads.

EPILOGUE

The Japanese researcher, Dr. Nakayami, began a lengthy recovery in Holy Cross Hospital, pending his own trial for first degree murder. Andi, Tommy, and Dr. Kingston visited him several times and even shared the gospel with him, leaving him a Bible and several books on prophecy and apologetics. He was interested and promised to read them in the hospital. To Ray's mind, he was a repentant man, and he hoped he would be offered some clemency if he cooperated with the prosecutors.

Lyle Hornum quickly found a literary agent and struck a 50-50 deal with Ray, Andi, and Tommy for their whole story. Their half of the advance came to over $200,000, more than enough to allow them to think seriously about getting a house once they sealed their marriage promises.

FBI agents and federal attorneys pored through the files at TWI, gathering evidence for the numerous murders perpetrated in the name of research. Willard's Funeral Home was temporarily shut down, pending a family resolution of ownership and the vague hope of a recovery from the media blitz, which dubbed them "the Georgia Avenue Auschwitz." Records were discovered cataloguing Martin Croase's talks with "Benreu" and Johnny Goge.

Three bodies were found in the helicopter wreckage—Croase, his girlfriend, Jillie, and the pilot, Bill Patton. Tommy and Kingston and Ray knew a fourth person had been in the helicopter, but no one was sure what had happened to him. The FBI was sure from the records in Croase's office that Johnny Goge was the alphabet killer. A manhunt was in progress. But Johnny Goge, for the moment, had disappeared with several million dollars and a supply of TUT and TUT-B, or so they believed.

Lou Miles was taken to Bethesda Naval Hospital and treated there for wounds to the chest and abdomen. He crustily informed everyone that he was still in the middle of an investigation and was out in a couple of weeks. Ray and Andi invited him over to the house in Silver Spring a week later for a feast of roast beef, baked potatoes, green beans, and a potent, dark chocolate creme pie.

Miles dug into the beef with infectious enthusiasm as Dr. Kingston, Ray, Andi, and Tommy chattered about the events that almost led to their mass exit from life. Miles was full of talk about the alphabet murders and his sudden new interest in theology.

"You know, for the first time in my life I've thought about Jesus as a serious contender for divinity," Miles said between enormous pink bites of roast beef. "If you people still believe in Him after you've been through all this, He must really be something."

Ray smiled at Andi. It felt good to be making friends together, and somehow they both felt this man would be a friend for life. "I'm glad you're thinking about it, Lou. Funny though, the circumstances that bring us together."

Everyone ate with relish. Andi had served up an excellent meal.

After a silence, Andi said, "Ray thought he recognized this guy Johnny Goge, didn't you, honey?"

Ray nodded. "I've been thinking about it. But he looked like someone I knew years ago, someone named John Godwin. When I was eight, he lived on my street—" Ray explained about his NDE.

"I could check it," Miles said, "see if there's any connection."

Ray shrugged. "It was probably just a resemblance, but it kind of gives me the creeps."

"This whole thing gives me the creeps," Miles said, taking another bite.

"I'll agree to that," Kingston answered. The professor then launched into a joke, and soon everyone joined in with stories of their own. After a while, they turned to the subject of heaven and their mutual experiences.

Andi commented, "You know, my favorite passage is in Revelation 22, where it says we'll see God's face. That's the one thing I never quite understood about the experience, why that didn't happen."

"God's not ready for that yet," Ray answered. "Not until the new heavens and the new earth."

"When we eat of the tree of life," Kingston said. "That's what I want to do. And there'll be no more pain, and Jesus will wipe every tear from our eyes."

"When I see all that," Andi began, "I'll for sure—"

Tommy gasped. "What did you say, Dr. Kingston?"

Everyone turned to look at the boy. "About the tree of life?" Kingston asked.

"No, every tear." Tommy's face was a picture of shock and amazement.

"It says Jesus will wipe every tear from our eyes."

Tommy gulped. "That's what happened to me."

Watching the boy's eyes intently, Ray said, "What do you mean?"

"I just remembered another thing about when I was in heaven," Tommy said, his voice rising with excitement. The scene flashed through his mind. Kartle, tall and shining, stood next to him. Tommy was weeping. He'd been thinking about his mother, how she'd wonder and worry and miss him. And he wanted to go back. Then the other person, the powerful one, stood before them. He never said he was Jesus, but Tommy realized He had to be. Jesus' eyes were friendly, a color that couldn't be described. His hair was white, but He didn't look old. He raised His hand and touched Tommy's eyes. The tears instantly dried and a strange, dancing joy filled his heart. A moment later, everyone disappeared, and he was back in his body.

After the story, Tommy concluded, "I felt so peaceful and happy, like all the bad stuff was gone forever."

Ray listened with wide eyes, his heart suddenly beginning to pound. "So He wiped the tears from your eyes?"

Tommy shook his head. "Do you think He really was Jesus? For real?"

There was a long silence. Andi glanced at Ray. "It's so incredible. Do you think it's possible that my son met Jesus Christ in the flesh?"

"In the spirit," Kingston corrected.

"I don't know," Ray said, still astonished. "But I'm not going to disbelieve it."

Tommy whistled. "Talk shows, here I come."

Everyone laughed.

Making a skeptical grimace, Andi said, "I don't think so, kiddo."

"Yeah, I know," Tommy said. "It's personal."

"Right," Andi said, winking at Ray.

"That's another thing," Tommy said. "Dr. Kingston and I don't think I have a gift at all." To Ray's mind, the boy had been more talkative in the last few days than he had the whole time he'd known him. Ray sensed it had something to do with his and Andi's telling Tommy they planned to get married and were only waiting on his blessing. He gave it with an exuberant yelp.

"A gift for what?" Andi asked, looking from Kingston to Tommy. The two had been having a lot of theological conversations of late.

"The TUT stuff. The other kind."

"The TUT-B?"

"Right."

Ray said, "You mean, you didn't survive it because you have some special ability or anything?"

"Right."

"OK. Then why did you live?" Andi looked at Ray and winked.

"Because God decided not to let me die. It was a miracle, just like how Kartle saved me."

Andi looked at Kingston, then back at Tommy. "Why do you think that, you two?"

Without hesitation, Tommy said, "Dr. Nakayami."

"Oh, you've been talking to him?"

"A lot. He told us. He said"—Tommy looked at Kingston—"he said there was absolutely no biological reason for me to survive. Right, Doc?"

Ray laughed. "Oh, so it's 'Doc' now for you too?"

"Right," Tommy said without missing a beat. "But that's not the important thing. The important thing is that Dr. Nakayami thinks Jesus had to do it."

Andi looked at Ray with surprise. "Jesus had to do it?"

"Well, he didn't say that, but that's what Dr. Kingston says. God just decided to keep me around a little longer." He grinned triumphantly.

Andi rolled her eyes. "Keep you around a lot longer than that, Buster Brown."

Ray grinned, then suddenly squinted at Kingston. "You going to start dealing with some of those heretics Croase brought into the seminary or what?"

"Definitely," Kingston answered, holding another forkful of roast beef at his lips before he answered. "Hal Gordon and a bunch of others are putting together a whole review. With what happened with Croase, though, most of the board has resigned and several people have been charged with murder."

After another silence, Tommy sighed and said, "Well, aren't you going to tell them?"

Andi glanced at Ray and said, "If he's referring to what I think he's referring to, you should do the honors."

After a brief nervous cough, Ray said, "Well, Andi and I have decided to get married."

Kingston immediately clapped Ray on the back. Miles stood and shook his hand. "You'll make a great team. Out to start a special commando agency or something?" Everyone laughed.

Sitting down, Miles said, "God's going to do some great things through you two."

As everyone finished the dinner in a sudden reverent silence, Ray thought about the complement Andi made to his

476

life. He realized much of his fear that God might take everyone away was more loneliness than anything else. He looked forward to their wedding, planned for Thanksgiving Day in less than two weeks.

His hand drifted over to Andi's, and he gave it a gentle squeeze. As he glanced at her, he noticed a glow on her face, a simple joy that made her look all the more beautiful to him.

Feeling and enjoying the warmth of Ray's touch, Andi thought about her love for Ray, how life was better than it had ever been. She knew he had his faults. He could be critical and impatient. Sometimes he was just too theological for her taste. But he had courage and compassion. He might let her down occasionally, but he'd been there for all the big things, and that strengthened her. She knew God could take it all away in a flash. But if He did, He'd have good reasons for it. She could live with that. And in the meantime, she'd enjoy every minute of what they did have.

Across the table, Miles mentally thanked God for sparing him. He knew that Croase could easily have finished him off. But for some reason the maniac didn't. If there was a God, as the other folks around the table believed so intensely, he resolved to make a new and committed search for Him.

Next to Miles, Kingston leaned back and closed his eyes a moment, to let his mind drift. He thought about the first time he'd met Ray, at that conference in Cape Cod. How at that time the Spirit seemed to tell him to give this kid his best shot as a discipler and leader. He knew he'd made the right decision there, even if he'd made a lot of bad ones elsewhere. He only hoped the Lord gave them a few more years together. Maybe he could be the father Ray had lost. And Ray could be the son he'd never had.

As Tommy listened to the silence, and looked at the faces of the people around him, he wondered again if Jesus was really watching over him and if Kartle had heard what they said. He couldn't be sure, but deep down he felt it was true. He figured life was pretty good, even if it had some bad things in it now and then. But even the bad things were ways to get stronger, and he decided if that was what God was doing with him, then he'd let Him do it.

He looked at his mother and her husband-to-be, the two people he loved more than his own life. He prayed silently, *God, let Ray love my mom more than she thinks he ever could, and let Mom be happier than she's ever been in her whole life.*

He picked at another piece of meat on his plate. Deep down, though, he sensed that somehow God would answer that prayer in a way that he could never predict, but which he'd know was right and perfect and beautiful forever.